Let the Secrets Die

The First Jewell Johnson Mystery

Andrea Wittwer, *Marple Ink*
10370 N Sawmill Road
Hayward, WI 54843
USA

www.awittwer.com

Let the Secrets Die

By
Andrea Marple Wittwer

**First Edition,
Advance Printing (2015)**

**Second Edition (2016)
CreateSpace**

Dedication

This mystery is dedicated to my beloved little mother, Mary T. Marple who was a voracious mystery reader; and to my father Eldon M. Marple who devoted himself to public service, research and study. They preserved secrets of the past. My beloved sisters Ina, Karin, Laura Nan and Ellen assisted and encouraged me for many years to get this book completed. Ina and Karin died too young, so they never read the finished edition. Instead, they are characters in the Jewell Johnson series. My brothers Wesley, Willard and James are also included in my many characters.

I dedicate my life to my husband Ron, and my five dear children; Amber, Gabriel, Jacob, Amanda, and Ara; to my ten sweet grandchildren, and many nephews and nieces. You are deeply loved.

Above all I thank my heavenly Father and my Savior, Christ Jesus and the Holy Spirit.

Acknowledgements

There are so many people who have helped me produce this first book from encouragement to proof reading. Naomi Cochran, Mari Bruckman Nelson and several trusted friends who read and commented on the first edition.

I have a unique opportunity here to give credit to those people who profoundly changed my trajectory in life. My life was greatly influenced by my 1960's Hayward school teachers especially Shirley Tiffany, Kathryn Coogan, Judy Bergren, Ken Toebe, and Mrs. Wyant. They contributed to my lifelong love for learning. I tip my hat to the superlative teachers in the Hayward Community Schools District.

I would also take this time to offer *Thanks* to our very dear friends- (*you know who you are*)-for their constant support in so many trials of our lives. When there is a crisis, there are some people you can always depend on to have your back and stand up for you. I hope we have returned that support.

The personal promise to complete this series was inspired by the struggles of my super students at the Lac Courte Oreilles Ojibwe Community College. They challenged me to stay - '*On Course*' and get this project done.

Forward

A **note to you:** I began writing my story about Jewell Johnson in 1981. The secrets and situations surrounding my characters are historical fiction. I think a truly fun mystery novel intrigues, involves and interests the reader. In the chaos of every-day life, there are little 'history mysteries' because life is filled with so many plots, comedies and sometimes dark subplots. My mother always said, "Curiosity killed the cat: but satisfaction brought him back." She also said that secrets kept, become tombs. I hope that my Jewell Johnson books will not only satisfy readers with historical information but also leave you entertained.

The world has developed international, intimate connectivity through the internet since 1971. Before that, our lives had shorter vistas and closer horizons, so we lived less complex lives. But less complex doesn't mean simple. Jewell is like many of us were in rural America back then: unsuspecting, guileless and a little gullible. We found life is like walking over the accumulated layers of humus under whispering boughs in a pine forest. We tread on this matted pine needle surface that resembles thin tumbled toothpicks, not comprehending the complex, living world beneath our feet. Growing up can be very painful. Love Andi

Isaiah 40

³⁰ Even youths grow tired and weary, and young men stumble and fall;
³¹ but those who hope in the Lord will renew their strength.

They will soar on wings like eagles;
they will run and not grow weary, they will walk and not be faint.

Contents

CHAPTER 1

EPITAPH ~ 1965

"Two more hours. I'll stop at the Sheriff's office and sign the complaint first thing in the morning. That should clean up this mess. He can serve papers and it's all over. Thank God, Dad finally told me the truth." Sigurd Johnson hit the steering wheel with his fist for emphasis. A set of passing headlights illuminated his worried white face, lined with tension and fatigue.

"I'll straighten everything out with Dad tonight. Why keep it a secret? Why couldn't he just tell me? What a damned fool I've been. May God forgive me; I've screwed up so many things in my life." He rubbed his fist on his forehead. "Oh, dammit, my eyes are tired."

Lights from the semi behind him reflected into his eyes.

"Why is pickup tailgating me? There's a rest stop. I'll pull over and stretch."

The Nissan Bluebird sedan rolled down the concrete exit into a graveled wayside parking area. Sigurd Johnson unfolded his tall slim body from the small car and stretched his arms wide. He walked to the water fountain by the wayside shelter, his face lined with fatigue and worry. He noticed a Ford Edsel parked near the little bathroom building and admired the smooth lines and creamy green colors of the big car. Noisy bugs swarmed around the light on the light post. A tall man appeared out of the darkness, walking up the sidewalk. He wore a plaid, short-sleeved shirt, with sharply-creased, grey work slacks.

"Headed north?" He had a pleasant, friendly, bass voice. "I had to stretch my legs."

"Yes, I am." Sigurd replied, surprised a stranger would chat.

"Looks like rain up north. You've got a cute little car there. Foreign job?"

"Yeah, Datsun. She was a special order. I just got her yesterday." He patted his new car with affection. The older man spoke up again.

"I like to drive at night, it's cooler. Less traffic too. I'm headed up for the weekend with my family near Hayward. Chicago's just too hot in the summer." He also stretched his arms up and twisted carefully at the waist.

"I'm just going up for a short visit with my dad at Philetus Spur." Sigurd replied, studying his hands in the near darkness. "I have some business to attend to."

"Really? I live up north, but I go back and forth. I'm helping my two sons with their business in the northern suburbs in Chicago."

"I'm from Madison."

"Izzatso?"

"My wife and I teach there. She teaches English at East High. I teach Anthropology at the U."

"Do you know Aaron Ihde? He's one of my old rowing teammates from back in '27'. We went to Nationals at Poughkeepsie. He's with the Meiklejohn House."

"I know him well. Aaron's famous around campus. I had a class with him too."

"I lived in Madison for six years while I got my degree in Agriculture Education. I did Ag Extension for the University in the northwest counties. For quite a few years, I was an education technician in the Civilian Conservation Corps."

"That's interesting. My dad talked about the CCC's. They did a lot of good back in the Thirties."

"Yes. Those young fellas from the cities got jobs and learned trades. Planted trees, pulled gooseberry bushes, built dams. Lots of 'em stayed and started families with local girls. There were camps all over the state."

"I went to the University back in 1927; thought I left the Northwoods behind me. Got my PhD at Chicago and worked here and there. Spent some time in Central America through the Big War."

"Interesting, I went overseas with the U.N. during the war. When I got back, I landscaped around San Diego, Kansas City, then Chicago – that's 'til a couple of years ago. We moved the family up to Hayward to live on my family farm after my dad died."

Sigurd smiled and nodded.

"That's interesting. My family has farmed near Philetus Spur since the turn of the century. My dad and his brother were immigrant Swedes."

"I guessed you were a Swede. You're tall and broad-shouldered. My dad was a cowboy who came up to Wisconsin in '14' after my mother died. She and her folks emigrated from Sweden."

"Your dad was a cowboy?"

"That's what my mother thought. She died after my sister was born and my dad left Missouri to raise sheep and farm. What's your family name?"

"Johnson. My dad is Sven; his brother was Lars."

"Why - I know Sven. Your mom is Elin, wasn't she? She's a lovely woman."

"My mom died last year. A car accident in Kansas." Sven shook his head sadly. "She was very special."

"Sorry. What a shame. And your dad?"

"He's okay. Maybe a little crankier now. He sold the Inn a few years ago, and they moved to my uncle's farm at Wolf Point on Lake Makoons."

"I retired too. My ticker's been giving me trouble. The Doc says it's stress. I had enough of Cook County anyway. Too many unions, too much corruption. I want peace and quiet now."

"But, crime is spreading up north. The gangs are spreading out."

"That's true. The underworld's been in Northern Wisconsin since the twenties. Even Capone had a couple of hideouts up here. I know about a few other types like Dillinger brought in his dirty business." He rolled his eyes and shook his head.

"Calling them "dirty" is an understatement. In my opinion, they're downright anti-American."

"I agree. But local people like the money they bring. Rural Wisconsin still holds many secrets." He looked around the poorly lit parking lot. "You never know who's listening, who they are, or the hole they will climb out." The two men stood silently in agreement for a few seconds listening to nature's orchestra – the crickets and frogs in the swamp around the rest stop. Marple ran his fingers through his thinning black hair and stretched again.

"Well, it was nice meeting you." The taller man reached out and they shook hands. "The name's Marple; Eldon Marple. When you get home, call the operator and get our number. Everybody knows us. Stop out at the farm."

"I'm Sigurd. I might."

"We'd be glad to have you. We'll talk about anthropology…or farming. My wife and I took the girls to Mexico. We can show you slides and some artifacts. I have some color slides of Tenochtitlan and Palenque."

"Really? I've been down there. I have some of Copan, Honduras and El Mirador."

"Sounds great. Mary and I have studied archaeology for years. I do genealogy too. I'm beginning a genealogical survey of the Lac Courte Oreilles Ojibwe tribe in Hayward. I found a treasure trove of information."

"It was a pleasure meeting you, Eldon. I'll look you up. I think I could use someone to just talk to. Life gets so damned difficult and complicated. And, it's strange - I feel like we've met before."

"Who knows; maybe we have!" the older man chuckled. "I get around. I guess I'd better hit the road though. My daughter Pandy is probably waiting up for me to get home. She'll be kneeling in front of her window upstairs waiting to see my headlights from the south."

"My little Jewell is waiting back home in Madison."

"Watch out for big wildlife in your little car." With a short laugh, a nod and a wave Marple walked over to his big car, got in and the Edsel purred powerfully off into the night.

In the suddenly quiet parking lot, the tired professor leaned over, rinsed his face with the icy water from the water fountain and wiped it with his cotton handkerchief. A pickup truck pulled into the end of the wayside and parked near the woods. He grimaced when he heard country music blaring out of the window. The orange glow of the driver's cigarette lit the driver's face through the darkness. Sigurd took a deep breath of the fresh northern air and stretched his arms out again. Patting the hood of his little sedan affectionately, he noted it was spattered with dead bugs from the trip.

"I'll clean you up, when I get back home."

Sigurd got into his car and started the engine. As he backed up, he noted a set of headlights across the lot, reflected in the rearview mirror. Opening his window to allow the cool, spring air to flood the car, he heard what sounded like skip-static from a two-way radio. Accelerating to highway speed and entering Highway 53, the small sedan slipped into the left lane only long enough to pass a slower-moving semi-trailer truck. Sigurd loved the power and agility of his new vehicle. He leaned back in the leather seat to get comfortable for the long drive he knew lay ahead.

4

When he glanced into his rearview mirror again, Sigurd saw the headlights of the semi he had just passed, steadily overtaking him.

Above, low clouds partially obscured the full moon, casting an eerie white light over fog-covered fields and forests in the hilly country beyond the steep shoulders of the highway. As he drove northward raindrops began to splat on his windshield. A loud black pickup seemed to appear out of nowhere and passed him. As he went by he and the driver exchanged looks. Within a mile, the truck slowed down in front of him. As he approached the truck, the headlights from a semi-trailer truck blinded his eyes in the side mirror.

"Dang trucker. Now why's he pulling up like that?" Sigurd tried to accelerate to move forward but the pickup ahead blocked him. He could hear the deep roar of a second semi right behind his little car, and saw its huge headlights blazing down.

"What tha' hell?" He realized something terrible was about to happen. "Oh, my God! Help me!"

Like giant plows, the two huge semi-trucks quickly bore down on the little car. The attack was so sudden, and the pickup blocked Sigurd's frantic efforts to accelerate or dodge the immanent disaster ahead of him. They squeezed him over and forced him to the ditch. As the Nissan's tires hit the soft graveled shoulder, it lost traction and flipped; tumbling, gouging the dirt and sliding down the steep embankment, landing with its hood mashed around a lone tree. Glass fragments, parts of the car, and its contents, exploded through the air and landed in the brush along the field. The semis roared off northward, their taillights disappearing into the night.

In a few seconds, the black pickup rolled backwards down the road to where the car left the highway. A man in a black leather jacket climbed out. He held a long metal flashlight in his hand, playing the light down at the little car.

"Hey you!"

Receiving no answer, he side-stepped and slid down the steep incline through the grass to the wreck. The roof and hood were crushed in, wedging Sigurd's body behind the steering wheel, with his lap belt locking him to the seat. The beam of light sought the wreck and flickered across his bleeding body. Blood spatters covered the seat and dripped from his cut face in several places.

"Yer done for..." The man turned off his flashlight, spit to the side, and turned to walk away. "Naw. Better be sure."

He returned, looking down into the passenger window where the roof wasn't crushed against the frame. Leaning in, he watched the injured man for a few seconds.

"I'll be damned, you're still alive!"

He reached in the window and smashed his flashlight on the side of the driver's forehead. He waited for movement and seeing none, turned away.

"Yep. That's done. Good enough." He smiled, wiped the flashlight on the wet grass and spun it in the air, catching it with satisfaction. Walking back up to his pickup, he clicked open a lighter, lit his cigarette and climbed in. Slamming the door, he turned up the radio and picked up his two-way radio mike. Barely a minute had passed.

"Breaker, breaker, one-two-nine. Northern Boy; ya got yer ears on?" His cigarette tip glowed, lighting the cab as he waited for the radio to answer. Static garbled the response, but he said; "Job's done, I'm Lincoln bound. Watch your back door for the bear and don't hand my ten-twenty to your grandmaw… I'm gone."

The pickup rumbled to life spinning its tires through muddy grass as it crossed the center ditch of the road to head back south. Under a stark, staring moon, there was no sound except the slow patting sound of lifeblood dripping from both the car and driver.

From the south, headlights crept through the night towards the wreck.

CHAPTER 2

Maidenhood

"Standing, with reluctant feet,
Where the brook and river meet,
Womanhood and childhood fleet!"
Henry Wadsworth Longfellow

SOME SPECIAL MAGIC

There must be some special magic tying your heart forever to a specific place on this earth. I think our hearts must be programmed to accept certain fragrances and sights as a place we'll always call "home."

My heart's home is due north in Wisconsin. She lures me to her deep green, pine and white birch forests; to the spring-fed lakes and moss-padded banks of cold and secret streams. Whispering in the breeze, her emerald boughs sigh and her laughter chuckles gently as burbling brooks tumbling over embedded rocks and logs.

Sometimes when I go home, I can hear my father's voice whispering softly in wildflower-filled woods, in cedar swamps and across small amber hayfields. Even in wintry blasts and blizzards, I am very sure his spirit lingers with his parents. His sudden, violent death drained and emptied me when I was only twelve. My child's sorrow still cries lowly like the sad midnight song of a solitary wolf. As if I died myself, my heart grew cold, when he left us.

My name is Jewell Johnson. Dad told me they named me Jewell, because my eyes reminded them of the way the sun reflected on Shadow Bay. Sometimes, he called me 'Migiziins' the Ojibwe name translated as "Little Eagle" because I could see things so clearly. When I was a child we came up to the Linger Inn from Madison every summer as soon as school was out, spending our days on the shores of Lake Makoons. Everyone in this area knew my grandparents, Elin and Sven Johnson. They built their home at the beginning of the century, and it slowly it grew to be a bed and breakfast, and then a resort. There's a village named Philetus Spur about a mile north from Johnson's resort and the Lac Courte Oreilles Reservation is just down the road. Let me tell you about my family and their immigrant history – and share the mystery that began in my eighteenth year in the summer of 1971.

The First Generation: 1908-1928

I loved to hear my grandpa tell the story of the Johnsons as we sat around the fireplace in the spacious living room. He said our family and several others established the village of Philetus Spur. Grampa Sven Johnson and his brother Lars came from Sweden on a small ship, bringing with them, their new brides Elin and Emilie. They had just enough money to begin a new life in the United States.

He said the two young couples found their way from the towering immigration halls of New York's Ellis Island, to the wide-open plains of Missouri. They planned to establish farms near other members of their family, but a cousin told them about "up north" in Wisconsin. He said it was a booming frontier where brawny men from many nations found work in the lumber industry. Women could easily find work in the camps as cooks and laundresses. Wild game, fish-filled clear lakes hid in the dark forests. The four seasons were much like back home in Europe.

In April of 1908 the four of them took the train up to Chicago and then to the ornate and crowded halls of the Union Station in Saint Paul, Minnesota. The huge depot was like the tower of Babel with a cacophony of chatter in diverse languages. A man in a suit introduced himself to them as they were resting on a couch in the huge marble-floored room at the new railroad station near the river. He gave them a pamphlet and encouraged them to go to the magnificent forests only one-hundred fifty miles east, in Wisconsin. He told them about towns like Spooner, Hayward, Radisson and Ojibwa were filling up and hard-working men could work in the woods all winter and farm all summer.

"Fertile black soil, clean lakes and rivers and plenty of firewood, fish and game to support your family! It's just like the old country only one hundred times better," the canny salesman told his astonished listeners in their own tongue. "Here in America you can buy an acre or a thousand acres!"

They were intrigued by his enthusiasm, it sounded like the perfect place for a new beginning. Surely, they would raise strong families and prosper in this new country.

They boarded a smaller train in Saint Paul and headed northeast into Wisconsin. They met another person who spoke Swedish, who was travelling back to his home. Along the way, they saw a snowy landscape studded with burned stumps, rampike trees and brush. The forests along the railroad were gone and enterprising farmers were pulling out the huge stumps or trying to farm around them. The conductor pointed out the St. Croix River, the Yellow river and then the winding Namekagon River as their new acquaintance translated for them. They saw dozens of small lakes and streams out the windows. The conductor was amused at their excited chattering when they saw wildlife and the new farms along the way. He told them to go to the land agent's office in Hayward and learn how they could purchase land.

"It's perfect, here in Wisconsin," he told them. "You couldn't find a better place to make your home!"

When they arrived at the bustling village of Hayward, the two couples said goodbye to their new friends and climbed down off the train to the crowded wooden platform in front of the clean white depot. They trudged through mud and manure past the city park, then on planked side-walks along the muddy main street to the Land Agent's realty office. Fortunately, he spoke a little Swedish, and he told the two men to get rooms for Elin and Emilie at Olson's boarding house instead of at the hotel. He said the women might not be safe on the Main Street with all the rough-housing at the bars. He cautioned the women never to go out at night, avoid the main streets. He told them to ask Mrs. Olson to introduce them at the Swedish Lutheran church and to show them the little public library where there were Swedish language books and newspapers.

Then he turned to Sven and Lars a sheet of paper with directions to some land for sale. They stopped at the Company Supply Store with wide creaking floorboards and silver tin-covered walls. They admired the ornate tin ceilings making the store echo as they walked in. Sven bought fresh bread and butter along with a little salami for supper and a bottle of milk from the dairy. They sat on the steps of the porch at Olson's boarding house and ate their first meal. They settled into the little room they rented and snuggled down under warm wool blankets.

The next morning, Grampa and Great Uncle Lars began to hike east on an icy, snowy tote road leading through a jumble of huge pine stumps, brush and small saplings. They bought a new gun because the land agent cautioned them about wolves and bear, but they had never fired a rifle. Grampa loaded shells into it and they took a few potshots at stumps along the way just to be prepared. They stumbled up slippery hills and slid down into sloppy pockets of icy water along the way. After a while they learned to walk in the brush along the ruts where it was easier to get along. Without a compass, it was best to stick to the tote road.

By afternoon they had hiked to the stopping place sitting in the middle on a flat field where a white and black sign announced, "Happy Land." There were several farms with small houses and sheds. Dozens of chickens, a few skinny black and white cows, and a small herd of sheep wandered around the buildings. The brothers were amazed at the dark, loamy soils showing between the patches of snow in the field.

Here they met a hard-muscled Norwegian lumberjack named Leif Haagestad. He was loading a wagon and heading to Hayward in the morning. Since he spoke a little Swedish, they fell into conversation on the porch of the stopping place. Haagestad said he was planning to take the train back to North Dakota to get his wife and children and trying to encourage his parents and sister to come 'up north' from Iowa.

"I bought a full quarter section: that's one-hundred sixty acres, boys," he told them. "It's alongside a lake a couple of miles from this stopping place. Let's go! We can walk there in less than an hour and you can see how perfect it is." They hiked northwest along a small tote road and at the top of a hill they viewed a wide blue lake, surrounded by uncut white pines. The water was still frozen in the little bay to their west. Leif said with pride he'd spent three winters in the logging camps and two summers building the railroad to earn enough money to buy his land on the little creek draining into the lake on the east side.

"North Dakota is no place to raise a family. I'm sick of the wind. It's blizzards and ice-cold in the winter and hotter than Hell itself, in the summer. Bring your wives here and build a cabin," he said. "You betcha, I'll come back in a month. We'll build a town together!"

Grampa Sven was deeply excited by this opportunity. He knew he had found his new home. This was just like the countryside back in Sweden: pine forests, and clear, clean lakes with sandy bottoms. Lars didn't see those possibilities as well, but he trusted his older brother. The three men hiked back to the stopping place and spent the night drinking whiskey, 'talking smart' and making plans.

Before dawn the next morning, they woke up with hammering headaches, to loud stamping, jingling harnesses and the snorting of horse teams. They pulled up their suspenders when they heard the clattering of breakfast. Any other time they would have eaten more heartily of the huge pancakes, biscuits and sausage gravy, but their bodies were not accustomed to alcohol. Leif laughed at them for their pain. With stamping feet, jingling livery and snorting clouds of hot breath, his team of horses stood hitched up to a rough wagon outside. The two young men lay in the back on baggage and straw bedding as the wheels bumped and jarred heavily down the tote road to town. The nausea was worse than being on board the ship when they came to America.

Overnight the mud puddles in the road froze solid and the team made travelled smoothly until they reached a steep hill where Leif and Sven wrenched on the brakes and they slid down frozen ruts. Leif told them by afternoon the road would be almost impassable again because the sun would warm the hillsides and soften up the ground. This was another important lesson they would need to learn. In a harsh country like this it is life or death to know when to move and when to hold still. The seasons in Wisconsin, Leif said, changed every day. The brothers realized there were many lessons to learn ahead of them.

When they got back to town they went to Olson's to get Elin and Emilie. The two couples agreed to make their way down to the land agent's office. Elin was excited to announce Mrs. Olson asked her to work at the boarding house for the summer. Emilie talked to the owner of the Dairy across the street for a job. They were all invited to dinner with her family and to go with the Olson's to church on Sunday. They agreed the most important thing they had to do was learn English right away.

At the agent's office, they looked at the land-looker's maps showing where land was available. Next to Leif's property was a parcel with one hundred and sixty acres of land including a high peninsula jutting out into Little Bear Lake. It was apparent they couldn't farm a portion of the property because of a marshy swamp but the tip of the point was never cleared of the original white pines and was a perfect place for a homestead. Later in the week, Grampa and Lars returned and walked over the whole piece of property and decided it was perfect. It was more comfortable for them to have nearby fresh water. Each of them would have eighty acres to clear and farm. They could cut a new road in from the tote road less than a quarter of a mile away near Leif Haagestad's farm.

My dad told me how Grampa and my Great Uncle Lars began early in the spring cutting off small trees and trying to get potatoes, beans and corn in the upturned ground around the stumps on their property. The women spent the summer in Hayward. Many days, Emilie slept in bed, sickened by a strange illness she caught on their trip. She made Elin promise not to tell Lars and Sven she wasn't well, because they would worry, visiting the doctor too expensive for them.

Gramma Elin said she worked from dawn until dusk at Olson's boarding house cleaning rooms, cooking and washing their laundry. All the money she earned went to support the two couples and she put some aside in a sock for the winter. In the evenings, she did darning and mending by candlelight for extra money and kept company with Emilie up in their little room.

Elin made friends with a couple of younger women and began attending the Swedish Lutheran church in town. She learned some helpful English phrases. At the tiny library, she got Swedish language books and newspapers for Emily to read. The minister and his wife from the church visited them in the little downstairs parlor to make them feel welcome to Hayward but that night Emilie ran a fever and was unable to come downstairs.

By the end of their first summer the two men had two one-room cabins, a chicken coop and a small barn erected near the lake. They bought a horse, and wagon, a flock of chicks and a pregnant cow. One cabin had a hearth and fireplace while other had a big porcelain wood-burning cookstove for heat.

"Elin, we will have sheep too!" Grampa told Gramma on a trip to Hayward. "We'll have our own wool. We'll build a barn and put up some fences, but the wolves and bear will try to kill our animals. You'll have to learn to shoot the rifle, Elin, *min älskling!*"

They learned to hunt and trap animals for food from a helpful and curious, elderly Ojibwa neighbor who knew they would need these skills to make it through the winter. In the summer evenings, they took the time to visit at the stopping place on the way to town to talk to the veterans of winters in the north. The brothers soon learned English and grew tough as hardwood trees and twice as determined.

Whenever my Grampa talked about those 'good old days,' his mind seemed to slip far away. One evening Grampa took out a box of sepia pictures he had locked in a wooden chest in his office. They were old photographs of the four of them, taken in a studio in Hayward. In one picture, Emilie stood behind Lars looking frail in her simple dark dress with a wasp-slim waist, her face framed by an angelic halo of tight curls. She was such a delicately beautiful woman, but I thought she looked hauntingly sad.

In another sepia-colored picture, Gramma Elin stood behind Grampa Sven's shoulder. She wore a blouse with a white lace collar and her luminous pale eyes seemed to probe the camera. Grampa told us he borrowed the suit he was wearing. There was a small postcard of the four of them, posed on the front porch of their boarding house in Hayward. The two men, muscular and darkly tanned, were leaning on the railings. The brothers were dressed in their work clothing with knee-high boots and full beards covered their faces. Gramma's blond hair sat, swept up on the top of her head in a pale mass. She had one hand protectively resting on Emilie's shoulder.

"Oh Gramma, you were so beautiful," I said in awe, but she just waved a hand and smiled, gracefully rising to go to the kitchen. Dad said when he was a child he remembered his mother's blond hair hung to her hips in a golden braid but now she usually wore it in a braid wrapped around the crown of her head.

"Your Gramma is still a very beautiful woman," Grampa said, as he watched her walk away. Later in front of the flickering fireplace, he and Gramma told us Emilie never got better. She developed a raspy cough and fevers but waved it off whenever Lars came to town. When he came back from the woods, she'd get up and dress and they would have dinner downstairs with the Olson's.

Gramma said Emilie died right after their first Christmas. She told us they all felt guilty because the four of them took a sleigh to church on Christmas Eve. Lars carried Emilie to the sleigh to keep her feet from getting cold or wet. He tucked her in, under a thick buffalo blanket and they sang hymns and carols. Unfortunately, she caught a chill in the unheated church and the next morning they found she was too weak to get out of bed or eat dinner. That Christmas day, she deteriorated quickly and ran a high fever. Mrs. Olsen sent Lars to get the doctor when she coughed up blood and then wouldn't respond in the afternoon. After checking her over, the doctor said she had advanced tuberculosis. Because of the lingering weakness, she was now unable to fight back pneumonia.

Lars was with her night and day; fearfully cradling her in his arms like a child, kissing her and wiping her lips with a cloth. There was nothing they could do, they just watched her fade away. The pneumonia took her quietly to heaven without a fight in a few days. With soul-wrenching sobs, Lars insisted on tucking a shawl around her body in the coffin in the boarding house parlor. Gramma Elin used her small savings and paid for a small pine coffin, the gravesite, and a simple white headstone. After a small funeral service in the church, they buried Emilie at the Greenwoods Cemetery in her black satin dress and her tiny high-heeled shoes. It seemed so sad to me she only saw her little cabin a couple of times before she passed away. Lars blamed himself for her death. Gramma Elin said he hardly slept and cried miserably for a solid week.

"Why did I bring her to this God-forsaken place so far from her mother? She will lay in this cold graveyard without her family around her."

Elin wrote letters to their relatives back in Sweden and Missouri, while Grampa and Gramma tried to ease Lars' pain. But now they now had their own hands full since Gramma was obviously pregnant and expecting in the spring. Grampa Sven decided to not return to the cabin until after the baby came: instead he worked in the huge North Wisconsin Lumber Company sawmill in Hayward. Lars also worked at the big mill, but he spent his spare time in the many bars around Hayward, drowning his pain and picking fights. Sometimes he slept in the livery stable or in Pastika's woodshed, rather than return to their rooms in Olson's boarding house. My grandparents watched worriedly as they knew he was struggling with his anguish and would listen to no words of comfort or guidance.

In spring, they persuaded Lars to come with them and the new baby out to their cabins. At first, he would just sit on the shore and watch the lake for hours or wander over to Happy Land to drink, but finally even Sven lost his patience.

"Lars, come on, man! You need to shake this off and pull yourself together. God did not put you on this earth to mourn and weep. He put you here to praise Him and live an honest and sober life. Our parents would not find honor in how you are behaving. You know Emilie is watching you from heaven and she would not be pleased you are acting like this. Finish your cabin, let's get our fields cleared and the crops planted."

"Your granddad was always a man of action," Dad told me. "My mom was very quiet, but she was a very strong woman. You can be proud of your heritage."

Several years passed and then my Great Uncle Lars met Naomi Isham, a young, soft-spoken Chippewa woman from the Lac Courte Oreilles Band of the Ojibwe. They met at the stopping place where she worked cleaning rooms. Naomi's family objected strenuously about her marriage to a white man, but she stubbornly won them over. At first even my grandparents tried to dissuade Lars from marrying her because they felt she was too young and Lars was drinking too much. Nonetheless, during their courtship she became great friends with Gramma, and they often laughed at each other for the way they tried to communicate with their broken English. Dad told me my Great Aunt Naomi taught Gramma many words in Ojibwe and English while she learned many Swedish words in return.

Naomi had many helpful things to teach the three immigrant Swedes. She knew many foods in the woods around them and could make medicines and teas out of roots, plants and tree barks. Her relatives taught them how to fish, tap maple trees and snare rabbits and they exchanged wild rice and venison for flour and potatoes. Naomi made baskets from reeds and bark and Elin taught her to knit with the carded wool from the sheep. They were both very talented and crafty ladies.

Dad said his aunt Naomi and Gramma matched each other in their determination to transform the farm. Shoulder to shoulder they dug deep, outside root cellars and cemented rocks together to make underground storage rooms like back in Sweden. Gentle Naomi took diligent care of Lars and bore him several strong boys. Lars continued to drink but he was always good to Naomi and got on very well with her extended family. Gramma was very proud of her young sister-in-law and praised her and the boys often. My four second cousins grew up tough and hard-working like their parents and took jobs at the lumber mill and in the woods.

In front of the original cabin, on the shores of Lake Makoons, Grampa built a large sturdy home for his family, using milled lumber from the sawmill he built on his property, and undergirded with thick cement and rock basement foundations. Along with farming, his growing herd of sheep and cattle, he began to accept logs from nearby property owners and mill them. In several years, he had the money to add bedrooms to the house for Sigurd, Greta Stina and even the new baby, little Alex Teresa. Then he added a larger kitchen and finally a second and third floor.

At first, Gramma rented the spare room out to sportsmen from the cities and then she fixed up the two original lakeside cabins to rent to fishermen from the cities who loved to fish on Little Bear Lake. As her reputation grew, she began to rent her second-floor rooms in the summer time. They added a boat-storage shed beside their parking lot for summer people to rent, storing their equipment over the winter.

They named the quiet estuary Shadow Bay and the road to their house from Philetus Spur became known as Johnson Road. Grampa, and Lars hired Naomi's two brothers to help build a sturdy T-shaped farmhouse on the opposite peninsula jutting out into Shadow Bay where the Johnson women could wave at each other over the water. They also built a small log school next to the river in the village and hired a young girl to live with them and teach. Their children attended school in the little building along with some other kids whose families bought property near the lake. Naomi refused to let her family's Ojibwe children attend the Indian Boarding Schools even though the Indian Service and the School District were persistent. Rumors were leaking out that the children at the boarding school did not eat properly and lacked shoes and clothing. The Philetus Spur community helped by stubbornly fighting the Government to keep all the neighborhood kids together at their rural school and providing for their needs in their own community.

Leif, and his wife Mari, constructed their farm nearby and sent their two younger children to the Johnson's school. Their eldest daughter returned to North Dakota to live with her grandparents to attend college at Minot. The Philetus Spur school was growing fast so when their first fifteen-year-old teacher promptly got married and moved away, the School District sent a good-natured Norwegian-speaking girl to be their teacher. She quickly met a young man from the lumber camp and they were married. Grampa sold them a piece of land near the Inn where they began their own small business hauling food and other goods back and forth to Hayward from the growing community. The last teacher was a girl who attended the school herself and showed her value as a teacher until the school closed.

Sven donated property and lumber from his mill to build a church. The Evangelical Lutheran Church in Hayward sent men, supplies and simple plans to help build a small white church with a tall spire and bell tower with a parsonage near the church. Not much later a slender pale young pastor and his wife arrived from Minnesota. Grampa's small lumber mill business grew and men around Little Bear Lake began to bring logs in to make extra money in the winter and to clear their own property. Grampa and Leif petitioned the County Board to build a better road from the depot in Hayward to the Lake. They met with the people who lived near them and organized the township and elected Grampa as their first county supervisor and town chairman.

Dad told us Philetus Spur residents created a comfortable, friendly little community cut out of the forests of great pines. They courageously endured the fierce winter cold and storms and the bug infested swamps. Leif and his family built a small log store and later a large building to warehouse produce to sell. The farmers organized a potato cooperative and sold their potatoes in the cities. The township hired a crew to build a small townhall on the hill above Philetus Spur with a wide deck and white round wooden pillars holding up a Greek style portico. The people used it for all community gatherings from elections and public meetings to dances and wedding parties. He said the community was very close and supportive of each other.

The years passed, and this village of hard-working families discovered the winter weather was becoming increasingly harsh, and summers too short for their small farms to make ends meet. The agricultural markets were too far away to make farming competitive with the growing corporate farms in the west. Instead they began to focus on the visitors who came up from the Illinois, Kansas and Minnesota to the Hayward area lakes and the Chippewa River. They took "blueberry pickers" and "sports" into their homes and rented extra bedrooms to them. Some came to ski and enjoy the snow. This became a second income during the summer and fall. Grampa and Lars added to their annual income by using their hunting and fishing skills to guide wealthy sportsmen in the forests, and on the rivers and lakes nearby.

One afternoon, Gramma was teaching me how to peel potatoes in her kitchen while told me how she and Naomi had very large gardens filled with potatoes, rutabagas, corn and carrots. They stored them in root cellars the two women built with their own hands. Naomi traded the fruits of their arduous work with her relatives at Lac Courte Oreilles for maple syrup and sugar, wild rice, and berries to expand their larder in the winter and shared them with Gramma. Naomi taught Gramma how to make Fiddlehead soup out of fern buds and dough gobs or fry bread. Gramma taught Naomi how to preserve their berries as jam and jellies with sugar. Naomi worked shoulder to shoulder with Gramma to clean the Inn.

The two women went to church together and gave teas along with Mari Haagestad and the pastor's wife Sophie. The two families were like one. For many years, the Johnson clan's lives were pleasant, busy and full.

The Second Generation 1928-1965

The next generation of Philetus Spur kids grew up close but gradually drifted off to go to college or to find work in larger towns. A few of the children remained to take over their family-run businesses or inherited resorts around the area lakes. Most of the families rejoined for holidays and vacations: like many rural communities, the village swelled to several hundred over the holidays or for a couple of months in the summer.

Dad told me he left the Linger Inn and Philetus Spur in 1927 to go to school in Madison. He joined the military Reserves and went to college. Alex Teresa stayed to help her parents at the Inn, but she suddenly died at seventeen. Dad said she had an appendicitis attack and died before the doctor could help her. The summer following her death, my Aunt Greta Stina met Uncle Oscar when he was a visitor at the Inn. They moved to Saint Paul after their marriage in the new little church at Philetus Spur.

When his enlistment was over, Dad finished University receiving his master's degree in Anthropology. Then he went to Chicago and got his doctorate. He lived and did research at the University in Madison but visited back home as often as he could get away. Mom and Dad met in Madison at the University of Wisconsin in the year "I Love Lucy" made its debut on television.

Dad was already a tenured professor at the University when he met Mary Chaney, a pretty college freshman from Spring Green, Wisconsin. She was studying at the Union cafeteria one fall afternoon when he sat down to read and have a cup of coffee at the next table. Mom said they fell in love when their eyes locked over her poetry textbook. Dad said he was worried because of their age difference, but mom convinced him and her parents, her age was no barrier and they got married at home in the spring. Dad promised Grampa Chaney he would see to it she finished her plans to teach and she would not waste her education.

I was an only child. I was born at St. Mary's Hospital in Madison one cold February morning. For twelve years, we were a very happy University family. We spent all our holidays, and two weeks in the summer, 'up north' with Gramma and Grampa Johnson at their Inn at Philetus Spur. I remember playing on the beach while Grandma watched from the deck or waved from her kitchen window. The three of us roamed the streams and forests, then also swam, water-skied and fished on Lake Makoons. We went further north to gather buckets of cool rocks and fossils on the beaches of Lake Superior near Washburn

18

and Ashland. Taking the ferry to Madelaine Island, to see new the Museum my dad's friends built was a thrill. Those were dear, sweet summer memories.

My world began to change rapidly one winter day when Grampa called to announce he'd sold the Inn. My grandparents were moving over to the Wolf Point farm. Mom and Dad looked at each other in shock and that day I overheard many unhappy phone calls back and forth. Once, Mom took me outside when Dad got a little too loud and angry. Then Gramma Elin died in an auto accident in Kansas City while she was visiting her Missouri cousins. It was a gloomy time for us.

Within a few months, the darkness closed in and my world lost color. I remember the day Dad died as if I were watching myself in a movie. On a gray June afternoon in 1965, my Grampa called Dad. After yet another stormy discussion over the telephone in his office, Dad stamped angrily around the house for an hour and wouldn't even talk to Mom. Finally, he kissed her and hugged both of us tightly. He made a few calls to arrange his schedule at work. I heard him say to Mom in the kitchen, he was going to "straighten things out" up north. He refused to tell Mom why he was going. He just said he would call the next day.

I knew Mom was terribly upset because they were always close and talked about everything. He chucked his suitcase and his briefcase in the back seat of his brand new blue Datsun sedan and headed out the driveway. From the hallway, I saw her worried face while she watched him leave.

Mom sat at the kitchen table all evening staring at a cup of cold tea. I wandered back and forth from the kitchen, to the window in dad's office to my bedroom. Mom wouldn't play Cribbage, so I finally got a book out and read it, sitting next to her. When the phone rang, she ran to answer it in Dad's office with me close behind her.

"Sig? Is that you? I'm so sorry!" she cried. There was a pause and I saw mom's face go white with shock, and she slumped into Dad's chair.

"*No!* Who is this? I don't understand," she said, "Is Sig okay? Oh, no – no; please say it's not true." Her hands began to shake, and she fumbled with the pencil she picked up clumsily to write down what he was saying.

It was the State Police on the telephone. He said Grampa Johnson was with dad and said she needed to come. The trooper gave her the details of an awful accident and telephone numbers to call. He was at the hospital she needed to come to Rice Lake right away. Mom's quakily dialed Dad's best friend, Jim Taylor. When she brokenly explained the situation he immediately offered to drive us. After calling Gramma and Grampa Chaney, we quickly packed a few things and ran to the car when he drove up. With tears streaming down her face, she ran to the car.

"Jim, they aren't sure Sig will make it. I can't believe this is happening."

The trip to Rice Lake took forever. Mom cried anxiously the whole trip; I struggled silently with grief and shock. I had a blanket and pillow, but no sleep would come so I watched the moon darting through the trees. As we drove northward a light chilly rain began to fall and headlights flashed through the car, my mother's sobs occasionally breaking the silence. We reached the hospital just after midnight. Mom ran in to see Dad first, while I sat in the cold hallway on a hard bench with the white glaring fluorescent lights reflecting on the granite floor. I'd never felt loneliness like this. My spring coat couldn't keep me warm as I shivered there and whimpered into the collar. It was late at night, few people appeared in the halls and I felt the big clock on the wall was ticking away my daddy's life.

Finally, Mom took me in to see him, but I could only kiss his cold cheek and touch his hand. There were tubes and bandages swathing him like a mummy. His eyes were swollen shut. I thought his finger moved against my hand slightly, so I pressed my cheek into his palm and whispered intensely, "I know you hear me, I love you, Daddy," my tears wet on his fingers.

The doctor returned, talking in hushed tones to Mom and Jim. A kind nurse took me to wait alone again in a cold uncomfortable chair across the hall. She gave me a thin blanket and I curled up, covering my face with my hands, and cried.

Within a few minutes, a dark, swarthy, man appeared in the shadows at the end of the hall by the dim "exit" sign. He just stood there, scowling at me under black eyebrows. My cold hands covered my eyes but between my fingers, I felt he made eye contact with me. It sent a shiver through my whole body.

Just then, I heard my mother's anguished cries coming from the Emergency Room. Like an evil shadow, the man disappeared through the exit door.

I jumped out of the chair and ran to be near Dad; wrestling away from the nurse who attempted to hold me back. I held Mom in my arms and we rocked back and forth as they covered my dad's face with the sheet. I was shocked, quivering and aching. These moments seared like burning scars in my brain. Mom was angry with the doctor who looked very unhappy.

"It can't be, Doctor! You said he was better!"

Everyone seemed to forget me, and time slowed to a crawl. There were endless details Mom had to handle. I heard her talking to the State Trooper, repeating what Dad whispered to her and Gramps, about someone running him off the road. Grampa said nothing, he hung back from us, his face blank and staring. He wouldn't confirm it when mom sobbed it again.

"He said, *"A semi pushed me off the road. He's got my briefcase."* I know what we heard! Dad tell him!"

The Deputy reached over and patted her arm, kindly explaining they'd make a note about it in the accident report.

"The only witness left before the police arrived. With no evidence there is little we can do. He was lying on the grass when the ambulance arrived. There was no briefcase. The report said his suitcase contents were scattered on the ground. He was either thrown from the car or he crawled away from the car. A passing motorist found him and called for help but then disappeared. The car is totally destroyed, the insurance company paid to have it hauled to the junkyard."

Mom sobbed and wanted to go to the accident site but the officer and another muscular man in a black suit talked her out of it. Grampa led her to a chair. Jim Taylor nodded understandingly.

"Mrs. Johnson, you are too upset. You and your daughter need to get some rest. Your husband probably forgot his briefcase at home. I'm afraid unless you want to pursue this with your own resources, there's no reason not to close the case."

No one in the room paid attention to me, a child silently watching and listening. At last, my aunt Greta Stina, arrived from Saint Paul and held me tightly in her arms. I melted there, painfully clinging to her with all my young strength. As the adults continued talking, she whisked me away to her car and to a hotel where she held me until I slept.

Mom's heart was broken. Her face looked grey and the dark circles under her eyes were frightening. I worried constantly she'd die too, staying by her side. I watched and listened. Neighbors and friends poured into our home bringing trays of food. Hundreds of people crowded into the memorial service at the University. Then we drove up to Philetus Spur to a family graveside service.

Grampa Sven knelt beside me as the workmen awkwardly lowered Dad's coffin on ropes down into the hole. Rocks and dirt clunked hollowly down on it. The pastor gently offered his condolences to our family and repeated the words he must have so often used,

"We have entrusted our brother Sigurd to God's merciful keeping, and we now commit his body to the ground: earth to earth, ashes to ashes, dust to dust: in sure and certain hope of the resurrection to eternal life through our Lord Jesus Christ, who died, was buried, and rose again for us. To him be the glory forever. Amen."

Aunt Greta and Gramma Chaney struggled to catch Mom when her knees gave out. She fainted right beside me onto the grass next to his grave. In shock, I dropped to my knees and sobbed over her. Aunt Greta gently pulled me away as several others crowded in to revive Mom and lead her away to Jim's car.

We returned to Madison the next day with Gramma Chaney. She stayed with us to help. Mom melted into her bedroom. I remember the bleak moments at suppertime when she would break down in exhaustion and cry, her bleak face cradled in her arms on the table. Other times, she'd find something around the house that stirred up some memory of Dad and run to her room to lay down. There were worrisome trips to the doctor and a couple times I ran to her when she collapsed to the floor completely, sobbing into the carpeting. After a while she would hug me tightly to reassure me.

"Things will be all right, Jewell. We'll be fine," she'd say as if to convince herself. One night I heard her tell Gramma Chaney, "Poor Sven; he's so alone. But I am eternally glad Elin didn't have to live through this."

To try to cheer her up and ease the gloom, I would play her favorite songs on the piano and tell her stories about my day, so she'd smile at me. I was so desperately worried about her, so afraid she too would leave me. Each night, I'd think about my Dad and make believe I'd see him in the morning, but then cry silently until I went to sleep. Nightmares about dark, scowling men, trucks and headlights, plagued the night. I didn't tell anyone because I feared it would cause Mom more worry and hurt and she had suffered enough. Night after night I would wake up crying and then not be able to get back to sleep.

But the seasons dragged by and they must have softened the pain of Dad's death for Mom, she seemed a little quicker to smile and finally returned to work. I was glad, but I mourned silently and alone, throwing myself into studies at school and soaking my pillow with tears at night. After a year, Mom began to spend extra time with dad's friend Jim. He would pick her up early in the evening for dinner, a play or a movie. I always waited up for her, studying or watching TV. When Jim left, I would silently go upstairs to my room. Mom would fiddle around the house for a while, then stop by my room to say goodnight. I saw her grow happier as the months went by, as spring turned to summer, summer to fall. I wanted to be happy for her, but it seemed to me as if she wanted Jim to take Dad's place. One evening she came to my room and sat next to me on the bed.

"I've come to like Jim very much, honey. We have a lot in common; there's so much to talk about," she said. She seemed surprised. "He's like your dad, so gentle and understanding. It helps me, he knew Sig so well." Mom hugged me tightly and kissed my cheek, but I just turned away, refusing to cry. To add to my sorrow, Grampa Sven had a stroke and passed away at the farm. Mom and my gramma Chaney tried to talk to me about my grief, but I turned away from them.

In the fall of 1967, I started high school at Madison's East High. Encouraged by my Mom and teachers, I studied and worked hard. I practiced swimming, took piano and guitar lessons and sang in the choir at school and church. I never missed a Wednesday night Bible Study. Later I was on the swimming team and where races and practice absorbed my spare time. I got excellent grades. A few boys asked me to school dances or dates, but I always found a reason to politely say "*No*." Life seemed dark, dusty and dry.

Mom married dad's friend Jim the spring of my junior year. The change I struggled to understand. I knew they were close. but I was too blind to see what was happening.

"Would you like to stand up for me, honey?"

"No, Mom. Not in front of all those people," I replied. "I'm too shy."

"Okay, sweetheart. I understand. I'm nervous too."

I sensed her disappointment and sadness, but she didn't bring it up again. I sat in the front pew during the short ceremony in St. Andrews Episcopal Church, a brownstone building near the Square. I watched as she stood with her back to me. Her long shining dark hair flowed over the shoulders of the simple cream-colored, empire waist dress. When she and Jim turned around to face the small crowd gathered in the church, the music swelled, and she smiled into my eyes. Around her neck on a thin silver chain was a tiny cross with a sparkling diamond twinkling like her earrings. The small and delicate bouquet of bridal veil and pink carnations was just like her. I caught my breath because I saw how fragile, sweet and feminine she was…no wonder Dad loved her so much. Her smile was for me but as applause filled the church, I swallowed a lump in my throat. I tried to smile back. Jim lifted her veil and kissed her tenderly. I looked away realizing he loved her too and I would have to share her with him.

Aunt Greta Stina sat next to me and I held her hand tightly. She looked down, nodded with a slight smile, and handed me a hankie. She always understood just what I was feeling. Even though she was in her fifties, she was so beautiful. Her fitted dress with a tailored jacket was ice blue, the same color as her eyes. My tall and slender Auntie Greta had a sprinkle of tiny brown freckles on her cheeks and the bridge of her nose just like me. I noticed a little grey was slipping into her shoulder-length pale blond pageboy. People often mentioned how much we looked alike and it made me feel happy.

Jim agreed with Mom not to move out of our beautiful brick house near Camp Randall until after I graduated. Instead, he moved a few of his things over, leaving most of his possessions at his house in Sun Prairie. The thought of leaving our historic home and garden was painful. Our house and yard resembled a picture in a magazine. I didn't have many friends my age living in our neighborhood, but I did love the elderly people next door. One afternoon, I walked out of the kitchen and saw Jim sitting at Dad's desk. A pang shot through my heart like an arrow, I had to close my eyes against the hurt as tears welled up. I had to walk away.

The last semester of school dragged by: my few girlfriends were now too busy dating and with their boyfriends, so I spent the evenings in our study. I took college placement tests then I was accepted and enrolled at the University of Wisconsin in Madison. By this time, I felt like I had become a part of the woodwork in my house. I jogged through the neighborhood and then around campus for several miles every day no matter what the weather was like. Mom worried about it, but I told her I needed the conditioning exercise for the swimming team.

"I have to keep my edge if I want to compete in college, Mom." I told her.

I graduated at the half-semester and got a part-time job on State Street near the Capitol building at a little triangle-shaped clothing boutique. I enjoyed the college students from around the world who stopped in to shop and chat. We had long dangling earrings, imported shirt-dresses, and jeans that were very different from styles at the new East Towne Mall. I even liked the flowery fragrance of the incense the owner burned in her office. Sometimes I went to coffee with a couple of the girls from work and even went to lunch with a boy from New York I met at the used bookstore. I shopped at Brown's Used Books reading through used text books and dusty old novels. Sometimes I went to the Union Mall or visited the Historical Society where I made some acquaintances. Other times I simply would sit by the fountain and watch the strange antics of hippies that came to hang out in the evenings. There was always an exotic smell in the air around campus where long-haired grubby boys played their guitars for tips. I loved the guy occasionally playing his sitar by the fountain. Mom worried about me going down there alone but she knew I was very careful. Since the bombing at Sterling Hall and I always was careful to be home an hour before dark.

One April day, mom called up the stairs from the hallway.

"Honey, can you come here?" She and Jim were sitting at the dining room table. "You can't just hang around Madison all summer waiting for school to start. Jim and I want to include you in our vacation up north for June and July. We are staying at the Linger Inn on Little Bear Lake just like we used to. I'll reserve the top bedroom for you like always."

"Mom, I don't want to intrude," I said, staring out the window through raindrops at the grey stormy day. "I'll stay here and watch the house for you. Besides, I have my job to think about."

"Angel, please. Your tuition is all taken care of. We want you to enjoy this last summer with us before you start out on your own. You loved the Linger Inn. This is your opportunity to relax and think about the future. This may our last opportunity to be together like this. The Linger Inn is right there on the lake. There's so many fun things to do. Remember swimming, hiking, canoeing, water-skiing, and golfing?"

"I don't know mom. I feel like I should be doing something constructive and useful. I'd be bored just lying around all summer on the beach."

"Honey, you are too serious. You've worked so hard in High School. I want to see you take a little time off before college. I would just love to spend some time with you where we were so happy, okay darling? You will come, won't you?"

"I guess so." I shrugged my shoulders, and walked back to my room, snapping on my desk light. As always, my Dad's picture smiled at me out of a walnut frame. The passing years didn't ease the memories of his death. Sadly, I touched his handsome face. I knew Mom understood and she talked to me about him and often tried to help me accept his death. But other times it exasperated her I couldn't accept Jim in our lives and left in tears. Something just screamed inside me when I thought about Jim moving into our house. I never intended to make life hard for her and I regretted it caused her pain. I didn't dislike Jim; it wasn't because I didn't love her. Dad had been the center of my life. Jim could never take his place.

On the last Saturday of May, we had just finished packing the car for the trip to Philetus Spur as Mom and I stood next to the car and the warm afternoon sunshine teased the fragrance out of the snow ball bushes in our yard. Madison was so alive with activity.

"You brought some warm things, didn't you honey? It gets pretty chilly in the evenings by the lake."

"Yes mom; I did. I remember those cold northern nights," I said, looking up at the blue spring sky and feeling Madison alive and humming all around me. I got my bike out of the back yard for my usual ride to Camp Randall and then over to campus. I stopped on State Street for a bagel and tea. At this point, I focused my life on attending the University of Wisconsin and then staying in Madison. There was so much to do. Madison had four perfect seasons and a ton of outdoor sports. I loved the festivals and museums. But I figured I would just use this time up north to catch up on reading, get a tan and prepare study plans for school. My few high school girlfriends were busy planning for marriage or for schools and careers. I packed a pile of miscellaneous paperbacks, Nesbit's fat History of Wisconsin and a packet of information from the University to read over into paper bag in the back seat. I didn't know how quickly life could change.

We left Madison early the next morning. Mom broke the silence two hours later, as we rose into the Northern Highland, the area where the climate and geography change in Wisconsin.

"Jewel, can you smell the 'Northwoods'?" Mom sighed. "Jim, I always feel the same once we get this far. It's a feeling saying we're coming home – everything is going to be ok."

"Can we take the old road, Highway 27, at Osseo, Jim?" I asked. I couldn't stand the thought of going past the place on the Hwy 53 freeway where dad was killed. This road was more interesting anyway. It wound ahead of us like a black ribbon sliding between hilly, cow-filled fields, around sharp corners and over narrow rock-strewn rivers. We stopped at Augusta for gas, coffee and donuts and then in Ladysmith at the café beside the four-way light for delicious hamburgers and fries. Our last stop was for coffee and a sandwich at Ojibwa and then we left the main highway to wind through the forests to the Chequamegon Forest. The sun was gloriously blue, and the sun's rays sparkled like diamonds on the dark blue water in each of the small pothole lakes we passed. We talked about school, work and the books I was reading, interjecting "*Oh look!*" as deer, raccoons, porcupines, and small critters scooted across our path and an eagle wheeled overhead to welcome us to the pinewoods.

After a while we passed the beautiful Lake Chippewa Flowage, climbed up and down steep hills and swung around wide 45-degree corners. After a few excited minutes, there was the little blacktopped road to the 'Flats.' That's what dad called the area where Grampa located the Inn and his farm. With a pang I remembered how Dad loved to teach geography. He explained this area was three miles by five miles, bordered on the west side by a high sandy terminal moraine shaped like a cigar. There were many small hilly moraines left when the glaciers melted back north. Beyond it was a deep valley with a winding river at the bottom.

He explained that the glaciers ground and shaped this area of northern Wisconsin thousands of years ago, dropping a payload of black sandy loam on this small plain. Lake Makoons was the eastern edge of the Flats. Dad groaned about picking up thousands of rocks and tossing them on Grampa's big hay wagon as Grampa drove slowly through the fields in the spring. Then he laughed because he remembered Grampa said spring rains made them grow like potatoes in the fields. They put all those rocks to good purpose.

The forest around this area filled with pools called perched water tables and then lumpy little hills filled with soft fluffy sand. Dad said Grampa learned a lot about the glaciers and soils from the University extension teacher and County agent who came up to help the farmers when he was developing this land. In his office at the farm, there was a wall of books about farming, business, classic fiction and geology along with several books with Swedish titles.

Storytelling was a tradition for the Johnsons. Grampa also loved to sit and tell us about long-ago. When the sun sank behind the pines, we'd gather in the living room under the large oval framed picture of Gramma and Grampa. He'd tamp a pinch of fragrant tobacco into his pipe and light it with a twig from the fireplace, and then lean back in his big rocking chair. One night he told us about stories of a silver mines discovered around the north woods by the Indians. There was one hidden in the forest up north of here that he said belonged to old

Chief Ice Feathers, and he said Aunt Naomi's uncle knew him. I learned about the "Windigo" a man-eating monster, the frightening winter spirit of the forests. Then to break the atmosphere of gloom, Grampa told us Paul Bunyan stories that made us laugh, and stories about working at the old lumberjack camps. Even though he farmed all summer and they had the bed and breakfast, sometimes he worked in the logging camps to help pay bills. Grampa said he didn't roll the logs on the river, but he told us about logrolling in the Chippewa River and camp life in the woods.

He also had a new joke or story every time we sat down by the fireplace. I always wished I'd written them down. He always began by saying that Swedes had no sense of humor. I loved the lilt of his Swedish accent and the smiles that passed between my parents whenever he persuaded me one of his stories was true. He told little stories about "the Old Country" and his family there but I don't remember them anymore. I remember one night that Dad started talking about Al Capone and Dillinger Gangs during the Depression. They had a gangster lair nearby. He simply said the only policing in this area was the DNR game wardens. Grampa got strangely animated and his English became very hard to understand as he talked about the gangsters coming up from the south.

"Dey bring der filth up ta here en den spread it aroun' town. Dey kill peoples and stick 'em in da swamps. Dumbbells. Don't chou be talkin' 'bout dis stuff. Dos guys are de vers kinds of mens. Drop da subject, Sigurd, and I don't vanna hear enyting about it in dis family effer agin."

I think Grampa's English slipped completely backwards because he was so mad, and so it stuck in my mind. It was the only time I remembered seeing Gramps angry. Dad immediately jumped up and stomped out of the room. Mom hustled me off to bed as Gramps grumbled, but then later Dad came up and tucked me in.

These memories of my childhood bubbled up one after the other as I lay across the back seat propped up on a big pillow. Around five hours after we left Madison, we finally drove into Philetus Spur. Pine trees and heavy armed oaks shadowed the short main road through town and the sun dappled down through their leafy branches. The leaves were lime green on the branches of the oak trees and fluttering popple trees between the homes that seemed to guard the road. Jim rolled up to the one-pump gas station to fill up again before we headed out to the Inn. A young man loped out right away and leaned in at the car window by mom before Jim could get his seatbelt off and get out of the car.

"I'll be darned. Hey, Mrs. Johnson," he said with a big, friendly smile. "I remember you."

"Hey there Ben. How are you and the girls? It's Mrs. Taylor now, dear." Mom reached across Jim and touched his arm. "This is my husband, Jim Taylor. It is so good to see you again. You certainly have grown to be a handsome young man."

I smiled and waved at Ben from the back seat, but I didn't remember him. He was extremely thin, darkly tanned and wiry. His longish, wiry brown hair escaped from his knit hat. He had on a ragged red and black plaid flannel shirt over a white t-shirt tucked halfway into patched and torn jeans with sprinkled drips of oil on them. His scuffed pointed western boots needed a polish.

"We're fine, Miz Johnson-uh, I mean Taylor. Leah got married last year and moved over to Saint Paul! She's got Johan with her for the summer but Abbie, Joanie and I are just fine. What can I get ya today?"

"Fill 'er up please," Jim said, smiling. "This great to have someone gas up the car. So many places are starting to make you pump the gas and add oil yourself in Madison."

"No problem sir. We're full service at the Spur Gas Station. Can I check your oil and wash your windshield?"

"I'd appreciate that very much, Ben."

Ben moved around the car quickly and efficiently, cleaning the mirrors and windows with his squeegee before the tank filled. Jim pulled the lever that popped the hood and Ben looked around the side after wiping the dipstick on a rag stuck in his belt. I smiled at the smear of dirt on his cheek.

"Oil's fine but I think you could use some radiator fluid. Should I take care of that for you?" he asked.

"Great, Ben." Jim laughed and while he reached for his wallet, Ben poured water from a long-nosed bucket at the pump. Jim handed Ben a ten-dollar bill and he took it inside the little station. He came back with a smudged handwritten receipt and a handful of change. Jim took the coins and handed Ben back a dollar bill.

"Did I add it up wrong, sir?" Ben said worriedly.

"No, Ben, that's a tip, just keep it. Thanks for your help. You should start saving for school!"

"Whoa, are you sure? Thanks!" Ben said and with a huge smile, extended his hand.

"We're headed over to the Linger Inn and we're planning to stay for a while." Jim answered. "I'll be stopping back for gas now and then!"

"Welcome home! Come in any time! Maybe I'll see ya round."

Ben stood in the driveway, smiling and waving as we drove down the road.

"Welcome home" indeed. I looked back and felt just right. As we drove away Jim asked mom for a napkin and laughingly wiped the residual grease off his hand.

"That's a very nice kid, there. He seems pretty sensible."

"I believe he is." Mom said. "He's the grandson of a homesteader here, Leif Haagestad. He sure has grown up. He was always such a sweet little kid. His mom died from complications after her youngest daughter was born."

"That's mighty sad."

"Yes, then I heard his dad was killed in a logging accident...there's five kids. I think I heard from Greta Stina that they live right here in Philetus Spur."

On the road to the Inn we passed Ingvar Olson, his shoulders hunched over the steering wheel on his tractor, pulling a manure spreader through the barn door out to his back forty.

"Things don't change much here Mom," I remarked. "Olson's manure spreader is still sprinkling greenish, stinky goo." I caught a whiff of it in the cool air, the fresh scent of natural fertilizer. When I waved out the window at him he waved back and smiling cheerfully, though I knew that he couldn't recognize me. I hadn't seen him in years. He looked older and a more bent over the wheel.

"Mr. Olson's got to be a hundred-years-old, mom." I said.

"I don't think so, Honey. But he's might be 85 now. That's still quite young when you consider that his dad died at nearly a hundred years old. I think it must be the fresh air and work," she said, smiling.

I rolled down my window to inhale the musk scent of moss, ferns and pine trees as we drove past the open farmland and into the pines that surrounded the lake. We bumped along down the gravel road leading to the resort and as we came around the last corner the Linger Inn sign was suddenly in view beyond a wide-open green lawn. The Inn posed sedately on the hill with a large Victorian veranda, fanciful peaked rooflines, odd-shaped windows and white cedar siding.

Behind the Inn, Little Bear Lake was azure blue and golden sunlight dancing on its surface. Little lichen flecked log cabins with moss colored decks lined the road as it curved around the wide lawn and flowerbeds and up to the side of the Inn. Across the lake, I could just see the tip of Wolf Point with the farmhouse and barn, where my Grampa Johnson and Gramma Elin lived when I was a kid. On the east side of the property down a short driveway I noticed a new looking very large metal storage shed half hidden in the pines behind the Inn's parking lot. At the end of the road I could see the boat landing down to Little Bear Lake with a broad white dock stretching out into the water.

As we pulled up to the front of the Inn, a slender woman with thin brown hair braided around the crown of her head stepped outside on the porch. Her faded dress hid behind a checkered apron and waved her dishtowel at us.

"Leave your bags and the car right there for now. I was real surprised to get your letter saying youse guys were coming back up, but I saved two rooms upstairs for you." She told us, as she squinted into the sun.

"Hi, Mrs. Swenson, this is my new husband Jim." Mom said brightly. "I wanted to show Jim Lake Makoons. We had so many times here with Elin and Sven."

Anna Swenson looked oddly uncomfortable.

"Well, isn't that nice, Mary. I'm happy for both of you. Come on in." Mom and I got out of the car.

"You remember my daughter, Jewell?" Mom put her arm around my waist and I nodded at her with a small smile. I didn't honestly like this lady. It could have been the acrid odor of cigarettes or the frown wrinkles around her dark squinting eyes. She returned my half-smile and invited mom to come in for coffee. "She was just a little girl when we stayed at the Inn, back when Sven and Elin owned it. I hope you saved her room."

Jim parked the car and joined us by the steps. He and I followed mom and Mrs. Swenson as they walked and talked down the short hall on the way to the kitchen. The sweet smell of baking bread filled our noses, leading us forward. I fervently hoped there would be creamy sweet Swedish coffee with fresh bread and butter. After a quick look past the lobby, I discovered Mrs. Swenson also had cookies, and cake with fresh bread on a backboard, ready for guests. The chocolate aroma lured me around the corner.

"It's good to have you here, Mrs. Taylor" she said, "Make yourself at home."

"It's wonderful to be back, Mrs. Swenson. I love this place. Pull up a chair, Jewel and Jim. We can rest a little while we work on a plate of these wonderful cookies and coffee."

CHAPTER 3

Nature, Poem 16: Secrets ~ Emily Dickenson, 1896

The skies can't keep their secret!
They tell it to the hills —
The hills just tell the orchards —
And they the daffodils!
A bird, by chance, that goes that way
Soft overheard the whole.
If I should bribe the little bird,
Who knows but she would tell?
I think I won't, however,
It's finer not to know;
If summer were an axiom,
What sorcery had snow?
So keep your secret, Father!
I would not, if I could,
Know what the sapphire fellows do,
In your new-fashioned world!

FORGET-ME-NOTS, DAFFODILS

After coffee with Mrs. Swenson, we went up to settle into the Inn. Mom and Jim were on the second floor and my old room was the only one on the third floor. At the end of the hall there was a door that opened out to a creaky wooden staircase onto a second-floor roof over the dining room. When I stepped back in and closed the door, Mrs. Swenson was right behind me.

"Remember, for emergencies, only." Mrs. Swenson looked at me sternly. She showed me how to unlock, and then open my door. "Always use the inside stairs, unless there is a fire," she said, wagging her index finger at me. I was relieved when she went back down the stairs.

I always loved my odd, little room. It looked out over Shadow Bay toward Wolf Point, looking right at Johnson Point farm. There were few changes in the small bedroom, tucked into the angled tower in the side of the building facing southwest. There was a line of towering white pines, standing strong and straight along the shoreline with smaller trees huddled in safety behind them. I remembered that when

33

the sun sank behind the opposite peninsula, the little bay would have deep shadows on the west side. It made me reflect that families are like forests.

The inside curve of the bay was rock-strewn, and the swampy shore filled with old fluffy cattails and tall grass. Mossy logs poked their heads up along the shore where they tipped over in the wind and they lay with their roots reaching upwards. I knew from experience there were small painted turtles sunning themselves on those logs, watching for lunch.

Today the bay was slate blue and glassy in the full sunshine. Occasionally tiny ripples feathered out as minnows jumped for the bugs that would be skittering around on the surface. The old Johnson farm was visible through the trees from my window. The "T" shaped, two-story house and the barn were shadowed by another grove of pines, which had been planted on the northwest side by my Great Uncle Lars as a windbreak. The barn still looked strong from my vantage point although I remembered it being old when I was a kid and red paint peeling off parts of it. I could see the one window at the front of the barn where my Grampa used to sit at his workbench to mend things, using the early morning light. He refused to have electricity in the barn, saying it was a waste since the animals didn't need light and he could get his work done in the daytime. He did have a few old oil lamps he used infrequently in emergencies because they were very dangerous around the straw used in the barn for animal bedding.

Grampa got up each morning before the birds and went to bed just after sundown. Dad said his father and Uncle Lars were professional farmers, even with some of their old-fashioned ways. Grampa learned to read and speak excellent English as they learned some modern techniques from the University Extension Agent from Madison back in the early days. They farmed just under two hundred acres, ran the resort and owned the Philetus Spur lumber mill. They hired Mr. Peters, a neighbor man to help with the machinery and get their crops in. I remembered Mrs. Peters was a gaunt-faced woman with six big blond sons and a very shy daughter. I don't remember ever seeing Mrs. Peters or her daughter smile. Short plump and balding Mr. Peters didn't talk much, but I discovered quickly when I was a child, his pockets had lemon or ginger candies in them and he could quietly slip one to me if his wife didn't catch him.

Mr. Peters managed the farming part of the business when Grampa got too busy renting rooms and taking care of the visitors in his big farmhouse now called the Linger Inn. Mr. Peters and Grampa were very close. I heard they were more like brothers after Uncle Lars died. Then Grampa bought the farm from my Great Aunt Naomi and she moved to live near her own family at the LCO Reservation. When I was eleven Gramps and Gramma moved to the farm. Mr. Olson, Mr. Haagestad, "Old John" and Grampa would meet around the table and talk about the old days and results of their activities. I'd hear their voices and laughter rumble below well into the night when I was upstairs in bed. I remembered hearing Mr. Peter's kids all moved away after he died. I don't remember hearing what happened to his wife.

I backed away from the large dormer window filled with a million recollections and let the thin white curtains fall back in place but as I sat back down on my bed, a glint of light caught my eye. As I watched, a car drove into the farmyard of the Johnson farm and someone got out. I opened the window, knelt and curiously peered out to see if our car was gone from in front of the Inn, thinking Mom and Jim had decided to drive over to Grampa's farm for some reason but our station wagon was still in the parking area. When I looked back toward the farm, the car and its passenger were out of sight. Although I was somehow uneasy about the situation, I guessed it could be tourists who were lost and looking for directions. The breeze up here was a little too cool for comfort, so I shut the window and returned to my daydreaming. I would mention those people to Mom later.

"What a beautiful place to live," I thought to myself. "Grams and Grampa must have been happy here in the Inn. I wonder why they sold out to move to the farmhouse. It would be so great to have some place of my very own. Mom and Jim are selling our house in Madison, so I can never really go home again. I wish I had my own special place."

I stared out the window at the picturesque but unkempt farm, resting my chin on my hands at the windowsill. I sat there for quite a while, but my reverie ended when my feet began to prickle. Rising, I began unpacking my clothes from my suitcases into the dress and closet. I laughed a little when I bumped my head on the slanted ceiling over the little dresser against the wall.

"How very typical. Everything in this room is too small now. I hope I'll fit in the bed," I mused to myself. At almost five-foot nine and a half, I am taller than most women. I discovered these slanted ceilings were a little short on one end for me. I needed Alice's shrinking potion, I thought to myself.

After I had settled into my room I went out to reacquaint myself with the building. The second-floor biffy was bigger than the bathroom on my floor. It boasted a footed porcelain bathtub and a rough wooden table with a ruffled cotton skirt. I walked down the hall to Mom's room where she was still unpacking their things and chattering to Jim about the people they had to visit right away. As I leaned against the doorframe nodding occasionally to her comments I decided to leave and continue my exploring downstairs. They certainly didn't need me to plan their day. Mom mentioned dinner, but I shook my head.

"No, it's all right, Mom. I'll probably just have soup and a sandwich if Mrs. Swenson has one in her kitchen."

"Are you sure honey? Remember, we want you to have an enjoyable time this summer," Mom hugged me around the waist.

"I will, Mom. Don't worry. I just need to settle down and unwind for a while after the drive up here. I think I'll take a bath, or I'll go for a walk. I'll see ya later." I said, backing out of the door. As I closed it behind me, my heart caught. I sighed, and I fought a deep wave of loneliness. I almost went back in, to take them up on their offer for dinner, but I took a deep breath and turned to face my own life.

I wandered slowly down the wide stair case, creaking along the maple hardwood floors and curiously examining the woodwork of the old part of the house. I traced the circular carvings and floral designs with my finger. The carpenter that helped Grampa build this house must have had a lot of pride in his work. Dad said in the 'good old days' they had higher standards for their work. The white picture rail around the walls of the downstairs rooms made the very tall ceilings seem a little less imposing. A small parlor was on the right at the base of the stairs.

I knew conversations were not private on the black rotary dial telephone that hunched importantly on a little wooden table next to the door, its numbers almost worn off. If you picked it up, you might hear someone already talking on the office phone. The burgundy velvet on the heavy antique couch and chair was prickly and well-worn. Dark floral drapes shrouded the windows in this room. A bookshelf filled with paperbacks and old hardcover novels, included an old set of Funk and Wagnall's encyclopedias. Tucked in next to them was an antique looking copy of "Productive Soils," "The Woodcraft Girls at Camp" and a beautifully bound, gilt-edged edition of "The Minister's Wooing" by Harriet Beecher Stowe. I wondered where they came from and who else would read them but decided I would have to further explore these shelves later.

The hallway that turned left at the bottom of the very wide stairway led to Mrs. Swenson's office and the kitchen. Walking straight ahead across towards the lobby, I entered the dining room, a spacious room with a wide set of glass doors opening out into the veranda facing the lake.

This morning the dining room was buzzing with several families and couples lingering over cups of coffee. From the snippets of conversation, I overheard, I assumed the whole neighborhood used this as their gathering place. A heavyset and deeply-tanned waitress wandered from table to table, laughing and refilling their cups. I didn't stay because I thought I felt their eyes searching me, although I couldn't imagine why. I bought a glass of lemonade from a young girl behind the small counter with a couple of quarters I found in my slacks pocket and went out onto the veranda.

I watched people and birds and the antics of some goofy squirrels for an hour then returned to my room. Pulling out my newest paperback, I settled down on the bed for several hours with my favorite brave and resourceful female sleuth. Later, after an interlude at the dining room for a hamburger, a salad and a bowl of the "Soup of the Day," I retired to my room for the evening. My sleuth and I finished her most recent adventure until I put on my pajamas and faded off to my usual dream-filled sleep.

Vacation days drifted by like a swirl of a quiet stream's eddy. I thought everyone knew each other here on the lake. Evidently, they were people who either came up in groups or had been returning to the Linger Inn and other resorts on the lake for years. They loudly and laughingly planned boating escapades, golfing, and scenic hikes, sitting around tables on the lakeside veranda. Mom occasionally made a fuss about me being with them, but I didn't choose to hang out with them and their friends. I had breakfast with Mom and Jim a few times but usually I avoided any group activities. When we first arrived, the water was still too cold for swimming, so I walked and jogged to stay in shape. It was all quite restful and very, very boring, even for me.

Mom checked in on me regularly between their outings and visiting schedule. She knew many people who were staying at other resorts around the lake who were from around the Madison area. Jim bought bamboo fishing poles, tackle and worms at the bait shop in Philetus Spur. Then they stood side-by-side on Shadow Bay's marshy edges, or a deep pool in the river just south of town pulling in sunfish and perch. I went along and watched, but I hated seeing the fish wiggling on the hooks. Their gross writhing worms were repulsive. An elderly part-time cook at the Inn who seemed to get quite a kick out of their activities and helped them pepper, flour and fry their "fish chips" for lunch. Mom laughed as she told me all about their adventures each day. Her tan grew darker and her shining dark hair a took on a golden highlight. Her happiness made me uncomfortably envious.

When I got bored, I tried out the large wooden console TV in the lounge. It was almost useless since you usually couldn't see any of the fuzzy programs due to the poor reception. In the evening, some of the kids gathered and sat on the floor to watch "Mod Squad" or "Adam 12" but sometimes the pictures were rolling and fizzling. I supposed the antennas were poor, but it was also a long distance from the TV stations in Duluth. I also decided I'd get myself a portable radio or tape player soon. Mrs. Swenson listened to a local station in the kitchen, loud enough for the twangs and strains of country music to waft up to my room or across the front lawn. I wished I could block her out. Back home, I preferred 'easy listening', folk music and classic orchestral music. Dad and I used to listen to WPR and WLS in the evenings and I doubted they broadcast this far north.

One delightfully cool morning, I decided to walk over to Philetus Spur. I was out of sun-tan lotion and wanted to pick some up at the little shop. I walked slowly along the blacktop road that wended through the wildflower and dandelion-filled fields and then crossed a creek where I entered the west side of the village. The Philetus Spur Church with her tall spire, reclined serenely against the hill on the north side of the road. Behind the church was a cemetery surrounded by a little rock fence and lilac bushes. I observed that the ankle-deep grass needed mowing.

I walked around behind the church and surveyed the graveyard. Towards the back, on a little hillside overlooking the creek was the Johnson family headstone, surrounded by a moss-covered cement footing. Sven and Elin Johnson each had small, flat, grey headstones. Between them was a large flower pot planted with beautiful red geraniums, surrounded by draped white petunias. At their feet was the pure white granite headstone that simply said "Alex Teresa, 1916-1933". Great Uncle Lars' headstone looked just like theirs. There was a bright bouquet of yellow and white plastic daffodils stuck into the ground in front of the stone. I sat down on a little stone bench nearby under a tree and felt sad that Emily was not here with Lars, that she was many miles away in Hayward. I thought I'd stop and visit her when I went to town. Behind them, was my father's grave under a perfectly conical blue spruce. I walked up and touched the cold grey granite headstone gently, noticing a little green lichen attached to the speckled surface. I knelt and scratched it off with my nail and brushed the stone gently with my fingertips.

"He is not here, he is far away," I remembered the minister saying, standing at the front of the church in his black suit. *"He is not here; he has risen, just as he said. Come and see the place where he lay."*

Above his name, Matthew 28:6 was carved under a small cross. When I felt the thin trickle of a tear run my cheek, I patted the stone and hurried away, back to the road. There was no reason to plumb this pain again.

"I'll be back soon, Daddy," I whispered and hurried away from the cemetery.

Along the blacktop a thin cement walkway connected the church to Philetus Spur's small-town hall. Chirping birds accentuated the otherwise palpable quiet. Beyond the grassy lawn there was a one-chair barbershop with a red, blue and white striped wooden pole hung next to the front door. The barber sat in his chair, engrossed in his magazine. A scruffy-looking little bar with a neon beer sign in the window and a wooden screen door crouched across the street under the sweeping branches of a huge oak tree. It breathed out the sour odor of cigarette smoke through the screened windows. My eyes rolled when I heard the faint sound of country music carried out into the street. I paused to look in the front window at the gas station on the corner, but Ben Widmer was not visible. Next to it was a small new building with signs for real estate sales and an insurance office. The cute old rock-walled mini post office was empty and boarded up. Instead, a new blue steel drop box sat next to the road.

I found my way along a half-buried, narrow brick walkway and passed under a new, carved wooden sign shaped like a fish that declared, 'Hagie's Bait' in green and white. It was a combination grocery and bait shop. A new cement sidewalk ran the full front of the building. Crimson and hot pink geraniums blossomed profusely from wooden planters that lined the full width of the store, while white petunias fluttered from window boxes. There was a wooden barrel filled with bamboo cane poles by the entrance. Standing there I could hear the echo of a water bubbler in the minnow tank just inside the front door.

I went into the store, pausing until my eyes adjusted to the low light. As I entered, a sharp buzzer attached to the doorframe summoned out a trim, white-haired woman from the back room. She wore a navy blue, polyester pantsuit with a red and white shell underneath. Above the sound of bubbling water was the creaking of the wooden floor as I walked to the cooler to choose Colby cheese curds, a box of crackers and a couple of apples. I noticed a box of used books at the end of the counter. "Take one - give one," the sign announced. I'd remember that when I finished the books I was reading.

I was never good at small talk so our exchange of money for goods was awkward, silent except for the "cha-ching" of her big, old-fashioned, cash register.

"Thank you. You're up for the summer?" Her voice had a musical lilt. It was soft and friendly.

"Yes. We're staying at the Linger Inn this summer."

"Well, did you find everything you needed?"

I nodded.

"I hope you have a pleasant day then."

"Thanks. You too," my words sounded vaguely unsociable.

"Stop in again," she encouraged.

"Oh. I will," I said shyly, but I didn't look up.

The sun drenched me when I walked out. It took a couple of seconds for my eyes to adjust again. I noticed a brown pickup parked on the gravel in front of the store, but no one was around.

"Odd. They sure showed up suddenly." I looked around the empty street.

"Hey Malin!" I heard a man's voice call out.

"Well, what a surprise, Jacob. I'm so glad to see you! Come on in, have a cup of soup." I assumed the woman from the store had a guest.

The spring on the screen back door squeaked and slammed the door shut and then the street was quiet again except for the birds. I walked away vaguely wishing someone would come along and break the walls of silence around me.

As I walked back to the Inn, I thought about the other families staying there. There was one young couple who spent their time playing with their two-year-old toddler or talking to each other. I heard him call her "Laurie." She was pretty, slender and dark-haired. She always looked up and said "Hi," in a friendly way when we met at the Inn. The three of them walked across the lawn every day, holding hands. They'd go down to the beach or wander off on walks, coming back up to the Inn for meals in the veranda dining room. Once, however, I caught his flashing black eyes staring curiously at me and I blushed; they seemed to see right through my clothes. After that, I took great pains to avoid him.

The other family included two teen girls. I was surprised their parents let them wear the miniscule bikinis, tight shorts and such revealing shirts. They posed on the beach brushing their hair and covertly watching to see if anyone was looking at them. Several times a week they took their father's car to Hayward and then on the veranda, they unpacked bags of t-shirts, post cards, and candy as they giggled loudly and made sure everyone noticed. Over breakfast, I heard them discussing outdoor dances held under a tent at Historyland in town and seeing big name bands. I couldn't believe their parents left them to their own devices so much. I hoped they didn't condone the beer they shared down at the beach with some boys from across the lake. After dark, other teenagers would show up at the dock in front of the Inn and they would party until well-after midnight. They'd play "The Stones," "The Dead" and "The Doors" on an eight-track player with an extension cord all the way back to the porch until shushed by someone in a nearby cabin. One of the boys had approached me near the dock one afternoon.

"Hey babe, yah wanna blow some weed? Wanna beer?" He had long brown hair and wore a tattered tie-dye tee-shirt with a black peace sign. He also needed a shave and shampoo. I shook my head at the proffered little bottle without comment and walked on by with my book, towel and a beach chair, struggling not to roll my eyes or scowl. I heard that kind of stupid in Madison, but drugs and alcohol just didn't fit into my concept of fun. I assumed the sunglasses he always wore, covered dilated pupils and reddened eyes. The girl said something under her breath, he flipped his hair back out of his eyes, and they both laughed loudly. It didn't make any difference to me.

"Pathetic," I said under my breath and stared straight ahead.

Later, smelling something familiar, I caught them sharing a joint on the back stairs draped all over each other. I wanted to rat them out to their parents. That night I overheard a girl giggling in the yard below my window. What kind of parents would let their kids run around with no supervision? They should at least wonder why these kids were so 'out of it.' Mrs. Swenson was watching them carefully, however. I'd seen her staring out the windows. I don't think anything got past her small dark eyes and was sure she couldn't condone them using drugs and alcohol on her property.

I shrugged my shoulders and grabbed a long stem of grass to chew thoughtfully as I enjoyed the sun and Wisconsin blue sky as I walked back to the Inn. The next afternoon I was quietly leaning against the porch wall and reading when I saw Laurie's plump toddler scream and dart down to the lake. Little Tamara crowed with impish delight when she knew she had my attention. Her newest way to get attention was to dance around and around, with her little hands above her blond curly head as she went into the water. She splashed water high with her feet and laughed gleefully. Her beaming parents sat shoulder to shoulder on a towel smiling their approval. My heart strings tugged sharply watching this family tableau. I remembered moments like these with my parents.

Suddenly a man's deep voice rumbled out the screen door from the Inn's phone in the main downstairs hallway.

"I know! Yeah, I heard ya. I'm watchin' for him. Yeah: okay, okay. You know I can handle it. No problem. Yeah. Goodbye."

I inched away from the doorway to avoid the appearance of eavesdropping and sidled off the deck. I was walking down the path when I heard the screen door slam and heavy footsteps scuffed across the gravel past the lilac bushes. When I got halfway across the grounds to the tennis court, I heard a car door slam and the tires spun on the gravel in the parking lot. I turned just in time to see a very dusty black pickup swing out of the circle drive and down the road in a cloud of dust. I wondered idly who "they" were watching. It could be someone from the Inn who got lost and they were looking for him or it could be just a lost pet. In any case, that guy sure didn't sound pleasant.

"I read too many detective stories," I mused to myself.

As I walked in the early summer sunshine, I wished I could find someone with a credible game of tennis. My racket and shoes were in the trunk of the car just in case I found someone to play. I was getting bored with reading, sunshine and sand. Lake Makoons is a spring-fed lake so the water was still quite cold, but I braved swimming out into the bay. I thought about walking in to Philetus Spur again or just going for a hike somewhere. I finally just spent the rest of the day sunbathing on a wooden recliner on the lawn near the lake and finished reading my last novel. The reviews I'd read promised thrills, but gnats and little black ants were too irritating.

By the end of the week I was seriously bored. Jim drove our wooden speed boat a few times so that Mom and I could waterski. I love to slalom because of the feeling of graceful power as the bottom blade cut through the water, building up enough speed by zig-zagging in wide paths to jump across both wakes at once. Mom and I would ski at the same time, laughing and crisscrossing under each other's tow ropes. Sometimes I would just take the boat out and cruise around the lake, watching the wildlife and enjoying the freedom. I finished all the novels I'd brought along and longed for something more physical to do. I began to regret spending the summer up here.

The sun warmed up the surface water in the middle of June, so I swam lazily out into the big lake and around the channel past Shadow Bay. Since my family still owned the property, I decided to hike around Shadow Bay from the Inn to visit the silent farm on Johnson Point. Returning to the beach, I wrapped my towel around myself and went up to my room. Towel drying my hair, I brushed it out, so I could braid it back away from my face. I put on a T-shirt over my swimsuit and pulled up white cutoff jean shorts. I buckled my leather sandals on and headed out. At the corner of the bay, I saw the path in the old tote road that led to the farm.

Meandering along, I knelt and admired at the tiny blue forget-me-nots. My heart took in the sparkling lake and the broad expanse of sky above me, now fringed with tall stately pines and birches. Early summer wildflowers out in the field were yellow and blue. Something smelled perfectly delightful, but I couldn't locate the sweet source. Pausing at the edge of the field I admired the world.

"There ought to be crayon named after this sky color called Wisconsin Blue," I mused to myself. "There just aren't any colors in a box of crayons quite this beautiful."

I admired the glassy mirrored image of the still green forest that stood guard across from me on the west side of the Shadow Bay. As I rounded the bottom of the bay on a little beaten path on the water's edge, I looked to see if Grampa's barn was visible from here. There was a clear view of the homestead with its frame of white birch trees. I stopped there, leaning against a tall oak, youthful memories flooding into my mind.

The white T-frame farm house looked like I remembered it. Thick vines engulfed the south side and overgrown cedars stood like twin sentinels at the little porch towards the driveway. The high-peaked roof had two little dormer windows cut into the bedrooms upstairs facing the lake. I remembered how those two little rooms smelled stuffy in the summertime. Their steeply pitched ceilings came down to within a few of feet of the floor on the outside walls. I could picture the walls, papered with old-fashioned pastel rosettes in a cream-colored background. In my memory, the floor was covered by grey linoleum with a faded pattern of big pink and magenta roses.

Mom, Dad and I stayed there for two weeks every summer when I was young. I recalled the smell of wood smoke, bacon and pancakes wafting up the stairs before the sun came up. Grampa always started the day with a hearty breakfast and a large cup of strong, sweet, and creamy coffee before he went out to the barn. Gramma rustled around the kitchen quietly serving food as she made fresh warm bread.

They were such handsome and interesting people. He was as talkative as she was quiet. His wide smile displayed straight white teeth and full warm-looking lips under a grey moustache. I loved to sit next to him at breakfast and then tag-a-long behind him as he did his morning chores. Kindly ice blue eyes would crinkle with laughter and he'd shake his head when I kissed the calves on their soft pink noses and talked to my favorites. Many times, I fell asleep in the barn with his dog, curled up in a pile of fresh straw while Grampa finished the chores. Often, I would wake up with kittens or cats licking my eyebrows and jumping on me, or the rooster crowing next to my head. I learned how to carefully pluck eggs from under Gramma's chickens in a little coop by the barn and gardens of flowers and vegetables on the sunny side of the house towards the lake.

Sometimes I sat on Grampa's lap in the evenings as he worked at his desk in his office, writing in his journals and adding the numbers up. Sometimes, I sat on his lap during this process, writing my own columns of numbers on a slip of paper. I wondered what my parents were doing during these quiet days when I was at Johnson Point. I didn't remember them except at meals and in the evenings.

Impulsively, I started across the little meadow towards the farmhouse picking some tiny bluish-purple wildflowers almost invisible in the long grass as a couple of swamp birds warbled above me, swooping back and forth overhead. The hot sun stared down through the cloudless noon sky as my tennis shoes crunched across the gravel driveway, around to the back door. I felt the familiar and unwelcome tickle of a woodtick and picked one off my ankle. Peering through the dusty window in the door at Gramma's kitchen I felt sad to see the linoleum peeled and cracking. It looked like rain and snow found their way through a small broken pane in the east window. The familiar cream-colored dishes were gone from the glass door cupboards, replaced with dust, cobwebs and dead flies. The sun shone down the hallway and into the living room beyond. I could almost hear Gramma behind me, holding a big pan in her arms, chatting to her chickens as she scattered feed in the yard. I rattled the door, but it was locked.

I followed the porch around to the lakeside of the little house, noticing the strips of peeling white paint on the thin wooden lap-siding. Wild pink roses grew in profusion, crowding around the beds where Gramma grew orange and black tiger lilies. As I stood in the dooryard surveying the farm, absorbing the sweet odor of early summer flowers and grasses, I imagined my Swedish grandparents together looking out over the bay, quietly satisfied with their claim in this "New World." I remembered them as old and white-haired, still speaking Swedish to each other and accented English to everyone else. I flashed back to one specific night, as we sat on this porch watching the lake and they sang a sweet little Swedish song "Det Mig Var" together. Grampa put his arm around Gramma Elin's shoulders. *"It was me,"* he interpreted for me.

A few years ago, I was terribly shocked when Mom told me that Gramma died in a car accident while she visited relatives down in Missouri. We drove up to the funeral in Philetus Spur and stayed at the farm along with Aunt Greta Stina. Then dad died, and it seemed not too long after that when we heard that Grampa died of a heart attack and we came up for his funeral too. That's when Aunt Greta finally locked up the farm.

"That's too much sadness to bear," I thought to myself.

Sudden memories rushed into my mind as I wandered around outside on the lawn. Grampa installed a funny little bathroom in the coat closet inside the back door when they moved over here from the Inn in 1962. There was a tiny sink so close that you could nearly wash your hands while sitting on the toilet. The window was right next to the toilet and so you could watch the garden. I don't remember ever seeing a shower stall as skinny as theirs.

Stepping backwards and looking up with a hand shielding my eyes, I noticed there were a few bricks missing from the two chimneys. Since nobody used the house after they moved out, overgrown tall weeds and grass surrounded the farm, the sheds were in ruins, and the back-porch steps were deteriorating. But it gave me a strong feeling of belonging to stand here in the farmyard. I heard a discussion a year or so ago that someone wanted to buy out the one-hundred-sixty-acre farm. They were going to tear down the farmhouse, use the fields for hunting pheasants and build a storage facility.

"Dad would hate that," I cried to mom. "Please don't sell the farm." Mom looked unhappily at Jim and nodded.

"We won't then, honey, not yet anyway."

Wandering around the house to a covered porch on the side towards the lake, my memories of Dad, Mom and growing up absorbed me. I stood looking out over Lake Makoons, leaning on the railing. Then, in the distance I heard the deep rumble of a nearby big vehicle moving towards Philetus Spur. When that noise faded, it was just crickets and bird calls again. I walked around to look at the garden. Gramma's fence around the old garden plot was sagging and the posts were loose. At its base, I found a patch of purple and yellow Johnny-Jump-Ups and some tiny white anemones. I was kneeling to pick one of those cheery little flowers when a cloud drifted over the sun and I suddenly felt I was not alone. Goosebumps rose on my arms and neck. It seemed someone was near and staring at me. I didn't believe in ghosts and I didn't hear anything, but I felt prickles of fear as the hair on the back rose as I slowly stood up and casually as I could, surveying the still-pleasant scene. There was the sound of rushing waves on the shore and the breeze gently rattling through the popples. I responded to my fear the way you learn to in the city, by staying alert and fully aware. I surveyed my surroundings as I headed for safety along the path back to the Inn, acting nonchalant and unafraid. I thought the woods might be dangerous---if, in fact, there was a danger---but the road back to the highway was just as wooded and it was further to safety. I shook my head and shrugged off the fear. After all, I had not seen anyone.

"Perhaps Grampa's ghost is watching over me–and I couldn't fear him." That thought made me smile and was comforting.

As I walked back along the little trail, it suddenly occurred to me it was odd that there should even be a trail from the farm to the Inn. This had not obvious to me when I had come across the trail earlier because I had been sightseeing and recollecting. My nerves relaxed, and I slowly surveyed my surroundings and still saw no one. Taking a ragged breath, I leaned up against a small tree to steady myself, then sighed with relief and continued down the trail. It was a narrow, definite path through the woods. It led across the bottom of the lakeside fields to the farm. As I walked up to the Inn, Mrs. Swenson was unloading bags out of her old green van in the lot behind the Inn.

"Hi, Mrs. Swenson," I cried, happy to talk to someone, and letting off a little nervous steam. "Can I help you?"

"Why Jewell, you'd better go inside and cool off. Your cheeks are pink as anything," she said, as she walked beside me towards the house and up the steps.

46

"I'm quite all right, Mrs. Swenson. Really. But I was just taking a walk and got quite a fright over by Grampa's farm."

"What? Why? What happened?" She swung around and frowned.

"Nothing. I mean nothing happened. I went over to Grampa's farm just to look around and I felt sure someone was there. I guess I am just an old scaredy-cat," I explained quickly. "I'm used to the city where you run first and ask questions later. It was probably just a cloud over the sun."

"You shouldn't wander around alone," she advised seriously. "You young girls need to be more careful. If you need something to do, there's always kids around here who can show you around. No, you stay away from there. You could fall in their old well-hole and they'd never know what happened to you."

She let the screen door slam between us and walked quickly back into the kitchen. I couldn't seem to make up my mind whether I should go in and ask her right out what she meant by her odd remark or go back to my room. Certainly, she wouldn't be afraid I would fall in the well-hole, it was filled in years ago when Grampa put in an electric pump. I finally decided I'd go look for Mom and Jim to see what plans they had made for lunch and ask Mom if there was a problem at the farm. Why would Mrs. Swenson act so weird?

Walking around to the front entrance to the Linger Inn on the way to my mother's room, I nearly ran over a greasy dark-haired man who'd been hanging around since we arrived. He tripped over his own feet trying to get out of my way.

"Hi," I said politely.

"Uh, yeah," he mumbled, shoving his hands deep into his pockets and skirting me as he strode around the corner of the building with his head down.

"Yikes, now there's a likeable guy," I grumbled under my breath as I opened the front door. I let the front door slam on the world and entered the cool dim interior of the Inn. I checked Mom's room, but she was gone, as per usual. I dug out my racket and went out to the empty tennis courts to practice my lobs against the fence. After an hour of desultory batting I gathered up the balls and went back to my room to change and join Mom and Jim for dinner. Mom looked tired and wasn't very talkative, so I excused myself to up upstairs. Later that night, when I was reading in bed, I realized that I forgot to ask mom about Mrs. Swenson and the farm but decided to finish my book instead.

I woke up the next morning to a cacophony of little bird songs and big black crows cawing at each other as they swooped across Shadow Bay. It was a gloomy and gray, summer-rain day. For some reason, it seems that the birds of this part of Wisconsin always sing they're hardest just before and just after a storm. Looking out the window I thought I had missed the storm. I sat cross-legged on my bed, and pulled the soft pink quilt up around me, grateful for its cuddly warmth. My bed was across from the window, so I could see the choppy water on Shadow Bay and the white caps on Lake Makoons beyond Johnson Point without getting out of my cozy nest. A veil of white mist hung low enveloping the Point itself and masking the pine grove behind Grampa's barn.

As I admired the technique of a blue heron's take-off over the swampy end of the Shadow Bay inlet, I noticed an orange light winking on and off in the little window at the front of the barn. I twisted to my knees and crawled to the window to get a better look. Could my eyes have fooled me? No light appeared again in the dark window of the big red barn as I strained my eyes to see any telltale movement. I jumped to my feet, trotted down the hall to the stairs to Mom's door and knocked.

"Hey, Mom!" She didn't answer the door, so I turned and ran back up to my room to peer out the window again. The light was gone.

"Now, where is she?" I grumbled, pulling on my jeans and sliding into a thin tee and a pale blue sweater. I grabbed my sneakers and yanked them on without tying the strings. Hurrying down the stairs, I made my way to the main floor.

The cook was clanking pots and pans in the kitchen I could smell delicious sausages and bacon. The odor of bread baking seeped into every corner. In the dining room was the usual hum of conversation. I found Mom and Jim in the corner booth by the fireplace, deep in discussion.

"Hi, Mom, sorry to barge in, but I need to ask you something."

"What's wrong honey? Sit down and have some breakfast." Mom pulled a chair over to the table and tugged my arm.

"What's the matter Julie, can I help?" Jim leaned forward as if he were interested. To be honest, I didn't like the name 'Julie,' but I never told Jim.

"No. Well I don't know. Mom did Aunt Greta rent out the farm or something?"

"No; not that I heard of, but I think she'd mention it. Why? What's wrong with you? Are you okay?"

48

"Mom, I think someone is hanging around the buildings at the farm. I've seen lights over there more than once…and then people in the yard." I spoke quickly, hoping Mom would take me seriously and show some concern over the suspicions bothering me. I wanted her to reassure me with some reasonable explanation for the lights, cars and people at the farm.

"Oh, Honey, probably someone was lost and just looking for directions. There's no electricity and the buildings are all locked up. Did you know that Greta took everything out of it when Dad died? Don't worry about it. Don't you agree, Jim?"

"Sure, honey. Julie, there's nothing there to disturb. I think even the barns are empty and there certainly isn't anything in the shed worth stealing." I imagined I could feel Jim's irritation over my interruption of their conversation. "We can take a drive over there, Mary, if you want to check it out, but I am very sure it is nothing."

"Yes, sure. Maybe we can do that later. Now, Jewel, what do you want to order for breakfast, dear? Pancakes, eggs, or bacon; or a Lumberjack Breakfast, with everything? You always used to love that."

"No, that's all right, Mom, I am not hungry. I just thought you might be interested," I added looking away. "I'm going for a walk." I ignored the look that I felt sure passed between them and turned away. I threaded my way through the dining room tables and out the door to the veranda.

"I wish I'd stayed home. I can't stomach him." I said into the mist as I strode quickly towards the beach. The lake was like glass and the opposite shore shrouded in a blanket of white. The air was pregnant with mist, stillness and silence. At the edge of the lake, I stood on a large rock, and leaned back against the trunk of a birch tree.

"It's a pretty view, isn't it?"

The deep male voice startled me.

"Aackk!!" With that loud, embarrassing squawk, I jumped involuntarily, backing away from the tree.

"Oops. Sorry. I thought you knew I was here."

I looked around until I saw a foot sticking out from behind my tree, then a fishing line extending out into the lake.

"I know, you think they don't bite this late in the morning. I was just resting. I really didn't mean to surprise you – sorry." A very handsome, smiling face appeared from behind the tree trunk.

"Oh, that's all right," I said, taking a deep breath. "I guess I just didn't expect anyone out here," I added. "You did startle me."

He had the most intriguing face I'd ever seen. His gingery curly hair was past due for a cut and accentuated the deep heathery green of his eyes. His thick eyebrows and lashes were almost white, and freckles were sprinkled all over his very pale cheeks.

"You appeared like the Cheshire cat," I said stepping back.

"Then I should be sitting on the branch instead of under, my dear Alice," he laughed loudly and slowly began to stand up – and that was a long trip.

"You'd better watch your head, you may still end up in that tree," I said as he unfolded.

"No, Alice, I'm not a basketball star." He laughed, looking down at me. This was an unusual feeling since I'm tall too.

"I'm sorry. That was rude. But you must get that comment a lot."

"I suppose you get those tall jokes yourself."

"Oh, sure. I get tired of it, but people also tend to leave me alone." I wanted to kick myself for sounding crabby. "Sorry, I didn't mean to offend you. Do you fish here often?"

"Nope. I can't do much of anything else and I'm totally bored. Even fishing is rather boring, but I catch some high-quality naps. I rarely catch fish. I suppose I have the wrong bait." He was almost apologetic. "I don't like to kill or eat them anyway. I always let them go."

"I guess relaxing can be boring," I said as I lifted my damp hair off my shoulders and shook it back. The mist was turning to rain, tapping on the leaves around us.

"Isn't that the truth?" he said, "I haven't really talked to anyone else yet today. I don't know anyone here at the Inn except the cook."

"I've met some of the people here, but I only really know my mom and her husband, and Mrs. Swenson. I haven't done much because they are on hegira most of the time."

"Hegira?" He smiled widely, and his eyebrows rose comically. "A what?"

"I mean they go on lots of odd trips with their friends, just looking at stuff, you know, - seeing novel places."

"That's a very odd word," he laughed. "But I like it. Hegira."

"It's called 'walkabout' in Australia."

"You know, it's getting wetter out here by the minute," His forehead wrinkled as he looked down at me and asked, "Would you like to have a cup of coffee with me at the dining room? You're as drenched as I am."

I hesitated, caught my breath and felt a blush in my cheeks. I dropped my head forward and let my hair cover my embarrassment.

"I'm sorry; we haven't been introduced!" he exclaimed, reaching out his hand. "I'm Jake P-i-e-t-e-r-s, that's spelled like 'pie' with a 't'. How 'bout it? Coffee?" He talked so fast and fired questions so quickly that I felt stupid and slow. I took his hand and he squeezed it in a hearty handshake. His big hand was warm and strong. I felt lost in it for a moment, embarrassed that I didn't let go right away.

"Jewell Johnson. That's with two J's and two 'ell's," I said with a smile.

When Jake laughed, I felt I had to laugh with him. His eyes crinkled up and met mine. The world slipped away for a second.

"I know. I asked yesterday. The Inn's cook can be very talkative. He knows your folks," he said. "You guys are from Madison. I ate Mike's hot cinnamon and raison sweet rolls early this morning and gleaned valuable information. I'm glad your name is Jewell; it fits, although you do look like my idea of an Alice – when she was tall. I hope you aren't into drugs like she was. Madison is rife with drugs." He looked at me meaningfully.

I was taken aback; no one ever even mentioned things like that to me.

"What?" I stammered, "Oh, I understand, I'm sorry. No, I don't do drugs, smoke or drink."

"C'mon, Jewell with two L's, won't you join me?" He reached out and took my elbow.

I was a little uncertain, wondering what mom would think if I walked in with this guy. But I deeply wanted to know him, it was like a strong magnet drew me. I instantly wondered if he felt it too.

He picked up his rod and small bait box with one hand. We turned and walked back up through the wet grass on hill in front of the Inn. I caught a sweet whiff of the hot pink wild roses that suddenly bloomed yesterday, crowding the edge of the lawn.

"Hey, you can keep up. That's cool." He said suddenly, "When I am with someone I usually feel I have to walk like a snail. You have a long stride. Are you in athletics?"

"I swim," I said. "And I play basketball, swim and play tennis."

"Competitively?"

"Yes, I've won a few swim-meets," I explained shyly, "I love being in the water. It makes me feel strong and powerful. I like running and riding bikes though, too. I was in the girls' basketball club at West High, in Madison."

"You are so graceful and beautiful. Do you model?" He looked sideways at me intently.

"Oh no," I felt a blush rise again. I cursed my shyness, looked down and let my hair again shield me from his probing eyes. We continued walking across the wide Inn lawn.

"What kinds of stuff have you planned for this summer?"

"Nothing. My mom wants me to stay here all summer and relax before I start college. I hope it isn't as boring as it looks like it will be." I said a little wistfully. "I had a job in Madison this summer and wanted to find an apartment of my own."

"That's not easy. It's tough to get a part time job that will pay for an apartment in the cities." He commented. "What's your job?"

"I graduated early from high school, so I was working part-time in the State Street Boutique and a couple of days a month at Brown's used Bookstore in Madison. That was, until we left to come here. I liked Madison. I could ride my bike to work. I've worked part-time in my High School's office and I've done secretarial jobs for mom at the U."

"It's hard to stash cash and pay rent with office and part-time retail jobs," Jake said. "Can you do anything with computers?"

"Oh, sure. I went to a student workshop at the UWCC before Sterling Hall was bombed and I took a programming class at the U last summer."

"Great, there you go; I think computer jobs might have a good future, at least in the government. If you live in Madison, you can live at home, can't you?"

"I suppose I could, but I don't want to. They are selling the house I grew up in and moving." Pieters cocked his head to the side.

"Why do you want to go to college," he asked curiously. Just then I looked up directly into his eyes. I completely forgot what the question was and caught my breath.

"Huh?" I answered lamely and a little breathlessly. "I, uh…don't know."

"Why are you going to college then?" he repeated looking back at me with a furrowed brow.

"I guess it's what my folks wanted. My mom and dad went to the University. I enjoy sports, studying and writing. What about you? You haven't said much about yourself."

"I'm twenty-four. I graduated from Denfeld West in Duluth but was drafted by the Army right away and was in Viet Nam. I invested a couple years in technical school, but I worked for the Superior PD until last fall."

"Oh, I see."

"I thought about going back to college, but I haven't got time." he said slowly as we walked up the steps to the veranda. "Right now, my time is strung out,"

"Why?" I asked curiously.

"Issues," he responded and looked back at the lake as he opened the door for me. Inside, I turned and nearly bumped into him. Stepping back, I looked directly into his face again and his eyes met mine.

"You live in Superior?" I asked awkwardly, tearing my eyes away and looking for a hostess or a table. Jake leaned his rod against the coat rack and put his little plastic tackle box on the floor by the hat rest.

"Duluth. After Nam, I moved back with my folks in Duluth," he answered. "I lived and worked on the Wisconsin side."

"Are you here alone on vacation?"

"No, I brought my entire harem," he said quite seriously. "Usually, I don't bring them along."

"Aw, c'mon," I laughed and shook my head.

"No, I'm serious. They always insist on coming along. My ladies are very jealous of other women!"

"Seriously, how did you end up coming here on vacation?" I asked as we walked into the lounge. I was very relieved to see that Mom and Jim were not around.

"I have a friend in the neighborhood, she suggested it" he said. "The Spur is such a quiet and restful place. I love the Inn."

"How about we sit over there by the fireplace?"

"Great, I'll throw a log in and you can order us coffee."

I sat in the warm armchair near the window and watched the lake between the raindrops racing down the glass. There was a grand view of Lake Makoons. The waitress came with two steaming cups of coffee as Jake came back and sat in the chair facing me. He smiled as I poured in a generous amount of cream and two teaspoons of sugar.

"What have you been doing since you got here?" I asked stirring my coffee.

"I'm here to rest," he explained. "Mostly sitting. I am not supposed to do anything. That drives me nuts."

"That's what I have been doing; nothing exciting," I said with a shake of my head. "Why do you have to rest? You look pretty healthy."

"I…well; I was shot on duty."

"You're kidding, how horrible!"

"It happens sometimes. That's the inherent danger in police work."

"I can't imagine it," I shivered. "Where were you hit?"

"In the parking lot." He reached over and touched my arm and grinned broadly as I rolled my eyes. "I am sorry, I couldn't resist that opportunity. I took a shotgun blast in the stomach. I've had a lot of surgery to patch it up."

"Good Lord. It's strange you wouldn't be wounded in war but got shot here at home." Regretting my words, I blew across the top of my coffee and then took a sip. It was still too hot. I stirred in a little more cream. "Why would someone shoot at you?"

"I'm Douglas County Sheriff's Deputy. I was on duty one night and apparently, I just got in somebody's way." His gaze slid by me out to the lake.

"What happened?"

"Hard to say, we don't really know. Some guy shot me at night in front of a bar just south of Superior. I went down in the parking lot, in full view of the highway and the bar, but nobody called for help. I pulled myself to the patrol and called in on my radio. I really don't remember anything else except a semi-truck pulling out of the parking lot." We both drank coffee at the same time and our eyes met over the rims. My heart twitched painfully. Could he tell?

"Can't they find out who shot you? Didn't they investigate?"

"Jewell, of course they investigate something like that, especially when an officer goes down in the line of duty. I've done some footwork on it myself, but I can't seem to make the right connections. But, I can't discuss an open case. The guys on the force will probably crack this one soon enough." Jake's deep voice absorbed me when he talked. "Murder and mayhem is a little rare up north."

"My mom said that my dad was murdered up here," I blurted out. "She was told someone would investigate it but instead nothing ever happened. He died, and nobody cared enough to find out why."

"Whoa, Jewell, I am so sorry. What happened?" He touched my hand softly with his fingers again.

I was suddenly, helplessly weak. Without warning, years of pent-up fear, pain and unhappiness simply poured out. I needed to talk about my Dad's death for the first time to another adult, nervously holding my arms tight across my chest.

"One night my dad got a phone call at home and told my mom that he had to come up here. She said it was just so sudden and so out of character for him. He was usually so careful and thoughtful. They argued about it, but then my dad left anyway. The State Patrol called later that night and said he went off the road on state highway 53, north of Eau Claire just before Rice Lake. It was cloudy and rainy that night but there was no good reason for an accident. My dad was an excellent driver. When we got up there, Mom said that Dad whispered to her that a semi 'got him' before he died. Mom tried to tell the officer what Dad said, and I heard the State Police guy tell my mom he was probably just out of his mind." At this point, I realized the muscles in my stomach cramped tightly, my forehead hurt. I felt sick to my stomach. "He was gone. Just like that. Mom begged the trooper, but he said there was no good reason to leave the file open. They thought he went to sleep at the wheel or was avoiding a deer or an animal. I don't think they tried to find out what happened. Sometimes I guess I still can't believe he's gone. Losing him was just so unreal- it was so fast." I found myself feeling strangely vulnerable with Jake. I put my shaking, cold hand over my forehead.

"I'm sorry Jewell. It must have been so hard for you and your mom." He reached over and patted my hand. It was awkward and yet comforting at the same time. "Drink your coffee but keep talking. I found that sometimes simply talking about this kind of stuff helps."

That did it. I buried my hot red face in my sweater sleeve and hiccoughed through my tears. I heard Jake move closer and I could feel his presence. I couldn't even lift my head to look at him. I wiped the tears off my face and Jake handed me a napkin. Lord, I must have looked just awful.

"I'm sorry." I whispered weakly. "I guess I've just never talked about it with anyone. It seemed so long ago and suddenly it is right here in my face again. I can see my dad's face and the blood on his hand."

With surprise, I realized as I said that, the lump that squeezed my throat released and I felt new unbidden emotions bubble up.

"I really miss my Dad. We were so close. My grandparents both passed away around that time too. Then Mom got married and now my life is shattered like glass. Jim is selling our house. They want to get rid of the farm. Why?"

"Come on, Jewell, let's walk somewhere," he said softly, "I think it would be good for both of us. C'mon." he said, helping me to my feet.

His warmth and strength were reassuring to my chilly heart. As we walked down the steps of the Inn and across the yard toward the parking lot, he held my arm and walked close to me. The mist was still heavy under the pines because the sun couldn't burn through the big fluffy clouds up above and the pines held the moist air low to the ground, but the rain stopped while we were inside.

Once we walked across the yard Jake turned and took my shoulders in his hands, so I faced him. Then, he lifted my chin and I looked right into his eyes. With a little embarrassment, I was glad the thick hedge of lilac bushes along the side of the lot shielded us from the Inn windows and the beach just beyond.

"You've really let the steam build up, haven't you? Why didn't you talk to someone and let it go before?"

"I couldn't. I think my dad and I were as close as you can get. We were two peas in a pod. When he died, the light went out in my life like a lamp switching off. I sometimes don't even want to go to church because I can't understand why God would take him away from me. I saw Mom suffer too, but it didn't make any sense to me at all. I still feel so alone. It seemed like there never was anyone else that wanted to talk to about it. I just feel awfully alone and empty."

Jake pulled a handkerchief out of his shirt pocket and handed it to me. He hugged my shoulders quickly and gently and then stepped back, but I didn't want him to. With his hands in his pockets he looked at the ground.

"I am really honored you shared this with me, Jewell."

"I am so sorry. I probably shouldn't have," I said, retreating into my stupid shell again. I blew my nose and then wondered what to do with the handkerchief. "I can't believe it. I do feel better."

"That's how it works when you bottle up something that big. Hey, let's just walk out to the main road." We walked along in silence for a little way, the gravel crunching under our feet. I stepped down into the grassy ditch to pick a purple sweet clover blossom. I bit off the nectar sacks with my teeth and savored the momentary sweetness. Jake laughed, saying he used to do the same thing. I picked one and offered it to him. A swallow swooped low over our heads and landed on the fenceline across the ditch.

"Tell me how you happened to come to the Linger Inn? Philetus Spur is off the beaten track and not a big vacation spot. How does a southern city girl like you know about clover?"

"Southern? Madison? Not really. The Johnson's, my dad's family, owned most of the land here on the north side of Little Bear Lake. My

Gramma and Grampa and my uncle Lars cleared and farmed all these fields. They also built the Linger Inn." I pointed at the farm, the Inn and the fields around us. "Grampa also built a sawmill over there by Philetus Spur. We always used to stay there or at my Grampa's farm when I was little. It was sold years ago, and my grandparents died. This summer I came north with my mom and her husband, Jim."

"That's quite a story! You say they owned the Inn," he said looking sideways at me.

"My Grampa Sven built it with his brother Lars back in the early 1900's. They were original residents on Lake Makoons."

"That's so cool, Jewell. Then why do you live in Madison?"

"Dad left when he went to college and only came back to visit in the summers when he and Mom weren't teaching. Sometimes we spent the whole summer over at the farm."

"The farm?"

"Yep, my Grampa sold the Inn to Mrs. Swenson after his brother died. Aunt Naomi moved back to the Reservation and Grampa and Gramma moved over to the farm."

"I see. I love it here at Philetus Spur. It is so quiet and calm," he said but Jake's face looked troubled and distracted.

We walked along the gravel road, watching tiny white moths dancing on daisies here and there as the mist vaporized. A couple of yellow Sulphur butterflies flitted on the breeze in front of us. I felt heat rising quickly along with the humidity, filling the air with the musk odor of sweet moss, lacy ferns and pine needles. Wildflowers filled the ditches with patches of purple lupine, yellow dandelions and blue forget-me-nots. Wild strawberry blossoms lined the bottom of the ditches near the fencerow, with their pointed three-lobed leaves as a green backdrop to their white upturned faces.

"My grandpa always told me when the berries are in full blossom this early in the spring it means good summer crops. He used to tell me a lot of farming things, little stories and folk tales. He came from a farming family in Sweden at the turn of the century. Dad loved the outdoors. They were really alike that way."

"Me too, I have always loved the woods." Jake was standing in the road with his back to me. He was obviously preoccupied by something else.

"I've thought about my grandparents so much. I went over to the farm yesterday and it brought back memories of the summers I used to spend up here. As a matter of fact, I had quite a scare." I shivered. "Suddenly it seemed like someone was watching me. I chickened out and scooted back to the Inn. It sounds ridiculous and weird, but I was really scared!" I laughed.

"It must be a part of my training, but you sound like you need a strong guiding arm—and maybe a bodyguard." Jake said with a slight wink and a smile.

"Sometimes I think I would appreciate a strong arm. I didn't realize until the last couple of days how lonely and empty I've felt. I've always had homework, sports and work to fill my time. This business of vacationing seems to have emphasized the loneliness. Bad dreams that I had as a kid are coming back so I don't get good sleep."

"May I offer to help for a little while?" Jake said with a coaxing smile. "I know all about bad dreams."

"Oh, I, I guess so." I answered shyly. I didn't look at Jake, but looking down, I smiled behind the shield of my hair.

Jake put his arm through mine and we fell into step as we pleasantly ambled along the gravel road. He didn't talk, and I retreated into comfortable silence. The sun shone through the now wispy clouds and it was quite warm whenever we walked out of the pine tree shade and into a patch of sunshine. It faintly surprised me that we matched steps so naturally. The feel of his arm was very comforting and the way his thumb gently stroked my wrist was wreaking havoc with my heart.

"So. Where is your grandpa's farm?" asked Jake, his eyes scanning the slowly clearing morning sky and the treetops across the field.

"Across Shadow Bay from the Linger Inn on Johnson Point: that's just what we called it. Grampa and Gramma owned the land including the Linger Inn and most of this section after my Uncle Lars died."

Jake's head jerked to look at me and his forehead furrowed worriedly. His eyes searched my face.

"You've got to be kidding." His hand covered mine firmly on his arm. "I was just thinking about that place."

"That's what I said. Grampa sold the Inn to Mrs. Swenson then he and Grams moved to the farm. Gramma died in a car accident and Dad died in a car accident too. Then Grampa died of a heart attack."

"That's odd." He stared at me for a moment and ran his hand through his ginger hair with a new worried look on his face.

"I have seen semi-trucks on that road twice now," he said. "I thought it was strange, but I just thought the drivers were lost. Then I went over there and saw the tire tracks in the sand on the drive, but nothing else. No one lives there, huh?"

"No, not since '66' when Grampa died."

CHAPTER 4

OUT OF THE PAST

"You said someone was there when you went to the farm yesterday?" Jake's cheeks flushed red and he stood with his brows knit and his fists on his hips, the sun glinted gold on his curly, fiery colored hair. He seemed to be torn in two directions.

"Yes, I thought so. I've seen lights and cars near the barn, from the window in my room at the Inn. Once I heard a truck on the highway just before that. What's going on?" I asked with growing anxiety. Jake swung around and started striding in the direction of Philetus Spur.

"Come on, I have to call someone." he said.

"Can't we just call from the Inn? It's too far for you to walk. You said you couldn't go far." I said trotting a little to catch up. "What's wrong?" I slipped on the gravel and nearly fell, but he wheeled around and caught me by the arm just in time.

"The phones at the Inn aren't private. You said your dad thought he was run off the road by a semi on the freeway, right?"

"Yes: the state trooper said he must have gone to sleep at the wheel. But Dad told Mom a semi ran him off the road and then he rambled on about the headlights. Then he couldn't talk anymore so the secret died with him." I explained. "We'll just never know what happened."

"Where did it happen?" Jake asked.

"North of Eau Claire, on Highway 53," I said. "He died in the hospital in Rice Lake."

"You never found out why he was going north? Where did he say he was heading when he got here?"

"He told my mom he was going to the farm to 'straighten things out'. Jake, what is going on, what you are thinking?" I demanded.

"I'm not sure---I don't know, not yet anyway." He began walking towards Philetus Spur again. "Your mom is here with you too, isn't she?"

"Yes, why?"

"Is someone with her all of the time?" Jake was beginning to labor a little and his breathing was ragged, and his lips looked a little blue. I grabbed his arm and pulled on him.

"You bet; Jim is with her day and night. Jake: really, stop. What the heck- tell me what is going on right now," I demanded, planting myself in front of him with my hands on my hips.

"I don't really know Jewell. It is just that suddenly a lot of loose ends jiggled together like a kaleidoscope and I have a whole new picture. I must get to my friend's house at the Spur and call someone I can trust. This might be the new angle I need to my case."

"Jake, what are you talking about? What case?" I asked with frustration. His answers seemed to be going around in circles.

"Not now Jewell: maybe later. I'm heading to Philetus Spur to call," Jake said, but his lips were gray and his face white. He bent over with his hands on his knees and gasped for breath. Just then a semi tractor-trailer rolled around the corner at the end of Johnson Road and rumbled towards Philetus Spur.

"That's it. Go back to the Inn," he pointed back and then started down the road away from me. I didn't know what to do so I stood dumbly watching him. He had almost reached the intersection with the main road going to the Johnson Point farm when I saw him stagger and slow down until he fell to one knee at the edge of the road. I sprinted down the road and reached him quickly.

"Jake, what happened?" I could feel prickles on my neck and fright tugged at my heart until I could barely breathe. "Jake, answer me, please!"

He seemed to have to concentrate hard to summon up all his strength.

"Jewell, I need my truck."

"What happened? Are you sick?"

"I guess I overdid it. Cramps. I need to move more slowly. Can you drive?"

"Sure," I replied.

"Could you run back to the Inn and get my truck, please?" he asked weakly. "My stomach is cramped up, bad: I can't walk any further."

"Okay, but don't you need a doctor? I can take you."

"It's alright, really, Jewell. Just get me the truck, please. Okay?" he asked, shutting his eyes. "It's the brown Chevy behind the Inn."

"Okay. Let me help you to the shoulder in the grass. I hate to leave you here alone. Will you really be okay?" He leaned up against an old rotted fencepost with the rusty fencing holding it upright.

"Yeah, sure, I'll be ok."

"The truck's over in the back, the left corner of the parking lot. Hurry up though," he said through gritted teeth. His face was now white and lined with pain. "Promise me, don't talk to anyone!"

"I don't get it Jake, but I will do it. I think I should talk to my mom and get my purse. I need my driver's license."

"No, don't. Just take my keys," he grunted as he unsnapped his keychain from his belt loop. "Please hurry, Jewell. I have to trust you."

"Okay, I'll do it. I'll be right back."

I took off at full speed sprinting down the road until I couldn't breathe and had to stop to regain my composure.

"Stay in control, be calm." I chided myself. I knew I was a long-distance person, not a sprinter. "Breathe evenly and trot steadily---breathe, step, breathe." I fell into the running pattern I developed on the trails in Madison jogging around the Arboretum. I made it back to the parking lot at the Linger Inn in just a few minutes. The truck sat right where Jake said it would be, but there was a dusty black pickup parked with the motor idling behind it. I jumped in to make sure I had the right vehicle. The key fit.

"I'm sure this is the same truck I saw in Philetus Spur at the store," I thought. "He must be 'Red,' from Hagie's store." The engine started with no problem, but the owner of the idling pick-up was nowhere to be seen. I pulled the emergency brake before I ran up the cement step to the Inn's back office door. Knocking, I called out, "Mrs. Swenson? Excuse me, hello, Mrs. Swenson?"

An unseen hand opened the office door and Mrs. Swenson called out.

"Who's there?" She was sitting at the big oak desk. "Why Jewell, excuse me. I have company here," she said.

"I'm sorry, Mrs. Swenson. My friend needs his truck, and someone is parked right behind him with the motor running." I said.

"Well, I never," she said with irritation in her voice. "It's your truck Buddy. Just hang on. The boys will move in just a moment. They were leaving anyway."

"That'd be great, thanks Mrs. Swenson, we're kind of in a hurry," I urged nervously and ducked back into the hall. I hurried outside and walked anxiously to the truck. I sure hoped I knew how to drive it.

When I got in I found it was a manual transmission, but I thought I could handle it. While I was checking out the gearshift, the two burly bearded men came out of the back door and got in the black truck. They looked at me and then laughed about something to each other, then swung themselves into the pickup and roared off down the road.

The engine stalled three times, but I finally backed out and started down the lane. It had been a long time since I'd driven a manual-shift vehicle or even driven a car and my reactions were very rusty. My hands shook as the minutes rushed by. The bumpy road was a struggle as I tried to keep the truck moving without hiccupping. Finally, I got near the main road and watched the ditches for Jake. I couldn't believe it; he wasn't where I'd left him. I stopped the truck near the intersection at the end of the lane and tooted the horn two long blasts and two shorts - out of habit I suppose. Dad said that was a "come home" signal.

"Still no Jake," I thought out loud. "Where is he? He caught a ride with those two guys?"

I wondered if he went to Philetus Spur. Maybe he recovered from his attack. Maybe the whole thing was an act designed to get rid of me, but that seemed like an elaborate ruse. I considered going back to the Inn, but my curiosity and a niggling fear got the best of me, so I drove on towards the village. I pulled into Philetus Spur a few minutes later, parking the truck and walked by the shady tavern windows and then crossed over to the barbershop, wondering where Jake might have gone. I went into the little grocery store but I a quick glance revealed nobody but a bored-looking kid at the counter and a guy looking at minnows. I got back in the truck and drove slowly up and down the one block of "downtown." Worry was replacing fear in my mind. I was driving a vehicle that wasn't mine, while looking for the owner, a man I had known for only a few hours. I didn't even have my purse and driver's license with me.

"I'll head back to the Inn and look for him again on the way," I thought. "Maybe he is cutting through the woods or something."

I drove slowly and scanned the bushes, hay and bracken ferns lining the ditches as I followed the main highway back towards the

63

road to the Inn. When I got back to the intersection with the gravel lane leading to the Inn, I turned around and turned the truck off, jumped out and began yelling "Jake! Jake!" to the empty road, my voice echoed back from the woods at the back of the 40-acre field. A fencerow and raspberry brambles bordered the open field on my left. I stood nonplussed for a moment, leaning against the fence, and ran my hands through my hair. A solitary mosquito's buzzing only added to the lonely feeling around me.

Finally, I walked back around and climbed into the driver's seat.

"He must have caught a ride back to the Inn somehow," I thought. When the truck started, it jerked forward—I was not very competent with the clutch yet. I was in mid-shift when my eyes caught a movement from the ditch on my right. The truck ground to a halt as I forgot to clutch and brake in the right order. I slid across the seat to see a hand and an arm reaching out of the weeds at the top of the ditch.

"Oh, my God," I yelped, frozen to my seat for a second. I broke through the fear and leaped out of the passenger side. Jake was lying in the weeds, his face and hands battered, his shirt torn and bloody.

"What happened? Where have you been," I cried.

"In the field. Help me Jesus," he moaned. "They'll be back. Hurry Jewell. We've got to get out of here. Help me up."

"I am taking you to the hospital, Jake. This is craziness!"

"Just get us out of here."

Struggling and straining, I finally got him to his feet with his arm around my neck. I used all my strength to support him and back at the truck I boosted him up to lie across the seat and pushed his legs inside.

"Go to the hospital," he moaned. I slammed the door and ran around to the other side to jump in. I carefully lifted his head up to rest on my leg before I put the truck in motion, spewing gravel. I turned it around in the road and then headed west towards Hayward.

On the way, Jake groaned painfully several times as some of the bigger bumps bounced us around on the road. This pickup wasn't built for comfort and the big potholes made the trip uncomfortable. I was surprised at the state of the road, as most of Wisconsin's back roads were kept in reasonable condition. Then I remembered Jim mentioning to mom on the way up from Madison a lot of the road damage was from the big pulp trucks and semis. He explained they used the back roads often to avoid the weight bans on the main highways on their way to the plants up north of Hayward. This highway must be one of those he talked about.

Without looking away from the road I checked Jake's pulse. His heartbeat seemed erratic and he was only semi-conscious, his was head lolling on the seat because of the bumpy road and his eyes were half-closed. His color was very pale under dried blood.

The road was narrow with soft grassy shoulders and at some points, swamp-water nearly overflowed across the blacktop. The road curved along lakeshores, dipping deeply between hills. White birches stood like toothpicks along the narrow ditches, reaching out into the road's clearance for sunlight with lime green arms.

Jake moaned again and suddenly opened his eyes.

"Jewell, where are we? What…"

"Shush, Jake. It's okay, we're going to the hospital. I know where it is. You have to get to a doctor."

"Don't talk to anyone."

"What? I have to tell them something," I cried, trying to keep my eyes on the road at the same time.

"Tell the doctor we had a fight and you won." He groaned through clenched teeth. He clutched his stomach in pain. "Ughhh."

"How can I tell anyone anything, I have no idea what's going on here? Jake, Jake, wake up!" I thought he passed out again. His hand was limp, and his jaw sagged slightly.

We approached Hayward from the southeast. I took the turn off the blacktop, slowing down when I saw the "Hospital" sign as I turned sharply up the driveway to the hospital. I swung into the emergency bay and jumped out to ring the bell at the door. A nurse came out and took the situation in at one glance. She spoke into a phone just inside the door and in a few moments two other appeared.

The nurse took Jake's name, and I explained to them I didn't know what had happened. The nurse flashed me a suspicious glance and told me to go to the admittance office as she joined the doctor who had just come down the hall. They lifted Jake out of the truck onto a gurney and then rolled him into the hospital. Just then Jake opened his eyes and raised his hand to me as they took him through the glass doors into the emergency room.

I went back to the truck to pull it around to the main parking lot and with dismay noted the truck's gas gauge buried at the bottom. I ran across the parking lot to the front door of the hospital. and as I approached the desk, I remembered I didn't even have my purse. I tried to look less distressed by self-consciously smoothing my hair and clothes. In the process, I had to pick off several pieces of grass on my light blue sweater. I felt a little warm and embarrassed by my appearance. I slid my sleeves up and spoke to the petite young blond receptionist.

"I came with a patient to the emergency room…Jake Pieters. Can you tell what room he will be in?"

"I'm sorry, if he is the guy that came in a little while ago - he is still in Emergency. They haven't checked him into any room yet. Are you his wife? I'll have some financial forms that need to be filled out."

"Oh no, I am just a friend. He should have the information in his wallet. I could go and ask him: I would like to see him."

"I can check with them. If you are not related, you can't go into the ER. I will tell you what they decide as soon as they let me know," she said and disappeared inside the office.

I walked across the room and found a leather chair near the windows. I felt out of place and embarrassed, even though there was only one guy in the room, who seemed oblivious to my presence. I sat still for a few moments, and then got up to look for a magazine or something to read. The little table had a couple of outdated Time magazines and a Fur, Fish and Game magazine. To my left I saw a washroom and I thought I should clean up. Rinsing my face and hands, I savored the feel of the cool water. It helped me relax. I tried to comb my hair again with my fingers and finally got it looking better. I dabbed at the blood spots on my sweater with cold water and soap on a paper towel until they weren't so noticeable. I went back into the waiting room, feeling more at ease, but still feeling out of place. I wanted my purse. I'd been in such a hurry when I ran back to the Inn that I hadn't even considered going back upstairs for it; I had thought I was only going to drive half a mile down the road and go back to the Inn.

"This is a fine mess I've got myself into," I sighed to myself as I wandered back to the lobby. A local advertising booklet called "The Visitor" lay on the low table next to my chair. I began to read a local history column about an interesting tour through the county that identified some historical locations including the town hall at Philetus Spur. I moved on to an out dated Time magazine and scanned the pictures. While I was reading, I'd catch the receptionist's eye and gave her a hopeful look. Each time she shook her head. After an hour she finally crooked her finger at me, beckoning me to her desk.

"Your friend was admitted to the hospital and he's in room 112 in Critical Care, down the hall and to your left. He's asking for you. Please check with the floor nurse first though, to make sure he can be disturbed. He was hurt badly, wasn't he? Was it a car accident?"

"N-n-no," I stammered, not knowing what to say.

"Oh," she frowned and shrugged. I took my cue and walked down the empty hall. My tennis shoes were silent on the shiny white tiles. Faint sounds of shuffling papers in the adjoining records room were the only signs of life as I walked up to the nurse's station. I waited a few moments there to comply with the desk clerk's request, then since no one came to help me, I quietly made my way to room 112. I entered the darkened room and pulled the door shut silently behind me.

Tightly pulled curtain block the light from the windows and the only light breaking the gloom came from a square light fixture near the floor by the door. I moved to Jake's side and reached out and touched him. His hand jerked up and gripped me, his powerful fingertips digging into my arm.

"Jake, stop, that hurts!" With my pained whisper, the pressure released immediately.

"Julie, I'm sorry, thank God you are here! Where've you been," he moaned as he tried to sit up. "Are you okay? Did anyone follow us here?"

"Oh Jake, I am fine. I didn't see anyone. What happened to you? Who did this?"

"I'm not sure. Now you're in danger too." He paused for breath and grimaced with the effort of talking. "It's not really safe here. I guess somebody think's I made a connection. Damn, Jewell, I don't even know what that connection might mean, let alone who *they* are."

I sat awkwardly on the foot of his bed. I saw the bloody stitches the emergency room doctor put in a deep looking cut on his forehead. Jake looked away momentarily and then looked back with a faint smile.

"I'm glad you are here."

"Can I get you anything? A drink or something?"

"You can help me get out. Just get my clothes," he said, trying to sit up in the bed and struggling with the sheets.

"No, Jake, you can't. Please lay down. You've got to give your body a rest. Surely, no one will come in the hospital. We are safe here."

"Jewell, you see what they did to me. I know what they look like. I'm thinking they will come back to get me again. If they know you are helping me, they will come after you too. They may have already made the connection because you took my truck. They came from the resort!"

"I saw two guys talking to Mrs. Swenson. I asked them to move the truck and they left. I guess it must have been them…there was no-one else around! I didn't look at them much because I was worried about you. I am just up here on vacation. There's no reason to connect me with you."

"Jewell, if I am right, this is not my first run-in with this crowd. I am still healing up after their first attack. Can you turn that bed lamp on?"

I turned on the small light and he pulled back the covers to expose his chest and stomach. I cringed at the sight of the ridged scars and healing skin under a light new growth of red-brown hair.

"This is serious, Jewell. It's why I'm worried about you. These guys don't play games. I don't want you to get in their way!"

"Don't you think I would be better prepared if I had some idea of what's going on Jake? What is the big mystery?"

Jake turned brooding eyes to the ceiling and lay back silently. I reached out and touched his muscular arm. He looked so out-of-place against the whiteness of the hospital sheets in the dim light from the bed lamp.

"Jake, tell me," I said softly. "Then I will help you as much as I can."

Maybe because his defenses were down, physically and mentally, or perhaps because I had reached out to him, I could see capitulation in his eyes as he turned to look directly at me.

"I haven't involved my family in Duluth, not even my close friends, except one. I guess I have to trust someone, and you already have a stake in the situation." His eyes searched my face in the dim light until I was uncomfortable.

"Tell me what is going on Jake. If I can help, I will. You can trust me," I said slowly.

He settled back on the pillows, gritting his teeth with pain as he adjusted a stretch bandage around his chest.

"I guess they broke a rib or something. Damn, my chest hurts," he groaned.

"Can I get you something?" I asked and stood up, wanting to comfort him somehow.

"Naw, I just want out of here. But I feel like my brains are floating around loose in my head and I have a damned bad headache. I suppose that's a concussion or something. What time is it?" I looked at my watch.

"It's 12:30. You were unconscious for about an hour."

"Damn. Sit back down. I'll tell you what I think is going on."

I scooted my chair closer and when I looked at him my heart skipped a beat. We were now comrades at arms, intimates, and yet I knew so little about him. It occurred to me that he might have a girlfriend, or even a wife. I was probably making a fool of myself over a stranger. I was determined to guard myself against that possibility. But everything about him screamed out to my heart.

"Do you think someone might try to hurt me too?" I whispered.

"It's possible," he answered. "You certainly need to stay away from that farm until I can check it out. I shouldn't even tell you anything about this mess, but you might see that you need to be worried. I couldn't stand it if you were hurt."

He suddenly reached out for my hand. I tentatively let him take it and he pulled me closer. I was surprised by his strength, but I didn't think to resist. For a long moment, our eyes locked, as he seemed to think about something deeply and something like electricity passed between us. He gently gathered me to him and kissed me firmly on the lips. My brain fuzzed out like a weak radio station and I had trouble breathing when he let me go. Catching a breath, I sat back down and fussed with my curtain of hair to buy a moment to gather myself back together. There was a long silence, and then Jake finally began to talk to me.

"Okay, I'm sorry if that offended you but I'm so glad we met this morning. I wanted to kiss you when I first saw you standing there in the rain. I needed to get that out of the way. I should have asked first."

"I...I guess that's okay." My heart was pounding so hard it was difficult to breathe. Jake reached over and took my hand and held it next to his chest. I could see he was gathering his thoughts and I was just staring at him. I took in every detail, his hair, his eyes, his lips, yes, especially his soft lips. I had to close my eyes for a second. That kiss was very nice.

"It's very serious, Jewell, not just to me, but to others as well. I don't trust anyone here except you and I hardly know you."

He paused, obviously trying to sort out his words. He shifted position and winced with the pain.

"A little over a year ago, I was working as a deputy sheriff in Douglas County. I was on patrol in the southern part of the county because Sheriff Bender wanted me to do a back check on a theft. That night I stopped at a little old country bar to ask some questions. The Sheriff said one of the men we suspected of being involved was a regular customer there. I asked the owner, but you can imagine bartenders usually don't want to give up names and he sure didn't want to tell me. He seemed to be on the defensive, so I didn't want to push too hard until I had something more to go on than just a suspicion."

Jake's eyes searched the ceiling in the effort of concentrating his thought.

"I was just leaving when the waitress stopped me near the door to ask about a problem she was having with an old boyfriend. I talked to her for a while and left her standing at the door. When I headed out to my squad the bar door shut behind me. I remember hearing a semi parked across the lot start up. The lights went on and then I heard sound of the air brakes releasing, but I wasn't paying attention; I was thinking about the case. About halfway across the lot headlights flashed on me and I saw the muzzle of a shotgun sticking out of the driver's window. I was a sitting duck. It was like Nam all over again and I froze."

"Oh, my God!" I shook my head in disbelief. "This sounds like a terrible movie."

"I know. I couldn't believe it either. The pellets hit me in the stomach. Fortunately, he was a little too far away. He just took off down the highway when I fell." Jake stopped here for a few moments, the memories obviously painful, even after this long. "I lay there for a few minutes thinking someone would come out of the bar to help me. Nobody came out, so I had to crawl the rest of the way to my patrol. I got the door open and fell in. I don't remember calling, but they said I made a mayday call before I passed out. I had six surgeries to get the pellets out and repair the damage. There were many times in the next couple of months, I swore I would find and kill that bast... oh, excuse me..."

I waved my free hand, leaning closer.

"I'm sorry, I don't really mean that."

"I don't get it, why would they want to hurt you? How could that girl not have heard the shot? Why would she not call for help? I can't imagine watching someone suffering and not helping."

"The Sheriff thought somebody gave her money to set me up. We didn't get a chance to ask her—she was gone by the time the Sheriff got back there. Her relatives said she'd gone off somewhere to hide out from her boyfriend. I want you to understand that these people are pretty ruthless."

"I get that, Jake. I just don't understand why I'm involved."

"Since that night, I've found a dozen clues that connect Superior to Philetus Spur. It's got to do with some guys who used to hang out together in Superior. They've been hanging out together in a cabin near the Inn. A friend of mine told me where they went. There's been a bunch of burglaries in the northern part of this County too. Over

70

the years, summer homes were broken into, but they are not being investigated and no one's been caught. I think somehow the Johnson Point Farm is involved, Jewell. Twice I've seen semi's there, but I can't move in to investigate. I am not working right now."

"What can you do about it now?"

"I'm thinking maybe your Grampa knew something and your Dad was on his way up here because he wanted to check it out. But I don't get how anyone could know he was coming."

"But why wouldn't Dad tell the police first, or confide in mom?" I asked. "And besides, that was six years ago!"

"I know. That's a big part of the problem. The burglary case I was working on had tips that stretched out over my whole lifetime and there's just a few clues linking them together. The same people and family names keep popping up between the cases, but the witnesses are dying of old age! I've just been chasing down hints."

"That's pretty strange!"

"I know. But it doesn't explain why I was shot. It was just a routine preliminary investigation. There's just some link I am not seeing."

"So, you sit by the lake and fish? Is that 'detecting'?"

"Since I got the latest tip, I came down here to keep an eye on the Inn. And, maybe it's all coincidences. A war protester could have shot me because I served in Viet Nam. Maybe I was shot by someone I'd ticked off for a speeding ticket or it could be anything – at least that's what the Sheriff thought. He even said it could be a case of mistaken identity. I just don't believe it."

"This is all too weird Jake. Why would I meet you now? What a crazy coincidence."

Jake looked at me and pushed my hair back with his other hand. He traced my jawline with a finger and tapped my lips. I felt mesmerized. I wanted him to kiss me again. I wanted to feel his muscular arms around me, holding me tight. Oh my gosh, I totally forgot to breathe.

"I think that's a kind of a miracle," he said thoughtfully, touching my hair. "It could have been that girl's boyfriend. There's no evidence either way…I just have this stupid intuition that I am on to something."

I could see that Jake was tiring, he looked gray and weak. I wanted him to relax and sleep, but I needed know what the connection was with my dad.

"So, tell me what happened this afternoon, Jake," I asked.

"I guess I should have had enough sense not to go rushing off like I did." He shook his head regretfully. "I got out of the hospital not long ago. The doctors said I should rest. My guts still need work. When you told me about the farm and your father's death, I overreacted. Then I saw that big semi pulling out onto the main road. I think that's how they are moving the stolen merchandise. There's no reason for a semi in that neighborhood. But, my head was pounding, and my stomach cramped so I leaned back in the grass in the ditch until I heard a truck pulling up. I thought it was you, so I didn't open my eyes. Then I heard a door slam, and somebody snarled, 'It's that deputy, son of a bitch!'"

"You're kidding. What did he look like?"

"Before I could get up he tossed a coat or something over my head. There were two of them and they started pounding on me with their fists and a bat of some kind. I couldn't fight back so I just played dead. When they heard you, coming down the lane in my truck, they must have panicked. They picked me up and heaved me into the bushes. They must have figured they'd come back later and grab me. I blacked out until I heard you tooting the horn and your voice calling me. I was sick with fear for you because I didn't know if they knew you were with me."

"Jake, this is nuts! You've got to call the Sheriff in Hayward."

"No kidding, Jewell! It's crazy. That's why I've gotta get out of this hospital. I'm a sitting duck here. I can't trust the cops, especially here, and I am not even sure about my own Sheriff. I need to get out of here."

That's when my worry turned to outright fear.

"No way, not until you've seen the doctor and talked to him. You could be hurt a lot worse than you think," I said pushing him gently back against the pillows. Just then a small, determined nurse came into the room behind me and looked suspicious.

"Excuse me Miss, are you related to Mr. Pieters?" When I shook my head, she said disapprovingly, "This patient is not allowed visitors yet. He needs his vitals assessed. You have to leave." She stood with the door open wide behind her, inviting me to precede her.

"I want her to stay in the room for now, nurse. In fact, I insist that she stay," said Jake firmly.

"Well! I guess I'll have to speak to your doctor about it," she answered, confused by his assertive attitude. "We have rules."

"Yup, I'd like to talk to him too," he countered.

"I guess I'll find the doctor and be right back." I watched her starched white back retreat out of the door and down the hall.

"Jake, can I contact someone for you? I should call your family and tell them what's happened to you right away!"

Jake squeezed his eye tightly shut and rubbed the back of his hand across them.

"No, don't. Mom and Dad would just be too upset, and my brothers would come tearing down here."

"Now, Jake, be serious. You can't just stay here in the hospital and not tell your family. That's not right. You're really hurt!"

"I just don't want them to know quite yet. I'll be fine. The doctor gave me quite a dose of painkiller, so I'll just sleep. He talked to my doctor in Duluth and they will decide if I need my folks here. I'll need to get back up to Superior."

Now confused and worried, I wanted to back up a day before these problems and dilemmas when I lay on my blanket on the beach chasing ants, buried in a novel. I wanted to go back to the rain and meeting Jake by the shore. I was playing a part in a novel myself; and I felt afraid.

"Jewell, please," he whispered.

He caught my eyes again and his magnetism radiated out to me.

"I have to get back to Superior."

"Jake, the truck is nearly out of gas and I don't have my purse or anything."

I could feel the tension leave when I said this. I sensed he knew he'd won. He smiled slightly.

"Don't worry about money - my wallet is in my jeans pocket. They're in that metal locker. Just get out whatever you need."

I went to open the cabinet door and gingerly pulled out his blue jeans. I brushed at the leaves and dirt on them as I got the trifold wallet from the hip pocket. Unfolding it, I saw his driver's license with his picture and name. A metal deputy badge was there too.

"At least I know that he really is Jake Pieters," I thought to myself.

"Just grab ten bucks," he directed.

"My mom will have a fit. How could I explain why I am driving your truck around?"

"Don't worry about it. If she asks, just tell her you borrowed it from me to go to town to get a Hayward T-shirt. Just don't tell anyone where I am or what's going on."

The semi-darkness was getting on my nerves. I walked over to the window and pulled back the heavy drapes to look outside.

"No. Close the curtains, Jewell." he said.

"What? Are you serious? There's nobody out there. It's just empty woods and a parking lot." I said and turned back to him.

"Whoever beat me up didn't finish the job because you came in the truck. They may have followed us here."

"Okay," I said "but I don't see anyone, and I find it hard to believe this whole thing. It's like a 'Spy versus Spy' cartoon. What do you want me to do?"

"Above all; take me seriously. If I'm right I am dealing with the mob and someone is worried enough to want to kill me. Local yokels don't kill people. The whole thing smacks of the Mafia. They don't blink an eye to kill if they think you know something. I think that they believe I know something: something big enough to be a problem. Now they know what I look like. That means they'll be looking for me and I don't even know who 'they' are. They think if they shut me up they're safe. It also means that somehow, they must know what my department knows, so there's a snitch somewhere. I don't know enough to tell anyone else or make a case. The worst thing is that I don't know for sure what it is that I know."

"What can we do then? Why can't the police deal with it?"

"I said I didn't trust the Sheriff's Department. Since you want to help, I think I need my buddy here. Can you go to town, get gas and while you are there, call my buddy, Randy Farrows?" Jake took a pen from the table next to the bed and wrote a number on a scratch pad. "Just tell him to come down here to the hospital. Other than you, he is the only one I can trust right now."

"Why can't you call from here?"

"These phones don't have long distance and I'd have to go through the front office. Anyone could listen in. Remember in these small towns, everyone is related somehow. Just go downtown and call at the public phone when you get gas. Don't take chances where someone might overhear the call. Remember; Randy Farrows. Hurry back, please? Don't talk to anyone else unless you've got to. Keep your eyes open. Please, be very careful."

"I will. I'll try to call my Mom to tell her I'll be gone the rest of the day. You'll be all right here. The nurse looks like a good watchdog."

"Sure. I'll be OK."

He reached out one hand to me tentatively. I took it and he gently pulled me towards him. I leaned forward shyly and kissed him softly and gently on the lips and let my hair shield my face again and blushing furiously. He reached over and pushed my hair back to see my face. He smiled up at me.

"Later?"

"I'll be right back." I sighed. As I walked out the door I still felt heady from his kiss, but uneasiness remained in the pit of my stomach. Something wasn't quite right; I was sure of it. But I also felt I was committed. It was very possible that I was 'in love' with Jake Pieters. I felt that my granddad would have punctuated that thought with a fervent "Uffda," and roll his eyes, so I did too.

"Uffda. Thank you, Jesus. So far, so good." I said. "Please take care of him - please." I took a deep breath and headed down the antiseptic-smelling hall towards the lighted EXIT sign.

CHAPTER 5

Love ~ Andrea, 1971

Lone eagle soars on thermal draft
The forest echoes the piercing laugh
On deep bent wings, feathered fingers ride earth's breath
Wide to glide on winds aloft unbound,
Unchained, untied to ground.
In inky darkness, to pale moon above,
Men have vowed undying love: but dark meets light,
Golden soldiers invade sovereign fields of night.
Love's unfettered, freedom gained
As day unlocks the mortal chained.

CALAMITY

I exited out of the front door of the dimly-lit hospital lobby into the bright hot sunshine and worriedly headed for the truck across the parking lot. Stepping off the concrete sidewalk onto the asphalt of the parking area, I was startled to see the back side of a man in a dark jacket leaning through the open passenger door of Jake's truck, apparently digging in the glove box. An electric shock zapped through me with a surge of adrenaline when I recognized one of the guys from the parking lot at the resort. Turning back, I strode quickly back towards the front door. I heard the truck door slam as I opened the door and when I sneaked a peek back out the window he was standing in the parking lot. He was scowling and red-faced.

"God help me, and protect Jake," I thought. Since that guy would be watching the truck I knew I couldn't dare try to take it. I could only hope that he hadn't noticed me outside. The hospital would be safe: the important thing now was to get Jake's friend here to help him. I went in the front door and stopped at the desk.

"How far is it to Hayward?" I asked.

"About two miles I think. You just turn to the left at the highway and then turn to the right on the first blacktopped road. That'll take you right downtown."

I waited in the lobby looking out the window until she went back in her office and then quietly went down the long, grey-tiled hallway to a door marked FIRE EXIT that led to a gravel driveway on the other side of the large brick buildings of the hospital complex. I stepped out and sped quickly across the pine-filled hospital grounds towards the highway that led to Hayward.

~

After Jewell left....

Jake adjusted the bed into a sitting position. His face wrinkled into a grimace and he winced out loud with the movement. He figured it wouldn't take Jewell more than a couple of hours to make the round trip to the Linger Inn, even if she changed her clothes and got things for him. If she called Randy right away, he would be here in about the same time.

He checked his watch to find it was just after 1:00 p.m. He tried to make sense of the events of the last few hours and relate them to his own shooting, but the strain made his head throb too much. He was sure he was close to the heart of the matter and felt so stupid that he couldn't see the answer. Right now, his thoughts were scattered and random.

"I hope Randy found the information I need about the warehouse on Hwy 35." He thought. "Maybe he located the name of the trucking company I saw on the semi in that Superior parking lot. I should have followed up on it myself instead of taking this danged vacation."

He reached for the bedside phone and called the front desk, leaving a message that would allow Randy to come to his room immediately. He thought of that beautiful, sober, unhappy young woman he met today. Jewell. How appropriate her name was...her eyes changed color like a mood ring every time he looked at her from dove grey to blue topaz. He wanted to take her in his arms, to hold her and to make her laugh. He had not reacted like that to any other woman, and he wanted her with him. With that thought his heart bumped against his ribs. The way the morning sun reflected on her white-blond hair reminded him of shimmering sunlight on water. Her calm self-control made her seem older than her eighteen years, but she was so vulnerable.

"Oh, my God, I think I'm in love," he thought with a shock. "That won't work. She's too young, she's so beautiful. I am too old ...and so broken."

Despite the painkillers, he seemed to hurt everywhere. He willed the nurse to bring the doctor. He needed to know whether there were any more internal injuries besides the obviously broken rib and concussion. The violence of the men beating him up brought back nauseating memories from Nam. He began to sweat and shake but he struggled to hold himself together.

"They take their time in this damned place," he said to the room. Just then he heard the voice of the nurse who'd been so snotty to Jewell, her voice echoing down the hall.

"No. You can't see him. I have Doctor's orders. Mr. Pieters can't have any visitors until the doctor sees him again. Please step back into the lobby or I'll call someone," she said with absolute certainty of her authority.

"Damn it. That dragon woman! Who in the hell does she think she is? *Nurse!*" he called weakly as he struggled to untangle his legs from the light blanket. She didn't hear him, and voices subsided down the hallway.

"It's too early for Randy, it's got to be Jewell, she must have some problem," he growled to himself. Clutching his belly in pain, he swayed and lurched across the room then pulled the door open to peer down the hallway. He could see people through the windows in the doors at the end of the hallway.

"Whoa," he muttered when he spotted a big guy facing the nurse's station with the tough nurse pointing her finger the opposite direction. He was someone Jake had never seen before. "What the heck?"

Just then another nurse approached them at the end of the hall and the nurse stood blocking the way with her hands on her hips, shaking her head.

"They found me. I gotta get out of here…I'm a sitting duck in this room. Dammit. Where's Jewell?"

He pulled the door shut quietly and stumbled to the little locker that held his clothes. Every movement brought him waves of dizzying pain, but the realization that the man was probably there to do more damage and the fear for Jewell, gave him the ounce of strength he needed. The nurses wouldn't stall those guys for long. Jake grabbed his pants and his bloodied, grass-stained shirt.

"There's got to be a fire exit or something," he thought. "It's better than laying here waiting for them to come back. This is crumby. I can't even leave Jewell a message. But I've got to get away from that guy in the lobby…"

He didn't know if he was talking out loud, but he couldn't think beyond this pain. He pulled the door open and peered down the hall towards the nurse's station. Looking to his left and he spotted a red fire escape sign all the way down the hall. He ducked into the hall and then painfully moved towards the escape. It seemed that most of the rooms were vacant with their door standing half open and the lights off. The hall was narrowing and pitching back and forth, the floor was soft and there were bees buzzing somewhere nearby.

"Stop it! Pull yourself together!" Jake said to the empty hall, hitching his broad shoulders back in pain. "Ugh - stop the damn buzzing."

Three dragging steps later was the solution. A bronze plaque on the door said it was a 'Quiet Room'. Jake took the handle and pulled the door open, stepped into the cool, deep blue, dark sanctuary. Soft curtains masked the windows towards the hall and outside. Silence and semi darkness shrouded the room. There was an oversized lounge chair, a small couch and a book on the end table. Jake staggered to the chair with its back to the doors and sank painfully between its big, soft, comforting arms. He dropped his clothes on the floor.

"Jewell…" he whispered, and the room slipped away from him. His head fell forward onto his chest and his arms to his sides.

A bustling, pink-faced nurse's aide whose nametag said "Edie" riffled through a pile of papers on a clipboard at the hospital head nurse's desk. She looked up, startled by a man striding past her desk. She rose quickly to her feet and blocked his path.

"Excuse me sir, I told you that you can't go in there. Is there someone you are looking for?"

"I need 'ta see a guy. I got the room number." He tried to move past her, but she stood blocking his way.

"But that wing is only for intensive care patients and their immediate families," she said firmly. "You can't go down there!"

"Yeah. Right. You need ta butt out girlie, I need to talk to this guy."

Head Nurse Reinhart came out of her office at the same time and immediately realized something was wrong.

"What's the problem here, Edie?"

"I told this man he can't go down into the Critical Care and he won't listen."

"I'm gonna see my buddy, he is back there."

"No. You can't see him," the Nurse said firmly. "I have Doctor's orders. Mr. Pieters can't have any visitors until the doctor sees him again. Please step back into the lobby or I'll call the Administrator," she said with absolute certainty of her authority.

"Bug off lady!" He pushed past her and went through the double doors labelled "Restricted", striding to room 112. He shoved the privacy curtain away from the bed and seeing the bed was empty, he checked the bathroom. He peered into the metal locker but slammed the door again and growled "Dammit!" He slammed his fat fist on the door of the locker and stormed back to the nurse's station where Edie was talking worriedly into the phone. She held on to the phone but refused to return to the front of the desk as he approached.

"Where's that guy in Room 112?" he yelled, pounding his big paw on the counter. "Where'd he go?"

"I don't know," she cried fearfully, "Let me check!" Her hands shook as she pressed the red button on the phone. The big man waited angrily for a moment and then abruptly swung around down the hall towards the front of the hospital. At the same time the hospital Administrator ran in with Nurse Reinhart.

"What's going on here? What's the problem?"

"I don't know, Mr. Mattson. That guy just pushed his way down to Room 112 and he screamed at me because his friend is gone. He's acting crazy: he scared us! I told you about the girl, you should have come right then!"

"Room 112? That's the guy that was nearly beaten to death at Philetus Spur? Help me, Jesus! Edie, that somebody is probably looking for him. Don't you read the charts when you come on duty? They said not to let anyone down there until Deputy Boyden gets here," he snapped as he ran down the hall and opened the door. Peering in, he turned back to Edie.

"Well, this is great. He's gone! The Sheriff won't like this at all. They said to make sure we held him until Deputy Boyden could talk to him. Sandy call the Sheriff immediately. Edie; go to the cafeteria and see if maybe Pieters slipped down there with that girl. I know he can't get very far with his broken rib and a concussion as bad as his. I gave him a strong dose of painkillers too, I can't believe he can walk. I'm going to check the other rooms on the floor."

The harried man ran down the hall, past the chapel, the laundry and the lounge to check the other patient areas.

~

Once outside the white and beige brick hospital building, I ran out to the highway along the shadowy driveway, lined on both side with huge old white pines and a row of trimmed cedars. I felt I had to get to the Sheriff's department quickly, no matter what Jake said. He needed protection right now.

An old red VW bug came out of the driveway on the other side of the road and an older lady with a familiar face waved out the window.

"Headed for town, honey. Need a ride?"

"Yes!" I cried gratefully as I ran across the road. She opened the car door from the inside. "Thanks a lot!"

"You know, you young girls shouldn't hitch hike like this," she said to me as she pulled onto the blacktop, spinning her tires and spitting gravel across the shallow ditch. I could hear it hitting the fence posts behind us. "City kids run into a lot of trouble, out here," she rattled on as fast as she drove. As she talked she waved her right hand in the air and the little car wandered back and forth across the lane. I gripped the door.

"I don't hitch-hike as a rule. I just don't have a choice right now. I certainly know it isn't safe," I added, trying to answer her quick questions in the right order. "I'm awfully glad you picked me up so quickly."

"Oh, I know about Madison, my dear. That's where they keep those legislators." She chuckled at her own joke. "You'd think Up-North doesn't even exist for them. That's okay with me if only they wouldn't come up here every whipstitch and complain about the way we do things. I think we should have stuck with Minnesota and Michigan to make a state, Minwimi: or maybe Mimiwi or Wimimin." She threw her head back and laughed. "And so where are you headed?"

She smiled at me, her wispy grey hair flirting around her head from the warm afternoon breeze through the open window. Her bright blue eyes smiled at life, surrounded by a web of suntanned wrinkles. She seemed very familiar.

"I need to find a telephone booth." I answered.

"You must be from out of town." She laughed. "We don't have any telephone booths in Hayward since the plow hit the last one at the top of Main Street in December. The driver couldn't see it under the snow drift, I guess. I can drop you at the Sheriff's office and maybe you can use his phone."

I was a little miffed at her assumption that I was just a tourist.

"My dad's family is actually from Philetus Spur, near Shadow Bay. My mom and I are up here for the summer."

"Oh, really?" She looked at me quizzically with birdlike curiosity. "I have the bait store at the Spur. I know you - you came in last week." She drew her peaked eyebrows together and I recognized her as the lady from Hagie's store.

"My dad was a Sigurd Johnson. Sven Johnson was my Grampa."
I answered. We were entering the Hayward city limits.

"Oh, really," she said slowly. "Sure, you would be. You have Elin's
hair. I knew your dad and your grandparents. They were fine people."
She smiled. "Yes. That was so long ago. Elin was so beautiful, and
Sven was so very kind. I was about your age when I left the Spur."

"I'm sorry, but I have to get going. Thanks for the ride, Mrs...I'm
sorry, I don't remember your name," I apologized.

"Malin. And yours?"

"Jewell," I said with a nervous giggle. "Maybe we can get together
some time and talk? I will be around all summer," I said hopefully, "I'd
like to hear more about my dad and his family."

"Sure, hon. I'm in the phone book or just stop in at the store. We'll
have tea." She laughed, waved and tooted her horn as she drove off,
leaving me on the short main street near the Sheriff's office and the
jail. A light wind cooled the afternoon off although the sun was still
bright. I shivered as I watched her drive away. Turning, I walked
quickly across the lot, and ran up the steps two at a time. The big
wooden doors opened into a room with echoing lofty ceilings.

"Hello," I said loudly to get the attention of the heavy-set man at
a desk. My voice echoed off the very high ceilings and glossy floors.

"Yes? What can I do for you?" he asked, turning around and
walking around a high counter.

"Can I make a telephone call?"

"You can use the phone if it is a local call."

"N-n-n-o, I have to call Superior, but I have money," I said.

"Sorry," he repeated, looking apologetic.

"Please, there must be some way you can help me. It's an
emergency!"

"I can wait until Deputy Boyden gets back from the hospital. He
has an emergency call out there, but he's coming back. Maybe he can
figure it out."

"At the hospital? I just came from there."

"Oh, don't worry: it's nuthin' much. Just some guy missing. Got
himself beat up this morning and then, plain up disappeared. Probably
a drunk."

"Do you know who it was?"

"Nope, can't say I can. What did you say your name was?" He got
up and walked over to the window.

"Jewell Johnson. Excuse me, what about the guy? Was his name
Jake?"

He looked back at me curiously and walked over to a short swinging door that was at the end of the counter.

"Maybe you should come around over here and sit down miss. I'll call the Deputy."

"Please," I whispered. "Can you tell me if it was Jake?"

"Calm down, the excitement is over." The officer came around the counter and took my arm. He guided me to a chair and I sat down, stunned. "The bad guys are gone; okay? Your friend probably just wandered off. Tom was headed out to question this guy when he disappeared. They have the staff and a city cop out there looking for him. Hang on, sit here. I'll call Tom. He will probably want to talk to you."

I covered my eyes with my fingers and massaged my forehead. What would I say? What was my mom going to say? It had been hours since I checked in with her and I didn't even leave a note. What happened to Jake, where was he? I was scared, hungry, thirsty and beat. I felt sick.

The radio chattered, and the officer walked back and forth for about fifteen minutes. Then a door in the back room opened and a tall dark-haired officer entered. His tan was almost as dark as his brown uniform. His face was serious, and his large brown eyes focused directly on me. I sat up straight and tried to look right at him clutching my hands nervously in my lap. My insides were shaking, and my stomach was tied in knots.

"Miss Johnson? Officer Hanson says that you need to make a phone call and you are a friend of Jake Pieters? Were you just at the hospital? Do you know where he went?"

"Yes, I am, I was, I mean…I'm sorry, I'm just nervous." I heard a quaver in my voice. What in the world was happening to me? I was whiney again.

"Just calm down," he said and handed me a tissue from the desk. "There. Come on into my office, I need some information about your friend." I followed him around the corner and down a hallway to his office. He was reading a note in his hand as he shut the door.

"Have a seat, Miss, Johnson," he said as he sat down in his own chair and leaned forward on his desk. I sat gingerly on the edge of the chair trying not to look as young and nervous as I felt. He had a way of trying to get me to make eye contact without saying anything. I let my hair fall across my face and then tucked it back behind my ear to buy some time.

"So. Your friend has disappeared. What are you doing here?"

"I need to call someone for Jake. I was supposed to call someone to tell him Jake is – was, in the hospital. There aren't any telephone booths and I don't know anyone here. I got a ride, but I didn't know what to do. I don't have my purse with me and all I have is a twenty-dollar bill. I just thought I could make a call from here."

"Mr. Pieters disappeared from the hospital less than a half an hour ago. The nurses said you were with him until another man showed up. He threatened the staff. Who is Mr. Pieters, and where have you been?"

"I left Jake in bed, and kind of sneaked out the back door. I came straight here from the hospital. I hitchhiked. The truck is out of gas. What man? I don't know anything about him. We were alone."

"Where is the vehicle Pieters drove to the hospital?"

"He didn't drive, I drove. I left his truck in the parking lot."

"Could I please see your driver's license?"

"I, ah, don't have it. I didn't have time to grab my purse when I ran back to the Inn to get the truck. I'd be glad to get it for you when I get back to my room." This was beginning to sound just awful.

"I see." He clearly didn't believe me. "Why didn't Pieters call his friend from the hospital?"

"Oh, I just don't know. Maybe because he wanted it to be private?"

I felt like a miserable liar, I hated not just telling him the little that I knew. He obviously saw right through me. I didn't know what I should say or if I could just trust him. After all, he and Jake were both police officers. Couldn't I just tell him everything? But Jake said he didn't trust the Sheriff.

"Can you describe his truck? Why were you driving?"

"It's brown, um…I don't even know. I can show it to you if you will take me back to the parking lot at the hospital. There was some guy digging in it when I was going to come to town. It scared me, so I tried to walk but I got a ride. Did you know that Jake was an officer in Douglas County? Can I make that phone call now? It is really important!"

Boyden looked at me with a half frown and waved to the phone on his desk.

"You can call from here. I am getting a cup of coffee and sorting this all out. Would you like some?"

"I would love something to drink or eat. I haven't eaten since early this morning."

"Okay, make your call."

"It is long distance, to Superior, is that okay?"

"Yah, you bet, if someone is coming down here that can help with Pieters."

Boyden walked out and left the door open. I asked for long distance and gave her Randy's telephone number. I thought about what I should say to yet another stranger and then took a deep breath. His secretary answered.

"Randy Farrow's office, Tanya speaking, how can I help you?"

"Your name, please?"

"I'm Jewell Johnson, I am looking for a Mr. Farrow," I replied and after a moment he came on the line.

"Randy, speaking."

"Hi, I am calling from Hayward. Jake Pieters asked me to call you. I think he is a friend of yours?"

"Yes, he's my friend." He answered slowly. "Who are you?"

"My name is Jewell Johnson. I met Jake this morning at Johnson Point Resort. We had coffee and went for a walk. Then Jake got sick or something and I went to get his truck. While I was gone, somebody hurt him. I found him. I brought him to the hospital. He sent me to town to get in touch with you and I'm at the Sheriff's office. He disappeared right after I left. The Deputy said someone was there, looking for him."

"What? My God, how bad is he hurt?"

"He was able to talk and sit up, but I think he's in tough shape. I don't know exactly because he didn't tell me much. He just said I should get hold of you and you needed to come down here. He was pretty out of it from pain."

"You said he disappeared?"

"Yes, the Deputy here said that he's missing. I left to call you, some guy came and now he's gone. He's in so much pain I can't believe he could even get up!"

"When did all this happen?" Randy asked.

"It started this morning: around ten. This is so frightening. Please come quickly, he said you were the only one I should trust."

"Okay, I'll finish up here quickly and come right down. Can you go back to the hospital? Jake won't do anything stupid," Randy asserted. "He may be hiding. I'll ask for you when I get there. Watch for me."

"I will, but hurry. He has a concussion or something and they are all worried." To my horror, I was having an awful time not breaking into sobs again. What was wrong with me? Perhaps tense, hungry and stressed out?

"I can't get back to the Inn now," I explained, "I have his truck keys but it's out of gas and some guy was digging in it and so I was afraid to take it to town to get gas and call you. It is still in the parking lot and I am afraid to go back!"

"Oh, my God. What a mess. Listen, hang in there. Jake's tough. I will be there in an hour or so. Maybe you can get a ride to the hospital. Keep your eyes peeled. Lock the truck doors, okay?" he said. "Don't go anywhere alone."

"Yes, I will. Good bye," I assured him. Before I hung up I heard a click on the line. At the resort that meant that someone was on the extension. Deputy Boyden appeared in the office door with a sandwich wrapped in waxed paper and a bottle of Coke.

"You looked like you needed some lunch. I had an extra sandwich today. Its meat loaf and pickles, I hope you like that."

"Oh sure, I'd love that."

"I suppose you're worried about your friend, huh?"

"I am." I wondered if it was him snooping on the phone.

"I thought you said you hardly knew this man, Miss Johnson."

"That's true, but he's in trouble and I feel like I should do something."

"I suppose I could give you a ride out there."

"Oh, thanks. I'd appreciate that. His friend just asked me to go back there and wait. I can't just turn my back and walk away."

"Do you have a way to get back to your home?"

"I am staying at the Linger Inn on Lake Makoons with my mom and her husband. I guess I can call my mom."

Deputy Boyden closed his desk drawer, picked up a notepad from his desk and stuffed it in his shirt pocket along with a clip-on pen. He adjusted his hat and waved his hand toward the door indicating that we should go. I stood up with my sandwich and drink then walked out into the hallway behind him.

"You're vacationing up here with your folks?" he asked casually.

"Yes, we are staying all summer," I explained. "My Mom and step-dad are visiting with friends today. I'm just a tag-a-long this summer."

We walked to his squad car through the quickly cooling afternoon air. A stormy grey thunderhead was building up in the northwest sky. I pointed it out to the Deputy as I got into his car. He adjusted his seat belt and we rolled past the main street towards the Hospital.

"My dad warned me not to walk in the woods or away from the farm when a storm like that was coming. He liked to tell me a lot of old lumber-jack stories like the one about widow-makers."

I stopped suddenly, feeling foolish and realizing that I was just jabbering to cover my nervousness. I felt weird riding in this police car.

"I'm sure it will miss us." He looked up through the window.

"You don't know what happened to Jake at the hospital?" I asked nervously.

"No, I'm sorry." He glanced sideways at me. "We have nothing. But I am concerned about this man who came to see him at the hospital. The nurses were threatened. Are you sure that this man is not a buddy of his?"

"I don't think so, but then I don't know a whole lot about Jake. I called his friend because he asked me to tell Randy to hurry down here from Duluth. I'm sure he thought he needed protection from someone."

"So how long did you say you actually have known Pieters?"

"I met him this morning; he was fishing. We had coffee at the Inn, went for a walk and then all of this weird stuff started happening." I covered my eyes with my hands to think.

"Yeah, okay. You just concentrate on that sandwich. We'll have a few minutes before we get there. This kind of thing doesn't happen often in this county, Miss Johnson. I don't mean to sound tough on you. I just need information to help Pieters."

I slipped a look at him and saw that he was carefully scanning the bushes along the road as we left the village limits. White daisies and Indian paintbrush were sprinkled around in the deep grass with some little yellow flower.

"Thanks, Deputy Boyden. I can appreciate that." I managed a smile at him. "I expect you work very hard to keep it quiet around here."

"Please call me Tom, Miss Johnson," He smiled, and his teeth were dazzlingly white against his tan. "It's orderly and clean in Hayward and we like it that way."

"Ok, Tom." I glanced sideways returning his smile. I guess I had been too wrapped up in my problems that day to even consider the deputy as anything but a "cop". I noticed he was nice-looking even with his very unfashionable short military style haircut.

As we approached the hospital parking lot, I squared my shoulders and tucked a few wisps of hair back behind my ear. I felt like a mess, but there was nothing to be done about it until I could get back to the Inn.

"I'll just go inside."

"Please stay near the nursing station. I need to look in his room to see if I can find anything. We don't have much to go on - yet." I followed his look as he stared over the top of the car at two officers. One was directing another in a rowboat in the lake. My heart skipped a beat.

"Do you think he's...?"

"Hard to say, we will search completely. Stick around. I'll want to talk to you again. Stay inside the hospital and don't wander around. Tell me if you find a ride."

"Okay. I sure will."

Tom turned and strode over to the two men. I hurried over to Jake's truck to check it out. When I opened the passenger door, his registration papers fell out at my feet. The glove compartment was open, and the contents tossed on the seat. I picked them up and tucked his registration back into the glove box, then locked the doors with the keys Jake gave me. I tucked the keys in my pants pocket and hurried down the tiled hall, watchful for any sign of trouble. The hospital lobby was so quiet you could hear a pin drop. Around the corner someone was talking in an office but there was no sign of anyone walking around.

As I moved quietly back towards Jake's room, I hoped I could find a clue they overlooked. At the nurse's station one nurse sat filling in charts and another chattered animatedly on the phone behind a glass partition. She would have seen me had she been paying attention. I watched all around me, half expecting that man to come out of one of the rooms. No wonder Jake could disappear. The rooms were dark and silent except for Jake's room. There were lights on and the drapes were opened. His clothes and shoes were gone from the open locker. I peered around and slipped back into the hallway.

I suddenly thought about my mom, wishing she was here to help me figure out this situation. I wondered how I would get home and if they would be able to find Jake, and what in the world had I gotten myself into. At the nurse's station two nurses were talking to each other and still not paying attention to me. Just as I looked, a man walked up to the counter. It was the skinny guy that had been digging in Jake's truck. The nurses talked to him, but I couldn't distinguish his words. I looked to my right and saw the words, "Quiet Room" on the door next to me and thought that looked good right now! I grabbed the handle, pushed the door open and ducked into the cool dark interior. I tried to find a lock as I quietly closed the door. I realized I couldn't lock it, so I pushed a chair under the grab bar on the door, so it couldn't be opened from the outside. Thick drapes covered each of the windows. There was nowhere to hide. I checked the windows but there was no way out without breaking a window. I was trapped. The only weapon would be that Bible sitting on the end table.

With a sudden shock, I realized I was also not alone. In the dimness, a completely silent figure sat in a chair facing away from the door. His head was bent as if he was praying but something looked very wrong. I stifled a shriek with my hand over my mouth. Looking closer I realized it was Jake.

"Jake," I whispered. "Jake, do you hear me? Jake are you okay?"

Then I heard voices coming down the hallway towards the room where I stood. I decided quickly that nobody, but Randy was coming into this room. My heart pounded violently until the voices faded on down the hall. I turned back towards Jake and dropped to one knee in front of him.

"Jake are you .... Okay?" I tapped him on the leg and then shook him gently. "Jake, please answer me..." I checked his pulse with my trembling hands. It was strong, but very slow and his temperature felt too warm. I reach up and took his face in my hands. "Jake, please wake up, are you okay?" He reacted slowly, lifting one hand up as if to push me away.

"Tired," he slurred. "Leave me 'lone."

How did they miss him here? I figured it would be at least another half an hour before his buddy showed up from Duluth. What could I do in the meantime? I didn't want to leave him here, although it was safe and quiet. He'd been fine the last couple of hours. Finally, after a few minutes of intense concentration, I decided to go to the front desk and leave a message for Randy to meet me here. As I rose, I saw a phone on the walnut end table across the room. It looked like this was simply a house phone and I could call the desk the same way a private room could. Dialing '0', I waited for the switchboard.

"Front desk, Sandy speaking. Can I help you?" she asked.

"Hi, this is Jewell Johnson. I'm waiting for a man to come to the hospital. His name is Randy Farrow and he will ask for me or for Jake Pieters. When he gets here, could you send him to the chapel in the wing by the Emergency Room?"

"Sure, Miss Johnson. That's Mr. Pieters, the one who walked away earlier?"

"Yes, it was," I said. "I am so worried about him"

"Of course, I'll send them down there as soon as they show up. I'm sorry about your friend." She said consolingly.

"Thanks a lot!" I said and hung up.

I thought that Jake's neck would be getting sore from sitting with his head drooping down, so I balanced on the arm of the chair with my back to the window and gently nudged him over to lean against my hip, gingerly putting my arm around his neck.

Jake moaned and pushed away, but then he seemed to wake up.

"Jake, it's okay, Randy is coming, and we are safe here," I whispered to him.

"Jewell, izzat you? Yore an angel," he slurred looking through half opened eyes.

"Shhh, Jake. Try to relax."

"Yep, an angel." He smiled and leaned his big shoulders against me.

I was worrying about the police showing up. Jake seemed certain about not telling them anything. I rested my chin on the top of his head.

"Mmrphnnah," he mumbled.

It seemed forever before I heard some footsteps in the hallway, but they paused a few rooms down. My ears strained, trying to figure out where exactly they had stopped. Was it Randy, Deputy Boyden, or was it that guy again? I took a deep breath and pulled my hair back away from my ears. I could only hear muffled voices.

I slipped away from Jake and over to the hallway window, pulling the thick curtain aside and peered out. Jake mumbled something and struggled to sit up.

"Shhh, Jake. Please!" I whispered and stepped back over to his chair, gently rubbing his arm. He struggled again to wake up and move forward. I held his face between my hands and whispered, "Jake, I think Randy is here. Hang on!" I reached over to pull the curtain aside a little. "Jake, look! Is that him?"

Jake's eyes fluttered open and his head bobbed up to look.

"Yes! Get him! Oh, my God my head hurts!"

"Sit down. I'll get him!"

I pulled the chair out from under the handle and gently opened the door. I was going to call out to Randy when I saw that skinny guy again. He was walking down the hall. I covered my face with my hand and keeping Randy between us, I cried out to him, "Oh Randy, Dad's gone, I can't believe it!" and I threw myself into his arms in my best sobbing act, hiding my face in his neck.

"What?" he said in a puzzled voice, trying to hold me back by my shoulders. I threw my arms around his neck again and whispered fiercely into his ear, "Shut up! I'm Jewell, come inside!" I hid my face in front of his shoulder pulling him closer to the quiet room.

"Okay, sweetie. I am so sorry. Take it easy," he said very loudly as we stepped inside the room and closed the door. I took a heaving breath and blocked the door with my body. Jake was unconscious again in the chair. Randy knelt in front of him. Because Jake's friend was here I was shakily relieved, and the weight dropped off my shoulders. I peeked out the curtain into the hall.

The skinny guy was moving back towards the nurse's station just as Deputy Boyden came around the corner. He asked the guy something and gestured towards the front door. The guy started to reach for his back pocket but instead he quickly reeled around and slammed his fist directly into the Deputy's face, throwing him into the wall and then battering his body with rapid-fire punches. The nurses stood immobile.

Throwing the door open I darted down the hall screaming at the top of my lungs.

"Stop it! Stop that!" I was screaming, waving my arms. "Help! Do something! Call somebody!"

He turned away from Tom and started moving towards me, but I darted into a utility room I had seen before – it had doors opening into both hallways. Slamming the door in his face behind me, I dashed back out into the main hall by the nurse's station, and then back around the corner to where Tom leaned against the wall, bleeding all over the floor, his face in his hands. Just as I saw Randy loping up the hall towards that guy, he pulled out a knife and brandished it towards us. Randy skidded to a stop and hunched with his fists up. I looked down and saw Tom's gun in his holster, I stooped down and unsnapped it. I'd never handled the cold steel of a gun before, but fear made me raise it in both hands.

"Stop it! I'll shoot! I swear I will!"

"No, Jewell," Tom yelled.

Randy ducked over against the wall. The other guy took one look at my shaking hands and ran right towards us. I heard an explosion and my arms flew backwards from a violent kickback. His face loomed closer and the last thing I remember was pain shooting through my shoulder and thinking I was going to die, blackness flooded my mind.

A moment later I heard someone calling my name.

"Jewell… Jewell!"

My head swam horribly, and nausea hit me in the stomach. I began to retch. I was shivering violently on the cold, tiled floor.

"Get out of the way, move it!" a woman's voice said with authority, "she's sick."

A cool towel enfolded my neck and a silver pan came into my view. I rolled over to my side and heaved. The nurse took away the pan and wiped my face with the towel. In a few moments, strong arms lifted me to sit upright.

"You're okay now. He's gone. It's shock." My shaking hands clung to the cold towel and held it to my face. I took a ragged embarrassed breath and looked around. Jake's friend Randy was kneeling next to me and staring with shocked concern. I was still on the floor in the hallway which was now filled with hurrying people.

"The gun?" I whispered.

"Nobody's dead. You were waving it around and it went off." Randy said, "Then he scratched you with his knife. You scared the hell out of him though. He ran right into the arms of the two deputies at the front door. They hauled him off." Randy chuckled.

"Jake? Tom?" I asked.

"Fine, as far as it goes. The Deputy's nose isn't broken but that's where all that blood came from; he'll probably have a fat lip and black eye. The nurses are icing him in the ER. They are taking Jake back to his room. It could have been a lot different if you wouldn't have jumped in. That was quite a show!"

Randy helped me up. I winced when he touched my arm.

"He's nuts. He's probably hopped up on something. That scratch hurts, doesn't it? That's your shootin' arm Calamity Jane." I looked balefully at him.

"Yeah, well it really hurts." I said, rubbing it gently. "Please stop calling me Calamity Jane."

"Then c'mon, 'Cat Ballou', if you are feeling better. Let's head over to see Jake."

My stomach was still queasy as we walked down to Jake's room. Jake was in bed with an icepack and a white towel over his forehead. Nurses were putting an IV line back in his arm, but his eyes were open.

"Good pain killers." He said. "They work fast! Are you okay Jewell?"

"Yeah, I am okay. A little worse for wear I think. How about you?"

"My guts are killing me, and my head is splitting but it is getting better. I think it's good to have a guard near now. I didn't realize just how nuts these goons are."

"Jake, what's going on?" Randy asked. "Quick before anyone else shows up."

"I think I stumbled into a hornet's nest." Jake groaned lowly. "There's some link with Superior. We can't talk about it here, too many ears."

"Gotcha." Randy looked at me and then the door. Just then, Deputy Boyden walked up.

"How are you doing," I winced, looking at him.

"Okay, a little worse for wear."

"Jake's a little worse for wear too."

"Jewell, how about you?"

"I'm good, okay, fine I guess. My arm hurts."

Boyden looked dubiously at me. I smiled slightly. He put his hand out to Randy.

"I'm County Deputy Boyden, you are…"

"Randy Farrow, accountant from Duluth. I am a friend of Jake's"

"I see." They shook hands. "The Sheriff's definitely going to want a full explanation of what's going on here."

Tom's left eye was swollen half closed: his lip was slightly gashed and still bleeding even though they put a little tape on it. "That was a damned dangerous trick to pull, Miss Johnson- Jewell. If you don't know how to handle guns you shouldn't touch 'em. I've got to admit I'm grateful you slowed him down though. He's a rough character."

"I am so sorry. I just reacted when I saw the knife. I didn't think about how the darned thing might go off. I don't know what I thought I would do with it.

"A gun? What did you do?" Jake looked surprised. "Did you shoot someone?"

"No, Jake, she was just waving it around for the effect and shot the wall." Randy laughed suddenly and broke the tension. "You're running with a tough gang, Jake. Where'd you meet Miss Ballou?"

"We had a breakfast date and things slid downhill on an icy slope, fast." Jake explained.

"Don't call me Cat Ballou!" I grumbled but Jake smiled weakly.

"I will want to hear all about it when the Sheriff gets here." Boyden said sternly. "The situation isn't exactly amusing."

"Sorry, glad to oblige. I'm a deputy officer from Superior but I'm on medical leave. My badge is with my stuff in the locker over there. Right now, I think I can't think, I am slipping away for a while."

Jake's head nodded back on the pillow and his eyes closed. Randy nudged my arm with his hand and nodded at Boyden to go into the hall.

"How about I take this young lady down to the cafeteria? When the Sheriff gets back this afternoon he can talk to Jake and then we'll head back to the Inn. I have an RV and he can rest comfortably until we can get him back to his room at the Inn. Some vacation! We'll have to come back up and get his truck anyway."

"I can't imagine the doctor will approve but that'll work. I want to get back to the office and get some paperwork done. I'll station a couple guys here to watch out for any more trouble. I'll have one at the front door and one out here in the hall." Boyden said. "Miss Johnson, this is a dangerous situation and I hope you know exactly what you are getting into. I think you should consider heading back to your parents as soon as possible. If you need a ride, I would be glad to take care of that." The two men looked at each other uneasily.

"I will see to it that Jewell gets back in one piece without any more incidents." Randy said without any inflection.

"Deputy Boyden, don't worry, I'll take care of myself." I responded seriously.

I thought I could feel Deputy Boyden's eyes on our backs as Randy and I went down the hall and into the basement where there was a very cool and sterile cafeteria. Several packages of cereal sat on the counter and the milk was in a big silver dispenser. There were dry-looking rolls and a tub of thin beef vegetable soup. I filled a melamine bowl, took some crackers and a small box of milk. I slurped my soup so quickly that I was nearly done when Randy plopped coins into a donation can on the counter.

"This feels good. I kind of lost my lunch back there."

"Did you want a bagel?" he asked. "There's some in a bag on the counter by the milk. There's even a packet of cream cheese but no butter."

"Sure; ugh-my arm hurts." I said, heading back over to the bar behind the food bar. "I could sure use a cup of coffee."

Coffee was one of my downfalls as an athlete. As a kid, my dad and I dipped toast in our coffee in the morning before school. Sometimes Mom served coffee at supper too. My dad would dump sugar and cream into his coffee and call it "Swedish coffee" and then laugh. My heart skipped a beat at that thought. The coffee carafe was almost empty, so I had to skip the idea anyway. The bagel was a little too chewy, but I finished it too.

"Thanks, I really needed something. I was getting dizzy!"

"Maybe we can find an aspirin too," Randy said smiling with me. "I hope this situation hasn't scared you too much."

"I'll be fine, don't worry. I can't believe I grabbed that gun. It was so heavy and cold; I just didn't expect that. I only thought I could scare the guy. Uffda!"

"Let's clean this up and head back upstairs."

Randy was confident and right now that was very reassuring. I noticed his creased slacks, striped business shirt and tie. He had nice blue eyes with light brown eyebrows and hair. It's odd how if there is commotion you don't see the people right in front of you. He seemed very gentle and considerate. We left the cafeteria and went back down the white and grey hallway to the stairs to return to the first floor. The afternoon was very quiet in the waiting area outside Jake's room and I napped for quite a while. Finally, the doctor returned and talked to Jake before releasing him.

Jake had finished signing all the insurance forms and checked out. The ER doctor wasn't too happy to let him go and looked on worriedly as he signed the insurance forms. Jake promised he would rest for a few days, drink lots of water and call back if he had unusual symptoms. He would contact his surgeon: as a matter of fact, he already had an appointment scheduled. The Sheriff called to say that he could not make it to the hospital and had Tom ask Jake a few questions about what happened. They made an appointment for Jake to return to talk to the Sheriff as soon as possible. Tom was also obviously not happy with how the situation was going but Randy and Jake were firm.

We were quite a sight as we left the hospital. Twilight was in the pines and the golden sun setting on the little lake when we walked out into the parking lot. Jake was in obvious pain and I was disheveled and tired walking beside the two men. I called the Inn and left a message with Mrs. Swenson to let mom know I was in Hayward and that I would be back soon.

"Where's the limo?" Jake asked Randy.

"I brought the RV, Sir. Your limo is in for a wash," Randy replied with a fake English accent and they both laughed.

"You dummies," I snapped, "How can you fool around at a time like this?"

I saw the amused look they gave each other and was thankful for no eye-rolling. We walked across the blacktopped parking lot to a small RV unit parked along the woods. Painted on the side of it was a panorama of a whitetail buck running through a swamp into a pine plantation. A doe and fawn were standing in snow in the background and an orange and pink sunset glowed behind the balsam pines.

"Where did you find an RV like this, Randy? It's beautiful!"

"I bought it a few years ago to travel around in and for hunting trips. My friend Deirdre painted the outside. She's not only a fantastic artist, she's a great mechanic as well. She does all the maintenance on my vehicles. Hop in front. Jake, you lay down on the bed."

Once inside the RV I decided to take the orange shag-covered captain's seat in front. I settled down and admired the RV's muted brown and orange interior with touches of olive green and gold in the curtains. The carpeting was soft shag in brown, orange and gold with a woven runner down the middle. Everything was perfectly clean. Jake made himself comfortable on the bed and Randy jumped up into the driver's seat.

"This is so cool, it is perfect!" I said to Jake.

"Thanks, it is my home away from home."

"My dad always talked about getting an RV but then we would talk about fixing up my Grampa's place at Lake Makoons instead. Grampa's place is that farm across from the Linger Inn." I noticed he looked in the rear-view mirror and looked back at Jake. I turned around and saw Jake motioning to Randy, but he quit when he saw me.

"Never mind, she knows some of what is going on Randy. I think we are going to have to fill her in for her own protection. She will be at the Linger Inn all summer and those guys probably know her."

"Jake, this could be too dangerous. Look at yourself. She can't take a beating like that. Jewell, it would be better to go back home. You can see this is not fun and games. This is no place for a girl."

"What? I'm not a girl. I'm eighteen. I certainly can take care of myself." I didn't like the idea of being treated like a child. I had enough of that with Mom and her husband. "I didn't run away when it came to defending Jake did I? I didn't like the gun thing, but somebody had to step up and I did."

"I am sorry, I didn't mean to put you down. I just thought that this situation should be handled by men, not a girl…um I mean a woman."

"So, that's it, huh? You don't even know me." I was getting mad now.

"Hey, you two - Cool it!" Jake's voice came from behind us. "Randy doesn't mean to sound like that. He's from Duluth, up in the snow belt, where men are supposed to take care of women. We Northwoods men are a little behind the times I think."

"Yeah, I'm sorry. I guess I just don't want to involve a stranger in this deal—and yes, I admit it, especially since you are a …girl. I'm no chauvinist. But dammit it, you really could get hurt." Randy shook his head.

I bit my tongue on the 'girl' remark. I decided he did care and he was seriously just protecting me. It felt kinda good, but then in a way it made me feel odd. At this moment, I just didn't feel like arguing with anyone. I stared out the window at the passing scenery in the dimming light.

The big RV rolled smoothly down the drive towards the main highway. I leaned back in the seat and tried to relax but my nerves and my muscles were tight, and my arm was painful. I concentrated on the surroundings outside the RV and tried to figure out what to tell my mom when we got back.

"It's so beautiful," I sighed. In the ensuing silence, I was still unsure of my relationship with these two men. They seemed so much older than me and with the drama over, I suddenly felt uneasy. I was a fish out of water. "I've never seen anything to match the coloring like that before."

"That's a northern Wisconsin sky I think it's a little peek into heaven," Randy finally said, "I am not sure why it is so different than everywhere else - it just is."

"There's absolutely nothing as beautiful as a summer sunset on Lake Superior, unless it is a fall sunset," said Jake from the back. He had stretched out full-length on the bed with his head propped up on big pillows. I felt oddly shy, even after protecting and defending him. Perhaps it was because the day seemed like an episode of "Kojak" or "Adam 12". I watched the sunset, and no one spoke. I faded off to sleep with a bunch of unanswered questions in my mind.

CHAPTER 6

Women Have Loved Before ~
Edna St. Vincent Millay

Women have loved before as I love now;
At least, in lively chronicles of the past—
Of Irish waters by a Cornish prow
Or Trojan waters by a Spartan mast
Much to their cost invaded—here and there,
Hunting the amorous line, skimming the rest,
I find some woman bearing as I bear
Love like a burning city in the breast.
I think however that of all alive
I only in such utter, ancient way
Do suffer love; in me alone survive
The unregenerate passions of a day
When treacherous queens, with death upon the tread,
Heedless and willful, took their knights to bed.

INTO THE MIST

When I woke up, I found myself alone in the parked RV. It was very dark. I uncurled from my seat and stretched. The doors were locked, and the silence was broken only when I popped up the thumb lock and opened the squeaky door.

"Not another disappearing act: where are they?" I don't know if I said that out loud. The silence was deafening. I got out and leaned against the RV for a second, looking at the twinkling stars in the moonless night. I didn't quite recognize the parking lot behind the Linger Inn, in the darkness but as I peered out across the front of the RV I could see the lights in the windows of the Inn.

Crunching my way across the parking lot and down the sidewalk to the lakeside veranda I found that the door was open. I walked quietly across the darkened dining room over to the stairs and up the two flights to my room. I saw was a note from my mom taped to the mirror on my dresser as soon as I opened the door. Tossing my room key into the flower shaped dish on the dresser, I picked it up to read:

"Hey Sweetie,

We had a wonderful day. Hope yours was fun, where did you run off to anyway? We missed you for dinner, but how about breakfast on the veranda at around 8 am? Jim hasn't met Dave and Jone Lambert, across the lake. Remember them? We are going over for a drink at the golf club with them, so I imagine we'll be home late. See you in the morning honey, ...Love, Mom"

"Sure," I thought with a touch of jealousy. "Maybe, when you have time to write me in your busy schedule!"

I was momentarily angry with mom. As I stripped off my jeans and sweater I threw them on the floor. I embarrassed myself with my childish tantrum. I picked up my clothes and folded them carefully, then set them in the wicker laundry basket to be washed. I put on PJ's, slippers, and the soft white housecoat Mom got me for this summer then went down the hall to the tiny wall-papered bathroom to wash my face and hands. A miniature window let night air in from the lake. I shook my head when my head touched the top of the doorframe and bumped the sloped ceiling over the toilet. I rinsed my face with cool water and lavender-scented soap to help cool my temper tantrum and padded back down the shag carpeted hallway to my room.

The face looking back at me as I sat at the dressing table mirror was pale and sort of sad. I brushed my hair vigorously and then braided it into a rope down my back. Looking up into the mirror again I thought I saw my dad's reflection in my own face and sat staring for a few silent seconds. Then I was startled by a gentle knock on the door.

"Who is it?" I asked rather crossly. I didn't want to talk to anyone right now.

"It's Randy. Can I talk to you for a minute?"

"I'm in my pj's. Can't it wait until morning?" I was a little nonplussed.

"Just for a sec?"

I opened the door and stepped back to let him in, pulling my housecoat around myself.

"Sorry, I just wanted to say I was sorry I abandoned you in the RV. I saw you in the window and thought I'd stop to see how you were doing. I had to get Jake up to his room, he isn't feeling too great. I am going to bunk out on his floor for the night. Are you doing all right?

"I'm fine. Thanks for the ride home. My mom was gone so no questions were asked."

"Do you have any aspirin? Jake wouldn't ask the doctor for a pain killer. He wouldn't admit he was in pain. How's your arm by the way? Does it still hurt?"

"Oh, I almost forgot about it, yeah it hurts a little. I have a tin of aspirin here somewhere." I said, digging in my bag. "Here they are, take the whole tin, I don't use them anyway. Randy, what's going on here?"

Randy took the little yellow and white metal container and then stared at me for a long moment.

"I don't think we should talk about it right now. I don't think I should be up here in your room, people will talk."

"I'm from Madison, Randy. Down there nobody'd notice. I do have some questions I want to ask you. I guess my mom might stop up later and I need to figure out what to tell her." I could see that I had made some impression on this tall, brooding man, and I felt just a tiny bit uneasy with his presence in my room. I glanced away at the window and saw a light blinking at the farm across the bay. I stepped over to the window and tried to get a better view.

"Darn it, I know I just saw those lights again. No one should be at the farm! Do you see them?"

"Hmm? What farm, what lights? Where?" Randy frowned, took a couple steps to the window and looked out.

"By my Grampa's barn – at Johnson Point. I've seen lights and cars over there and the whole farm is supposed to be deserted. My mom said that no one uses it. I'd hate to see someone vandalizing the farm. I guess I'll have to ask mom to contact the Sheriff in the morning."

"No, I don't see anything, I think you're just tired." Randy said seriously.

"No, I saw it, wait a minute. Hang on, I'll turn off the lights, I know I saw something past the barn!"

Randy knelt on one knee beside me and peered out the window too. I flicked off the lamp on my dressing table and returned to kneel on the carpet again. Night hawks and crickets sang in the evening and the light of a half moon and stars sparkled on the lake through a thin mist. Bugs bumped against the screen. The white house at Johnson Point was starkly visible, but the barn and the field were veiled in a silky mist. The breeze through the screens was almost chilly up here. I was aware of Randy's being so close to me that I caught an attractive faint whiff of his Brut aftershave. For the second time, I felt too close to a man I didn't know. I felt a little uncomfortable suddenly-maybe even afraid. I also realized that we couldn't keep kneeling here in the darkness waiting for a blink of a light.

"I guess it's gone." I stood up and moved away.

"Could have been a firefly?"

"No, it wasn't green. Why did Jake call you instead of his family," I asked, thinking that conversation would break the awkward pause.

"He was my best friend in high school. He doesn't want to worry his mom and dad. They went through a lot when he was shot last year. We agreed that he'd call me for minor emergencies. In this case, he certainly minimized his issue."

"And so, who are you, Randy? I mean other than being Jake's best friend? You know we really haven't been introduced."

"It's been a strange day." He rose with a slight shrug. "I'm Randy Farrows, I'm an accountant. My office is in Duluth. And who are you? How did you get so mixed up with Jake?"

"I graduated from Madison East and I'm on vacation up here with my mom and her husband. I just met Jake today, this morning, down by the lake." I explained. "He was fishing in the rain and I surprised him. We had coffee. Then we went for a walk up the road. While I was talking to Jake about my family, the farm and the things I saw over there, he got excited and decided to rush off towards Philetus Spur. Then he collapsed on the road and he sent me to get his truck. When I came back I couldn't find him. I drove over to the Spur and checked around but didn't find him, so I went back to the road. When I did finally find him in the brush by the ditch, he was all beat up. I drove him the hospital and I spent most of the day in one stupid situation after another!"

"That's crazy! What happened to him? What did he tell you?"

"I never had a chance to find out why he was running and hiding and who he was hiding from."

"We talked about that part while you were sleeping on the way back from Hayward. He said he wanted to get out of the hospital because he was afraid that guy might be looking for him. He tried to 'un-involve' you. He didn't think it would get so violent. He thought you should get out of this mess, but you seem to keep getting back in the middle of it. Because of the injuries, it's hard for him to take care of himself, let alone you too." He spoke carefully, and I could tell he was trying to find a way out of the conversation.

"Did it ever occur to either of you that I might be able to fend for myself? I'm eighteen and free to do as I please."

"You don't understand what I mean," he answered. "It isn't that we don't think you can handle yourself. I think Jake has a tiger by his tail and that tiger is pretty darned angry," he said seriously. "We don't know who they are or where they come. This isn't like a TV show. We can't just polka through a hail of bullets and capture the bad guy single-handed."

He put his hand on my shoulder and turned me to face him in the dim moonlight.

"Somebody shot and almost killed Jake. Now somebody beat him up and might have killed him if you hadn't showed up. They mean business, whoever they are. They may have recognized you by now, so we want you to stand back, Jewell. They might decide to hurt you. We don't want that."

I couldn't help liking these two guys as different as they were, even if they decided to treat me like a kid.

"How old are you Randy? How old is Jake?"

"I don't see that it makes any difference," he said, turning back to the stars out the window.

"How old?" He paused a moment, I guess he thought I might back down. The moonlight was drifting on a breeze through a million, chattering poplar leaves outside and it whispered in the tops of the pines but there was a loud silence between us.

"I'm twenty-five and he's twenty-four. Why?"

"I just wondered where you guys got all your experience and knowledge of such things as thugs and bad guys." I chided gently. "You need someone with driving experience and common sense apparently." I didn't look his way, just stared out the window. "Maybe you think it is stupid of me to horn in on your mystery, but it seems like there is some connection between Jake, our family farm and whatever is going on."

"Sorry: this is police business: well, kind of. It is dangerous. You were very brave this morning at the hospital. But, well, you just can't get involved. I mentioned something to Jake about that bar when he was shot. He decided to follow up for the Sheriff. It went horribly wrong and Jake almost died. I felt like that was my fault."

"What bar? What do you mean by that?"

"Damn," he said softly, and paused momentarily, collecting his thoughts. "I have to get back to Jake. He's not safe alone." He said, straightening up and moving towards the door. I got up and followed.

"I am coming. I want to see Jake again before you disappear."

"Shouldn't you get dressed first?"

"I beg your pardon. How long have you been here? I have a housecoat on and I don't care what other people think. I want to see Jake. Besides if we are quiet no one else seems to be around the Inn tonight. I am covered more than when I wear my swimsuit."

"What if someone sees you in the hallway?"

"We'll have to be quiet, won't we?" I said stubbornly, and I think Randy heard in my voice that I was going to stand my ground.

"I was just worried about what people would think!" he said as he crossed to the door and opened it, looking back over his shoulder he gave me a frowning look. "You're one of those women's libbers, huh?"

"You know, I really never gave it any thought. Like Popeye said, "*I am who I am*". At this point, I don't care what goofy ideas a bunch of strangers might have. I want to see Jake because I think you two have plans to vanish again. If he's awake, I'd like to say good-bye."

"Okay, come along then. I don't care." He didn't sound like he meant it. "I guess you can come down. Jake probably won't wake up for a few hours. He should sleep some from the stuff they gave him at the hospital."

Randy opened my door, peered out, then stepped quickly out into the hallway. He looked both ways, and then quietly slipped down the short stairs at the end of the hall. I was touched that he was concerned about what other people might think if they saw him coming out of my room. I swiftly joined him on the second landing and followed around the corner to #4. He unlocked the door and we walked in to find Jake, sprawled asleep comfortably in striped undershorts. For a split second before Randy flipped a chenille blanket over his friend, I saw new bruises and terrible older red scars on Jake's suntanned chest and stomach. Jake's face was puffy and bruised as well. I turned away and shook my head, wondering how anyone could be so vicious and brutal to another human being. I had never experienced something like that before. Randy turned an old wooden chair with a padded seat out from the corner and set it near the open window.

"It's pretty stuffy in here, but there's a little breeze coming in this window. Have a seat," Randy said and sat on the foot of the bed.

"This room is really nice," I commented. The walls were cool blue, and the old plaid, cream and navy curtains hung weakly on bent rods. An old brown dresser was stained, and the lamp was plugged into a brown extension cord stretched down behind the bed. A dark blue oriental rug lay on the gray painted wooden floor. Randy reached down under the bed and pulled out a brown bag.

"Want one? I stopped and picked some up a six-pack at the bar in Philetus Spur. I figured I'd get a little bored babysitting old Jake here. There's no TV in this room." He leaned back against the low footboard.

"Uh, sure." I shook my head. "But I don't drink. I'm thirsty, though."

"I don't have a glass, and water is down the hall. You're old enough to drink. Here, try one, Leinies isn't bad and I put them in the RV fridge for a while, so they are kind of cold. I'm sorry I didn't get back out to the RV and you woke up alone. That wasn't considerate."

I took a sip from the bottle. Randy was right, it wasn't bad, but it wasn't that good either.

"So how are you related to the folks at the Point? I'm just curious. You said something about your grandfather..."

"My Grandpa Sven and Great Uncle Lars Johnson owned this whole area. They came over from Sweden at the turn of the century. He and my Gramma built the Inn, but they sold it to Mrs. Swenson. Lars and his wife Naomi built the farm across the bay. He died years ago, and Aunt Naomi went back to live near her family at the Reservation. When Grampa and Gramma sold the Inn, they moved over to the farm. After my grandparents died, it wasn't used again. I think my aunt takes care of the farm now. The fields are rented out to Mr. Olson, but the house is abandoned. I was over there yesterday, and it felt so spooky that I ran all the way back here. Then Mrs. Swenson, the lady that owns the Inn, reacted strangely about me being over there. And there's that thing about lights in the barn." I explained while I sipped on the warmish beer. "I know I saw a car drive into the farmyard the first day we got here. I don't think that anyone has any good reason to be over there and it bugs me. There is nothing to steal so maybe it is kids looking for a place to party."

"Maybe you shouldn't be going over there," said Randy seriously.

"There you go, telling me what to do again!" This time I laughed myself at my instant reaction. I was getting to know Randy a little better and I wasn't so defensive.

"I'm sorry. I guess...well, I guess I forgot that it offends you," said Randy, apologizing with a wave of his hand and a grave smile.

"I'm not really offended. I just always have been an independent person and it seems strange to have someone intruding in my life or making decisions," I responded quickly. "That doesn't include my mom, of course."

"You don't have any sisters or brothers? Mine were always hanging over my shoulder," he confided, with a short laugh. "My older sister gave a kid a bloody nose once for picking on me. Dad gave her heck for it and then taught me how to defend myself. I have to admit that looking back on it, I appreciated the help but maybe that's what my dad didn't like!"

"What's with you northern guys then? What's feminine? A sweet southern girl hanging on your arm? Queen Guinevere? A fairy princess? What are women supposed to be?"

"Oh, I guess we're pretty conservative compared to Madison. Men are supposed to protect women, not the other way around." Randy looked uncomfortable with this new discussion. And since it was one I wasn't going to win with him, I backed off. I knew when to walk away and when to stand my ground. I learned a while back that it doesn't do any good to argue with men about stuff like this. In my high school the teachers talked about the 'Women's Libbers' and still the popular girls were the ones hanging all over the drippy football players.

"You know, Randy, I never worried much about it until I graduated and now that I am looking at schools, careers and jobs, I can see it might not be easy to be a woman and have a career. Where did you go to college?" I glanced over at Randy who was leaning back and staring speculatively at the light fixture.

"University of Minnesota, in Minneapolis. I have a Master's in Business. Why?"

"I have to decide what to do. My dad put aside some money for me. I can live at home and go to the "U" in the fall but I don't want to live with my mom and her husband. I have a scholarship for swimming and sports, but I can't figure out what I want to be 'when I grow up'. Sad, huh?" I laughed a little at myself.

"Where are your other friends going?" Randy asked.

"Most of the kids in my class are going to Madison or Milwaukee. Most of the girls just want to get married and have kids. I didn't have many close friends just a lot of acquaintances. I studied a lot and stayed home when I wasn't in sports."

"That's hard to believe - as pretty as you are," Randy said without smiling.

"Not really. Thanks though." I must have blushed because he got serious right away.

"I mean it. I had you pegged as the Homecoming Queen and head cheerleader!"

"Oh, c'mon, not hardly. I never got involved in that stuff. Mostly I just studied, worked in the library and I was a Candy striper for a while at St. Mary's Hospital. That's when I thought I wanted to be a doctor. The school counselor told me I would make a great RN instead."

"What else then," he asked, sitting up and moving back to the edge of the bed to face me. Randy was sincerely listening to me. I thought he could help me with his experience and opinions and it was gratifying to have his full attention. Breaking the silence, Jake stretched and moaned but then he slipped back to sleep.

"Oh, I don't know," I took a long sip on my bottle. "I think I'd like to be a manager. I liked to organize things in the store I was working for in Madison. I worked in the school library. I like to draw up schedules and stuff. I might join the Peace Corps for a couple years and travel."

"It sounds like you might like to major in Business Administration although I don't think there is a lot of demand for women in that field."

"Why would it matter whether you were male or female in Business?"

"I don't know. You just don't see many women doing that."

I was distracted by his face as he talked. Light brown hair framed his face and a small light moustache set off his full lips. I couldn't say he was very handsome, but I enjoyed his smile. There were crinkles at the corners of his eyes that creased with each smile and a long dimple cut down one cheek. Right now, there was kindness in his hazel eyes, but I felt I wouldn't want to cross him. There was a seriousness and tenacity etched in the lines on his tanned forehead.

"Do you work for someone else then, in Duluth?" I asked curiously.

"No, I'm on my own," he said, taking a long swig.

"It sounds like that wasn't your own decision," I commented gently.

"You read between the lines very well, Jewell. Every time I comment on your questions, I end up talking about something I don't want to talk about. Maybe you should be a journalist or reporter." He laughed shortly at himself. "Do you like to write?"

"Yes, I do. I wrote for the school paper and I have published some articles in other newspapers." I wanted to keep this conversation going. I had never talked on a very serious plane with anyone my own age and certainly not an older man. "I could talk all night long about the future. I wish I had some idea where I was heading. This fall is coming too fast. I don't know if I even want to go to college yet, it just seems like that's what everyone expects me to do. I don't want to just drift through without knowing where I am going. I want to travel. I have never really experienced anything outside of Madison."

"Then talk — it'll be a long night before Jake and I take off to Superior. We need to clean up some details. Here, have another beer." Randy handed me another bottle. I looked down and realized mine was empty!

"I can't believe I drank that bottle. I suppose I can have another. It is getting pretty warm in here though."

Coming down to Jake's room was my first unwise decision that night. The next one was finishing that bottle of beer. I'd never had two beers! I began to tell Randy my entire life story: my loves, my pains and heartaches. I even told him about a swim race I lost in 1968. Randy got bored with this tale of woe and I found myself hiccupping up the back stairs with him guiding and shushing me to my room.

"I'm okay," I said too loudly.

My head was spinning a little and I had this terrible urge to laugh at the fool I was making of myself. I sat down on the floor by the bed and buried my face in the spread. I let off the steam that was building up all day. I sobbed because I was embarrassed. I sobbed about the nights I spent staring at the moon out my window after my dad died. I sobbed about my mother leaving me out of her life. I sobbed because I was sobbing.

"I'm such an idiot. Just go away. I hate my life and everybody in it." I waved my hand at Randy fiercely. I felt a hand patting the middle of my back and looked up with tears dripping off my cheeks. Randy helped me up to sit on the bed, and awkwardly tried to comfort me.

"Holy cow, girl. Don't blame me. Ya' betcha it's the beer talking, and you'll feel better in the morning. You've had a long day and you'll need a good night's rest." He stood up. "I should have cut you off at one. I am so-so sorry. I just didn't realize…"

I tried to stand up but lost my balance, sitting back on the bed.

"Okay girl. That's it. Good night. I'm going back down to Jake. I hope we'll meet again."

I watched him quietly close the door then I curled up in bed with my housecoat on. My door locked itself when Randy left, so in no time at all I slipped off to sleep.

The muggy night turned into a dove gray, rainy morning. The room was chilly. Water droplets tap-tapped on the leaves below my window. The curtains slapped wetly against the screens in a light breeze carrying the smell of pines from the woods behind the resort. I thought about getting up to close the window, but the quilt was warm and cozy. I had a headache lodged right behind my eyes. I remembered last night and shut my eyes again.

"Oh Lord, please forgive me and don't let me remember how very stupid I am..."

I was embarrassed and unhappy but strangely elated at the same time. That was a nutty day. It didn't seem possible all those crazy things could have happened to me - Jewell Johnson. I felt as if I'd been in a funhouse at a carnival. I rubbed my hands over my temples to see if the aching would go away. I decided that I could just as well lay right here all day, reading the old National Geographic and a Life magazine on my bedside table. I curled up with my pillow like a child with a teddy bear, and closed my eyes, thinking about Jake's warm kiss on my lips, and faded off to sleep. I found myself sliding down into the same troubling nightmare I'd dreamt so often since I was a child.

I am in a dark glen. A fire burns in the distance and soft drum music is thumping like a heartbeat. Two huge knights in gleaming armor are jousting, their lances clanging in the semi-darkness. I am so worried that my sweet prince will be killed but I can't get to him. A yell comes from behind me and I spin around. There in the misty meadow is my prince on a white horse fighting a dark knight, their mounts dancing in circles, rearing and screaming. Then the black knight raises high in his stirrups and strikes the white knight. He tumbles to the ground. As he struggles to sit up he looks at me with his hand raised in goodbye and the black knight raises his sword with both hands.

"No!" I try to scream - but no sound can escape my lips. I want to run to my prince, but I can't lift my feet. The hem of my thin gown is wetly tangled around my ankles and a filmy scarf blows around my face blinding me. I hear maniacal laughter. My fallen, bleeding hero lies at my feet, a sword buried in his chest. Angrily I pulled it out and wield it at the charging black knight but the mist flows in and swallows them up. Sorrow wells up and chokes me, I feel my heart break. Darkness floods like a vortex into the hollow as thick mist envelopes me.

But this time, something new happens; a motor growls to life.

"Get up! Get up! The trucks are coming!" There's a voice calling from the woods. I struggle to lift my fallen hero who lies silently at my feet, eyes staring upwards. Now a new knight with flames pouring out of his helmet eye holes is galloping towards me.

"What trucks?" I scream, "I can't leave him! Mom, Dad? Someone help me!" The dark knight is charging me and there's nowhere to turn. As I look again, he and the horse became a truck whose eyes became glaring headlights thundering down the hill.

"What is it, dearie?" A honey-sweet faint voice calls from the bushes. It is my mother's voice, but I can't locate her. "You're a big girl now honey, you have to deal with it yourself."

"Mommy," I cry, "where are you? I can't see you! Mom help me."

"You're fine, dear. But I'm busy right now," she purrs and pads out gracefully from behind the bushes: she's a gleaming white cat. She delicately stretches her pink clawed feet.

"Mom, please, I need you! Why are you a cat?"

"A whaaat? I have to go, sweetie," she drawls, turning her head so that I see her large luminous blue eyes, but I am revolted to see a mouse tail hanging out of her sharp-toothed smile. She walks away into the dark woods surrounding the misty glen, her tail swaying from side to side. I look around and the truck is gone - I am alone.

"Mom? Don't leave me. Where will I go?" I cry into the mist.

"You'll remember, Jewell."

I jerked awake in a sweat. There was a latent sense of foreboding and fear in the room with me even though the sun had come out and voices outside were floating up from the veranda. I shivered, recalling the dream in detail even as I struggled to shake it off. I read that dreams are your subconscious interpreting your daily life and can help sort out problems. Images from your day intrude into sleeping thoughts. This one didn't make anything clear at all. As I thought about the nightmare, it dimmed. The message to me, so clear when I was dreaming: faded away. I was left with scenes and no web of a story in-between. The bits and pieces of fear made no sense to me.

I drew my feet up and leaned back against the headboard, pulling the quilt up around my neck.

"One of the knights could be Jake and the other is whoever beat him up. What was the symbolism of the horse being a truck? My mom is a cat eating a mouse? Am I crazy?" Psychology was obviously not my forte. I might want to take that in college. "Oh, who cares? It's just a dream anyway. There's no use getting upset about it."

I got up to see if the RV was in the parking lot. It was gone.

"I wonder if I will see them again." I caught my breath and blushed to think of Jake's sweet kiss. Jake and Randy were so different. And they are friends! And I threw myself at him. What would I say if I see them again?

"Oh man, I'm a total idiot," I said under my breath.

I stayed in my room reading until the sound of dishes clattering on the veranda announced lunch. Since it was getting hot and stuffy upstairs I thought I should take a swim after lunch. I dug out a tee-shirt and put on a velour aqua blue one-piece swimsuit. Although it wasn't very fashionable, it was my favorite. Swimming always seemed to make my life feel more organized. When I was younger, I imagined I would try out for the Olympics, so I spent hundreds of hours at the University pool. Since my mom and dad were professors I could swim all I wanted at the Natatorium. But in high school, my studies started taking up too much time and Mom said it would be too expensive to try out for the Olympics, so I gave up the idea.

I loved to swim out to the raft and dive off the board. I wondered if I should hunt up my mom and tell her all about yesterday. "I bet she'd find my experiences terribly interesting!" I said to my reflection in the old mirror. Right away, I realized she wouldn't even believe half of it. I didn't believe it myself. The thought of Jake's voice, his touch and his kiss made my knees weak again.

I went downstairs to distract myself. On the library shelf, I found an ancient copy of Edna St. Vincent Millay's "Collected Sonnets" to read. No one was in the kitchen, so I wrote a note to Mrs. Swenson's cook and grabbed two peanut butter sandwiches, a couple of apples and two boxes of 'Dairyland Fresh' milk before I headed out the door. The screen door clattered behind me as I walked out into the sunshine towards the beach, half hoping for Jake to come out from his fishing tree. I was a little disappointed to find the lawn empty.

It seemed like everyone was gone today, even the dock was empty. I sat on the edge of the white dock and ate my snack. The sun got a little warm, so I moved my blanket under a tree next to the beach. I lay on my side with my towel rolled up under my head, reading my book of poems as I tried hard to relax. I couldn't help looking at the farm now and then for any movement. Then I faded away thinking about Jake, his kiss, his arms and his eyes. I was troubled by the weird reaction of my heart with these random thoughts. I wondered if I'd see him again soon.

After a while a few kids wandered out to laugh and play on the beach. The sun stared down at me until it got too hot to lay on my blanket, so I pulled off my tee-shirt and slipped into the lake. I swam out to the raft for a few dives and then swam away from the shore. Rolling on my back and floated away from shore I watched the blue sky above and felt the hot sun on my stomach. My hair floated around me like a mermaid's. I watched a puffy little white cloud directly overhead as it shifted shapes.

"Jewell!"

I rolled over to tread water and looked towards shore. Tom Boyden was there, waving at me. A shock of apprehension zapped through my body. "What now?" I thought and swam in strongly.

"Hi, Tom!" I waved and waded up onto the sand. I grabbed my beach towel and patted my face dry. When my eyes rested on his bruised and cut face, I cringed.

"You didn't come up to my office to make a statement with your two friends, so I thought I'd check up on you just to make sure you're okay," he said.

"Oh, they left already? I apologize, but I told you we aren't close friends. I didn't have a car to get to town. I did promise you though, didn't I? Yesterday was such a crazy day. It slipped my mind this morning. Am I in trouble, then?" I wondered if Mom was looking from the Inn. It was uncomfortable being seen talking to a law officer. "I honestly don't completely understand what happened."

"There were no charges filed. Your friend didn't press an assault charge and that guy at the hospital had a rap sheet a mile long, so you won't have to do anything but answer some questions and fill out the witness report. The Sheriff released him to Douglas County this morning."

"I am glad I am not in trouble. I honestly don't know anything. The whole thing was so weird!" I grabbed my tee shirt off the blanket and slipped it over my head. I picked up my book, wrapped my towel around my waist, and slung my blanket over my arm. Nervously I didn't look directly at him.

"I hope you realize your friends are biting off more than they can chew. They didn't want to accept any help from us concerning the incident. Do you know anything about this guy who beat up your boyfriend? You need to be careful hanging around with guys like that."

"Seriously, he's not my boyfriend! I just met him. I don't even know if I will see him again." That thought made me feel a little empty inside. "They didn't tell me goodbye when they left or even tell me you wanted to talk to me."

"I suppose that's their loss." Tom said, smiling widely. Another very young officer walked over from the parking lot. "Dave, we're going over where the incident happened. I just want you to confirm some details."

"I'd like to get dressed, if you don't mind."

"No problem, I'll wait here." Tom nodded at his Deputy who began to walk back towards the parking lot.

I ran up the stairs and changed into pink Bermuda shorts and a white blouse. I quickly toweled and brushed my hair. I dabbed on some lipstick and then dug under the bed for shoes.

"White tennis shoes, or sandals? Sandals." I slipped them on and grabbed my purse.

When I got back down to the veranda, Tom was standing next to the door looking out at Lake Makoons. I noticed the kitchen curtain drop as I walked by. We went down the steps to the sidewalk and around the side of the Inn to the parking lot. Tom opened the squad car door and I got in the back seat. Dave filled out a form on a clipboard as I recapped the events of the day before, starting with Jake's collapse in the ditch until the time when the guy in the hospital was arrested. Tom drove down the lane and parked at the end of the road where the driveway met the County road.

"The guy at the hospital was named John D'Andrea," Tom said. "He has a history of assault, but never anything really serious, mostly drunken bar fights. He's been driving semi for a living and lives outside of Superior. We think he came originally from Chicago."

"Hmm, that's interesting. Does Jake know about that?"

"I didn't get the information on him until the Burnett County Sheriff called a report in to our office. Sheriff Swanson said you can't get blood from a turnip."

"So, you just turned him loose?"

"Nope, the Sheriff released him to Douglas County this morning. Are these tire marks where you pulled over? It looks like someone spun their tires."

"That was me. I am not good with the clutch."

I got out of the squad car and stepped across the narrow shoulders and down into the grassy ditch. I stopped for a moment to make sure exactly where I was and then started toward where I found Jake laying. Tom stopped me before I got more than a couple of steps down the slope.

"Hang on. We will want to check out the area. Hard to say what we might find, and you might step on something useful."

"You can see where the grass is pressed down." I said. I looked down at my feet and saw a broken pen. It looked familiar. I was going to pick it up when Tom's hand pushed my hand away.

"Wait! I've got that," he said and picked it up with a handkerchief. He looked at it carefully, frowned, and then rolled it up. He put it in an envelope and handed it to Dave. "It's just a pen but you never know."

They looked carefully around the area but found nothing that would shed any light on the attack. Tom stood with his hands on his hips and surveyed the fields around us.

"I'm pretty familiar with this part of the county," he said. "It is so quiet we don't have to come out here unless there's a fire or a medical emergency. It seems like these guys must have known each other before they met up here. It could be that they brought an old argument with them. D'Andrea wasn't drunk or high when we grabbed him, so it doesn't make sense that he'd jump your friend. I suppose he and some friends got drunk and roughed up Pieters for fun, but that seems awfully far-fetched. Mr. Pieters wasn't very helpful when he talked to us. He claims he never met this guy before."

"I have to say that Jake was pretty relaxed when I met him, and he didn't seem nervous or afraid of anyone when we were walking. He didn't say anything about it on the way to the hospital."

Tom turned back to look at me with his forehead furrowed in thought. He shook his head and took my arm to lead me back to the car. He waved Dave back over to where we stood.

"Okay, Dave. Can you drive us back to the Inn please?"

I was worried that I looked guilty or was headed for trouble since no one else was around to take the blame.

"I swear I don't know anything," I said as we approached the Inn. "It seems like you don't believe me." Tom looked at me seriously.

"No, I think you are telling the truth. You were in the wrong place at the wrong time. You walked into someone else's issue. Dave, go inside and call in our location. Find out if there's anything else to stop for on the way back besides what we've got. Check with the Sheriff too. Hand me that clipboard, would you? C'mon, I'll walk you up."

We walked around to the veranda facing the lake and I started up the steps.

"I believe you Jewell. It just seems like there's something being covered up-but not by you. I'll need some information for the case file. Fill in your full name, home address and your home phone number. I'm satisfied you aren't involved."

113

"Sure," I said and reached for the clipboard. I sat down on the wooden steps and caught his eyes on me as I wrote. A nervous blush crept up my neck and I hoped my tan would disguise it. I noticed that the pen was just like the one we found along the road. I handed the clipboard back to him and he startled me with another question.

"Say," he said slowly, "are you busy tonight?"

"Uh - no." Wow, that sounded awkward!

"Would you go out to dinner with me tonight? I thought it would be nice to try Madden's Resort. They have a nice dining room and the food is great. I think it might be what the doctor ordered, you should get out and relax a little."

I thought it over for a minute and didn't know how to say no. I swallowed and let my hair fall forward to cover my face.

"I - I don't know, Tom. I don't really have any other plans, but…"

"Then say "Yes". We could be friends and I think you need one right now. I am concerned about you." Tom smiled, and his deep blue eyes twinkled with inviting humor. "I'd like to see you smile and hear you laugh. I could pick you up around 5:30."

"Sure. That's fine," I said. I shivered slightly as a cloud covered the sun and a cool afternoon breeze swept up the veranda from the lake.

"I have to run and finish up some details at the office. I'll see you a little later!"

I watched him walk around the end of the building, admiring the way he looked in his tan and brown uniform. Tom was my height and slim, with wide shoulders and a narrow waist. He had a great smile and a natural grace. I wondered why he would want to date me. I only dated a couple of times in high school, but they were double-dates with friends. One of the guys had wandering hands during the movie that a fiercely whispered "*knock it off*" didn't stop. I angrily walked out and took a bus home. The memory still gave me the heebie-jeebies, and I shivered slightly.

Heading up the stairs, I was a little nervous about the evening ahead. I knocked on Mom's door on my way by her room and waited in the narrow hallway. Mom didn't answer so I continued up the next stairs to my room. About halfway up, I was halted by the sound of voices coming up the stairwell behind me. I recognized her voice: she and Jim were apparently just returning from another of their summer escapades. I leaned around the end of the stairs to call down to Mom when I heard her talking to Jim.

"Mrs. Swenson just told me the police came this morning and asked for Jewell. She went somewhere in the car with them and then came back. Jim, she's never been in any trouble in her whole life. What could have she gotten into? It's my fault for not keeping an eye on her. I'll have to talk to her right away."

"Mary, I am sure it was an error. Nobody's quieter and less likely to get into trouble than Jewell. There is a perfectly logical and reasonable explanation, I am sure of it. She is completely self-controlled."

I listened and even though I knew what he was saying was true, I felt insulted because he had no business saying it.

"I'm boring, quiet and never any trouble? I could be a chair for all you two care." I let myself into my room and slumped into the dressing table chair, grabbed my towel and began to dry my thick damp hair. There was a knock at my door.

"Ya?"

"Hi, can I come in? I think we need to talk."

"Sure, mom. What's up?"

Mom came in and stood just inside the door, surveying the room and turning her ring on her finger. That usually meant she was going to say something uncomfortable. I turned back to the mirror.

"Honey, Mrs. Swenson just told me that some policemen were here looking for you. What's going on? What kind of mistake was that?"

"It's Tom, the Deputy Sheriff. He just wanted a date for tonight." I covertly watched her reaction in the mirror.

Mom eyes widened and she almost stammered when she said.

"Oh. I get it, you're teasing. You almost had me there!"

"Nope, I met him yesterday and so we're going to Madden's for dinner tonight."

"You're what? How, I mean - when, could you meet him out here? You haven't really left the Inn!"

I felt an angry flush flow upwards in my neck and face and fought down the impulse to scream the whole story at her. She cared so little about what my life was like, it was all about her and her Jim. I decided to give her a tidbit about my day yesterday.

"I met a guy here yesterday morning. He got sick, so I used his truck to drive him to the hospital and I met Tom there." I turned to my mirror to brush my hair. I watched Mom behind me in the mirror.

"That explains the weird message I got from Mrs. Swenson. I thought it was odd. How's the guy in the hospital?" she had a worried frown.

"Oh, he checked out and came back here to the Inn last night. He and his friend left early this morning," I answered.

"I see…about this Tom, do you think it wise to go out with someone you just met? Where are you going?"

"To Madden's Resort, just down the road. Mom, seriously: he's a deputy Sheriff. I 'm not worried. He is really nice."

Mom moved to the window, stared out and fiddled with the curtain. She suddenly swung around and patted me on the back.

"I am so sorry Jewell. I simply tend to forget you are going to college very soon and you'll make your own decisions without my help. I know I was butting in, but it is because I love you. You know that. I'm sorry. You'll be careful, won't you?"

"Sure mom."

There was an uncomfortable silence that filled up with our thoughts. Mom was looking at me - I was avoiding her. I felt abandoned but then free at the same time. I half wanted to go back to her arms and be protected. I suddenly realized this was a defining point in my life. I think Mom felt it too and it left both of us feeling awkward and speechless. Looking in the mirror, I was shocked to realize my mom as an older woman. The dark tan she had acquired in the last few weeks, now accentuated the fine wrinkles around her eyes. Her wind-blown hair needed a trim. She looked like she'd lost weight. I wondered what she saw when she looked at me. She was frozen, waiting for me to say something.

"What do you think I should wear?"

Mom took her cue and sat on the foot of my bed breaking the mood.

"I suppose slacks, blouse and a sweater. The temperature drops so quickly in the evening now. Do you remember your dad used to say summer started in July and the first frost was in August? You look so beautiful in pale blue, what about the light blue sweater and white slacks?"

I froze a little, thinking that I'd better get those blood spots off the blue sweater.

"I've got that soft paisley silk blouse with browns and blue in it and a white jacket. I can wear that with white bellbottoms."

"That's a beautiful blouse. I love the colors. Do you have a scarf for your neck or maybe your hair?"

"No. I'll just wear light vest."

The conversation wandered off away from my date. Mom was standing by my window and looking out.

"Do you remember Gramma Johnson's garden? Your dad used to love weeding and hoeing in it when we came up. She always had such wonderful rhubarb and strawberries. He pruned her red roses back and mowed the grass for them. He loved late summer and fall the most, I think. When we came up we would have such a quiet, pleasant visit with Gramma and Grampa. I loved going with him in our row boat around the lake, fishing and swimming. Sometimes those days seem like a lifetime ago." Her voice tightened up and she rubbed her forehead.

"I thought you'd forgotten about him." I said into the closet, keeping my back to her.

"Oh, honey, no! Never," she said vehemently. "Sig was my first love and I will carry him in my heart until I die. No one can ever take his place. Sometimes I hear him laughing, teasing me or I think I feel him touching my face. Oh, no, Jewell. We were so happy together that I can't ever let his memory die. He always wanted me to smile…and so I try to smile for him. We were like two peas in a pod. There were no secrets until the day he died."

"I won't forget Dad either, Mom. Nobody can take his place."

"No one is asking you to forget him, just to open up to new people, Jewell. Jim would be happy just to be your friend. What is bugging you lately? Why can't you just accept him and move on?"

"Bugging me? You are the one that's gone all the time with him. It's like I don't even exist," I lashed out at her. "Where have you been recently? I needed you, mom. Whenever I have questions, you're not around!"

Mom stood shocked for a moment, staring at me openmouthed. Finally, she seemed to gather her thoughts, shrugged her shoulders, and moved towards the door.

"Jewell, I love you, but I can't make your decisions any more. If you want my opinion, advice is free. I suppose you are worried about college, we can talk. I'll help you as much as I can. I understand you have issues, but you are going to have to deal with them yourself. It's time you realized that."

"I can do whatever I want, if I just stay out of your way?" I stammered awkwardly.

"That's not fair; think about it a little. It's time you got your nose out of those romance mystery novels and think about your future.

Remember the decisions you make now will stay with you all your life. You have beauty and brains from your dad's side, but you'll get common sense from me. Use your gifts to their best advantage. Right now, Jim and I are heading over to Austen's cabin to play cards, and maybe tomorrow we can take a drive into town and shop. We can talk more then, okay?"

"Yup. Sure, Mom." I replied, sensing that to her, shopping was an alternative to our emotional issues. "Maybe we should talk things out a bit. Maybe we can find some excitement too."

"I don't think there's potential excitement here, Jewell. Perhaps a thunderstorm - that's about it! See you later, hon. Bring your young man to the lounge to meet us."

"Sure, mom. I'll do that." I said and after she left I rolled my eyes. "Sure."

I dug through my clothes in the drawers. I pulled out the white jean bells and the blouse I wanted to wear. Sitting at the dressing table, I put a little blue eye-shadow on my lids, with liner and then brushed blush on my cheeks. It barely showed up on my summer tan. The pink lipstick I had looked too light against my tan too. I tried drying my thick hair with a hair dryer. The soft water of Lake Makoons made it a fluffier that I was used to. I braided the sides of my nearly waist-length hair to hold it the rest of my heavy mane away from my face, clipping them in the back with bobby pins. As I looked at myself, I wished again that I had short curly hair like Hayley Mills in the *Parent Trap*. That was my favorite movie of all time…that is, next to the *Moon-Spinners*.

At five-fifteen I went downstairs to wait outside by the lake. I couldn't help looking again at the birch clump. No Jake sat there fishing tonight. A little fish plopped above the surface to inhale a water bug. The sun would soon slide down towards the trees behind Wolf Point. I carefully surveyed the farm, but there was so sign of lights or activity there tonight. Perhaps I'd get over there and check through the buildings tomorrow. I was day-dreaming about what everything looked like at the Inn when Grampa Johnson lived here, when a voice broke through my silence.

"Hi Jewell, ready to go?" Tom stood a few feet behind me.

"Oh, hi, Tom," I said, catching my breath.

"Sorry, you were so absorbed looking at the lake I hated to break in. Its sure calm tonight. It'd be a great night for bluegills. They'd hit like crazy on flies."

"You catch flies to use as bait?"

Tom looked at me carefully, decided I was serious, and laughed out loud.

"Fly fishing is not the same as using baits or worms. I take it you haven't heard about it before?"

"I've been fishing but I just don't know about fishing with flies."

He laughed and took my arm.

"Flies are little tufts of hair tied to a hook. You can buy them or make your own like I do. You use a different kind of rod. It's long and very flexible. Fly fishing is one of my vices. I love it. I fish whenever I am off work. I'm always looking for a reason to go fishing."

I was intrigued by his enthusiasm and passion for fishing.

"I hope you like to eat fish, that's the special at Madden's tonight. They have the best fish fry in the North."

"Oh, sure. We go to the spring church fish boil in Madison. There's a restaurant near us that does fish fry on Friday nights. We don't eat much fish at home though because my mom doesn't like to cook."

"Well, then this will be a treat, right? They also have dough-gobs, that's the same as Indian frybread. You can have it with cinnamon-sugar or plain. I bet you haven't had that!"

"I have. My father's aunt was Ojibwa and she made frybread right here at the Inn."

"Really? You'll have to tell me all about it tonight. Let's get going."

He looped his arm through mine and we walked across the lawn. Looking up at the veranda, I saw my mom and Jim just coming out the door to sit at one of the little tables.

"Do we have time to go up, so I can introduce you to my mom? She's up on the veranda with Jim."

"Oh. Sure. No rush." He guided our steps towards the building and smiled at me, "I would love to meet the woman who gave the world a beautiful girl like you."

I could feel the blush start up my neck and spread across my cheeks. "Oh, please be serious," I faltered, floundering around for a different subject, as we walked across the lawn.

"You're blushing! Don't all your dates tell you how beautiful you are?" Tom laughed and held my arm. "Now, don't get mad, I'm sorry. I don't remember girls blushing over compliments. You must not get enough of them! I'll try to catch you up, okay?" he said, looking down at me and pushing my hair aside with one finger.

I giggled, and the blush began to fade. I took a deep breath and smiled.

"There's Mom." I waved at her up the hill. Jim was there as always and this time he didn't bother to smile at me. We went up the steps to the veranda.

"Mom, this is Tom Boyden. Tom Boyden meet my mom – Mary. This is my step-dad Jim Taylor." Mom flashed her beautiful wide smile and pushed back her hair. Tom shook her hand and then Jim's.

"I can see where Jewell gets her beauty," he said. Mom looked at him with pleased surprise and surveyed Tom. She noticed his black eye, bruised cheek and cut nose. "Were you in a car accident?"

"Oh, no, didn't Jewell tell you about my little altercation yesterday? If it hadn't been for her I would have been in a tough corner. I've gotta say she's quite a brave gal, but she could use some shooting lessons." He patted my shoulder and laughed.

Mom stared at me. I avoided her look and concentrated on watching a little grey chipmunk chattering at a robin, holding some treasure in his paws on the deck rail. Then I shadowed my eyes with my fingers and watched the couple from Chicago resting on the beach. Tamara was covering her dad up with little buckets full of sand.

"Julie?" Mom's voice was strange and tight as she tried to question me.

"He's exaggerating mom, it was no big deal. See you later, huh? Don't forget our big shopping trip tomorrow to Hayward." I smile brightly and tugged Tom away with my elbow. He turned to my mom and Jim.

"Ok. Goodnight folks, glad to have met you. I think we'll be back early."

I glanced back and was rewarded by the hurt and curious look from Mom as she watched us walk away. I didn't know why it felt good to hurt her, but when Jim reached over to put his arm around her said something in her ear making her shrug her shoulders, I looked away angrily.

As we walked to the car Tom asked seriously "What was that all about? They don't like me?"

"Oh no, it's just how they react sometimes. I just don't think she needs to butt into everything. She hasn't figured out I'm a big girl and I need to live my own life."

Tom opened the door of his Dodge Demon and I slipped into the black, leather bucket-seat, without comment. I loved the purple color of his car. I'd never even seen a purple vehicle before or ridden in one like this. He walked around to the driver's side and slid into the bucket seat, buckled his belt and backed out of the lot. His hand gripped the gear shift and the tires spewed gravel when we pulled out of the lot. His car was powerful but felt light, like a wild animal being held back. I fiddled with the strap of my purse waiting for conversation to start as we speeded along Johnson Road.

"You were pretty unkind to your mother just now," Tom finally commented. "Why did you shut her down like that?"

"I have my reasons. If you don't mind, I'd rather not talk about my mom. I just haven't figured out how to tell her about yesterday yet and I just didn't want to waste our time talking about it tonight."

"I see. Okay. Family politics are difficult sometimes."

"I love your car."

"I just got it. I ordered the Hurst transmission and a special lift kit. She really sails! I can burn rubber in three gears!"

"That's incredible…but don't do that when I am in the car. I don't like it…okay?"

We drove in silence for a few seconds then he pointed to the left of the road ahead of us.

"Look there!" A doe and a tiny fawn stood at the edge of the trees close to the road. They seemed to be anticipating the waiting meal in the ditch filled with deep green grasses and wildflowers. Tom slowed down and slowly stopped within fifty yards of the graceful russet animals. He reached under his seat and pulled out a very professional-looking camera. Stepping out quietly, he leaned on the top of the car to focus and then snapped several pictures of the two animals in the fading shadows. He got back in the car and put the camera back in its black case.

"That's a great camera. Are you professional?"

"I take pictures for work, but I sell some of the wildlife shots I get. There's a pretty good market for pictures of animals in their natural habitat," he explained. "It helps pay for my unhealthier habits."

"You must see a lot of the great outdoors," I said wistfully. "In the city, you only see that kind of scene at the zoo or sometimes at the arboretum. I'd love to see some of your pictures someday."

"I'll drag them out for you some time. I have a dark room and develop my own pictures. I'd love to share them. I have a ton of albums and framed stuff at my house."

"Cool. That's great, look at that!" I said pointing to a deep wooded area where the forest floor was covered with white and pink flowers with three petals. "My dad used to say, 'trillions of trilliums". We didn't always get up here early enough to see them."

Tom slowed down so I could lean out the window and see the flowers better.

"Used to?" He waited patiently, and then said, "Are your folks divorced?"

"Oh, no! It's not like that! Mom is widowed, my dad died when I was a kid. He was killed in a car accident and she remarried."

"I'm sorry. That was nosy. Divorce is getting a lot more common nowadays even up here in the boonies. I didn't mean to pry. I'm just naturally curious…or it's my training I guess. Sorry about your dad."

"It's okay, it was six years ago."

As Tom took a series of sharp curves over a bunch of hills in the road, we chatted about our lives and compared the differences between "up-here" in Philetus Spur and "down-there" in Madison. Tom said he'd been downstate a few times and concluded there were just too many people and too many lights.

"You can't even see the big dipper or Orion's Belt there."

"But it gets awfully cold up here doesn't it," I asked, "and don't you get big blizzards?"

"Not really, there's a different quality of cold here. Forty-two below here doesn't seem even as cold as zero in the southern part of the state. It's a dry cold or something. Those who love it up here pay little attention to cold. There's tons to do. You can ski, ride snowmobiles, play hockey, ice fish just to name a few. I'd rather have cold than hot any day. You can always dress warmer."

"I'll be in school next winter," I said, looking out the window. "At the U, in Madison."

"Really? What's your major?"

"I don't know what I'm doing for sure. Maybe Business or Phy. Ed. I don't know what else I would do if I don't go to school."

"Not me, I got what I wanted from high school and left it behind. My classroom is the world and I majored in Social Activities. I ended up in Nam in '65 because I didn't go to college when my number came up. After I was drafted I spent two years in the Marines. It toughened me up, taught me about life and set me straight."

I studied his profile with interest. He seemed very dedicated to his job and good at it. It puzzled me that he was serious about having good times and rated education second-place. We swung around a corner and into a graveled lane leading down into the woods.

"In Madison when I was in high school, they were rioting to end the war. What do you think about that?"

"To be honest it made me mad. I was drafted. I hated Viet Nam and I hate war. I read that General Sherman said, "Some of you young men think that war is all glamour and glory, but let me tell you, boys, it's all hell!" He was damned right." Tom shifted gears and took a sharp corner. "You can't imagine how bad it was and I sure can't explain it. When we got back, people sneered and spit at us. Damned skinny, long-haired, whiny hippies sat at home and got stoned." His face was set, and he stared straight ahead. "Sorry, I said too much again."

I admit I was deeply shocked. I had never heard anyone talk like that. It was silent as we both stared out the windows.

"I'm sorry that happened to you."

"Yeah, well here we are," Tom said after a series of sharp downhill curves. We followed along a split rail fence until we came into view of the resort. The lane opened out into a large cleared field, with the buildings of the resort on the other side. "You'll like the food here, it's great."

It was a log structure with wide decks and big windows facing the south. Two wide doors opened onto a deck facing the field. The lawn was bordered with wild flower beds and a huge vegetable garden. Tiger lilies lined the sidewalk and frilly lime-colored ferns hung out over the cement walks. Big baskets of colorful flowers hung along the roofline. We parked in the graveled lot and walked past a rock garden with a little pool built around a huge tree to get to the house.

"The owner told me this big old cottonwood was brought as a seedling by his parents when they came here from Missouri or Kansas or someplace. They're pretty rare this far north."

"Oh Tom, this is just gorgeous. I love it! I would just love to live here."

"Wait until you taste the food." He took my hand and led me up the wide steps to the dining room of the lodge.

We were seated right away where the lofty ceiling rose above us. Outside of the huge window was a large pool surrounded by willows and beyond a fence line where several horses munched tall grass in the shadowy field. A goat wandered up to the fence and looked curiously at us.

"There's a path down to the river," Tom said pointing to the end of the building, "and maybe after dinner we can walk down by the lake to watch the sunset. It's like a painting."

We ate our fish and fries sprinkled with dark vinegar. I had never tried it that way and it was great. The hot fry bread was light and delicious. We dipped it in cinnamon and powdered sugar for desert. The coleslaw was a 'secret recipe' the waitress said. "I'd have to kill you if I told you how it was made," she laughed.

"I love this place and I love the food. Thanks so much, Tom!"

"I thought you would enjoy it." He was looking thoughtfully out the window. "You know, I am always surprised when people leave northern Wisconsin," Tom remarked, "it's probably just as well or we would have too many people around. Part of the beauty is the solitude."

"I love it here too, but I can't stay. My folks always planned for me to get a good education at Madison and then a job. I can't disappoint Mom."

"There are some things more important than school and money, Jewell. If you want to live up here you've got to give up some things but look around. See what you get in return? To my way of thinking, the sacrifice is to leave this behind. Can you eat in a restaurant in the city where they grow their own produce or catch their own fish? This is God's country. I can't imagine anywhere better."

"You're exaggerating Tom, just a little, don't you think?"

"Nope, you wait. You'll end up here. I can see it in the way you notice what's around you. I have dated other city girls. They hate bugs; they don't even notice trees and animals. They spend all their time worrying about their clothes and messing with their makeup. I like women like you. You have a natural beauty and don't glop all that stuff on your face to look like a magazine model. They're more interested in themselves than the guys they're with," he said with a broad smile. "You've got natural beauty."

"You are awfully tough on girls, Tom," I said, warmed by his compliments but remembering other times I'd spent worrying about my makeup in the mirror.

"I do know what I like," he said. He excused himself and walked back to the bar.

I felt the stupid hot blush flood into my face tried to cover it up by turning to point out the window at a couple of the colts who were jumping around like little kids. I felt very comfortable with Tom. He was easy to talk to and nice to look at. But the memory of Jake's kiss, the way he smelled, and his touch kept crashing into my mind. I felt strangely torn and confused. After rarely even being in the company of boys, suddenly here were two older men who were obviously interested in me. But then, Randy and Jake disappeared so quickly.

Maybe I was just imagining things. I decided to put them behind and focus on enjoying myself this evening.

The sun was slipping behind the forest in a sky ablaze with orange and purple when the waitress came to deliver the tab.

"Do you want coffee by candlelight or should we go out to the bar?"

"I'd like a soda, thanks. I need to get up and walk around after the huge dinner I ate!"

"Okay, I think the screens on the porch look like they will hold back the Wisconsin State bird. Did you see the t-shirts behind the bar with the mosquito on them? You know, I didn't notice it was nine-thirty already," he said piloting me towards the bar.

"Time passes quickly when you're having fun...or eating!"

"Too true. Are you worried about being out late? Will you turn into a pumpkin?" Tom dipped to one knee in front of me and checked my shoes. "Nope, no glass slippers here. We can dance all night, Princess!" He grabbed me around the waist and twirled me around with his other hand and then into his arms.

"Stop, Tom, stop," I said into his ear. "People are looking! There's no dance floor and there's no band!"

"Aha," he said cheerfully, "there is, however, a jukebox with Buck Owens and the Buckaroos and I love to dance. What do you like, country, blues, - or rock and roll?"

"Oh Tom, I don't care. I can't dance very well."

"No problem. Let 'Tom Astaire' lead you here on the porch." The music poured out the doorway and he gathered me into his arms. "Let me show you how. Just follow me."

My dad taught me a few simple country dance steps when I was a kid. He told me he used to dance with his parents at the schoolhouse in Philetus Spur. Dancing with Tom was very awkward at first and I stumbled over his feet a few times. But before long I learned a few simple steps and we were moving together to a country song. Tom held me tightly to him with his left arm around my waist and then held my hand in the air with the other. When he spun me out like a top I was surprised and laughed out loud. He stepped quickly towards me and held my hand high in the air again while he turned, and his muscular arms pulled me close to his chest again. He smiled into my face and then we danced for a while, laughing and talking between the songs. Once, we stopped and sipped our cold beers in the dark, Tom held his bottle up.

"I heard that the politicos are talking about raising the beer age," he commented shaking his head. "That stinks. A young guy is old enough to fight and die in war but can't legally drink a beer."

"Yes, that's pretty sad. You should be able to make choices when you are eighteen." I said. We paused a few minutes to rest against the porch railing. "Oh, look at the moon!"

"Have you ever seen one so big or near," he said softly, he stepped closer, his chest touching my shoulders. We stood there perilously close, admiring the profusion of stars and the brilliant moonlight flowing over the quiet landscape.

We were both conscious of our contact at the same moment. I half-turned to him to agree on the size and the beauty of the moon, when he pulled me close and his lips came down gently on mine. He kissed me first and then I kissed him back. I caught my breath suddenly wondering if anyone inside could see us and what they might think. His kiss was so warm. His lips were moist and firm. His left arm held me gently against him and his other hand massaged the small of my back.

"Why not kiss him back," I thought feebly. "It feels good, nothing else can happen here, and besides which I don't know any of those people in there." A slow hot flush moved up my neck until all conscious thought was blocked out. Tom took a deep breath: he was still holding me close with one hand on my waist. I wondered if he could feel my heart thumping wildly against his chest. His began to massage my neck and softly he began to kiss me on my cheeks, eyes and lips. His lips found my ear and he gently tugged my earlobe with his teeth. His breath warmed my ear and goosebumps trickled down my arm: my knees began to feel weak. I felt drunk with pleasure, happy, relaxed and totally thoughtless naturally responding to his demanding lips, matching him kiss for kiss. Without warning a sudden alarm went off in my head.

"Whoa!" I choked breathlessly, pulling away, but unable to immediately form a sentence. "Stop."

"What's the matter? You don't like it?" He chuckled.

His arms pulled me back close to him and took up on the kiss where we'd left off. My body felt like warm butter and I was afraid my brain was starting to melt. It was hard to stay focused on the moment. Just then he leaned back against the railing.

"Stop. Please." I whispered breathily. He released me, and I turned away. I looked up at the sky and caught a breath of cool night air, clearing my brain.

"I'll be right back, don't go away!" he said.

Tom went back into the bar but quickly walked back to me. He put his arm around my waist.

"My God girl, you're shaking. I'm sorry. I forgot you are so young. I lost my head. I'm deeply sorry. Are you all right?"

"Yes," I quavered, grateful that the darkness hid my blush.

"So, this was "making out," flashed across my mind. I was appalled by my inexperience. After mom mentioned sex, I stuck the whole subject on a back shelf. I had no use for that discussion. Sex education in our school had been a one-hour class on the physical difference between boys and girls. Nobody listened, the girls just giggled. Then our Phy. Ed. teacher told us not to have 'relations with men' and talked about menstrual cycles. I'd never had a girlfriend to talk to about this and though I'd had a few crushes, they were all unrequited. But this was crazy stuff! I couldn't believe how it messed with my mind.

"Come on, Jewell. I'm taking you back to the Inn." He took my hand and pulled me to his vehicle.

We walked away from the restaurant and then he held the door when I got into his car. As I sat there the reality of the situation hit me. I must look like a fool. He slid behind the wheel and turned the key.

"I should have asked permission first. You've never done 'this' before have you?"

"No," I replied quietly, so glad he couldn't see me blush furiously again.

"I'm extremely glad you asked me to stop, then."

"I didn't mean it at first." I giggled nervously. That broke the tension. He looked at me and we both laughed. His powerful car growled around the corners as he shifted gears. The golden headlight beams flashed cross-eyed against the trees along the road. I watched the sky for clusters of stars I recognized.

"There's the north star," I cried, as we passed a small field and the trees parted. "Look upwards; there's the Big and Little Dippers." I pointed through the windshield.

"You know, it's funny we haven't had northern lights this year yet. I don't even remember them last year, although I didn't spend a lot of time outside last summer because of work." He slowed down a little to look out too.

"Dammit! Duck!" Tom swung the car over to the edge of the road. With a roar and a flash of lights a huge black semi-trailer truck bulldozed through the night. His muscular arm kept me from hitting the dash with my head as I was thrown first sideways and then forward against my lap belt. I heard Tom swear, then gravel spewed up under my side of the car and the car jolted to a stop in the ditch sideways.

"You son-of-a-bitch-" Tom swore vehemently. "Are you okay? Sorry. Just hang on! I want to catch that guy."

Tom jerked his car up the steep incline over the gravel and up on the blacktop. It was instantly obvious that there was something very wrong.

"It's a flat tire. Dammit," he muttered and flung himself out of the car. "Can you get the flashlight out of the glove compartment?"

"Got it," I answered and dug out the flashlight. I climbed out of the car and aimed the beam at the tire. Tom worked efficiently to remove the lug nuts and replace the tire. With strength and coordination, he quickly packed the parts back into the trunk and we got back in the car.

"I am going to drop you off and head back to the office. I can't imagine where that guy was going. It's pretty unusual to see a semi down here because the roads don't really go to or from any city," he commented. "Something isn't kosher. Can you stash that flashlight back in the glove? Load up, let's get out of here."

The wheels spun again as Tom maneuvered the car out of the ditch, his headlights stabbing the tops of the trees on the opposite side of the road. He drove fast, with focused concentration, barely hesitating at the stop sign at the four-way intersection at the end of road to the resort. He pulled into the parking lot and jumped out to open my door. As I stood up next to him, Tom very gently took my shoulders in his hands and kissed my nose.

"Thanks for the wonderful evening, Jewell." He said letting me go. "Thanks for all of it, the conversation, the dinner and the dancing. You are a very special young lady and I would like to see you again. What do you think?"

"I…I guess so. Thanks for dinner. I had an enjoyable time," I said shyly.

"I will call you at the Inn, Okay? I've got to get back to file that report."

"Sure."

I quickly crossed the parking lot. There was the sound of people talking on the veranda, so I entered the side door and took the stairs two at a time to my room to avoid having to talk to anyone and break the spell. I unlocked the door and stepped into the safety of the darkness inside. The little room was so quiet, and I stood for a few seconds listening to the breeze rippling through the pines and popples outside my window. I went to the window to look out at the stars. In the silence, I felt I was not alone.

"Jewell?"

I recoiled, jumped and tripped over my dressing table chair.

"Ouch!"

"Shush! It's me - Jake!"

"My God! You scared me. How did you get in here?" I hissed back and rubbed my ankle. "Dang! What were you thinking?"

"Sorry! I was waiting down the hall. I just didn't want to surprise you outside. I guess it was kinda dumb; I scared you anyways."

"It's okay," I half-whispered. "Don't go. I'm getting used to being startled.

"I am sorry to barge in here. I just didn't want to sit around the living room waiting and then run into your Deputy friend. I kinda figured you wouldn't invite him up here. I let myself in."

"What are you talking about?" I flicked the little bedside lamp on.

"The lock; I picked it."

"No, I meant what do you mean about my 'Deputy friend'?"

"The cook said you were out on a date with Deputy Boyden. Knowing you, I figured you wouldn't bring him up for a nightcap…"

"Of course not! Wait: you talked to the cook?"

"Hey, Jewell, I can go. I apologize if I'm bugging you."

"No, forget it; please sit down." I pulled the little chair away from my desk and motioned to him. My little room seemed much smaller with him in it. I slipped my shoes off and sat cross-legged on the bed. I took a deep breath and looked closely at him.

"How have you been, Jake? You looked like grim death the last time I saw you."

"I stayed in Randy's RV and slept a lot. My doctor warned me again about exertion. I'll listen next time."

"That is, if there is a next time, Jake. You seem to have a knack for getting into trouble! I didn't expect to see you again."

"Really? I have an appointment with my doctor tomorrow and I just wanted to see you first. Hey, can I sit on the floor? This chair is awfully small and uncomfortable."

"You can lie down on the bed if you want, I'm sorry."

Jake sighed as he stretched out on the bed, leaned back against pillows on the headboard.

"That's great, I appreciate that, it feels much better."

I sat down at my dressing table. I couldn't look at Jake right now. It felt so uncomfortable to think that I just left Tom.

"What's up? Still looking for bad guys?" I asked.

"Uffda, I think I will go back to fishing for now. I don't think the search is very healthy! Whoever is involved in this, plays tough. It still just doesn't make any sense. It's like doing a crossword puzzle without the clues!" Jake smiled at me. "The sheriff seems to think that these guys were jealous boyfriends or something. He indicated they won't waste their time on it. Instead he warned me that a pretty girl like you could be trouble: bad for my health."

"That's really dumb. You've gotta be kidding!"

"You don't understand. The only real crime was shooting me and that went into the unsolved file months ago. Somebody gets beat up every Friday and Saturday night in bar fights in Northern Wisconsin. We aren't talking about a city like Madison or Milwaukee, Northern Wisconsin is a huge empty rural area and a Sheriff needs something more tangible than some guys in a fistfight to do any more investigation. Ask your boyfriend Tom Boyden. He'll tell you."

"He is not my 'boyfriend'," I snapped.

"So then, how serious are you about this Deputy?" he asked bluntly. I didn't look at Jake, but I caught his face in the mirror, he was staring at me.

"Jake, it was just a date! I never met him before yesterday. He asked me out for dinner!" I said, busily focusing my attention on unbraiding my hair. I blushed again, thinking how dumb it was that I blushed so easily. "We talked at the Sheriff's Office and again at the hospital because he is worried about me. He asked me to go out for dinner tonight. That's all."

"Where'd you go, somewhere around here?"

"Madden's Resort, down on the river. The food was great," I hurriedly said and began to blush remembering the night. I covered my face with my hands.

"Darn it, I don't mean to pry, I'm sorry. I hope you had an enjoyable time. You have been through a lot of stuff in the last day or so."

"Oh, yes, it was a nice dinner. We had the fish fry. It was great."

There was a silence as I put the combs in to hold my hair and glanced at Jake who was completely focused on his feet.

"I don't want you to get the wrong idea Jake." I felt shy and compelled to explain. "Tom was just cheering me up. You guys left, suddenly and I thought…well, I thought I wouldn't see you again."

"Did you want to?"

"Of course, I do, Jake! I have messed things up so far. I used to think I had everything under control, all organized. Now within a few days I feel so foolish. I've never dated before and I don't know much about guys all that stuff and I'm really confused." I said miserably.

"And you are so pretty with your hair in that braid. Y'know; when I woke up in the hospital I thought I was seeing an angel. The light makes your hair glow like a halo."

"Knock it off, Jake. That's not funny."

"I'm very serious right now. Maybe you don't know how lovely you are. I like you a lot and I need to know if you like me or you think you could. It makes a lot of difference to me right now. Do I stand a chance in your little black date book?"

"I don't have a date book I told you. I haven't dated. I mean-I don't often date. I was surprised Tom asked me out."

"Really? He'd be nuts not to."

"Can we not talk about this? I would rather talk about what you found out from Randy about the semis. Maybe I can do your legwork for you? I can drive and maybe ask people questions? Someone must have seen those semis if they were parked on the lane by the farm. Where else could they have seen us from? We would have heard them coming if they were on the main road." Jake was looking at me and shaking his head.

"I don't want you involved at all. These guys are bad. Maybe it's a clever idea to let everyone think you are dating a cop, they might leave you alone. And stay away from that farm."

"That's odd. That's what Mrs. Swenson said. My aunt, Greta owns it and I have a perfect right to go there if I want to. When I was there I only saw empty buildings and nothing else. It doesn't look like anyone has been there."

"I'm just saying don't mess with this. These guys have a screw-loose in their heads. Someone has connections across northern Wisconsin. I think they may have mafia connections, considering the roughhouse stuff, and they have been doing this for a while. They are darned sneaky. If you get in their way, they don't play nice. I can't protect you as much as I want to."

"What did Randy find out?"

"Randy put together a report that profiled everything we knew so far, about where the thefts in the warehouses were, what were taken, and a few of the things that showed up. He should have been a cop instead of an accountant. We tried to get information out of a truck driver, but he just smiled at us and said, "*I wanna call my lawyer.*" When the lawyer showed up he was a slicked back guy from Minneapolis. They got him off on a technicality in the paperwork."

"I don't understand how that works. How can that be?"

"Even if you are a criminal you have rights. Cops have the burden of proof and a lot of little leads that go in a bunch of directions but nothing that ties them together."

"What's really going on? You haven't really told me anything."

"Jewell, it's kinda complicated and we even have a tough time understanding it. It has something to do with new-fangled computers and using them to steal from warehouses. It also has something to do with drugs and burglaries in summer homes and cabins. We have even seen some prostitution in backwoods bars, but nothing ties together. We just can't nail down who is behind this whole deal. It might not be one person. We just don't know."

"I have built computers, Jake. They aren't that complicated. In high school, I was one of the best programmers and I know how to make them from the bottom up. I was helping set up a lot of the stuff at my high school because my teachers didn't even understand. Maybe I can help."

"Oh, well, ya... I don't know any women who are into computers."

"There are several girls in my school that are..." I said sourly.

"Ok, there's a few women in our police department too, Jewell. They do a respectable job, but they are mostly secretarial."

"I get tired so of hearing what women can't do. I can do anything I want to put my mind to. One time I took a test at school and it came back saying I should be a doctor, a lawyer or an engineer. They wrote my name wrong and thought it said Joel. Then the student counselor's office redid it and they said I should be a nurse or a history teacher. It is so stupid to base a job on your gender."

"I won't argue with you on that. Women have a unique perspective on things and it can help to get a job done." Jake paused for a few moments and the silence was heavy. He seemed to make up his mind about something.

"Ok. We think we're on the track of a ring of thieves. It has been going on for a few years now. They send fake orders to computerized telephone centers. The warehouse packs the semi-trucks including the false orders and drives off. We think the semi driver pulls off the highway and they move the fake order on another truck and deliver the rest. By the time the warehouse or the store discovers the missing merchandise, it is too late to hunt them down. Since we never know what warehouse or company they are going to hit, we can't nail them. There are hundreds of warehouses, stores and trucks. Half the time the company just claims it on their insurance or writes it off. In the meantime, these creeps are making a mint on the stolen stuff."

"You should be able to locate something in common between all the stores or company warehouses. I can't believe they can get away with this." I said in disbelief. Something was bugging me in that back of my brain. "Where do they keep all this stolen stuff? It can't be easy to hide."

"We are talking about Wisconsin, Minnesota, Michigan, Iowa and Illinois so far. I have heard that it gets converted into money through pawn shops. You wouldn't believe the number of stores and warehouses there are that order product by phone using code words to identify who is giving the order. But somebody's got to be getting the passwords and account numbers out of the stores and then they hijack the order before it get delivered to the store, using their own drivers and hidden warehouses. The stores don't know the order was placed and some stores don't even know they are paying for merchandise they don't get because they don't keep good records. We can't get anyone interested in it because most of the time insurance companies cover the loss. We can't even prove how much is missing."

"There still must be something in common, whether it is people, trucks or the warehouses themselves. You need to look at all of the data and find the way to look at it."

"I have piles of information, but I can't put it together. Randy says it would take months to get all the information. But I don't understand why would they attack me here? How did they know me? I must have hit on something because they jumped me here for some reason. I have been off work for months and I am technically on vacation now. That case I was on was about burglaries up in Superior. I just don't get it."

"How many burglaries are you talking about? How has Randy been looking for them?"

"Randy's been studying the books of the companies that have complained about getting hit too often. The orders are all on the telephone and there's no way to find out where the guy is at…they can use any phone and we can't track the calls to them. He thinks there's a small group of drivers that take the runs so there must be someone in the warehouses that know what's going on too. The guy the Deputy grabbed has a rap sheet for a half dozen other things from Minneapolis to Ashland, but the County jail didn't hold him when a slick city lawyer showed up. Superior PD is running a background check but so far nothing connects him to that bar in Superior or the warehouse heists. There's just nothing to link it all together. I am worried about you because they may have seen me with you."

"Tom said that they released that guy and they transferred him to Douglas County. Don't worry about me Jake. No one knows me outside of the village."

"Remember what I said, this is not the city, like Madison. Everyone knows everyone in rural areas. Besides, around here most everyone is related somehow, and people keep an eye on what's going on. Everyone has a reputation for something. In rural places like this it's important to know who you can trust. Randy feels like you are safer if you don't know anything. I think you'd better know enough to keep your guard up."

"Don't worry Jake, the 'bad guys' can't just carry me away. My folks are here too. You are way too serious about this, like its Dragnet or Hawaii 5-0," I said laughing.

"It is serious stuff, Jewell. I'm a real cop, not a TV cop. There are bad guys out there and they will do anything for a buck. They shot me with a shotgun and left me to die. That's dirty. Somebody didn't want me poking around in this deal, when they got me the second time they pounded lumps on my head."

"Ok, Jake. Seriously; I'll be careful about who I talk to and where I go, I'm not Nancy Drew! Now, what can I do to help you?"

"I don't know Nancy Drew. I thought you could ask your aunt if someone has asked about the farm. But listen to me. Don't go prowling around in the pucker brush. Find out if anyone has talked to her about it."

"Nancy is a fictitious detective. Didn't you know that?"

Jake shook his head and frowned at me.

"Never mind, I guess I could call Aunt Greta in the Twin Cities or I could ask my mom, but I don't think she'd know."

"Sure, keep track and I'll pay for long distance calls. Just ask whether they planned to sell it, or if anyone else has called to ask that and then who they are. That's a great start," Jake said smiling, "I've got to leave for a few days. I have an appointment with a couple of doctors up in Duluth."

Jake stood up from the bed and I saw him falter a little, so I jumped to his side, but he gathered his strength and stood firmly.

"It's okay; I just got up too fast." He smiled and patted my shoulder. "Thanks anyway, I have to get back to my room. It's getting late. It's good my room is pretty close."

"I can walk with you."

"Oh no, I'm fine. You stay here." We stood very close and he looked right into my eyes. "Jewell- I…" he said and touched my cheek. He kissed me softly on the forehead, then he turned and went out the door, closing it quietly behind him.

I stood for a minute not moving. I wanted him to stay and talk; I wanted to hear his voice…such a strong yet gentle voice and underlying it, a sense of confidence. I wished we had talked about something else instead of his mystery.

"Maybe I ought to check on him and make sure he got back to his room okay," I thought with mischief and smiled to myself as I reflected on the trouble I had gotten myself into in the last few days. I decided it wasn't a great idea and locked my door.

I put on my pajamas and laid my housecoat at the end of my bed. As I lay on my bed I reflected that I hadn't talked to Mom since my date with Tom. I regretted I didn't check her room on the way up to mine. We hadn't resolved our little tiff about Jim. Mom said she wanted to shop in town, maybe I should ask about that trip for tomorrow. I supposed she didn't need to hear about my date. Right about this moment I remembered the trip home with Tom. I forgot to tell Jake about the semi on the way back from Madden's. How could I forget something that important?

"I'll find him and tell him in the morning," I whispered to myself. It would give me a reason to talk to him again. I sighed again, curled up on my bed and slept. In the morning, I still felt washed out and weary.

CHAPTER 7

Fire and Rain ~ James Taylor, 1970

...I've seen lonely times when I could not find a friend,
But I always thought that I'd see you again...

HOME SWEET HOME

Sometimes memories are sharp and staccato crowding into my mind, while others are wispy and cloudlike. This morning they poured into my mind like a soft, summer rain. I got up quickly, dressed and hurried down to Jake's room but a petite and slender American Indian girl with long shining black hair and dark eyes was cleaning his room.

Disappointed; I said "Hi" to her and ran down to the dining room. Nobody was there this morning. I looked around the corner into the parlor. No Jake. I sadly slumped down on the big hard couch and fiddled with the radio dial until I found the local station playing a new song by James Taylor, "Fire and Rain". His voice swirled like syrup into my head and inside I absorbed the pain and the disillusionment of being young and growing up. I remembered reading about "Fire and Rain" in Time magazine- the first verse was about his reactions to the death of a friend. The second verse about struggling with addictions and then the third verse of that song was about his recuperation after an awful motorcycle accident that broke his hand and foot. I leaned back, closed my eyes and sank into my own melancholy contemplation.

After the song was over, I sighed and switched the radio off. I wandered around the Inn to see if were in but found Mom and Jim were gone. I went to the kitchen to see if I could use the telephone to call my Aunt Greta in Saint Paul. I startled Mrs. Swenson who was in her small office talking excitedly on her telephone as I came around the corner.

"How would I know? I don't have time to keep track of him…"

She looked up with a grouchy frown and put her hand over the mouthpiece. "Yes, Jewell?"

"I beg your pardon Mrs. Swenson, I just wondered if I could use the phone to make a long-distance call to Minneapolis today?"

"Um, sure…in a little while."

"That's great. I'm sorry I interrupted!"

"Close that door behind you, please."

I ducked out of the kitchen and back into the hall, climbing the stairs to my room to retrieve my wallet where I had the number to call. There was a telephone in the parlor for the visitors, but I would have to wait until Mrs. Swenson was done using the phone. I picked up some old postcards on the desk to pass the time. The people who waved from a ski-boat in the lake in front of the Inn looked vaguely familiar, but I couldn't quite make them out. One was a picture of a beautiful dark-haired girl in a swimsuit with a banner announcing, "Musky Queen". Just then, the kitchen screen door slammed, so I figured Mrs. Swenson was off the phone.

I dialed Aunt Greta's number and waited as it rang her home.

"Lindberg's, Greta speaking."

"Oh, Auntie Greta, it is so good to hear your voice! This is Jewell!"

"Hi honey! I am so happy to hear your voice too. You sound just like your mother now. What's up dearest?"

"Not much. Did you know we are in Philetus Spur for the summer?"

"No, I didn't. I'll have to come over and visit!"

"I would love that, Auntie. It's awful boring since Mom and Jim are always off gallivanting around the area. We have been water-skiing a few times, took the canoe out around the lake and we went out to dinner but that's pretty much it."

"I remember so many good times when you were a little girl, Jewell. Remember swimming and canoeing? I loved hiking in the woods around the lake. I always loved "Fish-fry Fridays" too."

"Me too, Auntie Greta. The lake has always been such a wonderful memory for me. I walked over at the farm to look around yesterday. You don't mind, do you?"

"Of course, you can be there, honey. The farm is a delightful place, but I am afraid it will not stay nice long if it stays empty. You are eighteen, now, aren't you? Done with high school?"

"I am. I guess I'll start college at Madison next fall. You haven't rented the farm out or anything?"

"Oh, no. It's just sitting there. I had Olson's cut the fields and sell the hay so that the fields stay cleared. A few years ago, the Muellers plowed up all the fields and planted corn. Other than that, the farm house just sits empty." There was a pregnant pause.

"I just love being here. It almost feels more like home than our house in Madison. So, it's okay if I go there, right?"

"Sure, you can, my dear. As a matter of fact, I've always hoped it would be yours. Sigurd agreed with me, that if you ever showed any interest in keeping the farm that I would give it to you. Did anyone ever mention that to you?"

"What? You are kidding, right?"

"No, I'm not kidding. After your Uncle Oscar passed away, Siggy and I talked about the farm. When Dad and Mom sold the Inn, we thought they made a terrible mistake. They sold it too cheap to that awful woman, Anna Swenson. Sig argued with him over it and was so angry because Mrs. Swenson was so pushy. Dad was determined to sell it and we couldn't change his mind. Mom hated that he sold it. But he said he felt that Mary and Sig would never come back home, and he didn't want to run it anymore. He said it was too much work for them. It was worth a fortune, but he literally gave it away to that woman. In a few months Mom died; and not long after that Siggy died. Dad was completely distraught. After he passed, I gave the whole situation to God."

"Auntie Greta. I am so sorry that all this happened to you."

"It's strange that just before Siggy died, he and I talked to Dad and we all decided that since you are the sole child between us the Wolf Point farm could be yours when you were old enough. Before Dad passed away he started talking about getting the Inn back again. He said he was going to talk to a lawyer. But that doesn't matter now. For you, there's the farm plus two-hundred and forty acres of fields and woods."

"This doesn't seem real," I could hardly talk. "I own the farm? It's incredible!"

"I'm surprised that your mom never talked to you about it. Your father and I always hoped you would keep Wolf Point in the family. There is a lot heritage there. I knew that you would love it like we did. I even stored Mom and Dad's stuff, like pictures and personal things, in case you wanted them."

"No, mom has never talked to me about that kind of stuff. I can't believe this! I am in shock, Auntie. I can't believe this is true. I can't take it all in."

"My dear little Jewell, I love you so much. I promise I will come over in July and we will get the papers set up if you want to. I'll get some help and I can bring a trailer with the furniture. There's no point in wasting time. I am not getting any younger."

"Of course, oh…Auntie Greta, don't talk like that. You are going to be there for me forever! I am just so surprised, and I guess I am totally floored. I don't know what I would do with the house and all."

"I shouldn't have dropped that bomb on you so suddenly, Jewell…but I have waited so long to celebrate with you. It is so exciting! I just can't wait to see you! I'm coming in a couple weeks. We'll go to Hayward and sign the papers at the courthouse."

I couldn't even respond. I was shocked, thrilled, happy, excited and my heart was beating like crazy.

"I am sorry, sweetie, but I have to run right now because I have an appointment."

"Okay. That's fine. Don't mention this to Mom right now. I just want to soak it in for a little while."

"I won't. It will be our little secret."

"I'll call you next week. I love you Auntie Greta, thank you so much! You know me like I know myself."

"I love you. You are certainly your father's daughter and I always felt you were partly my daughter too. I will make some arrangements, okay? Tell your mom I'm coming home soon!"

"Oh sure, I will. Goodbye!"

I stood for a few moments looking at the phone, and then I put it back into the cradle.

"My farm. I own a house…and I have land. My farm," I enjoyed saying it out loud. I rushed up to my room and threw my purse on the bed, grabbed my sweater and swept out of the room. I locked the door behind me and raced down the stairs taking them two at a time. Mrs. Swenson was standing in the hallway outside the parlor, staring at me. I smiled, flipped her a half-wave and hurried away. Turning down along the lake, I ran swiftly down the little trail to the farm. As I came through the bushes at the end of the yard, tears filled my eyes and I covered my mouth with my hand. I strode up to the house and opened the rickety screen door, and found the door was not locked. I pushed it open and stepped into the short hall outside the kitchen.

"My house," I sighed out loud. "Thanks, Dad. Thank you, Mom, Auntie Greta, Gramma and Grampa!"

The windows in the kitchen were dirty but I could just see Shadow Bay beyond the brush at the edge of the lawn. I pushed the dusty table from the center of the room over next to the window and then placed the two chairs at either end. The kitchen cabinets surrounded Gramma's big double porcelain sink in the middle of the wall. I loved the glass in the doors of the cabinets on the walls. I opened the tin-lined bin that tipped out of the bottom where she had kept her flour and sugar. The bottom was covered with mouse droppings and a grass nest. It made me sad because Gramma was so very careful with all her things.

I ran my hand along the smooth wood beams that made the arch between the kitchen and the living room. As I entered the middle of the two rooms I saw why Grampa built the house this way. The whole room focused on Lake Makoons and Wolf Point where a lone leaning pine cast a long shadow over the lake. Light was reflecting off the waves and twinkling on the ceiling. Because the house sat on an incline above the shoreline, I could see most of the lake. I remembered the pleasant breeze from the southwest that used to blow through the curtains and out the kitchen windows. I tried to open the window, but it was stuck in place. I loved the open rock fireplace with the deep and wide hearth. We spent so many evenings there popping popcorn. The narrow boards of the bird's eye maple floors in this room were in decent shape. Spider webs festooned every corner, but the room was still bright and cheery. I raised my hands in the air and spun around.

"My home. I am home!"

I nearly danced out of the living room into the other end of the hall where the stairwell went upstairs. I felt like bouncing and clapping my hands. Light streamed down from the window over the stairs as I creaked upwards. I remembered my childhood room with all the funny slanted ceilings and rosebud-patterned wallpaper. Pushing on the thin wooden door to the right I stepped in and was reminded of Alice in Wonderland again. Now the room seemed so tiny! In my memory, it was a spacious playroom. My head bumped the wooden board ceiling where it came down to just beyond the door.

There was the good old grey linoleum on the floor here too, worn and a little worse for wear. I turned back out into the hallway and followed the bannister to the other two big rooms down the long hallway.

"There will be some changes to make," I thought, touching some torn wallpaper. The other two identical rooms had shorter hip-walls with slanted ceilings and wallpapered in matching patterns. In the center of each hip-wall was a dormer with a double hung window. You could see the Inn through the windows. Grampa spent many hours putting finishing touches like fluted vines and whimsical flowers carved into the oak window and door frames. Every room had little built-in, mirrored cabinets. I remembered him puttering around out in his shop making wooden toys. His workshop was filled with projects that were later implanted into the house. Gramma would roll her eyes and smile with each new shelf, cabinet or box. I smiled remembering the time when I was little girl that I crawled around under his desk in the office and I found a little locked door in the floor hidden by a carpet. Grampa told me that the elves made it and we laughed together.

"This will be our private secret my Little Jewell," he whispered to me with a big smile and hugged me close. "Don't tell your "Mormor"!"

"Now what's this?" I opened the little door on the wall and saw my reflection smiling back at me in the small inset mirror. I wandered around for a little while checking the closets, looking out the windows and admiring the other special touches Grampa added here and there. I found the door to the attic in the closet of the larger bedroom, but it was locked. As I remembered, the attic was big enough for another bedroom, but Gramma and Grampa used it for storage. I'd have to figure out how to open it.

"This is so awesome!" I said out loud happily. My mind spun with all the things I wanted to do. I went back downstairs to continue my inspection and made notes in my head. I would have to clean, and I would need all kinds of cleaning supplies because there wasn't even a broom or dustpan in sight. I could get water from lake and the trash burner woodstove was still hooked up to the chimney in the kitchen, if I wanted to heat water.

I would start cleaning right away and not tell Mom until I got the whole house cleaned. I flicked the light switch in the kitchen but remembered Mom said the power was shut off. That was okay, I didn't need any power right now. I looked down the stairs into the musty basement, but it was too dark, even with the light from the little ground-level windows. Running into spiders in the dark didn't seem like fun to me. I walked through the office noting the smaller fireplace and then entered the lakeside bedroom. There was a short piece of a burnt candle lying on the floor. It seemed someone had been in here. I hoped kids weren't invading it.

"This will be my bedroom someday. The wainscoting is still perfect." I stood at the tall windows and again noticed the tall solitary pine tree at the point jutting into the lake. The overgrown lawn used to extend along the lake and around to the pine tree and a big boulder. "Maybe someday I will put a little monument to my family there," I thought. "That pine tree reminds me of Dad and Grampa Johnson, so tall and strong."

Leaving the house, I shut the door firmly. I would have to call and find out who had the keys. Then I could lock it up. Since I didn't have any paper, pen or money, I thought I'd return to the Inn and make a list of what I needed. Then I'd walk to Philetus Spur today and see what was at the little store. I had the two hundred dollars I brought along and had not used yet. That would probably do it! I trotted across the driveway towards the path to the Inn with a new sense of ownership. My head must have been in those puffy white clouds. It seemed like Star Trek's Scotty 'teleported' me back to the Inn.

In my room, I changed my sweater for a light blouse and vest. Jeans would have to do for now. I'd have to talk to Mom about a trip to Hayward to get my laundry done! I grabbed my wallet and slipped on my tennis shoes for the walk. As I walked down the road, I thought about the house and then Jake popped up suddenly in my mind.

"I wonder where he is and what he is doing today." I realized I had been so excited by this crazy turn of events I'd forgotten him. I also forgot to ask Aunt Greta any other questions. "Darn it. I'll have to call her and ask his questions, later."

The rest of the walk to Philetus Spur took about twenty minutes and I was thinking about all the things I would need. I got to the village and walked to the church and graveyard. This time I leaned on the fence and stood smiling at my memories.

"This is just perfect," I whispered. "I have to hurry but I will stop back later, okay?"

I hurried down the little cement sidewalk past the one-chair barber shop and the garage-gas station. Ben was working inside and caught my eye, so I waved cheerily at him. The bell on Hagie's door clanged as I let the screen door slam behind me. I had to pause to let my eyes adjust to the dim interior and then I began looking around. I found a corn broom, a copper dust pan, a mop and bucket. There was one small box of Spic and Span, so I tossed it in the bucket with a sponge, a package of rags and a scrub brush. While I considered my next item, Malin Haagestad appeared at the end of the counter and smiled at me.

"Hi there again, are you cleaning? Certainly, looks serious!"

"Hi. I'm very serious." I agreed with a big smile, "I was trying to find some window cleaner to wash windows."

"Oh, I don't carry that. It's cheaper and better to use white vinegar, and baking soda or FelsNaptha and then use a sponge or rags. I recycle newspapers to get a shine on the glass. A soft rag works the best, but I have a stack of old newspapers I can give you."

I must have looked a little surprised because she went on to explain.

"There's no reason to waste paper and poison the lake. Besides, it works much better. It works great if you have a rubber squeegee and I can borrow you one. You aren't the new cleaning staff at the Inn, are you?"

"No," I laughed. "I am cleaning up my grandparent's house over at Wolf Point. I hate it to look so empty and dirty inside."

"Oh yes," she said slowly, looking at me thoughtfully. "I can understand that. The soda will get greasy stuff off and you will need it because Elin used the woodstove right up until she left the farm. I've heard she was an amazing housekeeper and her cooking was legendary. I don't remember anyone living there since they passed away. Are you planning to live there?"

"Maybe later this summer." I said, as I packed all my stuff into the bucket. "My aunt, Greta Stina is coming over from Saint Paul. I wanted it to look nice."

"How lovely," she responded gravely.

"Thanks so much, Miss Haagestad."

"I wish you would call me Malin. We can be friends."

"That would be great, I would like that! I've got to get back to work now. I have to haul this stuff back to the farm." I handed her my twenty-dollar bill.

"Oh, no! I'll just put it on a tab for you until you finish the project. You can pay for everything when you are all done. Just sign here. Let me find Ben and see if he can give you a quick ride. I can keep an eye on the station for him."

"That would be so nice, thank you!" I answered and stuffed the bill back into my pocket.

"I'll be right back." She went out the door and it slammed behind her. Only in a place like this would you get to charge stuff and even get a free ride home! In a few minutes, Ben pulled up in his old Ford pickup. He jumped out and ran around the truck to open the door and he put my purchases in the back. After I got in he closed the door and strode around the truck to the driver's side.

"Malin said you needed a ride?" Ben hopped in and smiled at her.

"Sure, to Johnson Point Farm: I am so grateful for the ride, Ben."

"No problem, I was going to take a lunch break anyway, so I hung up my out to lunch sign." He drove out of the village, over the bridge and past the field where we had seen Mr. Olson a week ago.

"Looks like the first hay is in, I wonder who Mr. Olson will give it to this time. They don't need it and he always gives it away. He'll probably get a second cut with the cool weather and rain. I think 'Old Mr. Olson' wants to keep the field from growing over and he just plain likes to work," Ben said as he turned down the dirt road to the farm. The springs on his truck squeaked loudly as we bounced around the corner and into the circle drive. Ben pulled up right by the front door, hopped out and took my stuff out of the back of the truck. He reached over to open my door, but I was already getting out. I opened the screen door and turned the doorknob only to discover that it was now locked! I stared at the door for a second and then frowned at Ben.

"I was just here, and it wasn't locked. That's really odd."

Ben put down the bucket and cleaning supplies and rattled the door knob. He glanced sideways at me, wrinkled his forehead and thought for a moment. He walked over and reached in his truck behind the seat and pulled out a flat pry bar. He gently inserted it in the window in the kitchen and the window jiggled up.

"The old paint stuck that window closed, it'll open okay now," Ben said.

"Great. Can you boost me up through there?"

"Hang on," he said and got back in his truck. He pulled forward and then backed up to the window. I saw what he intended to do, and I jumped up in the back of the truck and clambered through the open window. I walked around to the hall and opened the door. Ben was already there with my stuff and carried it in for me.

"How about if I come in with you and take a quick look around?" I noticed uncomfortably he still had the wrench bar in his hand.

"Sure, go right ahead. I am going to get some water from the lake."

When I got back from the lake with a bucket of water, Ben was standing in the kitchen scratching his head.

"There's no sign of anyone being in the house. It's darned odd that the door was locked. I don't know if you should stay here alone, Jewell. There's no phone here is there?"

"No, but I'm sure it is okay. You need to get back to work, and I will just start cleaning a little today. I'll be leaving in a couple of hours."

"Okay, Jewell." Ben waved at me over his shoulder, hopped in his truck and disappeared down the driveway with a spray of gravel and a cloud of dust.

I decided to start with the floors, sweeping all the rooms on the first floor. My footsteps echoed as the dust started filling the air. I opened the windows on the south side of the house and then the kitchen windows to air things out. The kitchen window lacked a screen, so the bugs might be a problem, but the dust was worse. It felt good to see the floors swept up. I was going to need water to mop and then I'd tackle the windows. Just then, I heard the rumble of a motor. Looking out the window I saw Ben's truck bouncing back up the driveway. When he got out he opened the passenger side and a rather grave looking brown-haired girl got out with a basket.

"Hey Jewell, this is my sister Joanie. She said she would come and spend the afternoon helping you with the house and keep you company. She packed up a picnic basket for lunch too!" Ben waved and hopped back in his truck, bumping back down the drive.

"Oh, Joanne, how terribly sweet of you, I am totally starved!"

"I hope we aren't intruding. Ben told me you were here alone, trying to clean this big old place, and I couldn't help but volunteer. I hate to clean alone. I'll help you tidy things up and then Ben can give us a ride back before dark. Ben was right. This is such a great old farmhouse. Do you mind if I look while you eat?"

"Go ahead and explore. I love peanut butter sandwiches, and these are amazing cookies. Wow. Thanks!"

Joanne was gone for about ten minutes. I could hear the floor creaking under her feet upstairs and then down into the office and bedroom. When she came back she popped the top of two bottles of Coke and I finished the apple she packed in the lunch basket. We talked for a while about ourselves, our families and her love for gardening. I found out that she was just six months older than me, but she was responsible for Ben and her younger brother Johann, so she was busy.

"On Saturdays, I work at a resort, cleaning rooms for the changeover of visitors. I also help in the kitchen on Friday nights for fish fry. During the week, I make a little extra by sewing and doing alterations for people. Sometimes I work for my Aunt Malin at the store when she disappears on her business trips. My garden produces most of the food we need so I can our food. I have a closet full of jellies and jams from last summer. I can give you some if you'd like. I got the plums off the trees down the lane."

"You are such a busy person, Joanne. Do you mean Hagie's? Miss Haagestad is your aunt?"

"She sure is. She is the best."

"I met her a couple of times. She certainly is different."

"Well, let's get busy cleaning, Jewell. I think we can finish the whole first floor really quickly because there's nothing in our way!"

She was right, we finished before four o'clock. The windows were shining, the walls and windowsills clean and the floors were all mopped. The house smelled of Spic and Span instead of dust and mouse droppings.

"This is great, Joanne." I exclaimed happily as we surveyed our work. "I guess I can tell you, I don't think it has to be a secret. My Aunt told me on the phone today that this is going to be my house. Actually - I'll own it next month! I can't believe how fast things can change in life. Apparently, my Grandfather, aunt and my dad made sure it would be mine."

"My goodness, Jewell. That's wonderful! What will you do, sell it? You can pay for your college then."

"No, I don't need to. My dad put money away for my education when I was a kid. I guess I don't know what I will do. Auntie Greta is coming next month to sign all the papers and bring some furniture back from storage in Saint Paul. It just seems strange now to think I will go back to Madison for school when I own a house here. This is so weird."

"Well, I wouldn't worry about it right now. Just enjoy the feeling. You should sit down with your dad and mom and talk it over. It's like winning a jackpot in Las Vegas!" Joanne threw her head back and laughed but seeing my face she cried, "Oh, I'm sorry, what did I say?"

"I'm sorry," I whispered in embarrassment, "my dad passed away. He died when I was twelve and I miss him terribly. My mom married another guy, but he can never be my dad."

Joanne looked at me seriously and patted my arm with tears in her eyes. This was ridiculous. Here I was, talking about Dad again, making a fool of myself.

"I know just how you feel. My folks passed away too. My mom died right after Abbie was born and five years later dad was killed in a logging accident. I know what this feels like."

"Oh, no."

Joanne's hands were clenched in her lap. She shook her head and sighed.

"Yes. It was a terrible time for Ben, Leah and I but we've gotten used to it, I think. Maybe it's because there's so much to do. The little kids don't remember anything of course. My sister Leah got married and moved to Saint Paul last year with Johan. Ben and I decided to stay here with Abbie and take care of ourselves."

"That's so brave, Joanne."

"It's better now. Dad's death would have left us to fend for ourselves, but Aunt Malin and our neighbors helped us out. We found out how important it is to have neighbors. We had some shirt-tail relations in the area that took turns helping around the farm for the first year. Then some family friends bought it. Aunt Malin used the money to rent a small house for us right in Philetus Spur and opened a trust fund with the remainder. There was a lot more than anyone supposed."

"Oh Joanne, I feel so stupid. I'm so sorry. How awful for you guys. How do you manage?"

"The people in Philetus Spur are so wonderful. The folks in our church and the church in Hayward make sure we are always taken care of and we have the little fund that helps provide for us. Aunt Malin made sure we could stay together. I work, and Ben works. Leah has a little one of her own now, but she sends money when she can. Her husband, Don, is wonderful and has a good union job. We have what we need and there's always Aunt Malin."

"That's so strong. I want to be more like you. I grew up alone. I don't have any siblings or even many friends and I don't know most of my neighbors in Madison. I am sure I could never survive alone like that."

"Well, you will be friends and neighbors with us even if you are not here and we can certainly watch over the house for you. Ben will stop by and check on it to make sure nobody messes with it if you want him to."

"Would you guys really do that? That is so far out. I could come up here to visit since I have a car and all."

"And Ben sometimes drives down to Madison for his job! He picks up parts for the garage. Maybe you could even ride back up with him? I am sure he could help take care of this place for you in the meantime."

"Oh Joanne, I am so glad we met. I feel like I am opening a whole new world in just a few hours! We have so much in common."

"I feel it too. I have missed Leah so much and it would be wonderful to have a friend closer to my age, even if it is just this summer. All my friends are gone since high school. I broke up with my boyfriend and I am honestly too busy to go make new ones. You can teach me to swim and I will teach you to make bread and catch fish!"

At the same time, we just reached out and joined hands. I had to let go because tears were running down my cheeks from laughing. I wiped my eyes with my sleeve and leaned back, taking a deep breath. "Thank you, Jesus. You are so sweet to me." I whispered.

"Are you a Christian?" Joanne seemed a little surprised.

"Sure, I believe in God. I go to church sometimes..."

"Some time we can even talk about that, Jewell. Maybe you want to go church with me some Sunday? I have the little kids in the Bible School starting at eight on Sundays, but I could meet you upstairs for our service. Ben and I teach six little kids and we make sure they have breakfast."

"Do you think I could help?"

"Sure," Joanne answered. "We would love to have someone to help. Ben could go pick up Mr. Olson and his wife a little early then. This is wonderful. Then you can meet our Pastor."

Just then the rumble of Ben's truck as he came up the driveway flooded the kitchen through the open window. I moved over to the door and saw his cheerful smile as soon as he jumped out of the truck and loped over to the doorstep.

"Hey, how's it goin'? You guys done yet?"

"Hi Ben. No, we are not completely done! But we finished the whole downstairs! Joanne is an amazing cleaner."

"It's from years of picking up after me," Ben said with a huge lopsided grin. When he smiled, there were long creases on his thin tanned face and his crinkly blue eyes even smiled. He was wearing a red and black cotton shirt over a white t-shirt even on this warm day and I noticed his jeans were held up on his lanky body by a worn leather belt with a big buckle.

"Do you ride horses, Ben? Is that why you wear cowboy boots?"

"I exercise and take care of some horses for a family on the lake. It's just a part time job but I love horses. I always wanted a horse of my own. Maybe someday I will have a ranch."

Joan came around the corner with her empty picnic basket and broke into out conversation.

"Hey, Jewell and Ben. Enough chit-chat; you can talk in the truck. I've got to get home and get supper on the table soon. Abbie was over at Aunt Malin's helping but she'll be home too. I need to make more cookies for church."

"You bet, Joanie. Ben, I think I need a better lock on this door. I'll have to catch a ride to town for that. For now, I'll lock it from the inside and climb out the window again."

After we carefully closed the house, Ben and Joanne laughed watching me climb out the kitchen window into the back of Ben's truck. I decided to leave my cleaning supplies in the kitchen closet for the next round of cleaning. With a last look and a smile, I thought the house was homier now.

"I am so glad to have new friends. You guys are the best. I know you are in a hurry, so I can just use that little trail back over to the Inn. I want to thank you so much. I have your phone number and I can maybe call you tomorrow?"

"Oh, please do, Jewell. Why don't you just come to our house tomorrow morning? Our house is the first one past the post office."

"Great," I said. As they rolled around the driveway and out to the road, Joanne stuck her head out the window and waved at me with a smile.

It was such wonderful day. I wanted to skip down the path like a child, but I restrained my enthusiasm and turned towards the Inn. I looked back at the house when I got to the curve of the bay and smiled like an idiot at my house sitting sedately on the point of land. I was so happy to have real friends. It was silly, but "Feeling Groovy" lyrics popped into my head, "Skippin' down the cobblestones; lookin' for love and feelin' grooooovy!"

I was smiling so hard, it hurt. As I walked back I wondered if I should tell Mom tonight or nurse my secret for a little longer. Back at the Inn I looked around for her and Jim, but they gone again. I guessed they were at the golf course again because it was such a lovely day. I went down to the lake for a swim and finally went back up to eat dinner and spend the evening in my room where I could read my book and keep one eye on my little farm out the window as the golden sun sank in a hot purple and pink sky.

CHAPTER 8

CHARITY

Our Fourth of July celebration was low key. It was hot that day, so we spent most of our time on the lake, laughing and talking. For the first time, I could remember, I was comfortable and relaxed with Jim. In the evening, Mom and I packed a basket picnic and we ate sandwiches in our boat at the dock of the Golf Course and until ten o'clock when the sun slipped behind the pines on the north side of the lake. The owners of the golf course shot off some sparkly fireworks and a couple of big boomers over the lake. We were back at the Inn by eleven and I read myself to sleep.

I woke up shivering from another strange dream about being lost and frightened, running through a dark cold house with no furniture, hearing voices everywhere and looking for someone. I woke with a start and sat up in bed to recognize the Linger Inn's familiar wallpaper and the warm morning sun streaming across my room. It was cold again this morning and my comforter was on the floor. I sat up, reached for my housecoat, and there she was framed by the window-

"My House," I sighed out loud. She was bathed in early morning light across Shadow Bay, where the sun sparkled like fiery jewels on the ripples. After a quick trip to wash up in the bathroom down the hall, I braided my hair. I pulled on white hip huggers, a puffy-sleeved peasant blouse and a sweatshirt and slipped my feet into comfy clogs. My heels clattered down the narrow dark stairway to the hallway below where Mrs. Swenson stood in her office door.

"A little loud, young lady." Her lips were pulled into a frowny, old-lady moue. Her thick eyebrows were scowling at me.

"I'm sorry Mrs. Swenson!" I waved one hand with embarrassment and slowed a little as I went out the creaky screen door to the parking lot. The morning was fresh and a little breezy with small puffy white clouds floating in a sea of blue.

"It's gonna be a hot one today," I thought as I strode across the lawn behind the Inn. The sound of men's voices wafted out of the tool shed. I saw a white cube delivery truck parked along the shed and two uniformed men were unloading what seemed to be a new lawn tractor in a crate. I hoped that meant lawn mowing would be quieter in the future. Turning away, I hiked down the driveway towards Philetus Spur, admiring the daisies and the Indian Paint Brush in the ditches and thinking about Jake.

The beautiful morning was warming up nicely as I walked past the church and headed down the main street of Philetus Spur. From the front of Hagie's store I could just see the gas station. I nodded at Ben as I passed in front of the gas station Ben waved his squeegee as he washed the windshield of a large black and very shiny vehicle with dark windows. Enjoying the smell of fresh-cut grass and leaning down to sniff flowers I walked the last block to the house and climbed up the wooden steps of the Widmers' porch. As soon as I knocked, a cute little girl with curly pigtails opened the door. She wore plaid shorts, with a tee-shirt that was a little too small and just a wee bit soiled.

"Hi! You gotta be Jewell! Joanie told me about you. Come in," she said excitedly. "Joanie's in the kitchen!"

"Hi, then you must be Abbie. It's a pleasure to meet you." Her little blue-eyed pixie face lit up with a bright smile and she bounced down the narrow dark hall ahead of me to their tiny kitchen that looked out over the back yard. Joanne's smile reminded me so much of Ben's when she looked up from her work.

"Hi Jewell, please excuse my mess. I like to make bread early before it gets too hot. I made some coffee. It's right there on the stove. The sugar is on the counter in the jar and there is cream in the fridge."

I poured a cup of coffee from her glass percolator sitting on an old narrow gas range with cast iron gridwork on top. I could feel the warmth of the hot oven. Abbie followed me closely and followed every movement. Looking around, I loved the very old-fashioned kitchen. It was spotlessly clean but well worn. Open, rough-board shelves, painted bright glossy yellow, lined the walls. Colorful glass jars of canned beans, peas, and other vegetables and jellies, stacks of plates and a dozen mismatched plastic glasses filled the shelves. The big bi-level sink was sunk into a counter covered with the same linoleum as the floor. Abbie opened the boxy yellow fridge and pulled out a small glass pitcher of thick cream for my coffee. Joanne wore an old-fashioned brown floor-length dress covered by a cream-colored apron.

She was up to her wrists in flour as she kneaded bread on a board at the kitchen table.

"That's whole milk, I hope you don't mind."

"Not at all! My Grampa used to give us cream like this for our coffee. I love your house, Joanne," I said honestly. "It is so homey."

"Do you really think so? Sometimes I think it is just old and run down. But, it is home sweet home to us, I guess. Aunt Malin helped arrange it for us when dad died."

"Your aunt is a sweet lady."

"It was a God-send when she stepped in. At the time, I just thought it was a miracle that they decided to fix up this house and rent to us. It was right near Auntie Malin and the store, and close to my job."

"Then that's handy, Joanne."

"But I am kind of keeping a secret from her. The realtor who owns it wants to raise the rent and we simply can't afford it. There's not enough income from our Trust fund to pay the rent, heat, electricity and phone bills. We try not to waste money on food and new clothes. If I say anything, Aunt Malin always gives us what we need from the store. Ben and I talked about it and we think we'll have to move, even with Ben and me working."

"That's awful Joanne. I am so sorry. You'll have to tell her though. She will feel left out."

"I know. I planned to very soon. I guess it's okay. We'll get by. We always do. Ben works some nights and weekends and he will graduate from High School at midterm. If he gets a full-time job, we can move to town. Abbie will be closer to her Middle school and I can waitress somewhere."

Abbie slumped in her chair next to me. I put my arm around her shoulders.

"Abbie, cheer up, it will be okay. You'll like the Hayward school."

"I want to stay in the Spur by Aunt Malin." Tears rolled down her cheeks and Joanne leaned over to kiss her wet cheek but kept working on her bread dough. I could see how close she was to tears herself by her red rimmed eyes. "I hate those Townies. But nobody cares what I want."

"Sometimes we have to do things we don't want to. I have things I want in life too, young lady. And you know why I don't want to live in Hayward. We'll have to make sacrifices. Just be grateful for what we have, Abbie dear." Joanne punched her bread hard and reformed it into the pan. "God is good, He is watching over us and He will provide."

Abbie buried her head in her arms on the table, so I awkwardly patted her shoulders. My heart ached for her. Suddenly an idea began to coalesce in my head.

"Maybe," I said slowly, "you could live at the farm? Maybe you could be caretakers for me?"

Before Joanne could respond the front door slammed and the clump of work boots in the hall announced Ben's arrival.

"Hey, everybody! What's with the funky faces?"

"Hi Ben," I said: but Joanne just shook her head. "Abbie is unhappy about moving. Joanne was telling me about the situation with the house, and how you can't afford to stay here. My Aunt Greta just told me I was the owner of Wolf Point Farm. I just had a thought that maybe you guys could move over to the farm and be my caretakers."

"I don't know, Jewell. It sounds good but..."

"I'm sure we can work something out. The farm is just sitting there empty anyway. You guys would make my house happy!"

Joanne stopped kneading dough and stared at Ben. Ben's hands gripped the chair in front of him as he and Joanne locked eyes. Breaking the silence, Abbie bounded up and bounded for the door,

"I'm gonna tell Aunt Malin..." she cried. Ben tried to grab her with one hand as she ran by him, but he missed, and she disappeared down the hall in a flash.

"I'll call Auntie and explain, Joanne. Darn that kid." He turned to picked up the receiver.

"Just let her break the news," I asked seriously. "The house is mine and I can do what I want with it. There's no reason why you can't live there."

"I don't know..." Joanne said slowly. "I told Ben that you own the house now. I hope you didn't want to keep it a secret." Just then Ben broke in.

"I was thinking about your place last night. I was going to offer to fix it up for you...there's a lot to consider," Ben said. "There's a couple of broken windows. It's hard to say if the septic tank will work after so many years of not being used. You don't even know if the well will still pump water! The fireplaces look good, but I think the chimneys need a little work. The siding needs scraping, and painting and the porches are a little rotten. Still, it is a strong and comfortable house."

"What is a septic tank?"

"In the city, you have sewers under the streets. Here we have septic tanks to handle sewage. It is pretty interesting how they work."

"Ben!" Joanne laughed and smacked his shoulder. "That's too much information. Jewell can learn about it later."

"Grampa and Gramma lived there not too long ago. I'll bet that we can get answers to those questions. Maybe one of the men you know around town can come over and look at it and help us out. Don't just say no. I have a little money set aside and I think we can make it work!"

"Oh, it is too much. We couldn't possibly afford a big house like that on the lake. Ben, I would love to, but I just don't see how…"

Just at that moment Abbie bounced back through the door, pulling Aunt Malin with her. This time Malin was wearing a white pantsuit, a cute shell top with daisies on it and dainty little white moccasins. It looked so perfect with her dark tan.

"Well," she looked at us with a wrinkled brow. "What's going on?"

"I'm sorry Aunt Malin, she got carried away! Abbie, I could spank you!" Joanne fumed and finally stopped kneading. Her floured hands left small white hand prints on her hips as she glared at Abbie. "We are not ready to discuss this."

"Well, Abbie is rambling about you moving to Wolf Point farm. What's up?" Malin asked.

"I own the farm now, Malin. My auntie Greta just told me she is turning it over to me."

"She is? Yes," Malin looked at me gravely, "I thought you might be the Johnson's heir."

"I just said I thought that since I own Wolf Point farm, these guys could live there. Joanne was saying that their landlord…"

Joanne broke in.

"I am so sorry Aunt Malin. I didn't tell you the landlord raised the rent and we were thinking about moving to get better jobs. It isn't that we want to leave, we just won't have quite enough money to make it through this winter," she said with embarrassment. "I don't like to borrow from you."

Aunt Malin pushed her hair back off her forehead and gently scratched her behind her ear. She frowned then she pulled out a chair and sat on it, her hands on her knees, and stared at her fingers. We all held our breath. She finally looked up and broke the silence.

"Well, if Jewell wants to rent you the farm, I think it is a great idea. Nothing ruins a house faster than sitting empty. I was already thinking that when Johann comes home you guys would need and extra room anyway. I believe I can help you with the details. Jewell, there are some things that need to be fixed, right?"

"Like what Malin? I think it looks lovely."

"Well, for one, I would bet the shingles need replacing and the water and sewer systems need to be looked at. The siding is bad in a couple of places and it needs paint badly. You ought to consider installing a new, more modern heating system, maybe even propane, even though the fireplaces were fine for your grandparents. Rent would help pay the taxes and repairs on the building for now."

"I guess…"

"And the backdoor needs replacing. You need to get rid of that broken screen door. But of course, you will need to talk to your parents about it first. There are a couple of handymen I would suggest."

"I think I can make those decisions. I have a little money and I own the house, Malin. Or at least I will, as soon as my Aunt Greta Stina comes over from Saint Paul. She is bringing over all the paperwork."

"I know you feel like you can deal with this, but I suggest you get your parents' approval."

"Okay, if you think I need to. I will call Aunt Greta and ask her opinion too. My mom has ignored the house since my grandparents and Dad died and she didn't bother to tell me it would be mine. But if you think I should, I will talk to mom right away."

"That would be a good step before you make any more plans. You know, Lars and Sven built that house out of lumber from the mill. It's extremely sturdy. It will last another hundred years. It broke my heart to see it sit there empty, year after year."

"Malin, I am an adult now and maybe this will be my first big decision. I want the house to be taken care of and I think the Widmer family would be my best bet."

Joanne looked at her aunt, then at Ben, then at Abbie and finally at me. Her eyes misted up and Ben reached out and hugged her. I could tell that he realized it was a great idea.

"Please, please, please Joanie, let's do it!" Abbie was bouncing up and down with excitement.

"You will need a legal lease. I can write that up for you. Your parents should be the witnesses when Greta transfers the property to you. There will be rent income to handle. I can talk you through all the business aspects. I have a lawyer in town."

"You are wonderful Malin. I can't thank you enough."

"That is so true, Aunt Malin. How can we ever thank you?"

"You can take me to Fishfry on Friday! I should get back to the store; I just put up the 'Gone Fishin' sign. I will talk to you later about the whole idea, kids." Aunt Malin laughed cheerily, waved, and headed out the door.

Ben, Abbie, Joanne and I stayed, and the little kitchen was filled with laughing, talking and throwing out ideas for the future. Joanne could garden, and Ben could finally own a horse while Abbie just wanted a big flock of chickens and ducks. If Ben could buy a tractor and start planting crops in the fields, he could store hay in the barn and sell it to help pay expenses. Aunt Malin would surely let Joanne sell vegetables from the garden in her store. Laughing, Joanne said maybe they could buy cow and even sell her bread.

"Of course, it is too late to think about this stuff now, it is more important to put up wood for the fireplace and get the farm ready for fall and winter."

"Ben, you and Joanne are so practical!"

"Oh dear! Speaking of that, I have to get my bread into the oven," Joanne said suddenly. "We've been lollygagging around here too long!"

"I have to go to work!" said Ben. "I've got to do an oil change on Jim Minor's car."

"I'm going to go call Aunt Greta Stina and look for Mom."

"I'm going to go tell my friends, and call Johan," cried Abbie and everyone headed out after hugs all around.

"I'll give you a ride back to the Inn," Ben said as we walked down the sidewalk back towards the gas station. "This has sure been an amazing morning. It is so strange."

"Speaking of strange, what kind of car was that in the station this morning when I walked by?" I asked curiously as we approached the station. "It sure looked expensive."

"You mean the big, black Lincoln Continental Mark IV. It was darned impressive. It even had electric windows. The driver was wearing a suit and kept talking to someone in the back. He called him "Cappy" or some weird name. He was wearing sunglasses and looked like someone from Eliot Ness or "The Untouchables." He looked like a beefy, tough guy. A big tipper though. I liked that!" Ben snapped his fingers in the air with a smile and I hopped into his truck. "You wonder what someone like that would be doing here in Philetus Spur."

I made a mental note to mention it to Jake when I saw him again. He mentioned the Mafia too and I remembered hearing something about 'Capo' in a movie or something but it escaped me then. I stared out the window on the way back to the Inn, thinking about Jake with a jerk in my heart and wondering if he would come back.

"You sure made a good impression on Aunt Malin. I can tell she likes you."

"That's nice. I think I remember that she's from around here? She seems…quite different."

"No, not really. My grandparents, the Haagestads, came here around the same time your family did. They came here right from North Dakota and built the bridge and the store. They helped the Johnsons build the church, the school, the town hall and then a sawmill. But Aunt Malin left and went to college out west. My mom was Aunt Malin's younger sister Marte. My dad came from down near Baldwin. After our mom and then our dad died, Aunt Malin just suddenly showed up here again to take care of us kids."

"And she isn't married?"

"Nope. She was a secretary or a bookkeeper down in New York I think. Come to think of it, she doesn't often talk about herself. Dad and Mom never talked about her either. After Dad died, she just turned up and took over running the store. She bought it at my Dad's estate auction and the money went into our Trust Fund and that's what we live on. But I guess she really wanted to watch over us."

"It is such a cute little store. Does she live there too?"

"Yeah. There's an apartment and a warehouse in back that she fixed up. She did most of the work herself but had some guys come in from the Cities to help."

"She is really interesting."

"She's really smart too. She took care of everything for us and my grandparents, the Widmers too. They are in a nice nursing home in Baldwin. They were taken care of in that estate settlement. I didn't know my folks had that much. I think Hagie's Bait is a lot better than it ever was and the tourists love it. Then she helped the church when our pastor moved, and the church was going to close. Folks around here don't have a lot of money but she's a wiz for raising money."

"Some people have that knack," I said. "She said she likes to fish. Do you?"

"No, not really. I like to hunt and fish mostly, and I like fixing things. You know, it's funny, Aunt Malin owns a bait shop but now that you ask, I don't know much about her. I suppose she must like to fish but I've never seen her fishing."

"Are you related to anyone else in town? Where's your other grandparents?"

"We aren't related to anyone else here. My grandparents on the Haagestad side died before Mom did. But I think just about everyone else in this area is a shirt-tail relation to each other. It's kind of a joke. Anna Swenson at the Inn is related to the Sheriff, a cousin, I think. She has some relatives down in the village of Oxbo and I think her son has a delivery company in Chicago. I don't remember him up here, but her obnoxious grandson comes and hang out at the resort. I know he does drugs and I have heard at school that when he's here, he hands out weed and beer like candy."

"I think I know who he is now. That's terrible. I am sad to hear stuff like that. My grandparents used to own the Inn. I bet nothing like that happened when they were there."

"I forgot about that. And since you're from Madison, you know all about drugs, right? I don't like that stuff around my sisters.

"I don't know about drugs. I don't hang out with people like that."

"When Joanne was going with Deputy Boyden I felt a lot safer."

A sudden, shock of pain tore through my heart.

"Tom Boyden? Joanne went out with him?"

"Oh yeah. They met when he got back from Viet Nam in '67'. They broke up last year. It broke her heart. He started being different - all moody and grouchy. She won't talk about it. It makes things a little touchy because she still works for his aunt at Madden's Resort and he goes out there to visit. Why?"

"You said she works at Madden's Resort?"

"Yep. She's been there for a few years. She used to babysit for them as a kid and now she works in the kitchen and cleans cabins on weekends."

I resisted groaning and just looked out to window.

"Do you know how she feels about him now?"

"Well, I'd say her heart is broken," he said sadly. "She hasn't been the same."

"Oh brother," I whispered.

"Huh?"

I gulped uncomfortably hoping he wouldn't see me blush.

"I was thinking about what you said about Mrs. Swenson's son, down in Chicago."

"Actually, it's South Chicago. I saw his name on a truck at the Inn along with the address. I thought it was weird that they would be way up here. It isn't Swenson though. It is a kind of odd name, but I don't remember it right now. I have seen a few big trucks go to the Inn-maybe bringing stuff for his mom."

"You saw semi-trailer trucks here? Isn't that kind of weird?"

"Not really semi's. They were smaller cube trucks. Those big trucks can't get gas at the Spur because it's too small to fit around our pumps. Besides, they usually show up in the evening. Come to think of it they seem to be around more when the summer people are gone, in the fall."

"What happened to Mrs. Swenson's husband?"

"I never met him. I think he died. I don't think I ever met her son either. I think she was divorced or something. Nobody ever talks about it. I don't think people around here like her very well."

"That's sad. I have seen men delivering furniture and a lawn tractor."

"She must be fixing up the cabins huh? Now that you mention it, I guess it's kinda odd to get that much stuff. Maybe they are storing things for other people?" We arrived at the Inn and Ben pulled up to the back porch. I got out and walked around to his side.

"Do me a favor and keep an eye out for those trucks but just keep it between you and me. We don't want to offend Mrs. Swenson."

"If you want to know more you could ask Aunt Malin. She seems to know everybody and sees everything going on around here."

"I'll do that. I am going to talk to my mom and my aunt about the house. You and Joanne talk it over and if you are interested, we will try to make it work out. I would love to see you guys there making the farm a home. Maybe I could even come to the farm and visit you now and then?"

"That's an awesome idea. You are the best! Have a great afternoon!"

"I will, thanks Ben. Talk to you later!"

Ben left, and I stood on the porch leaning on the railing and enjoying the moment. As I watched the old truck disappear in a cloud of summer's dust I noticed two guys talking over by the utility shed. Their pickup was filled with a collection of dusty looking furniture.

"Maybe Ben was right. Mrs. Swenson was getting stuff for the Inn." I turned and walked inside thinking I should put my swimsuit on and go for a long swim in the lake.

The Inn was quiet. It felt cool and dark after being outside in the summer sun so much today. I looked around the downstairs but didn't notice anything new. In fact, all the furnishings looked old and well-used. I climbed the two flights of stairs. I found a note taped on my door.

"Dear Jewell, we are across the lake at the golf course. I missed you this morning! I thought we were going into town to look around!? Call over to the club and tell the manager if you want to have dinner with us, Love, Mom."

I wasn't unhappy about missing the day in town but with a sinking feeling, I felt bad that I had forgotten her. Perhaps it would be an appropriate time to mend some bridges. I went back downstairs to use the phone. I found the phone book and called the golf club.

"Hi Mom, can you come get me in the runabout?"

"Sure honey," she responded, "I am so glad you are back. Put your suit on and you can waterski back. We'll be there in a couple minutes."

"That's cool, Mom, I'll be ready."

I ran to my room, pulled on my bikini and picked up my sandals. I stuffed my favorite maxi dress in my beach bag to wear over my suit at the club. Mom always kept towels in the boat, so I walked down to the dock and saw that she and Jim were already headed towards me across the lake. Our slalom ski was on the dock. I slid my foot into the rubber shoe quickly. Mom was in the back seat ready to spot and Jim driving so when they rumbled up towards the dock, I threw my bag to Mom, she tossed the ski rope back to me. I settled the ski on the water surface and gave the all-clear signal.

When Jim powered the boat, I jumped up and smoothly sliced through the water off the dock. I loved the strength of a slalom ski, the way it sliced through the wake of the boat and the power when I jumped high in the air, waving one hand at mom. On the first wide swing, I dug the rudder deep and sent a sheet of water spraying several yards into the air. Water skiing was one of my favorite sports, but I only skied here at Lake Makoons. Fortunately, skiing is like riding a bike, once you learn it is always with you.

We circled around the lake a couple times and when we reached the other side of the lake I dropped off near the beach, gliding to smooth landing in the shallows and sending up another wall of water into the air beside the swimming area. I swam the ski up to the beach and heard a familiar voice call out.

"Bravo!"

Startled, I turned and looked towards the clubhouse and there stood Jake smiling on the lakeside, the sun glinting on his ginger hair. My heart flip-flopped when I saw him. I pulled my ski to the shore as Jake walked across the grass to the edge of the sand.

"Your hair isn't even wet!" Jake laughed and walked towards me as Mom and Jim pulled up to the dock. I loved his smile.

"That was great honey!" Mom yelled. Distracted, I met Mom and took my towel. Jim tied up the boat and strode over to us.

"Mom, this is my…friend…Jake." I explained touching Jake's arm.

"Well, nice to meet you Mr. … Jake. This is my husband Jim."

"It's a pleasure to meet you…Jewell's mom."

"I'm so sorry, Mom. I always forget introductions. Jim Johnson, this is my friend Jake Pieters. We met at the Inn a few days ago. He is staying there for a while. This is my mother, Mary."

"I see," Mom said, sizing Jake up and down. I could hear her questions in my mind about how I met two men so quickly. "Are you up for the summer?"

"Nope, just a quick visit. We came over to the Club to have dinner."

"Just a sec, I'll be right back." I went back to put my ski in the boat. I quickly slid my dress on over my bikini. Mom and Jim were chatting with Jake. It made me a little uneasy. Carrying my sandals, I took Jake's arm and propelled him towards the clubhouse.

"Who is your friend? Anyone I know?"

"I am not sure. Did you ever meet Malin Haagestad?"

"Sure, from Hagie's Store."

"Miz Hagie and I have been friends forever. As a matter of fact, she was close friends with my uncle."

"I met her at the store…how cool. She's the Widmer kid's aunt." I was going to tell him about Malin picking me up the day he was in the hospital and everything that was happening, but he interrupted my thoughts.

"That's right, Jewell. She is one heck of a lady!"

Mom interrupted just then as she and Jim caught up.

"Are you talking about Malin Haagestad from Philetus Spur?"

"Yes, Malin has been a family friend since I was a kid. She is kind of an auntie to me," Jake said. We entered the air-conditioned dining room and we saw Malin sitting quietly at a table near the windows, looking out at the lake.

161

"Why don't you join us," Jake invited.

"Mom?"

"I guess so." Mom and Jim moved around the table as we pulled up extra chairs. Malin stood up as Mom introduced him.

"Hi Malin, this is my new husband Jim. We are still living in Madison but decided to come back up here for the summer. We found a ton of friends around the lake from Madison."

"It is a pleasure to meet you Jim. It is wonderful that you have found happiness after such a tragedy. God is good, don't you think?"

"Why I guess so," Jim said a little uncomfortably and looked at Mom.

"The Lord has been very good to me in my life," Malin said with a cheerful smile.

"How is business at the store? We must have spent a hundred bucks on worms this summer," she laughed. "Jim loves that new bamboo pole he bought last week. We have been fishing at the pool just south of the bridge and catching lots of perch."

"I have to say I really love the store," Malin confided. "I enjoy the people here. I love everything about it."

"You were gone from here for a long time, weren't you? Your sister Marte ran the store."

"Yes, I left to go to college and when I got my degree I went out to the East Coast to work. I retired in '66 and came back up here to watch over the kids after Christ died. I was happy to take over Hagie's Bait. I'm afraid my sister didn't do very well there but I think I have turned things around. Most of all, I love spending time with the kids."

"You mean the s Widmer kids?"

"Yes, my sister's children, Ben, Joanne, Abbie, Johan and Leah. I never had children of my own. Marte died not long after Abbie was born. There's no hospital out here and when Christ drove her to Ashland she barely made it to the hospital for Abbie's delivery. There were complications and she didn't recover."

"How awful for those kids." Mom reached out and touched Malin's arm.

"Christ struggled to raise his family and I think he did his best. Sadly, I think he was drinking the night he died. He was out there alone loading a truck with logs and he never came home. Poor Ben found him, but it was too late. I was always amazed at how strong Ben has been for his family. He is quite a kid."

"He sure is," Jim added with emphasis. "I like that kid. He should go to technical school or something."

"Well, we'll see about that. After Christ died, there was no one to watch over them and so I stepped in. They are all good kids, but they need a little help now and then."

"Odd, I was thinking the same thing." I said looking meaningfully at Malin. "Mom, I have to tell you what has been going on as soon as we order." The waitress took our order and brought drinks.

"Wow, this fresh lemonade is delicious," I said and then I dove right into my story. "Well, guys, it's like this. I was talking to Aunt Greta Stina and she told me on the phone that the farm is actually going to be mine." I waited not wanting to even look up. The silence was deafening. I looked at Jake and his eyebrows were up. "She is coming up in a couple of weeks to do the paperwork and I will own the house and the property around it."

"Yeesss. That's true," Mom said. "Your father hoped you would love it here like he did, but I don't know how you could do that, go to school and have a career. It is too remote here to live a normal life."

Malin's eyebrows rose a bit and she concealed a smile.

"I love the farm, Mom. Aunt Greta is bringing the paperwork over next month. She said that there is furniture and stuff she wants me to have and she is bringing that too."

"Well, that's just lovely. And what do you intend to do with it?" I could see Mom was holding back. I looked at Malin and took a deep breath before I continued.

"Mom, I don't want to live there. I want to rent it to the Widmer kids. They need a new place to live because their little place at Philetus Spur is too small and expensive. It would be perfect for them and I can visit them there and I think they will be very happy and their rent will pay to do some repairs," I blurted out. "Please agree with me Mom. They are such wonderful kids and they would take loving care of it for me. I could even come up and visit with them there." She put up her hand to slow the outpouring. Jim and Mom looked at each other and he took her hand.

"I don't think it's in very good condition. The roof needs work; it should be painted and cleaned and so many other things. I think we need to think this through Jewell." Jim was not smiling.

"I already cleaned it up, Mom. I bought all the stuff I needed, and Joanne and I scrubbed every corner. It looks wonderful inside." I didn't meet Jim's eyes.

"This is a family matter, but might I intervene?" Malin was sitting quietly with her elbows on the table and fingertips tapping together.

"Sure, Malin."

She looked from me to Mom, and then to Jim.

"The kids came up with this idea. I admire their desire to help each other. I believe it's do-able. The farm house is basically very sturdy. The foundations and floors are in excellent condition. Lars and Sven built it to last a hundred years, like they did back in Sweden. I would only be concerned about the well, the septic system and the outside porches. The septic system is relatively new. Wells are cheap, and the roof is a minor concern."

"Are you sure, Malin? Where would we get the money to do all this stuff? How could those kids live there alone?"

"Joanne is nineteen and very competent. She has basically raised those kids and has done a wonderful job. She and Ben work, but Johan and Abbie help me at the store. If they rented the farm, Joanne will be able to garden and to provide all the vegetables they can eat. I'll make sure that the repairs are done and keep track of any expenses for Jewell. I will send you regular reports. I have worked out some of the details. I think she will get enough money in rent to pay all her taxes and make the repairs to protect her investment in the house. Ben and Johan are very handy carpenters and there are men in the area that would help. I can provide the kids with a down payment equal to a couple of month's rent just to get things going."

Just then the waitress brought our meals and there was a flurry of activity while we settled into eating. Jake had been quiet up to this point.

"Mrs. Taylor, Malin is right whenever it comes to money. If she thinks this will work, you can take her word. My folks always said she was the most brilliant bookkeeper they ever met. She is super practical too. My uncle Glen has known her forever."

Malin patted Jake's arm affectionately.

"Well, this is a pretty straight forward situation," she said. "I think that the kids can easily afford to pay several hundred dollars a month in rent. Twelve hundred dollars a year would take care of taxes. The rest can be put into the building that will slowly be restored. The fields, gardens and yard will be restored to the way Lars, Elin and Sven kept them."

"Someday I might want to come back here to live, mom. This way I will always have a place of my own! I just love the farm. It is a part of me."

Mom looked at Jim and then smiled.

"Then, I think it is a great idea if Malin can continue to keep the paperwork taken care of and it won't be a burden to Jewell in school.

She will need to focus on her studies. I can pay you Malin, for your time. I hate to see it abandoned."

Malin nodded thoughtfully and agreed with a fleeting smile.

"I will keep track of my time and we can figure that out."

From that moment, the dinner talk turned to golf games, fishing and summer fun. Malin was a lively lady and Jake chipped in with his own observations. I finished my dinner feeling more adult than a teenager. I was glad to get this load off my heart and I was glad Mom took it so well.

"Jake let's go take the boat for a ride. Mom, we will be back in a little while, I just want to show Jake the farm from the lake."

"Okay, make sure you have life jackets on. Check the gas too."

"Will-do, 10-4" I laughed, and we left for the dock.

"Do you want to drive? I am not real sure about the Runabout." I wasn't sure about driving on my own. "My dad's wooden speed boat is a Peterson. It was made locally. It's really smooth."

"Sure, I'd love to be pilot. What's our heading, Miss Navigator?"

"Over there, see where the pines jut out," I said as I held my skirts up and pushed the boat away from the shore. I climbed up next to Jake on the narrow bench seat and enjoyed the closeness.

"Jewell, you are such an amazing girl." Jake hugged me quickly and left his arm around my back. "I don't know too many folks that would step up like that and help the Widmer kids so quickly. Malin knew about this and didn't mention it?"

At this moment, my heart was doing flip-flops, so it was a little hard to reply. I could feel the warmth of his body on my arm, and I leaned in closer.

"We just came up with the idea this morning. It seems like such a practical thing to do."

"I think it is a great match. Those kids deserve a big break."

"There it is, see the house?" I stood up in the boat to see the driveway better. "We used to have a dock, but it rotted away. Hey, what's that?"

"There's tail lights leaving the farm."

A few seconds later, the lights were gone. Jake brought the boat to a stop. "Did you recognize the car?"

"No but I guess it could be someone lost…again. Maybe lost summer people."

"On a dead-end road?"

"I've seen lights and people at the farm three or four times since I got here! I keep wondering, why?"

Jake was silent, his hand on the throttle, the motor idling, staring at the farm.

"Tomorrow, I'm going over there to find out, Jake. Someone is going there, and it is my place!"

"Not alone, you won't."

"You can come along if you want. But I want to know what is going on over there. I might even call Deputy Boyden."

"Let's head back to the club." Jake swung the boat around the Bay and headed back towards the golf club. We pulled up to the dock and I jumped out to tie up and tossed my life jacket on the seat. Jake climbed out and we walked back to the dining room.

"Don't say anything to my mom, okay? She will get creeped out."

"Sure. But you must promise you won't go there alone. I will meet you downstairs for breakfast. Okay? Promise me."

"I promise."

We went back in to sit with the others for a little while and then Jake said he would take Malin back to Philetus Spur. He looked tired. Mom and Jim loaded our stuff in the boat and we skimmed through the dark, smooth moonlit water back to the Inn. I tied up the boat and we took all our stuff up to the boat house for storage.

"He is a nice young man…but it looked like he has been in a fight." Mom said pulling the leather cover over the boat and snapping it in place. She looked over at me with one raised eyebrow.

"He is a policeman mom, and a very nice person. I'm sure you will like him."

We stood on the dock and admired the beautiful sky above with millions of stars twinkling. Mom put her arm around my waist and leaned her head on my shoulder.

"I love you honey," she said and hugged me.

"I love you too mom; so much."

I wrapped my arms around and squished her. "I sure had fun tonight. Maybe we can do something tomorrow afternoon?"

"Sure honey. That would be awesome."

Walking back up from the dock I saw there a party was in full swing on the beach, complete with *The Who*, *The Zombies* and *The Stones* wailing and thumping out of their eight-track player. They had a campfire and the unmistakable odor of marijuana hung in the air. I looked at Jim and Mom, but they didn't even seem to notice. I decided to go up to my room and read, even if it was a little stuffy and hot. I was anxious to go to the farm in the morning and Jake was the real reason why. I remembered his smell when he hugged me. I sighed, curled up in my bed and slept very sweetly.

CHAPTER 9

"Nothing makes us so lonely as our secrets." – *Paul*
Tournier

SECRETS UNDERGROUND

It was already getting hot when I came down around eight. Jake was sitting in the morning sun on the deck reading a newspaper. He looked handsome in a light short sleeved shirt and blue jeans. I chose my favorite turquoise paisley peasant dress and a kerchief over my hair with sandals, and as always - a light cardigan for Wisconsin weather changes. Jake already had a cup of coffee and an English muffin.

"Hey there Sunshine! You are beautiful this morning."

"Thank you!" I felt so stupid for blushing. "I'm grabbing some orange juice and a muffin too."

I returned with a full tray of food. I just couldn't resist Mrs. Swenson's additional offer of oatmeal, plus I got some fresh homemade bread with melted butter.

"We'll use my truck when you are done with your breakfast. I know it is a short walk, but I want to conserve my energy today."

"No problem. It will only be a few minutes. I love oatmeal. It makes me think of being a happy kid." The minute I let that slip out I felt childish.

"Me too." Jake looked up from his paper at me. "My mom would say you're a 'hearty eater'. Did you know NASA is sending a ship to the moon? Apollo 15."

"That's crazy. Do you think they'll make it?"

"Hard to say. But it's awfully exciting to think about."

When I finished eating, I carefully put the napkin and silverware into the bowl and took my tray to the kitchen. No one was around so I rinsed the dishes out and set them in the sink. He smiled and put down the paper.

"Ready? Let's go! I hope the mosquitoes don't eat you alive," Jake said, looking down at my bare legs. "Walking on the moon, can you believe that? Wish I could go."

"I like my feet on the ground. I've got bug juice in my bag." We got into his pickup and drove down the long driveway out to Wolf Point. It was a half mile to the other road that went to the farm. Three rows of pines lined the west side of the drive as a wind break. On the other side, some of the old wooden posts were held up by the barbed wire fence and bushes. We pulled up through the circle drive at the door.

"Let me check first, you stay here."

"But the door should be locked."

"Stay here."

Jake stepped out of the truck and walked slowly to the house, carefully looking over the area. He looked through the door window. Reaching out he opened the screen door. Reaching in he turned the knob and the door opened.

"It isn't locked?" I asked. He shook his head. I got out of the truck and stood attentively waiting for him to return. In a few moments, he gestured for me to enter. As I walked in the house Jake was walking into the living room.

"I don't understand the door not being locked. Maybe Ben came back over for something and went through the window again. Don't you just love this place?"

"This is just awesome. It needs work, but man it is cool." Jake was standing in front of the wide rough stone fireplace. "I love how they built this fireplace. The rocks are so big I bet it heats the whole house."

As he was admiring the room, I crossed the hall over to Grampa's old study. I wanted to see if the Widmer kids would have a dining room.

Grampa's big old desk was gone now. It always sat so his back was to the built-in bookshelves that lined the wall. In my mind's eye, I could see him sitting there bent over his books. I suddenly remembered that hidey hole in the floor under his desk. As a child, I found it by mistake, stickling my little pinky in the hole. Grampa closed it carefully he held me on his knee and told me that it was "our forever little secret" and never to tell anyone else it was there. I solemnly swore myself to this secret. He showed me that it was just an empty place anyway.

I knelt, but my pinky finger was too big now for the little hole. I pulled a bobby pin out of my hair and stuck it in the knothole, gently pulling backwards. At first the board stuck in place but with a little tug it shifted. When I tugged again the board moved forward and it sprung open. The long narrow space was empty. Just then Jake walked around the corner.

"What do you have there, Jewell? Is the floor board broken?"

"No. This is my grandfather's 'secret place' underneath his desk. I think he used it as a safe or something. There was always a piece of rug over it. I found it by accident when I was little, and he swore me to secrecy." I looked up and smiled at Jake.

"Actually, until recently, I'd totally forgotten about it." I stuck the bobby pin in the hole. "There's a little catch that holds the board in place. See? Grampa had all kinds of cool little spaces in the house. He loved little secret things like this."

"Whoa. That is so cool. I want to get a closer look at that, I'm getting my flashlight."

Jake was back in a few moments and shined the light inside the hole.

"Look at that, the catch is even spring-loaded. He must have been quite a craftsman. The board fits perfectly. Hey, what's that?"

Jake reached into the empty space and pressed what looked like a nail back into its hole. There was a clunk and the board in the bottom popped open. It was about four inches wide and more than a foot long.

"Holy cow." Jake exclaimed.

In the deep hole lay a canvas covered bundle. Jake and I looked at each other in surprise.

"Open it. This is your house now. Maybe it is a map to pirate's gold!" Jake laughed and lifted the bundle out for me. "You never know in an old place like this!"

I untied the strap and unfolded the canvas fabric. Inside was a packet of yellowed letters tied with a piece of string, some legal looking documents and a note.

"Let's take it in the kitchen and lay it out on the counter where there's more light," Jake said.

We picked up the canvas and carried it into the kitchen, and carefully took each item out. Two letters were addressed to Sven Johnson from New York Safety Insurance Company. I opened one and pulled the letter out. Tucked inside was another small envelope and handwritten note. I read out loud:

> *Dear Sven*
>
> *Please keep these papers safe for me. It is a matter of life or death. I know I can trust you more than anyone else on this earth. They are my life insurance policy. If anything happens to me and you find out, get these documents to Glenmore Denks with the FBI in Minneapolis. There is an address on the envelope. I think I can trust him to follow up. It is so important: please don't fail me. I left them in our hiding place.*
>
> *With Love, Malin.*

"Malin?" I cried in shock. "Who is this Glenmore Denks?" As I stood staring at the letter I noticed that Jake was silently staring at the documents. Glancing at him I saw that he was more dumbfounded as I was.

"Jake?"

"Glenmore Denks is my uncle, Jewell. Malin is an uncommon name so I think it's got to be Malin Haagestad. She is a close friend of my uncle Glen's and I think she lived at Philetus Spur when she was young. What have we uncovered? What are those other documents?" Jake opened what looked like a stamped birth certificate and an ornate marriage certificate. He shook his head in disbelief. "This is a birth certificate from South Chicago and a marriage license from Illinois.

"And what's this?" I asked.

"It looks like a checkbook register or something. We need to go down to see Malin. Seriously, Jewell, right now."

"I am in complete shock, what does it mean when she says, "with Love, Malin"? What's this about? Grampa... and Malin?"

"Don't jump to wrong conclusions. It might look bad, but we need to talk to Malin first. She may be able to explain what's going on and she may wonder what happened to these things. She's a straight shooter, if it says, "it truly is life and death," it's not just a love affair - I am sure of it. I have known Malin all my life. There is more to this story. Help me bundle this up again and let's head down to Hagie's to see if Malin can explain it."

We got into his pickup and I held the papers on my lap.

"My Grampa just couldn't be a cheater," I moaned. "He was too good for that."

"But this might explain some things, Jewell. Hang in there. Let's wait and see what Malin says."

We were silent on the way to Philetus Spur. I stared out the window, trying not to think the worst. Jake pulled in behind the store with its shield of thick cedars and we jumped out. I carried the package tightly in my arms. The door jingled cheerily as we came in the back of the store. No one was in sight. Jake went to the glossy white door and tapped on it. He waited and then opened the door.

"Malin?" We waited but there was no answer. Jake walked up through the center aisle of the store to the front.

"Hey, Malin?" We waited again but there was only the sound of a ticking clock somewhere. "Malin, are you here?" Jake called out again.

"I am going out back to see if she is in her garden, hang on." Jake went out the back door again, jingling the bell loudly. I stood listening intently until he returned.

"What the heck?" Jake muttered. "Her car is in the garage. I am going to check her apartment. She may have fallen or something." He walked through the white door and I followed him looking around carefully at the tidy and organized white kitchen we entered. Jake called her name again but there was no answer. Jake went into the living room and called out again.

There was a muffled answer.

"It's Jake, where are you?"

"Wait in the kitchen." The voice was hard to hear but we returned to the kitchen. In moments Malin appeared, her cheeks pink and looking a little irritable.

"What? Is there a problem?" Malin flicked the switch by the door and flooded the kitchen with light.

"We were worried, there is no one in the store and you didn't answer me. I called you several times"

"Oh, I was in the basement cleaning. What can I help you with?"

"Maybe we should sit down. This is kind of serious."

Jake and I sat down at the little white table in her kitchen. I put the bundle on the table and opened it up, handing her the letter. Glancing quickly at it, she took a deep breath and looked at me intensely.

"I am sorry you found this. Where was it?"

"It was in my Grampa's secret place, under the floor in his office." There was a long silence…a clock ticked loudly in the kitchen.

"Jewell, did you read the note?"

"Yes, I did. Why did you do it? Did you and Grampa cheat on Gramma?" My hurt turned to anger facing the woman who disgraced Sven Johnson's memory.

"Cool down. Don't let your imagination get the best of you. The only thing that happened was that a very young woman gave away her heart. I was seventeen. He was married had a wife and kids and was thirty years old. That's all." She took a deep breath and continued, "Your grandfather was a handsome, wonderful man. He was a caring and devoted father. We fell in love, and I ran away before it could do any harm. It seems a million years ago."

Malin sat down and held her ashen face between her hands. Her slender shoulders shook with a sudden storm of sobs. Shocked, Jake and I both reached out at the same time patting her shoulders. After a few minutes passed, Jake went to her side and held her in his arms, stroking her white hair. I got her a drink of water and put it in her hand. Finally, the storm calmed. She gathered herself together and looked in my eyes.

"I hoped this would never come out into the light. I prayed that God would protect Sven and Elin from this moment. And I feel ashamed that you had to find out Jewell. But I have held him in my heart all these years," she sighed. "Finally, I can release a lifetime of grief."

Jake returned to his chair but moved it closer to Malin.

"What is this about 'life and death'? What was he supposed to give to my uncle Glen? Are you involved in a conspiracy?"

"Oh Jake, I hoped this wouldn't come out. I brought that package in 1958 and snuck up to the house. I needed to see Sven - just to see him! He was standing on the porch looking at the lake. I waited until dark to put it in our hiding place in the barn. Then I mailed this letter from Philetus Spur and went back to Chicago. But later when Sven had the stroke, I came to see him. He couldn't talk. He lay in his bedroom, the one downstairs towards the lake. That last night I sat by his side and held his hand for a while, when Greta was gone. All he could do at that point was move his eyes. Now I understand that he was trying to tell me the envelope was in the office. He looked at me with such sorrow and he slipped away. He couldn't tell me where he put the bundle. I have searched everywhere for it whenever I had a chance."   "It was right in the next room," I cried. "I bet it was you I saw over here from my room. Does that explain the lights at the farm?"

"Yes, Jewell. I thought I searched every nook and cranny in the house, the barn and the sheds. There is so much more to this story… I have been alone for so long."

Malin drank from the glass leaned sadly on her elbow. I handed her a tissue to wipe her eyes. After a little while, she collected herself and came to a decision.

"It is too late to stop fate now. I kept the secret for so long all alone. Now I think that knowing what is going on will help protect your future and might solve the attack on Jake. Come with me." Malin got up and walked down the short hall to a closet. Jake and I looked at each other and he shrugged his shoulders.

She opened the narrow closet door and to my surprise, as she flicked a light switch, the shelves of towels moved forward soundlessly. She stepped in and disappeared down a flight of cement stairs. We followed behind her down into a dimly lit concrete basement. When I reached the bottom step she flipped another switch and the doors closed upstairs. Walking over to the other side of the basement she reached into a shelf on the wall. There was a purring sound and the shelf moved over, revealing a door that she opened and beckoned us through. She flicked the lights on and what I saw shocked me to the core.

The beige-colored room was the size of a large living room. It was carpeted in thick orange, brown and olive-green shag carpet. Wooden bookshelves lined the walls filled with binders and her desk sat facing the doorway. There were maps on the walls, all kinds of electric gizmos, a copier and several file cabinets. The ceiling was a painted cement slab with hanging fluorescent tube lights. A small monitor was mounted on the ceiling above the desk that showed the front door of the store, the back door and a view of the road.

"Malin, what is this?" Jake slowly looked around astounded. "A bomb shelter?"

"Exactly. It was built back in 1958 as a bomb-proof bunker," she said slowly. "I had it built when Christ was living here. Nobody knows it is here. Glenmore supervised a very private contractor. It's my safe house. You see, I have spent a lifetime working for the FBI against the Mob."

"You gotta be kidding!" Jake shook his head in disbelief. We stood side-by-side staring at Malin.

"I'm not kidding. In 1916 I said goodbye my family and left here on the train to go to normal school in Minot, North Dakota. I was going to be a teacher. Instead, I got a degree in Business and then I got my master's from the college in Accounting. At home, my folks spoke Norwegian. As a kid in Philetus Spur, the neighbors spoke Swedish and German. I studied Spanish and Italian at school just because I have an interest in languages. In the summer of '21' after I got my Masters, a man came to the college to recruit me, and I was secretly trained to work undercover for the government's Bureau of Investigation."

"You? An FBI Agent?"

"Not really, they didn't hire women agents back then, so I applied for work as a bookkeeper and secretary with various companies they suggested. They made sure I got the job. I played the part of an eccentric old bookkeeper like an actress on a stage. I dressed like someone's mousey old cousin. I wore brown oxfords and old lady clothes and kept a low profile for years. Nobody looks twice at old women, so I became totally invisible."

"And Uncle Glen?" Jake asked.

"Glen was my contact, Jake. The FBI paid me in cash for the information I fed them. I had exclusive access to bank records, tax files and courthouses. I tracked spies, gangsters and white slavers pretty much on my own by using my accounting and developing investigation skills. I turned over the information to Glen or my handler and they took it to whoever asked for the information." She pulled out a chair for me and sat down in her desk chair. Tapping the papers, she brought down from upstairs on her hand, she explained the rest of the story.

"In 1926, my job was to work for the New York Safety Insurance company. I found out that the company was just a front for the Family. It was their cover for extortion, prostitution, drugs, alcohol and gambling businesses. I answered all the telephone calls and took notes for them and listened in on their phone calls. I reported everything I heard to Glenmore. He would take the information and give it to the Hoover guys. At first no one noticed me, but by 1930 things got too hot and I was transferred to Chicago."

"What did you do there?" Jake's bass voice startled me. I was completely absorbed by her story.

"By then the Bureau was the FBI. Because of what was happening in Europe, they were pretty much occupied with espionage. On my own, I got a job at the Cook County Courthouse and the word was spread around town that I was a terrific bookkeeper with a shady background. An attorney came and offered me a job in his office. I knew he was Mob-related. After a few months, he hooked me up with a South Chicago barkeeper. This guy wanted me to figure out how to redirect his cash into legitimate sales, so he would look squeaky clean."

"In South Chicago? By Calumet?"

"Yes, down towards the old harbor. I don't brag much, but I'm good at bookkeeping. I figured out how to clean the money like a laundromat. They never worried about me. I was only thirty, but I dressed and acted like I was in my mid-fifties, I even dyed my hair grey and wore old lady clothes. I'm an excellent accountant so they trusted me, and they began to make hundreds of thousands of dollars on legitimate investments. I never took anything but my wages from them and I lived in a nice little house in the 'burbs. I cooked their books in my office and snooped in their houses behind their backs. I made them rich. But finally, the Hungarian and Capone just got too big for their britches and then the killing started."

"The Hungarian? Who is that?"

"You don't need to know. He got into bed with men who were trading industrial secrets. It didn't work out well for them."

"But weren't you afraid, Malin? What if they caught you?" I was shocked at the confessions of this 'little old lady'. "How could you keep it up?"

"When I left Sven behind, Jewell, I knew I'd never love another man. I never looked for another. After a while of living with these degenerates, I didn't care whether I lived or not. I played my part, hour by hour, day to day and empty year after empty year, watching and waiting for 'them' to catch me but they never did. It was like a crazy chess game. They never suspected me, and I pretended not to care about them."

"What about Uncle Glen? What does he know about all of this?" asked Jake.

"He pretty much knows everything I did, but sometimes I only reported to the handler. Sven knew I couldn't talk about it."

"Who and what is a handler?" My heart was beating faster from this story.

"I don't know who. I never even asked. He was just a voice. We only talked by phone. He told me what I needed to know and paid my bills."

"How could you trust him?" `

"I don't know. I guess it was something in his voice. He never let me down and he made very generous payments exactly on time. He gave me just enough information to protect myself from the Family's little battles."

"So why did you quit?" Jake asked.

"In the 1940's and '50's, I discovered a rural burglary ring with moving alcohol, pushing prostitution and drugs, who were circulating stolen goods throughout the Midwest. There was a growing interstate operation. A gang with ties to northern Wisconsin was using the back roads to run drugs and alcohol up and down from Canada to Superior, over to Ironwood and then down the east through Green Bay and Milwaukee. The gang boss would even haul prostitutes up north in the summer to sell them out of the little bars along the main highways and at resorts. He traded goods for alcohol that his men turned around and sold on the streets. It was ingenious, and they would never have been caught except the trusty little old bookkeeper that worked

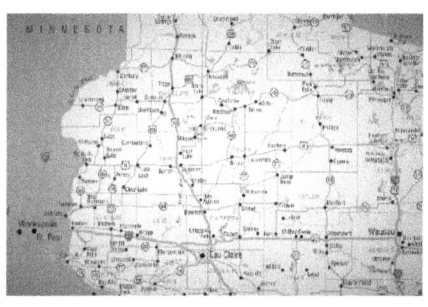

faithfully and quietly night and day," she laughed. "In the end, the Feds moved in crashed most of them right into Lake Michigan."

She put her feet up on the desk and leaned back in her chair with her hands behind her head and smiled with evident satisfaction.

"Then, in '57', I went to New York with my Mob boss for a big meeting where I reviewed their paperwork. I overheard that the scope of their plans was going national. They were talking about 'getting Hoover' so I decided it was time to get out. I knew there were too many police and Federal Agents working for the Family. I didn't trust them. I reported to my handler for the last time. Then I told the capo that I had congestive heart failure and arthritis, so I was retiring to South America. They gave me a huge bonus." Malin laughed and clapped her hands. "I cleared out of town as fast as I could. You see, I know the Family doesn't like loose ends."

"You are amazing Malin. I can't believe all that I am hearing." Jake said shaking his head.

"It's true. And I have been underground up here in Wisconsin ever since 1962."

"Oh, my God, Malin. I thought you were just a nice little old white-haired lady all this time. You and Uncle Glen are a crime-busting super-hero duo like Marvel Comics!"

"Not hardly Jake. I did my job. I did it the best I could. I had nothing to lose."

It was hard to digest all this information. I had read about this battle with the Mafioso in New York and Chicago in "Life" and "Look" magazines most of my life. I knew about the gun fights and murders in Chicago, Milwaukee and New York.

"What were you saying about the ring of burglars and drug dealers in Wisconsin? How did you figure them out?" I asked. "Did it have something to do with Al Capone?"

"The killing spree started with him and I know it continues until today. Evil never ends. It tends to ooze down a different road."

"Then what are these documents? Why are they so important?"

Malin picked up the bundle and laid out some of the papers. She picked up the rest and put them in a file drawer and locked it.

"These are my life insurance policy. If anyone finds out about me, I can use them for protection at the highest levels. I used everything I knew about detecting to find this stuff. It took me years."

Jake and I looked at each other and I reached over to touch his hand. He took my hand and moved closer.

"This file is more pertinent to you guys. Here is a marriage certificate between Joseph Szabo and Anna Varga, dated 1920 in Cook County. Go ahead, look here. On this one he claims he was a Hungarian immigrant working on the docks in Chicago in 1917. I found Joseph Szabo entered the United States from Hungary in 1919 and ended up in South Chicago. Here is a birth certificate and hospital records for a child from the marriage dated 1921. This document is a divorce dated 1922 in Geneva, Illinois. Look at the signature of Anna Szabo." Malin got up from her desk and went to a folder on a shelf behind her. She pulled out a document. "Back in those days it wasn't easy to get a divorce unless there was something pretty convincing."

"Now look at this land contract between your grandfather and Anna Swenson. You can see it is the same signature."

"Who is this Joe Szabo? You say he was Anna Swenson's husband? How could you find that out?"

"In '66' I began tracking her backward. The story was that she came to Ojibwa, Wisconsin from South Chicago, Illinois. I went to Illinois and I found out that she married a meat cutter in down there in 1935 named Gary Swenson. About two years later he was murdered. He was found beaten to death behind a bar where she worked. This clipping shows a picture of his young wife, Anna Swenson, with the District Attorney. His murder was never solved."

"You mean, Mrs. Swenson from the Inn?"

"Yes, I was there working for the Mob when this all happened, but I didn't realize it was the same girl from the Inn at the time. I got Anna's maiden name, Varga, from the obituary. The newspapers said that she had divorced this guy, Szabo. I went through every courthouse in the region and finally when I found her marriage records to Szabo, I found these birth records for a child named Bela Szabo in Joliet, Illinois." Malin tapped her finger on some official looking papers. "Then I posed as a Social Worker and talked to some relatives and found out that in 1938, she disappeared but she left her son in South Chicago and the man who owned the bar where she had worked confirmed the boy stayed with Szabo. Nobody would say why. It appeared obvious to me that she was escaping from a brutal, horrible man."

Malin went to a small cabinet in the corner and pulled out a cut-glass carafe. She poured herself a small glass of the dark liquid and looked at us.

"Anyone else need a drink?"

We both shook our heads. I could hardly take my eyes off her.

"This seems unreal, Malin." I was shocked by the revelations about this woman. Jake looked shocked too.

"It gets crazier. So then, Szabo turned up in Radisson in the winter of 1939. I tracked him by checking county courthouse records from Madison north, for land and tax records. The next year a new trucking company opened in Ladysmith. The guy also owned a bar and a gas station, but I never found any IRS records showing where he got his money. His name was Joseph Szabo. His son, Bela, worked with him. I never found another connection there between Szabo and Anna. That seemed strange because they were living in the same county."

"This Joe Szabo, lives there now?" Jake was pacing now.

"No. Joe's dead. He died in the late fifties when his getaway burned to the ground in a suspicious house fire in Southern Sawyer County. Some locals say it had something to do with the Mob."

"What happened then?"

"His son Bela inherited the whole operation. Now he acts like a respectable businessman. He has a charming home in town near South Chicago and a young blond wife who runs around in a cute little red sports car. They have a summer home on a big estate east of here. He also has a warehouse and a fleet of delivery trucks in Milwaukee and Waukegan. He also owns semi-trucks and a bunch of trailers that are parked in his three properties in Superior, Minoqua and Hurley.

But it seems his money seems to grow on trees. That, in my experience, means it has its roots in importing cocaine and other drugs from South America or Cuba." Malin looked at each of us seriously. "But no one ever says "boo" to him about flaunting his money." She assumed that thinking pose again, tapping her fingers together, like she was praying. Then she looked up and shared more of the story.

"I found that Anna Swenson worked near Ojibwa as a bartender from 1938 to 1948. Then the locals said she worked part-time at the Barker Lake Lodge. Since that was a gangster hangout, I figured that she was getting protection. When she bought the Inn for a pittance from Sven and Elin in 1957, I knew there had to be something wrong. This is a timeline of vengeance and murder."

Jake sat on the edge of the desk. He looked at me and then at Malin.

"I need to tell you about what Jewell and I are dealing with, Malin. Did you know her dad, in his own words, was run off the road by a semi-truck? He was on his way up here. The night he died he had an argument with somebody on the phone over something that happened up here. Last year, I was shot in Superior by a guy that got out of a semi-truck when I was investigating a bunch of burglaries between Superior and Ashland."

"Jewell and Jake, I knew about Sig's death. I was so heart-broken for you, your mom and Greta. Poor Sven lost his beloved son as well."

"This is getting convoluted, Jake." Malin got up and tapped the map of Wisconsin. "This is a 1957 map where I've kept track of reported house burglaries and robberies. Here on Highway 35 near the State Line is where Szabo has his other warehouse, then follow it up to Superior. See the clusters of robberies and burglaries? These roads haven't changed too much over time except that now there is the new I-94. I dated each crime. You can see they have been going on for years. Then follow Highway 2 over to Highway 51 to Hurley and down to Minoqua. Can you see the paths of thefts, burglaries and robberies? Now, trace the path across the state on Highway 8 to St. Croix Falls. What do you see?" her finger traced a triangle that encircled northern Wisconsin.

"I see a pattern along the highway corridors. You hit on something Malin." Jake ran his finger along the major highways. "I don't know if it is Szabo or his connections in Chicago, but there is definitely something going on here. I've been looking at the northern quarter of Wisconsin. But look at that string of crimes down Highway 13."

Malin went back and sat at her desk. She pushed her grey hair back from her brow and rubbed her forehead in deep thought.

"I ran across this Canada to Chicago corridor that went back up to Sioux Ste. Marie on Highway 141, by accident," she said. "Capone and his henchmen ran that route, but I could never find air-tight proof, just word-of-mouth. It was also by accident that I uncovered Joseph Szabo's connection. I think he and Bela Szabo took over and then Joe died, and Bela got everything. But again, I have no proof. I can't do anything without exposing myself to the Family. Now I have something to live for…five reasons. I can't expose the Widmer children to mob vengeance."

"You are right Malin. You can't fight with the mob. They crush anything in their way. But there has to be a way to stop this ring." Jake stood staring at the maps and tracing the main highways with his finger. "You are amazing, Malin. This is some fine detective work."

"It all started because I was so mad that Anna Swenson stole the Inn from Sven and Elin."

"What?" I turned around to look at her. "What are you talking about?"

Malin got up again and went to a little box in the corner. She opened it and took out a long brown cigarette. She rolled it thoughtfully between her fingers and then lit it. I was shocked. I had never seen an elderly woman light up a cigarette.

"Pardon me for smoking, it's a nasty habit. Don't worry. I have an excellent air cleaner. This is a very difficult story. Anna was at the Inn with her parents in 1916. They came north to avoid the influenza that came from Europe and was spreading in the towns and villages around Chicago. Anna saw him kiss me one night outside the Inn that summer." She shook her head sadly. "She kept it to herself, to use it at the right time. Then when she saw her chance she threatened him that she would tell everyone and ruin his marriage and his reputation."

"Poor Sven," Jake said. "What a witch."

"All those years I thought only three people ever knew about my operation," she held up three fingers. "That was Sven, Glen and my handler. I was erased by the Bureau in 1960. Then I got a note from Sven. He originally wrote to me in 1959 at my post office box in New York but I didn't get it until I got back from South America in 1961. Sven said that Anna told him she recognized me in New York. She was at the 1957 Family summit with the Chicago Mob and she saw me there. She recognized me from Philetus Spur. She remembered the mousey bookkeeper from Chicago and she wasn't fooled by my act. In '58' she was living in Ojibwa and must have come up here to the Inn. She told Sven she knew that I was using a fake identity and she would reveal who I was to the Syndicate. She told him they would kill me. She blackmailed him to get the Inn. He said at first, he pretended not to understand but then she pushed harder and so he said he wanted to retire anyway. She got it cheap, and then he and Elin moved to the farm. He was so worried that Elin would find it out or that Anna would tell her. Reading that note broke my heart. Sven didn't want Elin to ever know but he said he'd never forget me and wanted to protect me too." Malin paused and stared silently at the smoke of her cigarette. "When Elin died in 62, his world began to crumble."

"That's horrible. And Grampa was all alone?"

"I think he had friends here. That was the year I closed the books on these guys and that winter I read in the papers about all the arrests. It gave me a lot of pleasure, but I realized that we weren't stopping them because their roots went deeper. I knew I had to get away and come home. I told Glenmore I was done, and I came back here in the summer of 1963. My sister-in-law Marte died after Abbie was born. My brother-in-law Christ was miserable with grief while trying to care for his kids. Christ told me Sven was in mourning after losing both Sigurd and Elin who were killed in car accidents. It was not the right time to make an appearance, so I told Christ not to mention I had been home. I rented a cabin for the summer north of here where I could think. That summer Ben and Joanne spent a lot of time with me along with little Abbie. Leah stayed in Philetus Spur to take care of Christ."

"How could you keep track of all this stuff," I asked. "What made you consider this?"

"Crazy "coincidences". One after the other. I researched Anna Swenson after Sven warned me about her. I discovered a string of connections that I couldn't explain away including Joe Szabo, that tied her to the mob in Chicago. My plan was to turn her blackmail around and nail her with it. Then I heard one day that Sven had a stroke. They brought him home from the fields but there wasn't much hope. When I went to visit him, Greta remembered me and let me see him. She went to town for supplies and I was alone with him when he died. I could see he knew me; it was in his eyes. He just lay there silently. When I looked away, he sighed, and he was gone. After his funeral, I left and went back to my cabin and spent several weeks completely alone."

Malin picked up her glass and walked to the map wall staring thoughtfully as she smoked her cigarette. Jake got up and walked over to me, putting his hand on my shoulder. His somber voice broke the silence.

"There has been so much misery. Sigurd, Sven, Elin and you Malin: all of you were trying to do the right things. It all turned out wrong."

"Not wrong, Jake. We did the right things and in the long run, it will work out. I am just working on how to reveal what is going on here without putting our families at risk."

"But doesn't Anna know you are here now? She must know who you are…" I said.

"Yes, she does," Malin sat down. "When Christ died, I pretended I had just come home. Anna carefully avoids me now, but she hasn't said a word. She doesn't know who my connections are, and I'll let her think I am still allied with the Family. I am worried now because the word is out that Jake and I are friends and they have made some connection between the Inn and Superior. I think she or Bela jumped to the conclusion that he knows something dangerous to them so I'm guessing it might be why he was beat up. It was a definite warning, they wouldn't have wasted time simply beating him up. Until they know who my people are, I think I can protect Jake. I don't think they'll mess with the New York family without provocation. But I need to figure out my next move to nail her or shut her up. Now, it's like a dark chess game. I need to make my move, or you, your mom or Jim are in danger. I am not sure how far they may go. And then I have to shut Anna up for good without blowing my own cover."

"Malin, you don't mean..." Jake exclaimed sternly.

"Oh no, sit down. I've never hurt anyone. I need enough evidence to lock her away and shut down this ring. I can't trust the local cops. My only choice is to reach out to Glenmore. I think can still trust some of the FBI. I have strong suspicions that Sigurd was headed up here to confront Anna when he was killed. I would have told him not to do it."

"Oh no," I couldn't help crying out. Malin poured another small glass of alcohol.

"Yes, Jewell. Three years ago, I looked up the accident records. You and your mother wouldn't have recognized the officer who came to talk to you after Sigurd was killed and Sven died. I came to your house to question you. When I showed Mary my badge she naturally assumed I was a police officer. We may never know who or how they killed him for sure but from what Mary heard, I am sure it was no accident. I think Anna knew that Sig was coming up here and someone in her ring intercepted him."

"So, her son Bela, his son and nephew are up to their ears in this burglary ring? They must have decided to dispose of the threat." Jake said.

"What did you mean about not trusting the local cops? You can't mean someone like Tom Boyden." I said in disbelief.

"I can't say, but I have seen the Sheriff at the resort. He is Anna's cousin. I have been watching them by spying from the pines behind the Inn and from Shadow Bay. As a matter of fact, I watched you and Jake talking one morning near the lake. Right afterwards a truck pulled in and unloaded some stuff in the utility shed."

"I have seen men unloading a truck with big lawn mowers in it." I said. "They were putting them in the boathouse."

"Are you sure?" Jake asked. "Why didn't you say anything? That was the morning I was attacked. That's the link I am looking for. They must have thought I saw something that morning when we were walking behind the Inn. But how would they know me from up in Superior? I haven't seen anyone here that I recognize or know."

"That's what I mean Jake, they might be just warning me. When you deal with the Family, you don't ever know who they are." said Malin. "But it is likely through the police force. There is always someone secretly on the take. Sooner or later, that connection will come to light."

"What do we do next?" I asked.

Malin and Jake looked at each other. Jake turned away and walked to the map. He used his finger to trace the roads around Northern Wisconsin. Malin began to doodle on her pad.

"I am sorry, Jewell. This can't include you. Handling the Mob is like playing high stakes poker. You just don't have experience enough to deal with this situation." Malin was staring at stenographer's notepad on the desk. "We have to figure out how to protect you two, my kids and your family. I am not sure what this gang will do next or even where we are vulnerable." Malin began to write down a list.

"First of all; I am pretty sure Bela had something to do with your dad's death - but I don't know what. Secondly, Anna knows who I am. Third, she knows about Sven and I. Forth, she suspects I have Mob connections in New York. Fifth, she doesn't know if Sven told me about blackmailing him so me being here must worry her. Sixth, someone around her thinks Jake is dangerous enough to attack him viciously. But they haven't made any moves towards you or your mom. I feel like we have to hurry to checkmate their game."

"If she thinks you are in the Mob, wouldn't she think you'd be on the same side?" I asked.

"No, Jewell. You don't understand the way gangs operate. In New York, I worked with the head of the North Side Chicago gang. Anna's ex-husband was with the South Chicago gangs. There are gangsters in Milwaukee, Green Bay and everywhere in-between. They kill each other off regularly. You don't mess with them face-to-face."

"Oh. But we have proof that Mrs. Swenson blackmailed Grampa. Isn't that against the law?"

"It is against the law, but the penalty is only a year in jail and she has friends in the right places so it's not much of a threat. It's imperative to tie her into the interstate burglary, sex and extortion ring. Racketeering carries a heavier sentence and I can get backing from a congressman. I have been working hard to connect some of the dots and document the right information. But I need concrete proof to hand over to someone who can make big arrests. I want Anna to pay for what she did to Sven and Elin. I want her to get time if she was involved in Sigurd's death. We have to catch them red-handed."

"What proof would that be, Malin?" Jake asked.

Malin began to pace back and forth in front of the map of Wisconsin. Her forehead was wrinkled with the effort of the thoughts she was sorting through. I looked at Jake who was leaning forward with his elbows on his knees and his hands over his face in intense thought. I felt young and useless. Jake was leaning on the desk with his face in his hands. After a few minutes, I tried to break the tension. I stood up and then sat on the edge of Malin's desk.

"In movies and books there is always a last-minute clue that pops up."

Jake peered at me balefully between his fingers.

"I'm sorry, Jake. I read a lot of Agatha Christies and there's always a denouement! Why can't we just ask Tom Boyden?"

"I don't think that's a great idea, Jewell. Even if we trust him, Malin doesn't trust his boss. A Sheriff is elected by the public, not hired for their proven honesty or integrity. The Sheriff here could be in question."

"There might be other reasons why Tom would be willing to help us," I said, thinking about Joanne. "I think we should invite him to join us in this situation. He is tough, he's smart and he might surprise you!"

"Really?" Jake looked at me thoughtfully. Malin tapped her paper with the pencil.

"I must impress on you the importance of keeping this secret," she said earnestly. "We are dealing with corrupt local police, the FBI, the CIA and the Mob. None of them can truly be fully trusted at this point with what we know. Will you swear to not talk about anything until we get it sorted out?"

Jake and I looked at each other and nodded. Jake got up and put his arm around my shoulders.

"I am going to do a little reconnaissance before we make that decision." Malin got up and walked to the doorway. "In the meantime, I think we need to get upstairs and look around. We've been down here for too long. You two need to stick together, and I am going to be keeping an eye on the kids. As you leave the building look around first and see if anyone is watching."

We trooped up the narrow stairwell and slipped back into the living room upstairs. I noticed for the first time how few windows were in the little house and the odd cement block wall that ran down the center of the house. We went through the store where Jake attempted buy to candy bars, pop and a couple sandwiches but as usual, Malin said "I'll just put them on your tab".

We went out the back door and Jake opened the car door for me. Before I could get in he reached out and held my arm.

"This has been a weird day Jewell. I hope you are okay."

"It's just hard to hear about Grampa, but I think I understand more now."

"I am here for you, you know that - right?"

"Sure, Jake."

"Then let's get going. I am going to drop you off at the Inn."

I got in and he walked around the truck and got in. I think the emotional shock of the day unsettled my mind. As we drove back to the Inn I watched his profile. He was way too focused on his own thoughts to notice my scrutiny. I liked his face, the way his hazel eyes were fringed by those thick light-colored lashes and the strength in his jawline. He had this way of looking at you when he talked. He needed to shave...

"Hey, Jewell, did you hear me?"

"Wha-at?"

"Hey; stay with me here. When I drop you off, I want you stay in your room. Do you hear me? Wait for me, in your room. I need a private phone line and then make some calls. I will be back. Do not go off on your own. Do you understand?"

"Uh-huh."

He turned back to look at me and I smiled.

"Now Jewell, seriously…"

"Yup. I will, Jake."

"Jewell, are you okay? What are you smiling about?"

"I was just thinking about you - about Malin, Dad, all of it."

"I will be back soon to keep an eye on you and the Inn. This has been one crazy day." He paused for a moment and looked down. "We have to discuss something."

"Sure," I answered and our eyes locked.

"When I get back, maybe around six, would you meet me in the lounge?"

"I'll be waiting."

We arrived at the Inn and I hopped out of the truck. Leaning back in the door I smiled and said, "Later?"

He smiled and nodded. I waved in his mirror as he drove away.

"Uffda!" I sighed, with deep feeling.

CHAPTER 10

THE LAST SWIM

The Road Not Taken - Robert Frost *(1916)*

"Two roads diverged in a wood, and I—
I took the one less traveled by,
And that has made all the difference."

After Jake left, no one was around at all in the lounge or the halls, so I slipped right up to my room. I wondered where mom and Jim were off to this afternoon. I honestly didn't want to see them since I would want to blurt everything that was going on to Mom. Tom and Malin said to keep it to myself but I didn't like keeping secrets from Mom. I felt sure she'd know something was "up".

Digging out my bottle key on my keychain, I opened the bottle of coke and nibbled on the candy bar; then flopped down on my bed. Birds sang to each other as they swooped across the lawns outside and the soft, sweet odor of red roses wafted up into my window. I wondered about the Widmer kids and when they would be able to move to my farm. I thought it was a perfect answer for them and it made me so happy to be able to help them and I hoped we would all be friends for a very long time.

I thought about Jake, his face, his eyes, his lips and his muscular arms. He had that soft, reddish curly hair on his arms. Sighing deeply and rolling over on my stomach, I thought contentedly, "So, this is love."

I thought about his eyes, his lips and his arms again. I wondered if he loved me and within that thought, I relived each minute with him. With my eyes closed I smiled at them, one by one - the time passing very pleasantly.

Then, I thought about Malin and her life. It didn't make me angry at all now. I was just curious about why Grampa would gamble so much on her. She was awfully nice and must have been pretty when she was my age. I reflected on my child's-eye view of my grandmother. Gramma Elin, blond, beautiful, quiet and aloof - while Malin was so vivacious and positive.

I thought about all the convoluted things she told Jake and I about her life...I thought and pondered until I got up and shook my head. I'd given myself a mild headache from all the wondering. I took the kerchief off my head and brushed my hair slowly as I looked out the window. I could see Wolf Point across Shadow Bay... realizing suddenly I couldn't remember closing the hiding place in Grampa's office.

"Oh, darn it. I should go over and shut it. I'm sure I can be back in less than a half an hour." Without thinking, I pulled on shorts and a tee shirt, slipped on my tennis shoes and tied my sweatshirt sleeves around my waist. "It's a huge relief to know that the lights and the lights and people at the farm were from Malin's investigation and not something more nefarious."

The sun was an orange ball floating in a pretty, pink and blue sky. As I jogged slowly across the lawn towards the quiet path to Wolf Point, a lonely loon's cry echoed across the lake. Evening mist was settling down on the field. Like a gentle breath, the breeze changed direction and carried the cool moist smell of the woods and fields to me. The field on the north side of the Bay was filled with thousands of sunshine-colored dandelions that popped up as soon as Mr. Olson got done cutting the first hay and I could smell the sweetness of the wildflowers and odor of ferns in the fencerow.

I paused to think about how much I loved evenings in Wisconsin. I was still in the shade at the edge of the barnyard when I thought I heard a man's voice call out. I ducked down and crept through the deep grass to the back of the barn by the hill. Then I heard a loud thud. I thought my heart stopped. I sucked in my breath and dropped to one knee, crouching against the wall, listening carefully. There was another clatter sending shivers up my spine. Then a car rolled across the gravel and down the lane. I was afraid to look: but more afraid not to look. Feeling a little ridiculous and with my heart pounding, I peeked one eye around the corner of the building. There was nothing, the circle drive was empty. I took a shuddering breath and relaxed again.

"Dammit! Denny, get out of the way!" A door slammed on the barn. "Move it! We gotta get out of here quick!"

Crouching down in the shadows, I squeezed myself up against the wall. I felt so vulnerable and afraid and my knees were wobbling. Inside the barn a big motor growled into life. I heard gravel crunch loudly under moving wheels and then a vehicle slowly rumbled across the driveway. I took a chance to peek again and saw the rear end of a white delivery truck disappearing down the pine-shielded lane and away from the farm.

Was there someone still in the barn? Was I was trapped? Could someone be watching from the Inn? Then I realized that you couldn't see any of this from the Inn unless you were in my room. The house seemed so close. I could try to sneak along through the brush on the lakeside and go around that door to hide inside. The alternative would be to walk a mile and a half to on the darkening road in full view of the road across the plowed field. I took a deep shaky breath and shivered.

"Oh, God help me. Why was I so dumb to do this alone?" With my hands on my face, I thought frantically. I knew it would be at least a half an hour before the cover of darkness and I couldn't figure out what I should do. I peeked again and saw no movement at all. The shadows were darkening along the path and now I was afraid to go that way.

No one was in sight. I looked across the bay. I looked again at my room on the third floor of the Inn and desperately longed to be in it. How could I do something this dumb?

Right over my head was the window that was in Grampa's old workshop, so I slowly inched up and peeped inside. The shop was empty, and the barn doors were closed at the far end.

"Oh, thank God!" I whispered. I slipped around the west side of the barn, away from the Inn and cautiously sidled along the wall in the direction of the house. When I reached the front of the building I peeked around that corner and saw nobody in the driveway. "He must have gone with the truck."

With a sigh of relief, I ran crouched low, across the lawn in the deep grass to the house. I let myself in, quickly looking back at the barn as I flipped the deadbolt. With a deep sigh of relief, I peered around Grampa's office in the fading light and saw the hole gaping in the floor boards. Hurrying across the room, I snapped the little compartment shut and replaced the board carefully back over the hole. I heard the snick as it locked.

Just then I heard a noise behind me at the door. Someone was on the porch and rattling the doorknob. Sucking in a breath, I ducked away to the shadows along the wall to the front hall towards the lake. I let myself out on the porch and quietly closed the old screen door.

Hopping down off the porch down into the deep grass, I bent over low and crept close to the veranda behind the lilac bushes. I peeked around the corner of the building and saw that the man was now walking along the path to the Inn. I didn't want to run back in the open along the road to the Inn, it would take too long. It was only a few hundred feet across the sand spit and the opening of the bay.

I panicked and made a quick but poor decision. I'd swim for it. I knew I could race him back to the Inn. I'd be safer there. Without another thought, I kicked off my shoes and dropped my sweatshirt. I ran as low as I could to the tip of Wolf Point and waded quickly out to the end of the sandy area. I dove in and side-stroked powerfully, kicking my legs under water, silently as possible, towards the darkening beach on the other side. I prayed that he wasn't watching the lake.

After a minute or two, I heard a cracking sound and then a high pitched "pzzzzing" and something hit the water just ahead of me. Could someone be shooting at me? I dove down and swam as deep as I possibly could- powerfully stroking my arms and legs underwater until I had no more air. Breaking back up to the top I gasped a deep breath and pushed downwards again. I felt something hit my leg but forced myself to keep swimming.

Rising to the surface to grab another quick breath I heard the "ping" reverberate across my head and so I dove deep again, pushing myself underwater with all my strength. By now I was well over halfway across the opening of Shadow Bay. Breaking the surface, I stroked several times and a took deep breath. I was getting very close to the first dock on the point and saw the beach looked empty. There was no one visible but I heard another "crack" and "zing" as another bullet went over me. That's when I realized my leg was no longer working. I pulled powerfully with my arms under water one more time. This time when I rose to the surface I was within fifty feet of the dock. I swam beyond the Inn-side of the dock. I heard angry men's voices, a woman screamed; and then more shots were fired.

"Help!" I screamed weakly from the lake.

"Jewell!" I heard Mom's voice.

"Mom!"

"Where are you?"

"Over here! Help!" I cried weakly in a nightmare of fear. I struggled to dive down again and tried to use my arms to swim closer to the shore, but I had no strength left.

Floundering to the surface, I saw Mom running towards me across the lawn. Malin was shoving a canoe into the lake at the beach. A group of men towards the edge of the bay seemed to be fighting at the end of the tote road. I went under the water again, unable to fight any more.

Suddenly a hand grabbed my arm and pulled me. I tried to grab the side of the canoe. Malin, with desperate determination on her face, grasped my forearm and used my clothes to roll me over the side into the bottom as the canoe pitched back and forth. I lay in the bottom and stared in shock. Bright red blood was pulsing out of holes in my leg and pooling in the boat.

"I'm shot." I said in shock. My leg wouldn't respond.

"Lay down. Don't move. Now!" Malin commanded. There was a towel on the seat and she leaned forward and wrapped it around my leg, raising my leg to rest on the crossbar and her knee. With unreal speed, she ripped her shirt off and tied it tightly around my leg. "Lay still. Don't look, don't move a muscle!"

She turned the canoe around and stroked strongly back to the shore. Mom pulled the canoe to the beach and screamed when she saw me. I was weak and felt myself sliding away.

"Jake, Tom! Get a medical kit!" Malin screamed over her shoulder. "It's going to be okay, Jewell, stay awake, don't close your eyes. Hang on kiddo. Mary, take this towel; hold it tight." She inserted a stick in the fabric tied around my leg making a tourniquet below my knee. "Lean against your mom and don't move a muscle!" Faces appeared in a circle above me.

Jake knelt and he and Malin inspected the wound.

"The bullet's gone right through, it is a clean wound…but the bone is broken and she's losing blood. Keep pressure on that towel. We have to get her to the hospital as quickly as we can."

I could hear feet running pounding towards us, but I was feeling woozy and nauseated.

"Here's the kit, what do you need? I have medical training."

"Jake. There was a truck in the barn." I whispered and touched his arm.

"Shush, we got him. Don't think. Lay back." Jake said, holding me in his arms and exchanging looks with Malin.

"Tom, hand me those gauze pads. Use the bandage as a tourniquet, the towel is too big. Apply pressure right here, on that wound." Malin's voice sounded fierce yet fading. "Jake, get in there and call the hospital; hurry up! I'm sure the bullet nicked an artery. Tell them she'll need blood."

"Get her out of the canoe. I'll carry her to my car; I can get there twice as fast as an ambulance." He lifted me up and he carried me across the lawn to his car. Mom was sobbing, holding my hand.

That's all I remember until I woke later in the hospital with a pounding ache in my head and leg.

"Jewell," I heard mom's muffled voice from somewhere in the room. "Shush. She's waking up."

Then Mom and Jim were standing on either side of the bed. The lights were low, and I could hear whispers in the room behind them. "Jim, please ring the nurse."

"Mom, I am sorry. I shouldn't have…"

"I am torn between being so awfully angry with you and so grateful that you're alive. What in God's Name were you thinking?" Mom held my hand in both of hers, covering it with kisses. Tears dripped down her cheeks.

"Mary, just wait. She's too weak. We can discuss that later, Okay?" Jim said firmly. "Jewell, I can't tell you how incredibly grateful and glad we all are to see you awake and back with us."

I looked up at them weakly.

"My head, my leg… I hurt. Make it stop." I heard myself whisper.

"The nurse is on her way; they have something to help."

"Malin?" Things were getting further away.

"I am here, Dear."

"Thank you … rescuing me. Tell Jake … I'm sorry. He said … stay inside … we left Grampa's secret place open." It was hard to breathe.

"I'm here." Jake's voice floated around above me. "It's okay."

"Don't leave me alone."

"You won't be alone." Jake said firmly.

At that moment, a nurse entered the room. She brought a couple of fluid filled bags and hooked them on a hook over my bed.

"I need some room to work here. She has had severe trauma," she said meaningfully. "Mrs. Taylor, you can stay. Everyone else back."

Jim stepped away and the others murmured to each other out of my vision.

"It's best if she sleeps now. I am giving her something for the pain, so she won't know you are here." She fiddled around with the bags and within a few heartbeats I fell backwards into the darkness.

CHAPTER 11

"Because I Could Not Stop for Death"
~ *Emily Dickenson*

Since then – 'tis Centuries – and yet
Feels shorter than the Day
I first surmised the Horses' Heads
Were toward Eternity –

RESOLUTION

These were the worst days and nights of my life. I remember at some point I was in so much pain that my scream rang in my ears. Mom was always by my bed and Jim always seemed to be standing in the corner talking in hushed tones to someone whenever the nurse came in. When I was conscious, the pain had subsided quite a lot, so the nurse cranked up my bed to give me some water.

"Mom, is Jake …?"

"No honey. I think he is talking to Malin. She filled us in on a few details about the farm. They are coming back to talk to you around this afternoon. You are weak, you need to rest." She hugged me gently, ducking around all the tubes.

"Mom, I am so sorry. I should have found you and shared what I was doing. I shouldn't have gone back to the farm. I can't believe that I was so dumb."

"My darling, you could have bled to death in the lake!" Mom started crying again. "Dr. Wynatt says you lost a lot of blood. You had several transfusions in the last couple of days. That bullet went right through your leg, but it broke the bones. They can't try to fix the bones until the swelling goes down. In the meantime, we are watching for infection and a reaction to the blood transfusions. Darn it, sweetie."

"Mom. How could I know that guy had a gun? I thought he was going back to the Inn. I need to talk to Malin and Jake as soon as possible. Then I can explain more things to you."

"You need to sleep. I'll be here. Tom is here for protection until they find the other guy in the truck." I closed my eyes and slipped back into that grey dreamless chasm. I don't know how much time passed but the sun was setting when I woke up the next time. When I groaned, Mom jumped up and ran her cool smooth hand across my forehead.

"She's awake, Malin."

Just then Jake, Tom and Malin walked into my room.

"How are you doing Jewell," Jake asked and stepped up to look down at me. His fingertips softly brushed my arm. "It is good to see you back."

Malin moved over to the bedside.

"Jewell, I hope you are feeling stronger. We felt we should share some information with you all. I hope it will encourage you, Jewell. Mary, Jim, Tom: there are some things we are going to tell you that can never leave this room." Malin's voice punctured the quiet room. "There are some other things that we can't talk about at all. I've asked Jake's uncle, Glenmore Denks to explain what's going on. Glen, can you come in? Guard the door, Tom. Would you make sure that no one can listen? Thanks."

A tall, dignified gentleman seemed to fill the room. He wore a grey lightweight business suit with a white shirt and pink tie. I thought he looked like a wealthy banker.

"Well, folks," He said in a bass voice, standing at the foot of my bed. "I'm Glenmore Denks, a National Security Agent. Jewell, this is an angry hornet's nest you got yourself into and may I say it is very dangerous as well. There will be a few arrests made and possibly many more from several investigative strings joined together this morning by Malin, Lt. Boyden and Jake." He looked at each of us and then leaned on the foot rail of my bed.

"Young lady, you've held the key to so many secrets all these years and didn't even know it. Your Grampa built the perfect secret spot and hid some documents Malin entrusted him with before she left the country. His stroke kept them from being returned for all these years. I'm surprised you remembered it when you were such a young child. Jake showed Malin and me this morning and it is certainly ingenious."

"What are you talking about?" Mom asked crossly. "What secret spot?"

"When I was at the farm with Jake the other day I remembered playing under Grampa's desk: when I stuck my pinky into a hole, this door flipped open in the floor. Grampa told me that it was our little secret. Really, I just forgot about it. The other day, I remembered it again, and opened it with a bobby pin and showed Jake. Then he actually opened a safe by clicking a little button inside."

"What was in there?" Mom looked around with a puzzled look.

Glenmore raised his hand.

"We are not at liberty to discuss the answer to that question at this point," he said quickly. "I work for a government office that is

195

entrusted with secrets that protect our country. It is important for your own safety and for the sake of your country that none of you ever divulge that any of these events even happened or what you've seen. Because of her personal bravery and assistance, the Government is taking care of Jewell's protection and providing body guards. Her family will be monitored in the future for their personal safety. But no information can leave this room. Does everyone understand this?"

We all looked at each other and then nodded. Jim broke the silence.

"If this is dangerous, I think we need to have information to protect ourselves."

"We are discussing National Security Mr. Taylor as well as very dangerous people. The less you know the better. This is as much as you need to know. Most Americans know the underground crime syndicate in America is very strong, but few know how strong. They have legitimate and illegitimate ties inside our country as well as overseas. Sometimes they are simply too difficult to trace. Jewell and Jake have stumbled across a dangerous secret."

Denks looked at Mom and Jim and motioned towards the door.

"I am afraid that only Malin, Jewell and Jake may talk about the rest of the story. I'll have to ask the rest of you to leave the room. You can trust me. We are taking all possible precautions."

Mom began to object but Jim exchanged looks with Denks and guided her out of the door. Tom pulled the door shut as they left.

Jake and Malin looked uncomfortably at me as Denks went on in a deep voice.

"Jewell, you couldn't have known how dangerous it was to go to the farmhouse. There were people watching you and the Widmer kids the other day. When you began cleaning and making plans to move into the house, you stirred up two issues. Malin has been looking for her documents in the farm house. Plus, there was a burglary operation being run out of the Linger Inn right under our noses. Anna's grandson and nephew are in the Mafia Family. They've been openly using the barn and the storage unit and the boathouses at the Inn to store their stolen merchandise for years, but they were so stupidly obvious that no suspected anything was amiss. They loaded moving vans and semi-trailers with their loot to haul it to the cities to sell. It was only blind luck that they didn't get caught."

"I wondered why there was a wall of hay across the back end of the barn. I thought it was Mr. Olson storing bales. Apparently, they were parking a delivery truck back there. I didn't suspect anything."

Malin moved closer and patted my arm. "Sven and I had a secret place at the old sawmill and I was focusing my searching there."

"What?" I cried.

"Not now, Jewell. We can talk about it later." Malin looked pained.

"We don't think Sven knew the truth about Anna's husband, Joseph Szabo and their son Bela. Her husband was a spy. Szabo was a member of the National Bolshevik Party in Austria-Hungary. He immigrated over to this country after the First World War. His plan was to destabilize our country by blackmailing government officials. We think he made good money at it. He leaked secret communications about our relationship with Russia to our Allies and then blackmailed several congressmen by threatening to give the texts of secret agreements between the Allies to the newspapers. We don't know how he got his hands on them. We know he whispered secrets to try to stir up the State House against Congress just to cause trouble and was part of an organization trying to keep treaties from being signed in 1920."

Denks pulled the visitor's chair up to the other side of the bed and sat down. He continued with Malin's explanation.

"Here in Wisconsin was a small cell of men who shared his beliefs. He was just a vile and vicious man with some crazy fixation on Anna Swenson. He apparently kept hunting her. After she left Illinois, he moved to Ladysmith and he brought their son Bela with him."

"He's a war criminal then?" I couldn't quite understand why Malin was after him. Malin took up the story.

"Not at this point. You see, I wasn't looking for him. I was looking for information about the woman we knew as Anna Swenson, because she blackmailed your Grampa Sven. By this time, Anna was knee-deep in the Family."

"By coincidence, Malin's Family connections with the Mafia web linking the cities of Chicago, Detroit and New York, caused her to uncover Szabo's activities. It was like picking up a board and finding all the slugs and worms stuck to the bottom. In the process, she uncovered Anna's connection with Bela. Then you guys exposed his son Bela's activities up here."

Denks looked at Malin and nodded seriously.

"In this room, there is a woman who has devoted her life, over fifty years of it, to patiently uncover parts of the Mafia and anti-government elements in America. Malin is an incredibly intelligent, tenacious and brave patriot. She has saved hundreds of lives over the years by pin-pointing Mob family members and their activities for the FBI. Men like Szabo are the creeping crud around the edges of easy money in the Mob. His only focus was to create social havoc." Denks stepped away from the bed and over to the window. All our eyes followed him.

"At one point Malin's life depended on Sven Johnson. She gave him some documents that could wreak havoc in the highest offices across this country if they were released. She entrusted him with them; he was the only person, outside of myself, that she could trust. I was out of the country at the time and she had to make that decision quickly to make her get-away. She chose the right man and he took her secret to his grave. Jewell, you have returned that information to Malin, and therefore to the people who can use it to protect our country."

"I am no hero." Malin said, shaking her head. "I was angry. I wanted revenge on Anna for taking the Inn from Sven and Elin. And Joe Szabo deserved what he got because I am sure his own rotten son burned his house down around him. Jewell, it was you and Jake that brought everything together. I would not have connected Sig's death to the mob if you didn't draw those extra lines from Superior to Philetus Spur. It was like a story that unfolded in front of me."

"That's what happened to me too," said Jake. "At first, when Jewell started telling me about her family's farm and her dad I didn't think much about it. But then she said she saw people at the farm *and* her dad was killed by a semi. At that moment, I was trying to figure out how the burglary ring could move an entire house-full of furniture without drawing attention, and suddenly realized that semi's and storage units in strategic places could be how they did it. Just as I made that connection, I saw that semi going down the road. It was a crazy coincidence and it all came together in my head."

Denks put his hand on Malin's shoulder.

"Malin will not receive the medals and honors she deserves. Jake and Jewell, you are the only people that will ever know that Malin faced death as bravely as any soldier in WWII. When she left for South America she had no one to protect her, she could trust no one in our government and she was pursued by the worst people you can imagine. Her survival was amazing."

"You said you just walked away, Malin." Jake looked at her quizzically.

"Like I said Jake, the Family doesn't like loose ends." Malin walked to the window and looked out at the incredibly sunny day. "But by solving one series of crimes, we'll open the door for their backlash against us." Our eyes followed her, and my heart was filled with a strange ache. Jake reached over and squeezed my hand gently.

"Does this mean you are not safe yet Malin?"

Looking down at me, Denks awkwardly patted my foot and continued.

"Let's not worry about that now. This has been an extremely difficult day. You need to rest. I am going to have your folks come in for the last piece of the puzzle."

Denks knocked on the door and Tom ushered Mom and Jim back into the room. They all looked very worried. Denks indicated Mom should sit down.

"Mary, there is one more thing to discuss. Our analysis of the whole situation is producing one definitive answer. It looks as if the same gang that shot Jake in Superior, probably murdered Sig."

Malin put her arm around Mom.

"I couldn't report that I discovered phone calls from your number at home to the Linger Inn and the Farm the day Sigurd died. Then there was also phone call made from the Inn to the Sheriff's office. I'm sure that someone up here knew he was coming north. More strange coincidences have provided us with a bona fide witness who met Sigurd at a wayside just before he went off the road. He could identify Bela's son and his vehicle- they left that wayside right after Sigurd. We just need to have corroboration to link him back to the crime."

Mom started crying again. Something was distracting me, a memory that bubbled up at the edge of my consciousness.

"I tried to tell the police what Sig said," mom choked out. "Sig said he was attacked and he was right. Now the truth will come to the surface and justice served."

"We will do our best to bring him to justice, Mrs. Taylor, but there are no guarantees when it comes to gangsters." Denk's face was grave as he shook his head. Jake took my hand in his stroking it gently.

"I am guessing that the guy that shot me was also Bela's son." Jake broke in. "He was in Superior with a crew apparently moving stolen merchandise down to Saint Paul and then to Chicago. We checked some other informants and it looks like he and his men would load the trucks at night from warehouses. That night they just stopped at the bar. I stopped in and was asking awkward questions, so I'd guess they thought I tracked them down. They acted on their own and thought they were covering their trail. But Karma wasn't good for them. I lived, went on vacation, met you and those crazy lines of fate started converging."

Tom's voice came from in the corner by the door.

"I have been watching a few strange things here in the county for the last couple of years since I became Lieutenant. There were too many break-ins that never got solved and Sheriff Liski just wouldn't pursue investigations. At first, I thought he was just lazy. Thieves cleaned out houses during the night and left nothing behind. Deputies never reported finding finger or foot prints or clues. No one ever saw anything. Somehow, they knew which cabins to hit. I knew it had to be something more than casual burglary. I asked the Sheriff about it more than once and he just shrugged it off." Tom shook his head angrily and walked over to my bedside too.

"On my own, I began looking around at other counties in the state and they had the same problem. There was never a witness, no clues found, and the cases piled up unsolved. I was seeing semi-trailer trucks driving on the county roads. I knew Hayward is the only place in the County with a store big enough to need a semi-trailer and trucks don't come here without reason. Remember the night we were coming back from Madden's Resort, and that truck ran us off the road and disappeared? That road has nothing but small resorts and bait shops. I asked everywhere but I couldn't find where it stopped or where it came from. My guess is that it was the one in the barn at Wolf Point farm."

Tom shook his head with his arms crossed in front of his chest. "Knowing what I do now, I'm glad I didn't bring my thoughts up to the Sheriff when Jake was roughed up." At this point, Jake jumped back into the conversation.

"Jewell, the day we were walking, and you told me about seeing lights and people over at the abandoned farm; I remembered seeing a semi-trailer truck on the road. It seemed a little odd. But there was no reason to connect it until we kept talking and you said your Grampa owned the farm and then you said your family used to own the Linger Inn. Then there was a link between your dad's death and Philetus Spur because you said he was run off the road by a semi and your dad had a big beef with someone up here. When Malin, Tom and I joined forces over the last week, the different pieces of the puzzle started to come together."

"That's crazy," I said weakly. "I don't see how all these coincidences could come together like this."

"What looks like a coincidence is often a string of connecting events and we just don't see the pattern they are making. The problem we have right now is we need a specific link between Bela Szabo and the murder of your father. We know about Jake's shooting, Anna, her cousin the Sheriff, and a gang of Mafia thieves." Malin ran her hands through her hair. "I would still like to know what was in Sigurd's briefcase."

"It is possible that after Anna talked to Sigurd on the phone the night he called the Inn, she told Bela to intercept him and have him killed." Jake said. "Bela lived in Ladysmith - his son was staying at the Inn. She may have threatened to tell Sig about how they were using the farm and the Inn to store stolen goods. My guess is he or his men cornered Sig on the highway."

Tension was palpable in the room and I think everyone felt it. They looked at each other and then moved around to shake the strain. Denks and Malin stood together at the foot while Mom and Jim moved over to the edge of my bed looking down at me. Tom stepped closer to stand beside Jake on the other side. Then Malin spoke up.

"Jake accidently stumbled into the situation when he was there on vacation. They may have recognized him at the Inn and thinking he was onto them, they tried to kidnap him near the resort. But then you returned and scared them off. When they tried again at the hospital and they ran into you and then Tom. I am guessing the Sheriff called them off. That's why the guy wasn't charged at the hospital. It takes their kind of craziness to simply barge into a hospital."

As I lay there, a frozen moment in time came to life.

"I have the key," I weakly quavered. "The night that Dad died, I was sitting in the hall at the hospital and this guy came in. I remember him so clearly even now. He stared right at me. I watched him standing in the hallway. I heard Mom scream, and he left through the back door of the hospital…not the front. He was so creepy. What if that was Bela Szabo?"

"Jewell, you never mentioned that. Why didn't you tell me? How horrifying!" Mom reached out and took my hand holding it carefully, so she didn't dislodge the IV bag and needles.

"Mom, I didn't want to upset you. You already suffered too much. I still have terrible dreams about him because he was so scary. He was like the Angel of Death in a black leather jacket. I tried so hard to forget him, but I never could."

"Could you recognize him if you saw a picture?" Agent Denks asked.

"Oh yes. I could draw his picture from memory. He had a mean-looking, round face, dark hair, black eyes. I think there's a resemblance to Anna! He had her eyes: squinty, dark, and empty but he also had bushy brows and looked like he was snarling."

"That sounds like Bela. I will bring in some photographs and we will see if you can identify him. If you can point him out, it might match the witness's identification. In the meantime, don't tell a soul." Denks looked at each of us in the room. "If it is Bela, he is even worse than his dad. Until we get this taken care of I will make sure you have a guard, one of my best, 24/7."

"She will have me nearby until that day." Jake said. My mom and Jim exchanged glances.

"I think we should go back to Madison." Jim said. "She needs to be far away from here and back where there is more police protection."

"No, I disagree, Mr. Taylor. It is too crowded to protect, too close to his people in Rockford and Milwaukee. He'll have people inside the State Patrol, police and sheriff departments down there too." Agent Denks moved towards the door. "I am getting that picture. I'll be right back. We'll have to work fast. Lt. Boyden stay by the door. You know who should and shouldn't be around here. There are agents outside."

As the hours passed and we waited, Jim produced a pretty vase of daisies he had delivered from the flower shop, along with a card and some Trembley's fudge from Hayward. I tried some right away, it was so creamy and chocolatey delicious. I was feeling a hungry and hoping that dinner would come soon. Jake sat silently in a nearby chair, sometimes studying his hands and other times staring out the window.

Tom poked his head in the door and everyone turned to him.

"Hey folks, supper is coming down the hall and Mr. Denks called. He will be here in a few minutes."

I sighed with relief, both for dinner and because the tension was getting to me. My leg ached, my head ached, the IV needle was irritating my arm and I was just plain tired of lying in bed.

"Thank God, for small favors." I said. "Mom remember Grampa saying that?" Mom leaned down to me and smiled.

"I do honey, I am remembering a lot of things. You and I have some things we need to talk about and some time we need to spend together!" She kissed my cheek and pushed my hair back.

"We will, Mom. I promise." I whispered, smiling at her.

The nurse came in with a tray of food but not quite as I had hoped. Chicken soup, crackers and Jell-O was not my idea of dinner. The nurse cranked my bed up and I sipped my soup. The Jell-O slid down smoothly and helped allay my hunger. I was nibbling on my crackers when Agent Denks entered the room with Tom. He handed me a black and white photograph and I saw with an electric shock the man I had feared all these years. His dark eyes scowled at me even though the picture was fuzzy.

"It's him, isn't it?" Malin asked. "You went pale." I nodded and looked around the room.

"I will get a warrant as soon as I can to search his offices," said Denks. "I have to get some information together. In the meantime, your family, Tom, Malin and Jake are going to watch you like hawks. You must not, under any circumstance be left alone. Do you understand, this time?"

"Yes sir. Will I have to testify or something?"

"No, we have to erase the link between you, Anna and Bela Szabo. We have our ways."

"He won't have to stand trial for Sig's murder?" Mom cried angrily.

"No. We won't be able to charge him with your husband's murder. There is no direct link unless he confesses, and he won't. But we will be watching Szabo's every move and we can get warrants with reasonable cause. We will get him on racketeering. That will put him away for many years. The important thing is that he will pay in the long run. What we don't want to do is stir up his anger at your family. You must stay away from this investigation at all costs. Bela Szabo comes from a line of angry, vengeful and vicious killers going back to Europe. I am leaving right away but I will find ways to keep in touch. Thanks to you Jewell, at last this man will be stopped." As he left I saw him give Malin a look and she followed him out.

"Jake, I am sorry. I should have listened to you." I said. "I just wanted to shut the little door in the floor. I didn't listen like I should have."

"It's okay Jewell. This is my fault and you got hurt. I am the one who needs to apologize." Jake came over and stood by my bed, looking down at me with concern.

"But Jake, we figured out who killed my dad, didn't we? We figured out the mystery, just like Agatha Christie! We are a team, like her Tommy and Tuppance." Jake smiled thinly and shook his head.

"Yes, we did." Then Jake looked away. I saw tears in his eyes.

"What's wrong?" I reached out to take his hand and he held mine gently stroking it for a few seconds. Then he leaned down and held my hand to his face. His cheeks were wet. I tried to talk but he put his fingers on my lips and my hand back on my chest.

"Jewell, we will talk when you are well again. Right now, will you concentrate on that? Uncle Glen, Malin, Tom and I are making sure you will be safe." He took a deep breath and settled his shoulders back.

"When I get well you'll take me to Duluth to show me around?"

"Sure, I would love to," Jake said and returned to his chair. Just then Mom walked in from the hall.

"You need to sleep honey; Jim and I are going to the Ranch to have something to eat and then back to the Inn. You seem to be so much better today. We will be back first thing in the morning."

"Can you bring me a real meal tomorrow?

"We sure will, honey. You need to rest. I love you."

Tom was waiting in the hallway for Mom and Jim to leave. Then he returned to his seat by the door. He smiled in at me and waved with a half-smile. I waved back to him as the door shut.

I slept painfully all that night, I remember the nurse coming in several times to fiddle with the IV in my arm and give me medications. Suddenly I jerked awake, from a horrible dream that a dark being was crushing my leg. I must have screamed because Jake jumped up from the chair and held me while I clung to him.

"It hurts!" I cried. "Oh, my God! My leg! It hurts so badly! My head hurts so badly!" I choked out. I was unable to control my reactions.

"You're burning up. I'm getting the nurse," he said.

"Please don't move. I hurt." I was moaning as I pressed my forehead into the coolness of his shirt to stop rolling nausea. Jake leaned across me to press the nurse's button. He stared into my face with wide-eyed concern as I began to shake uncontrollably.

"Jake, what's wrong with me? I'm so sick. The room is spinning."

"Lay still, it could be the wound; the doctor said this might happen. You're spiking a fever. Hold on, the nurse will be here in a second."

My brain was on fire. I couldn't breathe because each beat of my heart sent flames of pain from my leg up into my body.

"Jake, pray for me" I cried with my teeth chattering. "I think I'm dying!"

"No Jewell don't talk like that." Nurses ran in as Jake held me in his arms. One took my temperature and blood pressure as Jake tried to calm me.

I heard someone tell the nurses to call mom. The other was yelling for help. There were lights, loud noises, more faces and suddenly a sickening crash. The muscles in my body tightened, my back arched up…and then…blackness.

CHAPTER 12

Anne of Green Gables ~ L.M. Montgomery

"When I left Queen's my future seemed to stretch out before me like a straight road. I thought I could see along it for many a milestone. Now there is a bend in it. I don't know what lies around the bend, but I'm going to believe that the best does."

A NEW DAY –

(oshki bimaadiziiwin)

I woke very slowly. It was like coming up from under dark water. At first, I whimpered, because I couldn't breathe. I was floating in a pool of pain. There was something over my nose and mouth. The room was dark, but orbs of light stared down at me. Mom appeared at my bedside staring intently into my face.

"Jewell? Oh, thank God. Nurse! Nurse, she's awake!" Mom had tears streaming down her face. "Oh, honey bear, you gave us such a terrible fright. Welcome back, sweetie."

"Mom, what happened? There was a crash." My chest hurt when I tried to breathe…there was a disgusting taste in my mouth.

"Oh honey, you were so sick! You're in a critical care room. You have been unconscious for three days. Your leg was septic, and you had a seizure. I thought we lost you!"

Nurses seemed to appear from everywhere, checking bags, adjusting the mask on my face, checking my pulse, touching my forehead with the back of cool efficient hands. One nurse swished water in my mouth.

"Ugh-I am so sick to my stomach," I said to the nurse.

"It is the fever coming down. It will pass in a few moments. Heidi, get another IV bag. Mary, quick, hold this compress on her neck. Crank the bed up slightly."

Dr. Wynatt appeared at the foot of the bed and stood reading a clipboard. He looked at me gravely and told mom he would be right back. When he returned, he checked my reflexes, looked in my eyes and moved my arms up and down.

"That hurts, Dr. Wynatt. My back hurts. When you move my arm, it hurts everywhere in my body."

"I am sorry Jewell. This is a necessary. I am going to check your leg and then review your vitals." He pulled the sheet back from my leg and I saw Mom look away with tears in her eyes.

"Mom?"

"You are going to get better dear. We just have to be patient and let your body heal."

"Jewell, you'll have to be strong," Dr. Wynatt said, "This will hurt; but I am going to spray a little Novocain on it. I need to remove a couple of stitches. Lillian, could you adjust her IV for me, please?"

I let the medicine in my IV slide me back into a dark, deep and dreamless slumber. When I awoke again it was night, Dr. Wynatt was gone and the nurses were back, rustling around the room and talking to Mom. I looked around and motioned her to come closer.

"Mom, where's Jake? I haven't seen him in so long."

"He went back to Superior." Mom squeezed my hand. "He had appointments or something to deal with up there. I think he had to see a doctor. Hold on a little honey, I should call Malin Haagestad. She'll want to know that you woke up again. She has been frightfully concerned." Groggy with pain, I just wanted to see Jake.

"Mom, when is he coming back?" I whispered.

"I don't know honey, he just left suddenly. I am sure he'll call." She was still talking to me as I faded back to sleep.

Weeks passed before I was well enough to even sit up, eat or watch the birds on the feeder outside the window. My body felt like a weak sack of skin and bones. I watched with a sense of detachment when the nurse, Lillian, gave me a bath. My mind was cloudy, and I couldn't concentrate. Each day nurses removed and changed the white bandages that swathed my leg. I saw that my foot was purple and swollen. Bags of fluid hung around my bed and painful IV puncture bruises lined the inside of my arms. Time faded in and out with no nights or days. There was Aunt Greta's short tearful visit and Joanne Widmer came with Ben when they brought flowers from the farm and a card.

Finally, I was moved into a private room that overlooked the lake. A series of muscular men in black suits were posted outside the door of my room and they checked in on me regularly. I was too weak to use crutches, so my nurse helped me into a wheelchair and pushed me to the window, so I could watch the sun glint on the little lake below the hospital.

Mom offered me food. Jim brought me little gifts. When Aunt Greta came, she brought me several beautiful silk pajama sets. The nurses cut the pajama's leg off, so I could put them on. At some point a physical therapist tried to teach me how to get up and use the crutches. He gently tried to move my leg, but it seemed frozen and even the pain killers didn't help. It was so hard to even lie in bed because I was so skinny that the bones hurt my muscles. I was getting bedsores on my back and bottom even though my nurse, Lillian, helped me move and rubbed oils into my skin. The nurses explained to mom that I wasn't eating properly, I had no appetite at all. When my hair began to come out in gobs on my brush, it was the final straw. I broke down and weakly sobbed.

Finally, Dr. Wynatt came to talk to me. Mom sat holding my hand and Jim stood next to my wheelchair. Dr. Wynatt said that if I had not been in excellent health, I would have died. He explained that the muscles of my left leg were damaged severely when the bullet went through and it left fragments of bullet and bone in the muscles. The bullet nicked the artery in my calf as it broke through the bones, so the bacteria entering the wound, caused an anaerobic infection that quickly spread throughout my body. He said they could fight the infection with continued antibiotics, but it could be a hard battle. They were concerned that the many blood transfusions they gave me saved my life but caused my body to go into shock and could cause my organs permanent damage.

"With therapy, you will potentially be able to walk again. We saved your leg and the surgery to reset the bone went well, but you had a reaction to the transfusion because you received so much blood. That caused pneumonia." Dr. Wynatt patted my arm sympathetically. "The pneumonia is better, but the antibiotics are killing the beneficial bacteria in your stomach. Because you went so long without eating solids, your natural hunger is gone. All of this is sapping your strength. On top of that the pain drugs are depressing your appetite, so you aren't getting enough nutrition. You must drink more water, eat all the chicken soup you can!" Dr. Wynatt smiled and continued, "You need to eat yogurt to restore your body's natural immunity. You must be stubborn and fight back. The last thing is that you must start moving more to get well. You must fight the pain. It is all up to you."

"Try harder, Jewell. Please," Mom cried.

"I will Mom. I just don't think I have any strength left to give!"

"You must try, for your Mom," Jim encouraged.

"Sure, I will," I promised weakly.

After that day, time still passed in a fog. It was late in August when the bandages came off and Doc Wynatt let me look. I covered my face with my hands in shock when I saw how my leg muscles wasted away. There were circular red wounds from the bullet passing through the calf of my leg and the muscles were twisted, swollen and distorted by the infection. My leg lay, ruined from the hip down and when I tried to move it there were sickening waves of pain. I sobbed. Dr. Wynatt said the bones were healing but it would take a long time. Mom held me.

"You can be grateful that it didn't completely shatter the bone too, Jewell. You might have lost your leg completely. We are grateful for small favors at this point. We will do everything we can to restore your mobility. I'm adding anxiety pills to your treatment plan."

I wasn't too sure. The next day mom and I decided to cut my hair short. It was tangled and thin, too difficult to take care of in bed. A beautician came to the hospital and cut my hair in an ear-length pageboy. She did her best to make me feel better about my looks, but the mirror revealed a hollow-eyed, sallow-faced girl who was still haunted by fear.

That night, I tossed and turned. Outside the window, a huge summer thunderstorm brewed up. Finally, unable to sleep, I called the nurse to help me crank the bed up. I watched the lightening and listened to the thunder as the front moved in. With the lights turned out in my room, I could see the black branches of the trees whipping in the wind and the rain pelting the window. I cried alone in the darkness. When the nurse returned, she encouraged me lay back down and gave me a sleeping pill, so I slipped away, dreamlessly.

Malin came to see me the next afternoon and I asked her about the burglaries and the man who shot me.

"Who was he Malin? Is he locked up now?"

"Jewell, we are better off not discussing this right now. I am so sorry that you got caught up in this terrible situation. You are the innocent bystander and you have certainly suffered the most. I pray constantly that your body will heal quickly."

"Malin, when I nap I have terrible dreams. And unless they give me pills, I can't sleep at night thinking about all this stuff. Because of the pills, I can't read books because I can't focus. I don't even know what day it is most of the time. And where is Jake? He hasn't come to visit me. He doesn't write or call. Do you know where he went?" Tears dripped off my chin. "I can't go on like this."

"Jake had to leave - for your sake he felt he had no choice. You have to be strong for now Jewell."

"He said he really cared for me. I believed him."

"You are safe; you are getting good medical care. You have to focus on your recovery."

"But Malin, I think I love him. I want to see him. I thought we had something special. This isn't fair." Malin sat quietly with her finger tips together in that 'thinking posture', I was beginning to recognize.

"I want to share something very personal and difficult with you, Jewell. Jake is going through a tough time right now. He is struggling with issues that he experienced in Viet Nam a few years ago. Getting shot, meeting you and then nearly losing you have worsened his condition. He is doing what he needs to do. He isn't avoiding you." Malin suddenly looked so vulnerable and sad.

"I remember the night I said 'Good bye' to Sven. He said we should leave together, but then he talked about how much he loved his kids. I knew he loved Elin. I loved him with all my soul, Jewell. He had such a magnetic, dynamic personality. But, you see, I knew the right thing to do. I had to walk away and hope our secret would die. Of all the things, I have done in my life, that was the hardest, by far."

"But Jake isn't married. He said he loved me. There's no reason why he should avoid me." I wiped tears off my cheeks with my sheet. "I have suffered so much. I don't understand why God has put this burden on me.

"The world is a fallen place, Jewell. God is with you right now and you will heal. Jake is fighting another war. You fight yours - let him battle his own."

"I don't understand Malin. I honestly thought we had something special. I keep thinking I did something wrong and he just walked away."

"Life is so complicated Jewell. You'll have to trust me. It isn't because of anything you did and certainly not because of his lack of feelings for you. For now, the best thing you can do is to remember what you had and let go, dear." Malin turned away from me to look out the window. "We have to struggle on in this life, as best as we can. I will be here for you; your parents and your friends are here while you heal."

"You are so sensible. I need to have you around, Malin. Otherwise, I only have my mom, Jim and my aunt Greta. My Gramma Chaney is older and far away. Mom is busy with Jim and I think she'll go back to work at the University very soon. I feel like my life is changing too fast. I thought I was going to help Joanne and the kids, and I was so excited about restoring Wolf Point farm. Now I can't even go to college. I can't focus enough to even read, and I can't walk on my own.

I had such a good life and now I am going to be crippled, I might lose my leg and my life is completely ruined." I finally broke down and sobbed like a baby, hiccupping with my eyes dripping and my nose running.

Malin hurried over to the bed with a washcloth, wiped my face and kissed my forehead. Gently smoothing my hair back, she smiled and patted my shoulder.

"But that is part of what I came to tell you. I have some perfectly amazing news. Greta and I spent some time researching at the courthouse. We will soon have a deed transfer ready for your signature. You own the farm and all two-hundred-forty acres of land. The kids are already working at the farm and we will have the septic, pump and fireplaces ready to use in a week…then they can move in. The rent will start very soon into a special bank account for you."

"Oh, Malin." I sighed with a shudder. "That is such good news. At least their lives will be better, right?"

"But there's more. Greta and your mom wanted me to share this. Your Grampa was such a smart guy, honey. Anna and Sven signed the sale document for the Linger Inn - but Elin did not!" She smiled broadly at Jewell. "Her interest was not transferred by the deed. The sale of the Inn isn't legal."

"I don't understand."

"I talked to your mom this morning. She's hiring a lawyer to handle it. Sven hid a new will in the papers you found, and a note to me stating that Anna coerced him through blackmail, but he outwitted her by not completing the deed forms correctly."

"He did?"

"Yes, and indeed, Anna was fooled. Just between you and me, in his letter, Sven said that his feelings never changed for me. That's given me some peace. Now I respect your grandma Elin's memory and Sven's even more. Sven was so honorable that he couldn't follow his heart. He told me how he felt, and said it was wrong to inflict pain on the innocent.   Now, we can do the right thing and let it drop like a rock. Jake agreed. I think you'll agree to not ever tell anyone about our secret."

"I do. Now I understand, Malin. It's a real-life story with a sweet, but also a sour ending, right? Are you trying to tell me something about Jake?"

"Your story can have a different kind of ending. Jake is around - he is just working through some issues." Malin's face was filled with compassion. "Confronted with the truth, and the fact that she is implicated in the burglaries, Anna is very willing to settle for a quick sellout to pay for her legal troubles. She's looking at prison time and that is awful for a woman her age. Thus, you will end up owning the Inn too. ---You are Sig's sole heir."

My heart jolted. Shaking my head, I stared at Malin.

"You're serious? Mrs. Swenson's going to jail, and the Inn is mine? I own Wolf Point Farm too?"

"Yes, dear." Malin sighed with a smile. "You are very well off now. If you manage your money well, you will be a very wealthy young woman."

"I can't believe it. Does Mom know all of this?"

"Yes, dear. And that closes this chapter for me. I will be able to sleep again. You returned those darned documents to me, so they can be stored in a safe place. Our country is a safer place. On top of everything, now Anna will pay for what she did to Sven and Elin. Her Karma got her good."

"Malin, I could never let go of my dad's memory. I have suffered since dad died from terrible dreams. I have missed Gramma and Grampa so badly. On top of that I carried the memory of that guy glaring at me every night. I think those days are behind me too." I felt a surge of strength rising like an eagle inside of me, a feeling I only felt at the beginning of a big athletic challenge. "I think now I might be truly free."

Malin took my hand and patted my face.

"Atta girl, Jewell. Build yourself a secret place in your soul; a safe place where you can be everything you want to be. It builds your confidence."

"I am confident, just not about the future."

"I was twenty when I memorized this from "Hyperion" by Henry Wadsworth Longfellow. "...let us so enjoy it as to be still young when we are old. For my part, I grow happier as I grow older. When I compare my sensations and enjoyments now, with what they were ten years ago, the comparison is vastly in favor of the present. Much of the fever and fretfulness of life is over. The world and I look each other more calmly in the face. My mind is more self-possessed. It has done me good to be somewhat parched by the heat and drenched by the rain of life."

I looked at Malin with surprise.

"I'm a little foggy… what do you think it should mean to me?"

"Actually, I am surprised that it is so applicable to my life now. For you…don't waste a minute of your life. Drench yourself in the rain of life. You are young, so innocent. You have many years ahead of you."

"I guess that's right. Perhaps I can go to college school at Rice Lake, Ashland or Superior when I get well, Malin. That will let me be close to Philetus Spur. Maybe I could even do home-study and I can learn about business then use it to run the Inn! You could help me. Joanne and Ben could be my staff, I could even hire Johan and Abbie. You would help us get started, wouldn't you? They can walk to work. I can stay at the Inn until I am strong enough to help. There's the cook, Susie and Rosie."

"That may be a while, Jewell. We were thinking, at first you could stay at the farm with the kids, so they can care for you. Of course, I'll be here for you. Your mom, Jim and even Greta too. There are some quality vocational schools near here where you so can start your education by mail in the beginning."

"I think my dad would have wanted this for me because he loved it up here. My mom will get used to it and her vacations at the Inn would always be free!"

"I know you'll have to have some serious conversations with your mom. I think she'll agree the Inn has tremendous potential. I have talked to old Mr. Olson and persuaded him to sell his fields to me. Between us - you and I own the entire cove area. Later, we can build more cabins to rent out. I would love to leave something for Christ's kids - something that will give them a future." Malin stood up and patted my shoulder.

"Malin, this is such a marvelous dream."

"Yes, but you need to rest now dear, I think you got too excited."

Malin straightened up my sheets and blanket, tucking me in. She reclined the bed's head and said, "You get some sleep now. We will talk more after your mom has time to get used to the idea. I can understand why she wasn't thrilled about having you stay up north. Tomorrow afternoon I am bringing Ben, Abbie and Joanne up to visit you. They miss you and are very concerned."

"Malin, you are wonderful." I smiled yawning wearily. "Will you say "*hi*" to Jake if you see him?" I closed my eyes and sighed.

"I will see what happens, honey. Keep your faith in him."

As Malin passed through my door into the hall I heard her talking to someone.

"Eldon, how are you? Are you visiting someone here?"

"Hello Malin. Good to see you," a bass voice replied heartily. "No, I am doing research on old hospital buildings. I'm writing a story for "The Visitor" magazine about the Hayward Indian Boarding School. Are you here on business?"

"I was visiting my friend Jewell. You have some things in common. I want her to meet you." Malin stepped back into my room and pulled a very tall, tanned man about her age into the room. His kindly blue eyes twinkled from behind wire rimmed glasses and under bushy grey brows. His nearly shoulder-length, black and white-streaked hair with a full, white beard resting on his chest made me smile. Gaudy hippy beads with a big peace symbol, contrasted with his plaid cotton shirt.

"Jewell, this is Eldon Marple. He is the local historian, a writer, a teacher, a world traveler *and* my favorite character. We shared some adventures in Europe, years back." The pause was exaggerated by smiles that passed between them. "Maybe we'll share that story when you feel better."

"Hi," I replied. "Any friend of Malin's, is a friend of mine."

"Eldon knew your Grampa, Jewell."

"Did you? Cool!"

"Sven was a pretty clever guy, an amazing carpenter and a great farmer. Men like Sven, Lars and my dad settled around these parts around the same time, in the Cut-over. My mother was Swedish and looked just like your grandmother. I met your dad, too." Marple looked at me and nodded thoughtfully. "He seemed like a good man."

"I'd like to hear more about them from you." I smiled at him. "I love history."

"That's great. My wife and I study history too." He looked down as Malin took his elbow and guided him to the door. "We love uncovering secrets."

"But, we can't stay now...Eldon, you and I need to talk - and this young lady needs her rest."

"Malin will bring you to our farm when you are strong again. We'll perk some coffee. I'm sure Mary has a spare Fig Newton to share."

"We will definitely make that a date. Good-bye; Jewell dear I'll be back tomorrow. It will be a new day and a new beginning." As she and Marple left, I heard their voices echoing down the hall.

I pressed the nurses call button to see if it was time for a pain pill and settled back wearily into the smooth white pillows. I snuggled into the soft pink blanket Mom got me, and smiled, thinking about my future. Tomorrow I would get to see my friends, the Widmer kids. Owning the Linger Inn was a dream come true. Now it would return to my family, as it belonged. I couldn't wait to get up and get going with my new life. I decided firmly that I would not give up...not on Jake or on healing my body. I knew now that I truly loved him. I'd fight back. Wisconsin was my home, and I would stay in the Northwoods.

"We'll be together again soon, Jake. I feel it in my heart."

This is not The End…

You betcha, I'll see you later!

Luke 12:2

"For there is nothing covered, that shall not be revealed; neither hid, that shall not be known."

CHAPTER 13

SECRETS ABOUT THE AUTHOR,
Andrea Wittwer

The youngest of the eight children, I grew up next door to the Lac Courte Oreilles Ojibwe Reservation in Hayward, WI. After graduating from Hayward High School, I married my sweetheart, Ron Wittwer. I'm proud to be a graduate of the University of Wisconsin with a BA in Anthropology. I took classes at the UW Superior in Secondary Education and for Business at WITC in Rice Lake while Ron and I raised our five kids in Hayward.

The Book Store on Main was my first retail business, then Handy Andi's and Marple Farms Pubs. Ron and I have also owned Grey's Barber Shop since 1976. I worked for WHSM Radio and thirty years in retail hardware at the Northern Lakes Coop. I was an adjunct instructor for the Wisconsin Indianhead Technical Institute and for the Lac Courte Oreilles Ojibwe Community College. While working for LCOOCC I was 'behind bars' while teaching in County jails.

Community service is central to my life. I've served on many community boards. The twenty-five years I served on the Board of the Sawyer County Historical Society/Museum and the Wisconsin State Historical Society Office of Local History were the best.

I went on a mission trip to Guatemala to serve, not long after Hurricane Stan. While I was there, I discovered a whole new country to investigate and study. I made many return trips to Guatemala City, and then up to the volcanic highlands near Lake Atitlan. I developed many important friendships. I hope to help the world not forget what was done to the indigenous Mayan people, in the villages of the volcanic highlands.

After years of study, I was ordained in 2011 by the Wesleyan Church. Starting in 2011, I served as pastor at the Woodland Wesleyan Church north of Danbury, WI until I retired in 2015.

I am so thrilled to finally complete and publish my project, "Let the Secrets Die." I look forward to finishing the JJ Mystery Series. In my next two books, "Done Running" and "The Secret of San Pedro La Laguna", Jewell will mature and face challenging physical and spiritual adventures as she uncovers more of the secrets hidden in her family's past.

www.ingramcontent.com/pod-product-compliance
Lightning Source LLC
Chambersburg PA
CBHW071330250626
47159CB00004B/1538